To Zuky,

Really ho!
enjoy

CW00516565

THE AUTODIDACTS

Thomas Kendall

Whisk(e)y Tit
NYC & VT

Published in the United States by Whisk(e)y Tit: www.whiskeytit.com. If you wish to use or reproduce all or part of this book for any means, please let the author and publisher know. You're pretty much required to, legally.

ISBN 978-1-952600-18-0

Cover design by Matt Lyne.

For Cami and Dylan

CONTENTS

PART 1

1

THE
LIGHTHOUSE,
1982

There is a man living in the lighthouse. At night he governs the lamp across the sea. The lantern's beam a secondary, weightless moon folded through waves and governing nothing in its turn. No boats have landed here for a hundred years or more and the lighthouse has fallen into a state of disrepair. Rust climbs its walls like a rot of fire.

The man is sat at a desk in the service quarters of the lighthouse. He opens the desk drawer and removes a photograph. He places the photograph over the text he has been writing. The man cannot remember the words the picture is obscuring. It turns out the world is sad enough.

The man stares at the photo and touches his face. He recoils. There is something that wants to come out of him, that his face could not survive: it is as if there is another body conceiving itself within him.

There are times when the man does not remember who he is, or how he came to be here. Times when he seems to act out the script of a desire that is not his own.

Either this place is cursed or I am, he thinks.

The man lies down on his bed and bends his arm over his eyes, his eyes that insist on being open though they comprehend little of what enters them. He turns on his side. Tonight, he will not pass the light across the sea. Tonight, he thinks, he will figure out how to leave this place.

Under the loose floorboards, a rotary telephone skips into the air. He reaches for it.

– Hell, hello…Hell, Helene?

The man is remembering himself.

Now everything remembering is pain.

*

This is a small town and one she has never really wanted to escape from. A town artlessly arranged, braiding the cliffside with property which falls brazenly, fiscally, through the landscape. Cliff-top mansions and hotels give way to judders of shops, housing estates and wild closeting fields that sad, homeward called children pock with abandoned toys.

Helene had been among those children once, part of a pack roaming their containment. The park was a no man's land, council designated. She and her friends, all dirty faced, leaping out of the too tall trees, ankles twisting on impact with the roots ridged out of the hillside. Those hard wood tentacles gathering notches of bone. She can still see the odd broken bottle glittering the dirt, and friends, gone now, with teeth poking through lips, gurgling mouthfuls of blood, their knees having been driven into their gums as they landed.

The park was where they met. 'They' as in everyone. Almost.

Helene considers the verticality of her life. The accident of her being here, in this house. In this house at the peak of the cliff. In this house that fixes and dwarfs her. She is steeled, she hopes, against all possible futures. Still, there were things she found herself wanting. Wanting against herself.

And why now and again?

Still, she couldn't help feeling that it was wrong to believe your life mattered.

And so it must be for others, for one another, for one other. Life that is.

She must be someone else.

For life.

And yet, the way she acts, the things she is suddenly doing. She felt she must be someone else to do them. She felt unbelievable.

How stupid, she thinks.

Helene looks through the French doors that frame the lighthouse. She stares into their elongation.

In a cot, in the corner of the room, her baby begins to cry. Helene goes to her. She picks up the baby and walks towards the French doors looking at the lighthouse. She stops in front of the table. The table with 'the elegant walnut finish.' On the table with the elegant walnut finish there is a telephone, the slight spill of her hip, and a small ring box displaying her future.

Helene holds her baby and the phone receiver in each hand, not exactly. The child cleaves to her, comfortingly. The knuckles on the hand squashed under her ear lean into her cheeks at the sound of his voice.

*

The man in the lighthouse returns the phone to its cradle. He is very still. He is still for longer than they spoke. But not for as long as their silences were connected by the telephone. He walks towards his desk and removes the picture from what he has written. The man can still hear her voice, can feel her name mark the eddy of his blood. He understands now, he thinks.

His hand moves across and around the pages of the notebook. This has all already happened. There is nothing left of him. He stands up and moves as if he is no longer part of this world, as if the world as it stands was no longer there for him.

The man walks towards the lamp room. He points the lamp toward the cliffs. He stands in front of the lamp and stares into its lens.

Click.

*

*

*

The phone brackets her breast and collarbone, static crumbling like crushed snow through the receiver. The receiver falls and bounces around her knees. Helene begins to rock her baby with both arms. The baby's small pink hands are cuffed by the telephone cord which she grabs and straightens only for it to return to its scrawled and looping curls. The baby cannot understand why the telephone cord insists on remembering itself. It is a trick she is not yet victim to. She runs her gums around the straightened wire, encasing it in gloopy, plasticky, spittle. The baby lets go of the cord and again the cord springs agonized into its ready-made position. The baby wears a frown that puckers her image.

Evelyn, Helene says bending to pick up the receiver. Evelyn, please stop crying. She jiggles the tiny bundle of her daughter rhythmically as other, tinier, poorly held things patter and fall within her. But Evelyn has not been crying, though her frown threatens to ingest itself in the rumpled cushion of her face.

Helene places the receiver back on top of the phone. She looks at Evelyn directly for the first time since picking her up. Evelyn though does not reciprocate her gaze. She is frantically trying to turn around in her mother's arms. She is turning her small body towards the lighthouse, her arms asking to be carried by some invisible other.

The room is blinded. The mother and daughter radiantly erased by a flood of white light. Helene's mouth forms a tiny, teethed void. She cannot believe what she is thinking.

Helene is in the corner of the room hunched behind the sofa, holding the strangely quiet infant when her fiancé enters five minutes later. Enough, enough, he says. The Fiancé is a black hole in the centre of the sun. You encouraged him. Lawrence, no I…

He drags the telephone from the table and sets it at the base of Helene's feet. Crouching, Lawrence dials the number nine three times, each time allowing the dial to click back to nought before tersely dialling again. He speaks briefly to the police, turning away from Helene as he does so. Something has to be done, he says more than once. He places the phone back on the floor, takes Evelyn from Helene and walks to his car. At the sound of the car starting, Helene screams. She screams to silence the clamour of being, to staunch time, but the scream itself is an act of irony and it ends, as it must, in exhaustion and defeat.

A further irony has occurred, Helene has become the ghost of her scream. A ghost standing up and walking through the light, through the French doors and garden, a thing immaterial floating up and over the cordoning fence.

Helene drifting. momentarily, over the cliffs.

*

Lawrence is giving a statement to the police on the beach. The power to the lighthouse has been cut. Two policemen are rowing out towards it. The rest wonder what they can do. They rub their hands together and maintain radio contact. They pass Lawrence a mug of tea which he blows shyly into.

Evelyn has remained in the car, arms outstretched, torso fixed in a large H. A police officer is tickling her. The police officer leans towards Evelyn, her mouth open and in full coo as Evelyn, triggered by the surprise and the various sensory inputs of the tickling hands, defecates violently. The police officer's expression changes from clownish to rictus stricken to clownishly rictus stricken. The officer places her arm on the roof of the car and inhales deeply. She looks around for the father. She gestures at him. Lawrence waves back and then, confused, returns to his tea.

Evelyn is crying hard. Her hands attempt to grip and remove the straps holding her in place. She stops breathing. Her face looks like a planet coming apart.

The police officer continues to gesture at Lawrence who frowns and walks towards them. He walks past two policemen, listening to them while they are on the radio:

> – Crackle, there's crackle no crackle crackle sir
> – No one's come ashore over.
> – Crackle, crackle?
> – No one has come ashore over.
> – Crackle boats crackle here over.
> – All of them? Over.
> – Crackle, crackle. Over.

The constable lifts up a different radio to his mouth.

> – I want a crackle party now crackle!

Lawrence is asking the police officer if he can return home, Evelyn needs changing and he is tired and needs to get some sleep before work.

He can answer their questions tomorrow, he says, but right now he and his daughter need to sleep. She tells him that he has been free to leave since he gave his statement.

He thanks the officer for looking after Evelyn and drives up the hill.

*

Helene is lying on a shelf of rock. Her arms and legs are askew and there is a curtain of blood opening across her knee. She tries to sit up on her elbows, to crawl backwards. She moves up the slightly bowled curve of rock that she fell, or rolled, or dropped into, or onto. She can't remember. Perspective is hard and variable. Helene can see the police lights discoing the sand.

James, she says. She knows he is gone.

A helicopter noses around the lighthouse, its searchlights cast towards the darkly ruffled waves. The pilot scrutinises their surface for the shadow of some monstrous thing blooming underneath. Nothing. The pilot circles back towards the cliffs for another pass. The lights of the helicopter catch something irregularly slender and smooth amid the craggy rock face. The pilot edges towards it. Helene's dress unfurls over her head like a party horn.

*

Lawrence enters the house and calls out for Helene. No answer. His shoulders slump. He lays Evelyn on her changing table and begins to dissemble her nappy. He calls out to the empty rooms again. He shouts that he's sorry, that he's not to be hated. This is what he's saying, essentially and in other words, as he liberally peppers Evelyn's behind with talc before folding her neatly within clean linen.

He calls her my little sushi roll and then, smiling, picks up the dirty nappy and walks towards the kitchen. He stops in the centre of the room and calls for Helene again.

I'm sorry Helene, he says, I'm really sorry. Please don't be mad. I'm sick of that weirdo. Somebody had to do something. Please? The telephone rankles from the floor. Lawrence stoops to unlatch the receiver and draws it to his ear. It is the hospital calling. Lawrence presses the nappy against his cheek and then, realising, jerks backwards, the nappy unfurling and spilling its contents over the rug. The receiver is stretched out in front of him; he brings it to his ear again. He can hear Helene in the background, her voice farmed out to the painkillers she's taken. Lawrence stares at the nappy on the floor. He thinks she doesn't know what she is saying. He drives to the hospital.

*

Helene changes the channel on her bedside television and rolls onto her back. She stares at the ceiling. Her eyes may as well be one of the fixtures there for all of their input. She was discharged from hospital at around seven thirty a.m. Lawrence drove her home before leaving for work. That much, at least, she knows.

Helene can hear the cleaner moving around downstairs, dismantling and then reconstructing the domesticity of the house. She's not meant to be here today, Helene thinks, Lawrence must have called her to look after Evelyn. The sounds from downstairs, oddly inhuman and strangely gear-like, rumble under the carefully constructed optimism of her bedroom t.v's plethora of voices. Helene closes her eyes and unburdens time, time that shifts tectonically within her, forming chasms into which her consciousness pours.

A voice is communing with her in the television. Helene tries to follow the indistinct murmur that comes to her now in the dark of herself. The murmur is constellate, faintly musical— first near and then far— before drawing itself together in binding accusation. The television is asking Helene about her pain, it is asking her about her child, it is sternly asking her to participate in a duel to the death. Helene's mind stands back-to-back with herself and separates, falls into nothingness. She opens her eyes. For a moment, Helene believes she has gone blind and each muscle in her body contracts around this fear as if in sudden audit of itself.

The cleaner is stood in the doorway clearing her throat. Helene whips her head towards her, a rash of relief and then annoyance colouring Helene's face. The cleaner is eyeing Helene's bandaged foot but catches the ragged look in her eyes. The television is playing an old Western. The cleaner turns it off and begins to speak.

*

I've just the bathroom to do and then the stairs. Was Mr Muir unhappy with the way I cleaned yesterday?

No, no. I suspect he was just wanting to have you in the house and not knowing how to put it. I've had an accident you see.

The cleaner nods, looking at Helene's foot. Helene stares at the ceiling again. The cleaner remains in the doorway. The cleaner is younger than Helene. Helene thinks, 'she doesn't haven't a bucket, where is her bucket?'

Helene's mother had been a cleaner. In this house Helene cannot remember her mother. She cannot remember whether or not her mother would have looked how Helene imagines a cleaner in her house would look if the cleaner in her house were also her mother. Helene begins to hate herself, lying there, half listening to the cleaner.

If you like I can stay and look after the baby. That's what I was asking before, if you wanted me to stay?

Helene is reaching for her medication by the side of her bed. Helene and Lawrence had gone private just after Evelyn was born. Helene remembers Lawrence spending an inordinate amount of time in the hospital's corridor staring at a painting of a lake during sunrise. He had kept saying *it makes me feel calm and that's what I want*. She remembers that he'd even tried to buy it during that first excruciating session. Now, Lawrence plays golf with the doctor on a weekly basis. He has never won a game though he still comes home beaming, wearing his bobbled flat cap and those ridiculous trousers and saying things like:

– I'm getting better, closer today.

And.

– I really feel that I have a handicap now

And

– How are you feeling?

And

– I love you.

Helene is telling the cleaner that yes, she would like it if she could stay until four at least. The cleaner smiles and says good and then pauses as if she still has something to say before wordlessly leaving the room. Helene is alone again. She sits up on the bed and shakes some pills into her hands.

Last night James disappeared.

Last night.

James is gone.

She picks up the glass of water from her table and swallows the pills. She sits there clutching the glass and praying for their gifts to erode quickly into her blood. She puts the glass down.

– Evelyn, Jim has gone and he is not coming back.

And what would that ever mean to her? Probably nothing. There will be answers that you couldn't pretend to have the questions to. James used to say that. He said it once. She remembers.

*

The cleaner has been working for Helene for ten months now. She started a few weeks after Evelyn's birth. They have grown, the cleaner believes, if not close, then attached. They have sat for cups of tea together and talked over biscuits, often in bitter declamation of the biscuits! Helene has allowed Diane to bring her children to the house whenever she has pulled them out of school for whatever obscure reason Diane is always dragging her children out of school.

Diane is grateful for this. She likes Helene. In small, polite ways she has tried to save her. Literature has been discreetly proffered and politely accepted and then left to age at an unnatural rate in the secondary bathroom as if intently browsed.

They have talked about Him before of course, the subject of Him marking, with an increasing regularity, the end of the biscuits. 'God between the crumbs' is how Helene would have liked to describe it to someone, had there been anyone she believed capable of listening to her.

Diane picks up the last brochure she gave to Helene. She knows something is wrong, that Helene is in a great deal of spiritual pain, that she has a duty to try and help Helene. Diane though does not know how to help Helene, what could she say to bring her to God?

> – It is not for us even to direct our own steps.

The line makes Diane flush with beauty. She has said it out loud, accidentally, almost tonelessly. It cannot now be caught. The words are suffusing the heavenly white enamel of the room and Diane feels their truth physically emerging from the gleaming tiles, the words floating towards her and becoming a buoy on the spiritual plane of the here and now.

> – Become a fisher of men

(and women)

Diane believes herself spoken through. She thinks *Helene is ready to come to God. God wants Helene.* She stands up and washes her hands. She picks up a magazine next to the toilet and walks to the bedroom. She will tell her the good news.

Helene is staring blankly at the oval portraiture of the door when the cleaner's slender frame takes up residence there again. It takes Helene a second or two to register the change. She lifts up her hand. There's a pant of a smile on her face and her lips are browed with sweat. She hears Diane say something. The drugs capsize. Helene falls out of them and into the room.

– What did you just say? What did you just say?

Diane steps back frightened by the edge in Helene's voice. Helene feels replaced— literally replaced— in space and time as if she'd just been abducted and had her memory re-organized. She doesn't know when she is. She takes a tentative account of herself. It could be years before she discovers what's lost or missing.

– Are you talking about last night? Steps?

Diane's hands wring the top of the magazine she's now hiding.

– Last night, I fell in the garden. Down the steps. I twisted my ankle. Thank you.

Helene leans over and takes a drink from the glass of water on her bedside table. The glass is quite out of keeping with the rest of the room.

It is a plain pint glass stolen from a pub several years ago and which she has kept much to the baffled chagrin of Lawrence. She stole it in nineteen seventy-eight. She remembers the very night then grows sadder. She hates how that equation works.

– What's my remainder?

Jim.

Helene begins to cry. Diane steps forward. From behind her skirt a child bursts through the door. His arms are whirred out and he is flying a car in irregular looping patterns through a fantasy roller coaster.

– Henry!

The child stops short at the sound of his mother's voice. He looks at his mother and then at Helene. He brings the car down to his stomach and shines it with his thumbs. Henry's hair is tousled into a rough fringe that hangs above a straight nose. The child has a thin mouth that at rest settles into the shape of an upside-down canoe.

Helene tries to smile reassuringly at the boy. Fails. You mustn't panic, she thinks. She pats her face and eyes until the last traces of sorrow sink under her skin. She tries again. Helene feels herself to be a sifted person, barely held together, prone to scatter. Her smile has a submerged quality like an animation grafted between the stasis of her skull. Henry can see it floating around her face, not quite fixed. He stares at his car and then at his thumbs as they buff the immutable surface of the metal. There is something about the car that he does not understand, that he will remember not understanding. The bare fact of its existence under his gaze, or something. Helene looks at the child's wan face. It is as if you could see the adult crouching unbidden in him, she felt. Not a strong adult or a glimmer of the person he would become but rather the adult of sadness fossilised in his youthful stare and weighted with permanence within him. Helene recognizes this look. She gave her own youth to trying to discover its secret. Jim.

°

Henry walks towards Helene and hands her his car. He maintains eye contact. After he has given Helene the car he walks towards his mother in the doorway and stands there holding her leg. Helene leans off the bed and rolls the car towards him, the car jackknifing across the carpet and bumping his toe. Helene asks Diane if she could bring Evelyn into her. Diane turns to leave, gesturing at Henry to follow her.

> – He can play here if he wants. I was just going to read to Evelyn.
> – Would you like that Henry, do you want to stay here?

Henry looks at the floor and then his mother, his mouth shifting from side to side, his elbows splayed out. Diane smiles, tells him to stay here and to be a good boy. She leaves and brings back the baby and hands her to Helene.

Helene pats a space on the bed and Henry climbs up into it. Evelyn falls between them, grabbing a tiny fist's worth of his cheek.

– She's little isn't she Henry?

Henry nods.

> – Would you be her friend? She is going
> to need friends soon.

Henry steers his eyes from the carpet and lets a tear glaze in them.

> – I want a friend.

Helene nods. She opens a book.

> – Once upon a time
> – In the beginning?
> – Yes Henry, in the beginning.

*

Monoliths shorn from the cliff face compose the visible bulk of the isle from the shore. The largest rocks jut nearly thirty feet into the air and form a nest of calcified javelins that roughly encircle the hidden heart of the island. Out of these the lighthouse rises like an exit wound.

Detective Richard Fort is standing on the island. He is looking up at the lighthouse and dashing off equations in his small leather notebook. Equations he'll erase moments later with a tense flourish of his wrist. Every few minutes he reflexively shakes his left foot. His left sock sodden with water and wrinkling under his heel. The rubber of his shoe having been skewered on the island's staggered rocks as he disembarked. Richard Fort limps towards the entrance to the lighthouse.

The day brightens then dulls as he walks, a Theremin light shrinking and expanding with an almost sentient feel for the 'crime scene aura.' A slow wash of salt appears across the wood of the door in the wake of the sun's tides like a granulate residue of dead light. Richard Fort presses his hand against the door and pushes. The door swings against the web of shattered locks behind it. He walks to the edge of the island.

Richard Fort is on leave due to the recent break-up of his marriage and some interrelated displays of insubordination directed towards one Sergeant Dawkins. Richard Fort should be at home or whatever amounts to a home for the broken-hearted. Instead he is here, walking the length of the island, counting his steps and closely monitoring his breathing for tremors or halts. He understands that his sadness is not only ugly but burdensome to those around him. He believes that each of the people around him serves a principle whether they are conscious of that principle or not. He understands that although morale has few rational edicts it is a necessary component for the principle they serve to be effectively, i.e. rationally, applied. He doesn't want to be seen; he just wants to work— to feel the fidelity of his labour— and so Richard Fort is here in a 'semi-official' capacity investigating a dead end disappearance he's certain that no one else on the force is at all interested in.

At the edge of the isle he plunges his hand into the water. The water is shallow. There is no sudden drop-off in depth. He turns around and looks up at the lighthouse. At the top there is a dome surrounded by a balcony. The balcony runs circularly around the outside of the glass dome like a wastebasket. The sun glares in the wastebasket like a dropped egg. Richard Fort enters the building and finds the switch. Light clatters up the hollow. He mounts the stairs.

In the living quarters of the lighthouse there's a scrappy looking single bed with springs rising like tornadoes through the covers, a threadbare rug piled with books that Richard Fort is diligently writing down the titles of, and a desk cramped with items that, as is Richard Fort's M.O, he's leaving till last to investigate.

Richard Fort was in the year above James Burke at school. He doesn't remember much about him though he recognized the name over the radio and the bizarreness of the allegation had piqued his curiosity enough for him to pull James' file the day after. There wasn't much to it. A few minor drugs charges, a count of vagrancy, one or two logged complaints of harassment by Lawrence Muir and that was all. He looks at the photo of James Burke and the accompanying description.

James Burke: 33 years old
                    Caucasian male
                    Brown hair
                    Green Eyes
                    6ft 2
No other distinguishing features.

Richard Fort kneels and touches the frayed rug. He looks at the telephone in its crib, half-submerged in the floor, and pulls it out. He searches under the loose floorboards. There's nothing of interest there. He walks over to the desk. A lamp cranes over the desk. Richard Fort turns it on. On the desk there is a notebook. Next to the notebook is a photograph of a woman. It is a photo of the woman that Mr Burke is alleged to have been harassing. Richard Fort looks at the photo without touching it. The photo is of a personal nature. Richard Fort pulls open the desk drawer. He finds a plastic baggy turned inside out and possibly licked clean and one small syringe. Richard Fort takes a Polaroid of the desk with the drawer open. He holds the Polaroid up as it begins to develop. He senses a poetry might emerge in its composition that'd render it inadmissible as evidence. He puts the Polaroid into his top pocket before it has finished developing. He picks up the notebook. He flicks to the last few pages. These last pages are filled with a series of drawings of varying detail and technical ability.

The first drawing is of a child with long hair, presumably female though otherwise featureless, standing on a ledge and looking out towards a lighthouse half her size. The child is embraced conically by light. The light is represented in the drawing by two divergent dotted lines emerging from the lighthouse that extend to the top and bottom left corner of the frame. The last dash at each corner is half the size of the preceding ones suggesting— Richard Fort notes— that the light continues exponentially along its path. The second picture shows a delicately shaded close up of the child's shoulder separating from the torso. The third is a detailed drawing of a leg separating in three places: Hip, knee and ankle. The areas of separation— both the appendage and its former joint— appear smooth and curved like a pebble, as if both were either immediately cauterised or never truly connected.

The depiction of light is constant in each picture and signified by the same diagonal lines at the edge of each frame. These lines occurring either to the bottom left or top left of the frame, or concurrent in both, and suggesting— it would seem— that the light is somehow destroying the child. This supposition being confirmed to some degree, Richard Fort felt, by the final picture and the title underscoring it.

The final picture is a close-up of the child's face. It is at once the most intricate and inscrutable of the drawings. The picture takes up the whole of a page. It is of a face drawn and then neatly erased, scrubbed, of all identifying aspects with the exception of the lips which are drawn up in either pain or, more disturbingly, pleasure. The drawings are collectively entitled "The Death of the Jubilant Child". Richard Fort extracts a Dictaphone from his pocket. He relates, as best he can, the details of the pictures.

He picks up the picture of Helene from the desk. Helene is naked in a portion of sea, haloed by the lamp of the lighthouse. It is night and she is turning towards the camera with one arm riding across her chest. Her other hand is cupped around a smile that escapes it and her back is slightly bent in laughter. There is a faint suggestion of her ribs written under the captured movement of skin. The ribs look like mounted wings waiting to emerge from the luminosity of her flesh. It is as if her skin is being x-rayed by joy. Richard Fort turns the photograph over. The date 07/06/80 is written in pencil on the back of the photograph. He turns it over again. The waves are fringed white. Helene's hip is lightly curved around the onyx reflection of the pier's hulk in the water and there is a small silvery arrowhead of light glistening at the base of her spine. The whole sea seems to lap at her.

Richard Fort places the photograph between the pages of the notebook. He walks to the lantern room.

The room is domed and the windows are stained with filth. Several generations of spiders have left their webs to grow freighted with dust, to bend greyly in cremated rainbows around the darkened glass. Richard Fort stands in front of the disconnected light and then turns around until he is facing the cliff. He can make out the victim's house and three to four other building sites. He takes the notebook out of his pocket. He starts to read it from the beginning.

*

Lawrence Muir is sat gingerly at his desk visualising an aqua blue inflatable rubber cushion, one donut shaped and recently extracted from a large industrial freezer. He is visualising it being gently inserted under his clammy thighs, a coolness finally coming to rest there, the ring of the cushion encircling his own within its oval frame and somehow, he hasn't quite worked out how yet, creating a tunnel of soothing arctic air that'd waft up that troubled passageway in a soothingly holistic breeze.

Lawrence has lifted this technique from the self-help book *Imagined Success You Can Have It*, gifted to him by his Doctor and golfing partner.

Other images Lawrence Muir has used in an attempt to alleviate his current discomfort have included: a lake composed of placid moisturising lotion soundlessly quenching a burning asteroid in some incredibly humid jungle setting, a frost like a graft of skin settling over the scarred earth of a drought ridden plain, and the well-lit interior of an industrial fridge filled with frozen corpses.

All these, however, have failed to adequately distract him from the gush of evil he's had repeatedly torrent out of the lit oil well of his stomach over the last few hours.

Lawrence Muir's stomach is prone to complaints anyway but the stress of last night and the cold coffee he drank and the egg and cress petrol station sandwiches he bought and ate only the filling from, not to mention the promotion he is pushing for and which he expects to hear about soon, very soon he hopes, have all adversely affected his stomach to a degree he's never before tenanted. Lawrence has just returned from the staff toilets for the eighth time this morning. The temperature of his extremities is unholy. He has been at work for only three hours. This means he has been to the bathroom once every twenty-two and a half minutes. If you factor in the amount of time spent in the bathroom as well as the time expended travelling back-and-forth he has spent only fifteen consecutive minutes at a time at his desk working.

This ratio and its negative implications cannot fail to have been noticed, he thinks. Lawrence Muir looks around the office. At each desk there is a person apparently engrossed in their work, heads bent in fierce concentration. This striking him as somewhat suspicious, conspiratorial.

In between his trips to the bathroom Lawrence Muir has struggled to decode his co-workers' hushed conversations. He has strained to hear anything of pertinence or sense in those opaque and frosty tones that have run half-lit around his head like the strips of fluorescent lighting strafing the office's ceiling. Eight trips to the bathroom coupled with his unheard-of tardiness and not a glance from his co-workers or an excruciating innuendo levelled at him by his boss. Perhaps they have heard something about Helene and are choosing to ignore him out of embarrassment, he thinks. Lawrence reassures himself, *how could they know?* The moment Lawrence threatens to relax a subtle but distressing change occurs in the stress of his reasoning:

– How *could* they know?

Lawrence Muir is working himself carefully towards the seat's edge. His cheeks, tensed into two peaks of barely qualifying muscle, attempting to tippy toe towards freedom. It is a doomed attempt.

Something sour and anachronistic is gathering within him. He steers his sight across the map of desks, oceans of space slowly drying up around him. His stomach gargles. The stomach gargle sounds like the weakening drone of a dying fly, its low battery death bent by universal affect. His body seems to have gone into shock in reaction to the enlarging sting of pain that spreads and opens now onto the spiritual world of his soul and denounces it. Yes, it is a soul-denying shit brewing within him, one, though in truth it is legion, held back only by the rhythmic resistance of his metronomic foot. His testicles feel like two shelled peas.

> – Why am I always so conscious of my
> balls?

Lawrence holds his stomach, a fountain-shaped sweat breaking out across his back. He turns and looks for the minuscule icon of the toilet marked 'male'. He has the pose of a man heroically confronting a fatalistic future. A tear forms in his eye. At the same time a piece of paper is dropped and then blown down the aisle by some errant rotary fan. The crushed paper tumbling past him just at the moment that he blinks a large hot tear.

– Hey Lawrence you look just like that famous Red Indian guy!

That is all he would need someone to shout now.

In order to make it to the bathroom Lawrence must negotiate twelve sets of desks. He is calculating a new route to the bathroom, one that must vary significantly from the last few trips. He has used the same route for the last couple of trips as he did the first.

– Have I become so short-sighted?

Lawrence stares into the wild plain of his desk. A pen grazes it. He leans forward and rests his elbows on the table. He turns around slowly and tries to discreetly plot his way to the bathroom. It is impossible. The tops of each desk preclude any strategic view. Each desk is heaped with complexly arranged objects either drained of, or charged with, totemic life. Symbolic figures snatched from the lives their inhabitants dreamt of, still dream of, though these places, or the shades of these places, existed somewhere outside of here in the crumbling reality of their leisure. Those that have staked out a career in the office, journeyed into a heart of rendered grey, their desks are among the most savagely and sentimentally enjambed.

Lawrence hopes to reach the bare, touristy, singularly lined desks of the temps before any serious accident occurs. Lawrence straightens up. The pain seems to have alleviated a little in a rare moment of grace. He is going to be fine, he thinks. All done. Lawrence is smiling vacantly as his eyes fix upon the watercooler in the corner of the room. He watches a thick gelatinous bubble rising up in the large plastic container. It is followed by another and then another. Lawrence can sense the babble of water, understands that the bubble's infraction in the still of the water is not at all placid, understands it on a seemingly cellular level. His stomach replies in kind. The two have started to converse.

Lawrence cannot take his eyes from the water cooler. He watches a slow bubble, of significant circumference, forming in the base of the cooler. It rises tortuously at first, as if too heavy to float, and then with increasing speed careens clumsily to the surface. Lawrence watching as the rim of the bubble becomes oval, impressing itself on the surface limit, indented, breaking, splitting at the sides, exploding, releasing…

> – Not now, Jesus, no, not now Jesus. Oh
> Jesus, Jesus, Jesus.

Lawrence Muir is on his way to the bathroom for the ninth time. He is past the first three sets of desks with relative quick footed ease when, distracted by the sight of a co-worker rising to greet him, his elbow brushes a plant pot off of an empty desk. The liberated cactus has landed in

the classic pose of a murder victim, the white peat
providing the iconic outline.

The cactus and pot belonged to Susan
Donaldson. Susan Donaldson is even less popular
in the office than Lawrence Muir, though for
wildly different reasons. One reason being the
care and attention she likes to lavish on this
cactus during her breaks, the whispered sweet
nothings that have either been overheard or
crassly imagined and then hastily scribbled on the
toilets' walls.

Lawrence is hastily picking up and tossing the
cactus back onto the desk when a provident
shadow engulfs him.

– You ok there Lawrence? You look a little
worse for wear, heavy night?

It is Ian, Ian of all people, the office prince of
the office fuckwits. Lawrence stands. He is
sparkly with sweat.

> – You've killed that cactus, wow. It's
> definitely dead. Cactuses they can
> – Cacti
> – They can survive a lot, but not that I
> think. Susan will be dressed in black for
> a month.
> – Erm yes. She is, er, absent
> today…fortunately for her or…er.. us.

Lawrence, having tried to convey in his words
and manner the casual friendliness of a parting

witticism, smiles and leans forward at the same time. He almost butts into Ian who remains inured to the plea in his voice.

– Ha! Ha! Haahaha...ha... In all seriousness though, Susan is pretty ill, we shouldn't be laughing.

Lawrence murmurs an 'oh' as he cranes his head around Ian and begins to employ the breathing techniques he had memorised for Helene's pregnancy.

> – Yes, she's in the hospital with a kind of stomach flu. Ate some dodgy sandwiches from a petrol station I think. My wife said that...
> – Susan is in the hospital? Since when? Are you sure?
> – Yeah my wife is a nurse there, she told me that Susan really did not look well. Come to think of it, you look a little like how she described Susan being. Pale, sweating. Have you been having any auditory hallucination? Because that is not a good sign if you have. CAN YOU HEAR ME? BLINK TWICE IF YES. Seriously though I think you should sit down. You don't look well.
> – I'm fine, I just need to
> – You don't look fine. My wife is a nurse I should know. She is always telling me medical facts that would make your hair

curl. I'm sure she exaggerates. Actually,
and this is funny, this one time
– Your wife is a nurse at the hospital?
– Yeah, anyway this one time she starts
telling me I must have been cheating on
her because there's this terrible rash all
over my groin. It came up literally
overnight I tell you, on a Sunday of all
days.
– She was working last night?
– Yeah all last night, and I say there's no
way, 'I haven't been cheating on you' etc
because I really hadn't been cheating on
her, I would never do that. I mean, I love
my wife. But there's this rash you see
and she's a nurse and it has got me to
thinking about how I got drunk at
Sam's, you know Sam right, Sam in
accounting? You know him?

Lawrence nods vigorously.

– Well I got drunk at Sam's the week before
and I couldn't remember getting home. Lots of
beer and vodka, a sort of wahey the lads kind of
evening, and we went out somewhere and then
that's all I remember, and so I'm starting to think
maybe I should just confess except I'm adamant
that it's not possible that I cheated on her, no way
except…you know… *is* there?
– I have to go now.
– And my wife she starts saying that she knows

100% that what is currently tearing burgundy up my balls and shaft is a V.D and I should just come out and be a man and admit because she's a nurse and she knows exactly what it is I've got and how I've got it, you filthy brute, cock sucking bastard etc etc and so she goes to the kitchen and grabs this knife and comes back into the bedroom where I'm still bare naked and all but ready to confess

Lawrence shoulders past Ian who spins around, his hands finned around his crotch, a manic smile at play on his lips.

Lawrence can hear every pen scratching, every word processor clack, he can hear the quiet desperation of the room very clearly, can hear it as if the 'quiet desperation' was in fact screaming very loudly and insanely in his face. Ian, raising his voice to a hoarse shout:

– Turns out it was all a hilarious practical joke! She'd gotten hold of my allergy tests and decided to play a trick on me. Of course what she wasn't to know was what the long term effects of inducing this rash would be or the effect it was to have on our...

Lawrence quickens his step. The toilet door is visible to him now. The woman closest to it looks up at him, frowns, how many times has this woman seen him today? Her desk being unavoidable bringing up, as it does, the rear. The association puns on his

abdomen. Onwards, regardless, he pushes the

bathroom door open and enters a grey tiled room charged with latent grace and a smell of poverty. A bathroom not unlike a school bathroom with toilet rolls more akin to tracing paper than the double woven, gently moisturised, tastefully embroidered tissues he generally likes to see a toilet furnished with.

Lawrence begins to fret now, allows himself that luxury, as he lowers himself onto the hard enamel rim. The police have yet to call. He hopes that they do not call at all. He hopes that there will not be a scene and that they will not enter while he is still in the bathroom, sat here with his trousers netted around his ankles certainly not catching butterflies. He is remembering now as the first umbrella of shit gives way— its form forged only through velocity—that Ian has a wife and that Ian's wife is a nurse in the hospital where Helene was treated. Also, the secretary has a husband in the police force while Clarice, in marketing, had a relative admitted to the hospital only a few days ago. Lawrence feels the world closing in around him, the world shrinking to the pain in his stomach, the world exiting him with force.

He wishes to be recognized for his contributions to the company, to efficiency. He does not wish to be known because his wife has a stalker or because his wife has a penchant for throwing herself down cliffs— of all things— in her free time.

Don't be so harsh, he thinks, you love her. You. Love. Her.

A lot.

He loves her so much.

Lawrence places his palm flat against the cubicle wall and tries to master the burning sensation. He leans his back against the cool tank. Sweat breaks around his temples in morse code:

..-. ..- -.-. -.-

F   u   c   k

– Muir, you in here? Muir!

It is his boss' voice.

– Muir, you in here? Muir!

Lawrence watches a pair of shoes crossing the row of cubicles. He leans forward and silently unlatches the door, inching it forward. His boss is standing with his back to the cubicles regarding his reflection in the toilet's large horizontal mirror. Lawrence can make out the man's eyebrows meshed up like a scour across his forehead. His boss begins to pace in the military fashion across the sinks. Lawrence closes the door, takes a deep breath and pulls the chain. Two expensively attired yet condescendingly manly feet instantly plant themselves just outside of the door. The door begins to tremble and sigh as a knee brushes it, once, twice.

The latch, Lawrence has forgotten the latch.

– Muir, you're in there aren't you?

Answer me dammit! I don't want to have

to get on my knees and check, you hear?
You're to come out immediately.

– Just a second sir.

– Muir!

– Please, sir, I will just be a moment.

The door creaks open just as Lawrence stands
pulling his trousers up. The boss examines
Lawrence with a wrinkling look of distaste.

– Come with me Muir, we're to have a serious
chat.

Lawrence walks behind him, his body cold with
sweat, arms drooping towards his knees,
mortified face sloping away from mortified skull,
his flesh puddled towards the door's slip with
each condemned footfall. The boss opens the
door and the light bears painfully down on
Lawrence's brow and then there is a sound,
sprinkled and repetitious, gathering in portions
of the office as his dehydrated form enters,
blinking, into the room.

Lawrence trying to refocus his eyes in a
headache catalysing light. That sound, both
forced and lackadaisical, is it— could it be—
polite applause? Polite applause being the sound
Lawrence most clearly associates with success.

He sees a banner wishing him good luck.

– Congratulations Muir, you're moving up in
the world.

*

Are you aware that James Burke kept a journal? Richard Fort asks as he glances up at Helene. She is lying in her dressing gown, bandaged ankle elevated by the sofa arm's snailish recoil. Richard Fort is sat to the right and slightly behind her, legs crossed, body therapeutically bent in posture if not purpose.

James never kept a journal, she responds. There are crescent moons ripening under each of Helene's eyes to a marbled red. In fact, gelatinous tissue appears to have been chewed and wadded under her skin as if stemming the internal flow of some subcutaneous intrusion. Richard Fort nods at her words, an ambient whine roosting in his nasal passages. His lips complete the hum, lend it body, the lips harmonising with a softly flapped burr that flattens out to an inquisitive, consonant heavy, whisper.

–

Helene sits up slowly in tenuous response— leg tentatively arcing down in front of her— and draws a slim cigarette from the pack on the table with the elegant walnut finish. She's leaning back and lighting it as Richard Fort reaches into his pocket for Jim's notebook.

Helene feels a wash of repulsion as Richard Fort raises the notebook to shoulder height, the book standing up vertically like a tract.

Helene thinks: I hate this man.

The notebook leans limply back and forth in his hand.

The sharp tang of whisky on Richard Fort's tongue has turned to a mound of greasy slurry. Sat in his car outside of this house he had felt surprised at the lightness of his hip flask, a lightness which had felt giddy in his hand, as if the bottle might rise through the car's ceiling with the merest of synaptic twitches. Strictly speaking he shouldn't be here right now.

Richard Fort gestures for her to take the book, to look through it, to familiarize herself with its contents.

Helene stares at his outstretched hand.

– That's not his journal if that's what you're trying to say. I told you he wouldn't write a journal. That's the information I'm trying to give you here.

– If this isn't his journal, what do you suppose it is?

Helene attempts to smile 'witheringly' at Richard Fort. The affected gesture casts coins of skin into Helene's eyes. This both sharpens and undercuts the effect of her expression like a nail sticking out of some ornately carpentered frame.

Helene gestures for the notebook. She looks at the front and then the back covers, opens it randomly somewhere in the middle, flicks through a couple of pages, glances briefly at the scrawled 'crippled fly walking across the page' (oh, Jim) handwriting and shrugs pointedly.

> – It could be anything. He used to say that he was writing a novel. It could be the notes for his novel or even his supposed novel but it's not a journal or a diary. He could never keep one of those.
> – Why not?
> – He found anything to do with real life embarrassing.
> – Embarrassing?
> – Yes, embarrassing.

Helene holds the book out, bridging the space between them with it. Her other hand is holding the top of her dressing gown, bunching it together just above her heart though her hand rose there long before she leant toward Richard Fort. Helene is signalling that she wishes to return this book, this book that she does not understand, that does not register within her at any point.

Richard Fort's hands remain funnelled in his lap.

> – It mentions you by name you know.

Helene's face is quantitatively the same except time has passed so now it is completely different. A sine wave flutters briefly across the amplitude of her smile. The flexed dimples in her cheeks begin to cramp. Helene slowly, gingerly, releases her expression. She lets her eyes pour through Richard Fort's hands. Helene looks up at him and then away. It's a gesture Richard Fort is inclined to read as disingenuous.

> – This is so misguided, I'm tired of all this.

Helene leans back against the sofa, the book still in her hand, and crushes the half-smoked cigarette into the ashtray. The fizz of its extinguishment laundered within an unmistakably real sigh. It is a deep sigh that exits Helene now, a fire drill of the soul that hangs there, indisputable, like the must we go on of some indivisible remainder. A sigh that is hurrying after and displacing the smoke teased silken around her otherwise studied breathing. She lifts her leg and places it on the sofa arm and lowers herself into a horizontal position. Richard Fort crosses and uncrosses his legs.

Helene opens the notebook and begins to look through it. She is turning the pages slower this time though it is apparent that she is still not reading, that the words are not entering her, that she is resistant to their meaning. Richard Fort makes a note.

At the sound of his pencil scratching away, Helene begins to talk.

– Listen, James always wanted to be a writer.

Everyone knew that. He used people he knew as the basis of his characters and often he didn't even bother to change their names. He thought it was a literary technique but to most people it sounded like a mean trick... The simple fact is that he had a big problem with names, whenever he thought of one it would sound wrong, too... something or other, never right. He couldn't be realistic even with names, it was a hallmark of his character... and of course it did turn out to be a mean trick, what he did with our names, but not in the way we'd thought it was going to be. He'd use mine or his friends' names or nicknames to try and keep himself honest, I think, or tethered or something but all anyone ever felt when they read his writing was more alone. I'm not denying that we used to know each other well but James was sick, really sick and he was harassing us, he was harassing my family, he was obsessed. Is it surprising he'd make stuff up about us?

She glances at Richard Fort and then back at the book.

– There are dates, times, places...things that I suppose could be verified were they to be officially looked into.

Richard Fort is lying. He hasn't found any of these things in his hastily cribbed reading of the notebook. There aren't any names at all, just letters standing in for characters (H, E, F) and no real plot that he can discern. There are just a series of non-narrative events, increasingly unfathomable abstractions, manic references to a curse and, from what he can figure out, a teenage girl in trouble at the centre of it all.

> – Why are you doing this? Do you even know where James is?

Richard Fort looks down at his notes as if he were embarrassed for Helene, his voice and body language acquiring an official, passively aggravated, tone.

– Could you characterise your relationship to James Burke, before, when you knew him please?

Helene has just found the photograph of her naked in the sea. She fingers its gloss.

– More than friends.

– Lovers?

– You could say that.

Helene turns the page.

– What would you say?

– Probably what everyone else said, in hindsight.

– And what did they say?

Helene sits up and pivots towards him sarcastically.

– Why do you want to know?

– I'm trying to understand why James Burke might shine a however many kilowatt bulb into your house and then disappear without a trace. You're right by the way; we don't have a clue where he's gone. The doors were bolted from the inside when the officers arrived at the scene and it's unlikely that he could have jumped from that vantage point without landing on the rocks, in which case we'd have found him and I wouldn't be here. The lighthouse didn't have a fire escape or any other exits. That's one of the main reasons I'm here, we've got nothing. No clue. Nada.

Helene reaches for and then lights another cigarette from the table with the elegant walnut finish. She can feel the French windows glower with light behind her. The light and heat streaming through the window pane plays with her hair, contracts around her scalp, bunching the roots together, before releasing them slowly in an echo of that way she used to like, Jim, whenever a cloud passes.

Last night she was flooded, erased, by light. She tries to fill her mind with that light. She is trying hard to remember how it felt.

Helene takes a long, meditative drag on her cigarette.

> – Just that he was no good; that he'd
> never amount to anything, that he was
> useless. These were all comments from
> people that liked him too by the way. I
> remember my father, who was actually
> fond of Jim and who liked to paint as a
> hobby, nothing professional mind you,
> sailboats and the like, well he would
> make a light blue slash of watercolour

on his canvas, so pale it was barely there
you understand, and he would point at it
and say 'look it's Jim' and then titter to
himself. The joke was amusing but it had
a point to it. Later when things, when
things with James, got bad with drugs
my father was more serious but he still
cared for him. Other times Jim would
say bullshit things like his ambition was
to be a stained-glass window. He'd be
stoned at the time he said admittedly,
but then when wasn't he stoned? He had
all these ideas about moving away and
becoming an artist but he was just
completely impractical. I mean the guy
didn't know how to make his bed until
he was twenty-five. He wasted every
chance and opportunity his intelligence
and privilege afforded him until he
became such a joke that no one even
listened to him try to make the same
points he'd made more convincingly,
more cogently, when he was a teenager.
So people just said, you know, 'James is a
loser, he'll never come to anything, what
are you doing with him?'
– What did you say to them?
– I said that I loved him. It was true back
then and I was committed to it but I
failed. Later, I was less committed to it
but it was still true and then, after a long

while, I even stopped loving him completely. It wasn't just like that of course, it even came as something of a surprise to me to find out about it. I don't feel much about him but anger now.

– Were you actively in a relationship with him when you realised that you no longer loved him?

– I don't understand the question.

– Yes, you do.

– What is this about, Richard?

– Where's James Burke?

– I don't know.

Richard Fort leans forward and takes the notebook from her hand. He turns the book over and over in his hands. He looks up at Helene who is putting out her cigarette.

– I think you have some idea.

Richard Fort is about to continue when he catches a dark glimpse of himself in the table with the elegant walnut finish. The expression on his face isn't what he had expected. He looks puffy, used up, distorted. Richard Fort realises that he has been swallowing more than usual, that his throat feels bruised. He is trying to control the tremble his hands are suddenly possessed of though his mind feels calm and clear enough.

– James Burke left the town for a little over 8

months two years ago. We know he was living with friends. We know that he was holding down a job. From what we can gather he had no more ties here at all. So, what I'm asking is, why would he come back? He was living in the lighthouse, did you know that? It's a cold, damp place. A night in there must have been torture, sheer torture. It's obvious that he was mentally unwell and I have to say at this point I'm as concerned for his safety as I am yours.

Helene is growing sadder and sadder, in steadily increasing increments of sadness, until it feels as if Helene cannot get any sadder any faster. The velocity of sadness approaching, verging upon, a timelessness which, being timeless, begins to seem like it will never ever end, only somehow barrenly accrue unless, or more realistically until, the sadness collides with something so unapologetically real and irreversibly eventful that it will physically alter in some non-utilitarian way her entire body. Helene takes a drag on a cigarette that she cannot recall having lit and exhales quickly.

> – If you could tell us why he came back, any possible trigger that might help explain his return then maybe we can find him.
> – Your job isn't to find him, it's to protect us.
> – I'll decide what my job is.

> – I want to talk to someone else, I want
> to speak to someone else.

Richard Fort is noticing how the red rims underneath Helene's eyes look like how a sunset would look if the sun suddenly scabbed up or started to show its age. He turns away from her glare— pretends to make a note— leans on the silence between them.

The trembling in his hand seems to have stopped, his hand and the notebook coming to rest on his lap as Helene opens her mouth to speak.

> – The lighthouse, possibly, it has been
> associated with his family for nearly a
> hundred and fifty years. I think, well I
> know, my fiancé is involved with a
> company that is trying to buy the
> building to convert it into…something.
> The lighthouse is protected, it's a Grade
> A listed something or other but they
> could get permission to renovate and
> convert it. I think James must have been
> against that. The lighthouse was like a
> church to him and he believed, or
> wanted to believe, in the stories around
> it. To see that all lost and turned into an
> apartment…he'd have hated it.

Richard Fort shakes his head.

– I know you've seen the photo in here.

– ….

– When is your husband…

– Fiancé

Richard Fort glances up.

– When is your fiancé back from work?
I've a couple of questions to ask him too.

– I don't know; he works late
sometimes.

– Do you have the address?

– I can write it down for you if you like.
Aren't you going to ask me about why I
had to go to the hospital last night?
Where I was going when it happened?

– I don't think anything you'd tell me
would tell me anything, even if you were
able to keep it to the facts. I can guess
what you might say though. Would you
like me to?

Helene puts out her cigarette.

– You were disorientated, threatened.
You didn't feel safe in your own home.
Your fiancé, Lawrence, had taken off
maybe to fight James but he's not really
the type so you were sure someone
would get hurt and you didn't know
what to do so you did something stupid.
Now, of course, you're embarrassed by

> your theatricality, by the fuss you've caused. You're sorry for everyone involved, for the brother and sisterhood of fellow taxpayers even, but the fact remains that you were scared, that you are scared, and that you only hope this nightmare can come to a definite conclusion very soon by our finding James and ensuring your safety.

There is a wailing sound ghosting through the baby monitor and Helene, already adrenalized by her growing anger, attempts to stand.

Pain branches electric through her form. She cries out. Richard Fort rises and catches her by the arm as her body slews against him. He is gripping the fabric of her dressing gown and trying, using his knees as the fulcrum, to slide her back onto the sofa as the cleaner appears, Diane helping to lay Helene down, to fold her dressing gown into place before resting her cool hand upon Helene's forehead.

Diane looks at Richard Fort. The look she is giving Richard Fort is pitched somewhere between reproach and understanding, a look of forgiveness unasked for but strangely welcoming. A smiling forgiveness that carried within it the first news of the sin. Richard Fort finds his face unable to master a reciprocal expression.

Richard Fort sits down confused.

Diane tells Helene not to worry, that she will

go and check on Evelyn for her. Helene is about to tell Diane not to bring Evelyn down, that she will come up in a moment, when the pain in her ankle erases her sentence. Helene rubs her leg. She thinks 'drugs.' She thinks 'Jim.' Helene reaches for the pack of cigarettes. It is empty. Helene is blaming Richard Fort. She tries not to. She can't remember what she is or isn't blaming Richard Fort for. Helene fails not to blame Richard Fort. Helene thinks, 'this is a long silence.' Helene thinks, 'Jim.'

> – How old is she?
> – What?
> – Your daughter.
> – Oh, she's just under twelve months.
> – I see.

Richard Fort looks at his notes. Helene watches him, frowning

> – I've just one other question to ask you before I go.
> – Go on.
> – Does the phrase 'the jubilant child' mean anything to you?

Helene's face is impassive, then confused, then relieved in its innocence. Has Helene come to think of herself as guilty? In reality she has never stopped.

– No, not at all, sorry. Why?
– No reason, it's just that this last entry caught my eye.

He passes Helene the book. Helene is looking at the drawings. Richard Fort studies her for a moment or two before being distracted by the crouching reappearance of the cleaner in the room. In front of the bent over cleaner he sees a small boy carrying a baby across the threshold of the room.

Henry is looking at Evelyn with tenderness and ignoring the world. Diane is behind him, steering him through it. She is beaming with pride. Diane is going to say— is about to say— that Henry had insisted on carrying her. As an afterthought she'll add that she, of course, would not allow him to hold Evelyn until they had reached the bottom of the stairs. She is about to say all this as she looks up and sees Helene's face rotated and screwed by the tears her eyes inadequately plug.

The notebook is lying open on the floor, its pages slowly flickering back and forth. Henry stops and looks at it. He is instantly transfixed by the image of an arm separating from its body and the expressionless face of a child there. He recognises the lighthouse from its stripes and rust and knows that it is out there, in the world, through the glass of those doors, and what does this mean? Henry is instinctively aware that this was something that he was not supposed to have seen. He is fascinated by how it feels to have seen this secret. To have seen it and to understand nothing. The fascination sets off a world inside him.

Richard Fort gets to his feet. He picks up the notebook. He glances at Henry without knowing why. Evelyn begins to shift in Henry's weakening arms. His grip loosens, Evelyn slips. She begins to cry, her crucifix form suspended just above the floor, her chubby legs dangling helplessly. Diane takes her from him. Helene has stopped crying and is apologising to everyone and no one, talking about her medication and its side effects.

Richard Fort stands in front of Helene as she cleans her face with the sleeves of her dressing gown. He places his card on the table with the elegant walnut finish.

– I think we ought to talk some more, when you're ready.

He nods at Diane in wordless apology as he leaves. She turns to watch him out of the door, her lips maturing steadily outwards into a sill of confusion.

*

Lawrence is smoking a cigar behind the wheel of his company car. He is not sat down, his feet are not resting on the pedals and neither are they under or atop the hastily kicked-up rubber mat slid unevenly beneath their vulcanised hammers.

Lawrence is crouched before the wheel of the car in a squatting stance – knees parallel to the horn – feet tucked underneath the tipped scale of his trousers – forward leaning torso inclining at an increasing rate towards expectant windshield as the seat spreads out in a pit below him. His thighs are fired with pain and he knows that soon he will have to extend one of his arms towards either the steering wheel or the passenger window if he is to maintain his balance. The knowledge of this panics him.

He pushes the cigar around the carving of his grin. The cigar goes from left to right and up and down. His mind is calmly observing the movement of the cigar and calculating how best to transfer the sodden butt from one corner of his mouth to the other while the rest of his body continues to torture him at the periphery of what he can stand.

The cigar smoke is only a mask. There is another physical, weighted smell pursuing an increasingly territorial policy regarding the car's subsidiary of air.

Lawrence has recently shat himself. The cigar is helping with the odour but that is not its sole function, cigar smoking being a conventionally celebratory activity.

And Lawrence is going to celebrate his promotion, however unconventionally. He has thought to himself *I am continuing to celebrate my promotion* anytime a thought has threatened to threaten. Lawrence's squat position becomes a skier's ready position as he extends his legs until his back is nearly touching the roof. The new position lacks the hoped-for stability as his calves tremble above meridians of sock. It is untenable.

His hands claw at the steering wheel as the cigar teeters dangerously over his lips like a coach full of horny teenagers.

The manager had taken Lawrence to the office, given him the promotion and then he— Lawrence Muir — shat himself. The cigar tumbles to the floor, rolls under a pedal. The smell of rubber now added to the car's cauldron of aroma.

– How do I. How do I. What. How, do I, how?

It is custom to smoke a cigar with your manager after being promoted, there being something appealingly atavistic about it, about standing there like a fertility god with a displaced sense of oneself.

The manager had been in the process of handing the cigar to Lawrence when it happened. The manager's large mottled hand had continued to move over the desk without agency even as the fact of the shit had become undeniable. Lawrence had taken the cigar from the hand that rose like a question in his direction, then backed away, thanking the manager graciously as the sweaty palm of his hand slipped around the brass doorknob. Then there was the tripping over of the rearranged desks, Ian's puzzled face looking in his direction and the surreal sight of a row of hands moving like synchronised swimmers to hold their noses as he scrabbled by.

Lawrence leans forward, grabbing for the cigar butt, afraid of tipping over.

Lawrence is going to try to drive without sitting down. He is pulling on the wheel and stretching out his right leg in front of him. His left leg remaining underneath him. The idea being that he'll be able to transfer the right foot from accelerator to brake as needed, thus keeping the seat of his trousers suspended above the seat at a near forty degrees from vertical so as to reduce the possibility of any further incriminatory slippage. Given the capacity for thought in a moment like this, it had seemed the only solution.

There is a wire mesh fencing off the car park five feet ahead of Lawrence's car. Holding the wheel with one hand and still leaning back— his foot trembling on the pedal— Lawrence turns the key in the ignition. The wire mesh becomes pregnant with car. Lawrence untethered by the seatbelt sperms about the car front of the car— his forehead butting into the windshield— his neck disappearing into the collar of his shirt. He falls sideways onto the passenger seat, the gearstick piercing his ribs. Shit flows out of his pants. Tiny perfect squares of light harlequin his face as it flows through the mesh. Lawrence lays breathing heavily for a minute or two. Shadows cross his face. There is a knock on the window.

Lawrence rolls his face away and waits. Whoever it is leaves to call security.

Through a complex series of movements Lawrence resumes his position and grips the steering wheel again. He sets the car into reverse. The wheels slip tongues of mud from the wall of the ditch they're overhanging. The parched mud lays spat behind the car, shrivelling on the concrete in the bright afternoon. Lawrence opens the car door. He places one foot on the concrete. There is a welcoming firmness to it. He ducks under the frame of the door. He pushes the car, an avalanche of sweat and excrement tumbling down his back and legs. The car backs out of the ditch. Lawrence sighs. He looks at the car seat. He shakes his leg. He sits down and pulls the door to and visualises a fresh tube of minty fresh toothpaste being squeezed somewhere around the middle. He sighs. The cigar is a sodden plug in his mouth. The car jerks back onto the concrete and swivels away.

*

Helene is on her knees in front of the sofa playing with Evelyn. The cleaner is upstairs, supposedly getting her things. Helene has been trying to send her home since the detective left. She can hear the vacuum being turned on for one last run at the upstairs hallway's clingy dirt. The cleaner stalling for time, out of kindness Helene supposes. She closes her eyes. The roar of the Hoover above her could sound like a waterfall if the drugs were working. Helene tries to pray. She has no words for it.

Helene opens her eyes and the world and her failed prayers fuse into a small, anonymous, looking boy peering at her with hazel eyes. She seizes Henry's shoulders and kisses his cheeks frantically. She gathers him into herself and holds him through the rapids of her settling panic. Henry looks at the ceiling as his body is crushed into her softness, his face broad and emptying. Henry does not know the name of this feeling that erases him. It is not love though love is a component of it.

– I don't know what to do, I don't know what to do. I've lied to everyone, forgive me.

Helene's whisper has toppled like a beam into the room. It lies between them. Helene holds his shoulders and looks through his eyes. Henry has never been looked at for so long. He looks back. On the carpet Evelyn falls back and giggles.

Upstairs, Diane has switched the Hoover off. Henry and Helene both look up and then Henry steps toward Helene and hugs her with all the heroically lacking strength of love flung against an impossible. Henry's small arms exhausting themselves around her.

Evelyn tugs the cuff of Herry's trousers.

– Herry, Hairy.

Helene begins to smile for the first time in forever. It doesn't last.

– hairy, herry hainreee

These are not the first words Evelyn has said, 'dada' having come a few weeks earlier while Lawrence tickled her under her chin and she burbled over with love for him, but these are the first words Helene can remember Evelyn having said since.

She flushes with shame.

Henry has secretly been trying to get Evelyn to say his name for weeks now, in private, whenever he has seen her. He is smiling and pointing at Evelyn and he is stamping his foot and when he glances at Helene he can no longer understand or even notice the way Helene's smile is weakly withdrawing from the world. Evelyn giggles and rolls on her back. When she manages to sit up again, she's completely lost.

Helene can hear Diane's footsteps begin to sound with an anticipatory directness above them. She tries to raise herself onto the sofa, struggling to get into place before, before what? Henry feels it too, he wants to help. Evelyn has turned around and is trying to follow the dull sounds moving diagonally across the wall while grabbing at Henry's ankle.

Diane is skipping with a clipped pace down the staircase. She doesn't feel right about leaving like this— not at all— but her elderly father has been looking after Jude all day and she can't keep him waiting any longer. She pushes the front room door open. There's a tableaux quality to the way their bodies tense into painterly lines as she enters the room. Henry attending to the wan woman's wounded heel. Helene taken aback, her hands clawed around the raft of sofa. Evelyn sat there cherubically holding Henry's ankle and craning her chubby neck towards Diane, her eyes wide open and cluelessly severe as any old symbol of observant innocence. Henry stops and picks up Evelyn and shows her to his mother.

– Listen mum, listen, I'm a word.

Diane tells Henry to say his goodbyes. Helene kisses him on the cheek and ruffles his hair. She asks Diane to pass her the crutches which she does. Diane picks up Evelyn and places her within her creche. Evelyn keeps saying 'Herry, Herry'
    – Mum, I'm her first word.
    Diane looks at Helene whose lips ease into a distracted but polite smile. Diane nods. Helene stands using her crutches and walks them to the door.
    Henry is smiling, he says

– In the beginning was the word.

Diane's hand rises up and comes down hard across his backside. At first Henry's mind can't conceive of the blow and then his face curdles and he begins to howl. Diane holds his collar and brings her hand up once more. Henry senses it. He tries to run up the wall. He is cycling through the air like one of his cartoons and for a moment he truly believes he will escape. Henry falling back to earth as Diane's hand rains down expertly across his twisting rack of legs. She lets him go. Henry Road Runner's to the car crying. Helene wants to say something but her jaw won't open. Diane makes her apologies and leaves. When she gets to the car where Henry is leaning and trying to control his tears she turns and waves gaily at Helene who is still watching from the doorway.

Henry stares at his mother. Helene closes the door. Diane looks at the door and then at Henry. She says

-You know why.

Henry says

– I wasn't, dad says
– Well, your father

Henry's mother unlocks the car. Henry climbs into the passenger seat. He picks up and opens a Spiderman comic his father gave him that his mother barely approves of. Diane doesn't say anything.

The car pulls out of the driveway and trundles down the hill towards home.

– How come Jude gets to stay at home?
– He's small enough that Granddad can look after him and you're usually well

behaved enough to bring along to work.

Henry nods and then looks up.

> – Will God forget dad when dad dies?
> Because I won't.

Diane strokes his head. She can't answer that. A husk of something peels down her throat. She changes gears.

> – And will God forget my friend too?
> – Who?
> – From school. I told him yesterday that God was going to forget him and that the four horsemen of the apocalypse were going to ride over him and that his neck would break under their hooves and that he would be trod into the dirt. I think his mum is going to phone you.

Diane turns the radio on.

> – Mum?
> – Yes?
> – The teacher called a child a fiasco yesterday. What does a fiasco mean?
> – Well in Spain they go to sleep in the middle of the afternoon and they call that a siesta.
> – What?
> – That's what a siesta means.

– You're not listening. I said Fiasco.
– What?
– This kid, he farted on Jimmy
Anderson's head and then the teacher
called him a fiasco. What does a fiasco
mean?
– I don't think I like the sound of this
boy.

Henry is no longer listening. He is flicking
through his comic book. Spider-man levels a
witticism at the Green Goblin. Doctor Octopus
smashes through a wall. Spider-man says
something self-deprecatory. There's panes
composed of dust and detritus clashing
everywhere in garishly candied colour. Spider-
man leaps out of view. The way that you can tell
that he's leapt out of view is that there are these
little exclamations of light outlining his absence.
Doctor Octopus and the Green Goblin look
around for him. Henry thinks of his front room,
the dinner table, the chair by his bed at night
and all the other places he tends to remember his
father being. He draws lights round them. Henry
begins to think of his own secret identity,
whether he is good or bad. He desperately wants
to be good.

Diane glances at Henry. Henry catches her look
in the rear-view mirror. Her lips form a spout
on the left-hand side of her face. Henry begins to

laugh. He knows what is coming. Diane begins to imitate the stern voice of her father.

> – You need a haircut.
> – Nooooooo!
> – You need a haircut. You look like a giiiiirl.
> – No please, no please! I don't look like a girl!
> – You do, your hair is a sin against nature.
> – Noooooooooo!!!

Diane rubs his head. The sky rushes past blue winged and cloud tailed. Henry shakes the fringe from his eyes. His mother begins to sing along to the radio. The song is American Pie. It is the only song Henry has ever heard his mother sing along to though she never remembers the lyrics correctly. The car reaches the house before the song finishes. Diane abruptly turns the radio off and Henry unbuckles his seatbelt. The house is at the bottom of two hills so the car is parked on a slope. They swing their legs out of the car in tandem and let their knees brace against the steeped concrete. Their dogs Amos and Elijah are barking. They are always barking. Diane unlatches the gate and Henry follows. The face of the house is the face of an evil robot to Henry as he paws back an overgrown bush. The dogs rush out and entwine themselves between Henry and his mother's legs. They are no longer barking but whimpering. The dog's tails bookmark their hind legs.

– They must be hungry

Diane strolls on, opens the door and shouts we're home down the hallway. One of the dogs, Amos, has followed her and he walks in a brief semicircle around Diane until his body is horizontal to her legs, barring her way. The dog looks at her and then at the stairs with that characteristic indecisiveness of servitude. Diane kneels down and scratches the dog under the chin. She notices the tail hanging between the dog's legs and frowns. The dog's paws go up and down on the spot and his whinge intensifies. Diane straightens up and walks to the bottom of the stairs. She shouts we're home again. Henry unwraps a chocolate bar in the hallway; he'll have to share it with Jude he knows but it needn't be exactly half and half. Diane runs up the stairs. Henry suspiciously observes the space left behind her and then fills it.

– Mum?

He looks up the stairs and at the photos of him and his brother lining the walls.

Henry will always remember how normal the house looked at this point.

2

WELCOME TO
THE WORLD,
1981

A car enters the outskirts of the town. Diane is driving and next to her in the passenger seat is her husband Mark. His body is slouched in the seat and his head appears glued to the passenger window. He is wearing an ill-fitting leather jacket. In the back their two sons and Diane's father sit in postures delimited by the stockpiled possessions they are transporting to their new house.

The Grandfather is talking to the eldest son

Henry. He is telling Henry that he, Henry, will never die.

– You will never die.

The Grandfather points to the literature he is holding as proof.

– It is all written here.

The Grandfather passes the pamphlet to Henry. There are many illustrations in the pamphlet but the largest and most detailed spans the front and back pages. Henry unfolds the pamphlet to better examine its panorama. In it, lions nestle against sheep and the sky is laced with transparent, electrically veined clouds. The clouds, pink rimmed— billowing— hover at the end of the pages shepherding the scene. Under the clouds, in a large meadow, people of every colour laugh and smile at nothing in particular. There is no impression of aloneness anywhere in the picture. God is nearer than the moon.

– Would you like to live there?

Henry nods slowly.

– I must work for God to remember me; you must strive for him to recognise you.

Henry sticks a finger in his ear. The sound of his Grandfather's voice suggests to him scales dropping from eyes (whatever scales may be), stones rolling back from the mouths of caves and the very great fear of being forgotten by God. Henry removes his finger and examines the palette of it. The coin of wax is darkly furred.

Henry frowns. His ears are still blocked. If he had a mustard grain of faith Henry could say

> – Hey wax, move over here and hop into my palm. Become a pillar of wax.

And it would. It would have to and that'd be ace unless his ears were too clogged to hear his mouth tremble the words. And just imagine if God didn't exist? Henry attempts to drive his head against the back of his mother's seat in order to expel the thought. The seatbelt restrains him.

The Grandfather looks down at him and places a hand around the back of Henry's neck. The Grandfather's fingers begin to roughly massage Henry's neck.

> – And Jude? What must Jude do?
> – What we all must and more.
> – For God, his mother adds.

The Grandfather's callused hands are imparting a lesson to the soft muscle of Henry's neck. They are whispering to it that death covers life, that death can manipulate life and that death swims through the skin of the living towards itself just as life moves naturally through the borders of nonexistence and God creates everything forever and ever and ever amen.

The car is stuck in traffic. Henry's father leans over and presses the car horn.

The Grandfather says

– Impatience is a sign of this system of things.

He says:

– We should pray now. Close your Eyes. Listen. Dear Father in heaven thank you for our lives even though we are stained with sin and fully deserving of death. Let us come to know you and in knowing you shake of the dust of this world. Amen.

–

His Grandfather's hands come free of his neck, releasing Henry into the darkness. Henry opening his eyes to see his shoes dangling inertly in front of him.

Henry's stare careens through them. He cannot feel his feet or, come to think of it, his ears or the planes of his face either or his abdomen or his frowning belly button if it is— in fact— even frowning anymore. Henry grabs at his belly but cannot move his neck. He is becoming a statue, he's sure of it. Henry turns stiffly towards Jude, his lips pursed in a grotesque parody of a kiss out of which his last breath pipes suddenly hot and shortly whistled— the gusty form of it breaking against Jude's wide open and near incredulous expression. Henry hanging there—frozen— in front of his brother.

Jude bursts into a delighted giggle. He pats and

pulls Henry's face, remodelling his features, bringing Henry back to life. Henry closes his eyes again, lets his body thaw out.

Diane looks in the rear-view mirror and regards Henry. His mother's smile is wide and vacated and her eyes seem to possess all the unfixable memory of the sky above them. Henry can't find himself there.

Henry turns and looks at the profile of his father who is slack-jawed and disinterested, the father's gaze attending only to the repetitive scenery streaming across the passenger window. A greater portion of his father's face is transparently reflected in the windscreen and Henry turns his attention now towards this double whose expression reposes, slightly suspended beyond them all, in the glitch of houses and the vaguely harassed boredom passing through his features. Henry has the impression that his father is travelling faster than anyone else in the car, at light speed.

He knows that it only feels as if their father is going away from them.

*

Lawrence Muir does not believe the art on the walls of a hospital should consist primarily of red smears. He is sure of this one thing. The hospital is confusing, last night was confusing. He has sat with Helene and their newborn the whole night.

He has sat with them because he must love them. There is no other explanation he can think of for having sat there— utterly awake— for the past six hours.

Lawrence has not slept. It is seven forty-five am and Lawrence has been attempting to leave the hospital for almost twenty minutes. He has been up and down this corridor with the arterial/menstruate slashes of art on the walls twice already.

He moves into the centre of some conjoining corridors and performs a 360-degree turn.

He is late for work.

He is late for work and clumsily pirouetting in an NHS hospital. He looks down both corridors and begins to tap his foot. The foot tap, gradually putting on weight, climaxes in a pathetic stamp and begins again. Lawrence adds a stick of gum to the wad in his mouth and struggles to tame it. Lawrence has gone through twelve packs of sugar-free spearmint gum in the last six hours and the clump in his mouth is now roughly the size of a small, withered appendage. Lawrence turns right and then left. He is in the maternity ward again. The light from the incubator room forms a pale square on a wall otherwise coloured only by a deficit of light. Lawrence stops. He leans against the wall. He looks around. Where are the nurses?

Lawrence's teeth work the hardening gum into a fist. He begins to chew the fist of gum with vigour, his forehead arrowed towards his nose in a half-willed dramatisation of a sizeless abstraction. The exaggerated frown providing a reassuringly physical tread to his thoughts' otherwise ungraspable surface. The flexed mat of forehead lays out no welcome, writes out a stanza of annoyance clear enough for anyone to see, and he wants them to see it, demands it be seen!

There is no one around though. There is not even another new father turned listless with emotion to whom he might explain his agitation, his great fears, and who in turn would jocularly reassure him— this perhaps not being the hypothetical man's first child— with broad and affable statements of solidarity before sentimentally reeling off anecdotal cliché after anecdotal cliché regarding the rewarding labour of parenthood.

Lawrence sighs and rubs his eyes one after another circularly with the palm of his hands as if working away a knot of muscle cramping in the centre of his vision. He takes a deep breath and endeavours to pull himself together. He's going to be a father after all.

He turns and looks into the glow of the incubator room, towards a mass of new and striving life in which all the love of the world must surely be assembled. The presumptive serenity of Lawrence's expression quickly mutates into horror. Thirty to forty babies lay suspended in white rectangles raging impotent and mute behind the window, their bodies writhing in a disjunctive orchestra of need.

Lawrence wheels around and then staggers to the end of the corridor. He turns left and then right, lost in the labyrinthine hospital. He is sweating profusely. He opens another set of doors— he is sure that this is the way out now, it must be. He looks up, a canvas blank but for a crucifying spear of red bounds down towards him in judgement.

Lawrence slumps against the wall. A faint clinking like the jangling of a janitor's keys disturbs the ambient hum of the hospital. Lawrence's ears twitch towards the sound as he inhales deeply, eyes closed, his spine straightening out against the reassuring solidity of the wall. Finally, he thinks, someone has come that he can ask the way out.

He can hear footsteps now.

Lawrence opens his eyes and, between that movement and its completion, is already ready to ask— the words stirred through his jaw bone activate within the muscles of his lips and tongue— 'do you happen to'— Lawrence almost asking right now without looking, asking whoever it is— a janitor, a nurse jangling some catheters, a doctor irregularly drumming on his clipboard with a pen — who cares, Lawrence can sense it, the sound of his voice already tuning up somewhere in the ether, set to emerge abstractly into the physical to address 'them'— 'do you happen to know the way'— but Lawrence, eyes now fully, definitely, open and seeing— lips engaged and rigged— finds in the narrowing aperture of his pupils, and right in front of his mouth, only an incomprehensible head, not even a head really but a face, a set of eyes with— he notes now— some green *matter* entangled in a darker matter above them and the faint glint lower down of something metallic at a height that's worryingly intimate. Lawrence finding all of this pressed up and *impressing* upon him so that the active sculpture of his question dies flat on its larynx as tongue and lips and jaw continue to grind soundlessly through his asking and the face actually *breathes* on him.

The smell of hot dogs + alcohol clings to a crop of Lawrence's nostril hair. His hand slaps instinctively at it. The face withdraws. The mouth asks him is it you?

> – No? Well, in a way it, if you say it like that.

The face, Lawrence can see now, has a body— a body replete with limbs and appendages and something extra that he's trying to ignore.

> – Um Hi, why were you…oh.

Lawrence is disturbed by the man's hand and the man's attitude to his hand that the man has raised now— wholly unconsciously it would appear— in greeting making it, the hand, impossible to ignore.

The length and arcing array of the hand currently held upwards in greeting, acknowledgement or possibly, Lawrence thinks now, warning is supplemented by a fork stiffly protruding from under each fingernail. Lawrence attempts to turn his attention to the man with the forks in his fingers' face. Lawrence surmises that were he first to address the existence of the forks in the fingers, even implicitly, he might further imbalance an individual evidently so unstable as to be apparently unfazed by his being mutilated with and by cutlery. Concurrently, the existence of those forks in his fingers is undeniable and they exert a magnetic pull on both the tone and direction of Lawrence's consciousness. Consequently, Lawrence is unable to really 'take in' the man with the forks in his fingers, and the patina of impressions he's deriving from this figure seem hampered and obscure, so that his consciousness of the man with the forks in his fingers continually refocuses and hovers around a sensation of confusion that's completely overwhelming in its clarity. The man with the forks in his fingers has a rakish fringe of dyed black hair, evidently woven with a frond of seaweed, and a pale fin of a nose that regally partitions his lopsided expression. His age is indeterminate and he is dressed in mismatching clothes, torn jeans and two jackets: a brown duffle coat over the top of what appears to be an Elizabethan doublet. None of these details really coalesce in Lawrence's mind becoming instead little irradiated figments of his perceptual failure.

The man with the forks in his fingers' hand remains raised.

Lawrence pinches the bridge of his nose. Frowns.

> – I know you.
> – I really don't think.
> – This is different and happening. Can you see me?
> –

–   I need help.

> – I can see that…hmmm…. They're really jammed in there aren't they.
> – I'm looking for an accident and an emergency.
> – A&E?
> –
> – I wish I could help. Do you happen to…
> – What is happens…or doesn't…definitively, what is this?
> – Yes but…

A bead of blood forms and then rolls down the man with the forks in his fingers' hand and elbow. It falls onto the floor with a muted slap that exists primarily in Lawrence's mind. A skin begins to slow over the surface of the blood there.

Lawrence stares at it.

> – I know you.
> – What? No. I'm not entirely sure that

The man with the forks in his fingers pinches the bridge of his nose. Frowns.

> – You now. Us. The light. You think otherwise?
> – Excuse me, I need to…
> – Of course, of course.
> – Thank you.
> –
> – What?
> – Is it you?
> – No, no, well, as I said before, if you phrase it.
> – And you are?
> – Never mind, here, here.

Lawrence reaches into his pocket and hands the man with the forks in his fingers a business card. This being an effective way to curtail conversation with just about anyone, he has found. Lawrence walks away, then stops and turns. Thinks *oh what the hell.* The man with the forks in his fingers is still staring at the card. He looks up. This time Lawrence will ask, he will.

The man with the forks in his fingers begins to speak again.

> – You are.
> – In development yes, listen I wanted.
> – I know you from here.
> – Well perhaps, perhaps I have spoken to you before during one of the company's community events, now.
> – The lighthouse, do you know about it?
> – Well we were interested in it that's true but it is very complicated.
> – Yes complicated. Phenomenally so. Do you know about it yet? I need help, I need help because it is happening.
> – I can see that. I think I saw a nurse.
> – You saw? A girl, I'm looking. I need to help them.
> – A nurse went thataway, ha hum, a little while back. Listen do you happen, do you happen to know the way out?
> – Straight on.
> – Straight on?
> – Straight on.
> – Really?
> – Straight on.
> – Great.
> – Who are you in all of this?

Lawrence already walking away: GOODBYE. Within five minutes Lawrence enters the commercial hub of the hospital. Every balloon in the lobby seems to incline toward him as if attempting to camouflage the exit. He remembers the babies' silent red faces in the incubator room and shudders.

The automated doors slide open. The morning light lays over the car park like a pane of glass. There is barely any wind. The absence of any activity makes time feel suspended. Lawrence walks across the eerie, light-trapped court and slides uneasily into the car. He pulls down the mirror. Light orbs in the centre of it then swells, rotates and splinters over his lap all at a speed he can't comprehend. There is something dissociative in the heat's partial covering of light. His testicles retract slightly. He looks ahead and notices two faint yellow eyes revolving in the steel trunk of the car in front. He has left the headlights on all night. His hands strangle the wheel. Lawrence bows his head, turns the ignition, the car miraculously whinnying and retching into life. Two eggs of sweat sit incubating under his armpits. He drives towards work. On the hill leading down through Sunnyside Avenue the car stalls and then simmers into sleep, the wheels trolling the pavement as Lawrence relentlessly feeds the steering wheel through his hooped hand.

*

Henry picks out a toy from the pile of objects walling off the car-boot causing a slight avalanche of dried pasta to skitter down over his Grandfather's shoulders. The Grandfather's eyes scold him. The toy he so coveted and which he now guiltily turns over in his hands is an action man. There is a button on the back of the action man's head that moves the toy's eyes left and right. The action man should be a eunuch dressed in combat gear, then the moveable eyes of the action eunuch might denote cunning, intelligence and stealth against some presupposed enemy. Henry's action eunuch, however, is dressed in knitted trousers and a knitted cardigan that his mother painstakingly handmade over the course of several toy delaying weeks. The shifting eyes of the action eunuch now denote a kind of caged terror, suspicion, a sense of being trapped in a reality inseparable from neutered toil. Henry faces the figure in his hand towards his Father's reflection. He lifts the figure's arm up and extends his own towards his father's chair.

The toy's hands were cast to bear a plastic submachine gun and not the ambiguous questions of a child. The Grandfather's hand snuffs out the plea returning the toy in one movement to Henry's lap. Henry glances up at his grandfather. The Grandfather's shirt is painfully white and charged with sun. Henry holds the toy in front of him and frowns.

  – You are no part of the world Henry, and that

toy in your hand is its too violent symbol. Put it away now.

The car shrugs forward at last continuing to weave through a succession of oddly bent and declining roads until the house, their new house, rises from the dip of the hill to meet them.

– What's that, what's that man doing?

Up ahead Lawrence Muir is waving them down, the lapels of his shirt wilted around the twin ovals of his shoulders. The car stops.

Lawrence Muir is talking to the Grandfather. He is making a pitch about investment opportunities in his company by way of thanking the Grandfather for helping jump start his car. He cannot seem to quite get the words straight.

The whiteness of the old man's shirt is making Lawrence self-conscious about his own wrinkled shirt. Lawrence's shirt, which he can now hardly consider white, is being overpowered, harangued even, into admitting its shortcomings in the face of this other, imperial, whiteness.

– I'm just a, I mean I've just had a baby you see.

The Grandfather says nothing and wipes his hands on the tiny flannel Lawrence keeps in his glove compartment for drying off after particularly taxing games of golf. The Grandfather thinks *the wages of sin* and rolls his shoulders back revealing more of the same luminous fabric. The wrinkles of Lawrence's shirt begin to resemble dirty fingernails. The fingernails leach at his torso.

Lawrence looks at the young mother who stands rapt by the old man. The look has a quality of appeal and, Lawrence is surprised to note, a buoyant plume of lust climbing back after it. He hands her his card, says *if there's anything we can do*, and begins his pitch again.

– Actually I'm looking for work.

Her husband kicks stones around the car, scuffing his black Doc Martens. The toddler is veering towards the grilled pond, falling into a bear crawl and trying to lift with his impossibly chubby fingers the metal cover. Henry, the little boy that Diane is now introducing to him, just stares and stares at Lawrence. His large indeterminate coloured eyes enveloping his face, dripping down, the child's face resembling some terrorised conscience made flesh. The boy stands by the Grandfather half-hidden by the trunk of his legs, the two of them burning in the air though one casts a light and the other stands consumed.

Lawrence continues to jabber. The Grandfather curtly thanks Lawrence while he, Lawrence, is still in mid-sentence. The Grandfather turns and walks into the house. The rest of the family follow at a subdued rate. Diane follows first. She scoops up the toddler scolding him for playing with the pond's cover and then beckons Henry, who Lawrence is avoiding looking at for fear that the child's expression might imprint somewhere behind his own.

Diane turns on the doorstep and waves.

Lawrence lifts his hand up, syncing it over hers across the distance, their two hands locked into something mutual, except, Lawrence realises now, that Diane is not waving at all but rather beckoning her wayward husband who shoulders past Lawrence and walks reluctantly towards the house. Lawrence gets into his car.

*

James 'Jim' Burke arrives at the hospital ten minutes after Lawrence leaves. This despite appearances is in no way premeditated, appearances being less than convincing on closer inspection. Jim is unshaven and wearing a suit slicked with patches of scuff and wear, a vinyl stickiness to the fabric akin to the wet scraped skin he used to find around his knees during the long lost and barely specifiable summers of his youth.

Here he is then, unshaven, unlaundered, his pupils an enlarging spot of black in the spoiled fruit of his eyes, thought patterns gone AWOL, defected in deference to a ragged swarm of digitised colour blown around like confetti by the jigsaw winds of his perception. There's a bunch of flowers that he stole from an elderly woman's garden in his hand, the dirt still nattily dreading the stems and forming an organic webbed candelabra under the base of his fist.

He is full of stories or anti-stories that knit and

chain together, tangled in images that no mouth could shape nor ear disentangle. How to explain to Helene what happened to him today on the way to see their child or what looped Road to Damascus revelation lurked behind their sequence. Jim walks through the car park rehearsing all the things that he'll shed, in an instant, on seeing Helene's heart-shaped face.

He wants to tell her about the old lady on the bus with her wrists crossed stoically above her shopping cart. How she pointedly ignored what must have sounded to her like obscene chatter from the teenagers behind her but which Jim knew held all the necessary, ugly fecundity of youth. He wants to tell Helene about the old lady's hands, how they were ridged with veins the way great rivers are rendered on a map. How he knew in this moment that he too was some celestial body, a planet amid planets coursing through exploded space, full of lifeforms and possessing only the burning consciousness of a star nudged from its path.

Jim steps forward and the doors of the hospital slide cleanly open, an airless hum sucking the sound from his ears. A cold regulatory blast of air conditioning straps around his body, his skin coming to attention now in a Mobius strip of goosebumps.

Jim feels a sudden rush of exhaustion that's warm and vaguely sensual at first but which is followed by a quick disavowal of that pleasure.

His cells grind. Jim feels the muscles of his body stretching like a long strand of spit. The flowers begin to weigh in his hand. He looks at them. They have wilted on the bus ride here and point downwards now as if peeled from the air.

They were supposed to prove something else entirely.

Jim ducks inside the gift shop. He picks up a bunch of expensive roses and begins to weave the stolen daffodils into their array. The bouquet has become clownish, smeared with a carnival yellow behind which the serious red of the roses break through in little patches of suggested depth.

– Another self-portrait Jim?

He imagines Helene laughing as she says this. Sees her touching his hand and leaving a white half-moon of shooed blood where her finger rests. He pictures their child being transferred to his arms, a weight his body has missed all these years and in which each of them swirl and gambol and mutate, the child a new being to go beyond each of them, bound for the stars or somewhere else at least.

The excitement is making Jim's fantasies childish. All his hopes have this quality of having been arrested in youth by sadness. He has been sad for a long time. The sadness seemed to reproduce itself in all his wayward strategies to cope with it, a disease that proceeded to colonise all the settlements of his self.

The girl behind the counter of the flower shop

is trying to flirt with him. He barely notices. She lays her fingers on the counter and rotates her hips towards the register. There are large rings on each of her fingers. She takes the flowers and scans them while lightly bouncing her hip against the drawer.

> – What are you here for?
> – I'm a dad... I think. I think I'm a dad.

The girl turns to him now, leans over the counter.
– You think?
– It's complicated.
The girl presses the change into his palm.
– Best of luck with that.

*

The man with the forks in his fingers is growing suspicious. The nurses— these intemperate blue angels of the bedpan, of the white hallways— are conspiring against him. He's sure of it. The man with the forks in his fingers has watched them round corners just ahead of him and then disappear into thin air. He suspects these nurses of ducking into closets, changing into informal dresses, posing as patients and then walking back past him. The man with the forks in his fingers having almost verbally assaulted one or two of the more extravagantly prop heavy disguises of these nurses: the old man in the wheelchair, the pregnant teenager, the cancer patient.

The man with the forks in his fingers is tired of looking for the emergency room. He has not been helped once. In fact, he has been continually misdirected, held up, at each and every turn. He needs help, genuine care, not to be gawped at or prodded with stares as if to see him that way, as a dancing bear, a bearded lady, some fork-nailed Christ, would ever be acceptable. The man with the forks in his fingers is a real human being in very real corporeal pain: he suffers, and he must be cared for.

The man with the forks in his fingers has had these forks in his fingers for a long time— longer than he can say— since breakfast at least. If anyone were to ask, to sincerely ask, he is sure that he could outlay a series of rationally sound events that led to these implements being so solidly stuck.

For instance, the man with the forks in his fingers is missing his wife. He misses her terribly. That could be something.

And his wife, when did she leave him? Every morning she would bring a glass of water with the funnies then soft-boiled egg and soldiers. Breakfast was always a soft-boiled egg and soldiers, the routine being of importance to him. Often orangey egg dripped, unseen, from strips of buttery toast onto his time-paled pyjamas. Egg that would then dry and resolve, tightening around the cotton fibres, into a pastille yellow stain. Stains he would sit and finger blandly for hours on end. The man with the forks in his fingers unconsciously rubs the business card in his pocket.

Was she, after all, his wife, this woman? The tips of his fingers let out yards of pain, switching the tracks of his concern. It is unimportant now. The man with the forks in his finger must find someone who will care, that is all that matters.

A man walks past him and into the room ahead. He is not a doctor unless these are hard times for handsome doctors. The man leaves the door ajar.

The man with the forks in his fingers peers into the room. A woman is on the bed. He watches her push herself up into a sitting position. The man is standing at the foot of the bed, his arms lowered to his side, a pitiful bunch of flowers just hanging there.

The man and the woman are about to talk. They will converse and then something definitive will happen. There is intimacy in that room, the man with the forks in his fingers thinks. Maybe it's them, he thinks. After all, maybe it is them. The man with the forks in his fingers remembers. He is looking for someone in particular. He is looking for that person to see him.

He lingers.

The man with the forks in his fingers edges

closer. He does not hear what they are saying above the sound of his own whispered prayers.

*

– Hey Hell, you look beautiful.

– I'm pretty tired Jim.

– Can I see h…h-uh…h-e..r-h..i-m…

– Her, Jim, It's a girl. I've known it was a girl for months.

– What's her name?

– And no, I don't think you can see her. How did you know to come today?

– I called around. There are people who still know you even if.…

– Even if what?

– Please, Hell.

– She's sleeping.

– …

– No, Jim. They've put her in the crèche. You can't see her, it's logistically not possible, you understand?

– I'll get to later though, won't I?

– I don't know yet, it doesn't seem possible.

– What's her name Hell?

– Her name is Evelyn, Jim. *We* called her Evelyn.

– That was one of our names though, wasn't it?

– As I remember you weren't that into…
– It *was* one of our names though, Hell, wasn't it?

Helene lifts her eyes from the sheets they've been sucking light from. She looks at Jim. She looks at him squarely, Helene holding his gaze as it falls apart. When Jim's face falters, when it reveals a bridge over which a desire wishes to meet you, it is heartrending. As in, here is something so open and yet narrowed into you that on every side of it the world fractures, falls away. Helene can feel her resolve beginning to give way but she knows she cannot trust this feeling. She knows that this sincerity, as true as it is right now, is a temporary charm and that if she tries to really grasp the reality behind it, she will find that what is left of him is only this transmission, a charged airy tunnel between her body and his, a shadow of an urge or a plea, a stateless signalling that constitutes a leap of faith that she is sick of having to take again and again and again.

– Jim you know why.

The bed sheets haven't changed much around her, a few new ripples, a couple of dunes that'd be easy enough to smooth out or rearrange. Jim tries to bore his eyes with them. They quieten a little.

– I'm ok now. I don't do any of that anymore.

– Please don't lie to me. It wouldn't
make a difference now if I believed you
anyway, so please don't lie. Look at you,
what were you doing last night?
– That doesn't make any sense.
– What part?
– Any part.

Jim is staring at the floor now with tears in
his eyes. He glances upwards. Helene looks away.
Jim focuses on a tile beyond the bed. The muscles
in his face wriggle like Houdini in a sack, then
smooth out. The magician of sadness appearing
to have escaped, that's the illusion. Jim smiles
mirthlessly, dimples stapling his cheeks. His
expression harshly cinched. Helene tries to sift
through his eyes. They've become as hard to farm
as the desert.

– James I think you should go.
– I thought you might want me to be
here.

The door tilts open, fingers clanking around
the edge of the frame.
– I hope I'm not intruding but…I feel that I'm
here for you, because of you.
Jim and Helene stare at the man, their glances
dropping to the forks extruding from his
fingertips and then staying there. Jim is the first
to turn away telling the man with the forks in
his fingers to just please fuck off as he does so.

Helene continues to angrily stare. The man with the forks in his fingers cannot believe it, he was sure that these were merciful people. He raises one forked finger in steely accusation, the handle bobbing under the fluorescent light. A pea of blood hatches and splits down his index finger as his mouth begins to shape the protesting syllable and, just as he is about to issue forth this accusation, James 'Jim' Burke's turns towards him, his face just caving in, his features becoming wet cavities.

> – James go, please.
> – I want to see her, don't I deserve that?
> – I'm not sure that you do, Jim. I'm not sure you know what the fuck you're doing here.

Helene staring inquisitively at the bunch of flowers in Jim's hand as she says this.

> – Helene, Hell, please

The man with the forks in his fingers is still standing there, embarrassed now, the handle wobbling at the end of his outstretched finger. The finger trying to illustrate a point quite beside the heaviness of the room. The man with the forks in his fingers does not know how to apologise for his intrusion and yet he must exit this situation, and quickly, but how does he leave now, how can he extricate himself?

– Get the fuck out of here. Both of you.

The man with the forks decides his losses are there to be cut. He uncurls his other fingers and toodles goodbye. The man with the forks in his fingers dashing out of the room. He looks around for a nurse and then throws himself around the corner of the corridor. He is remembering something.

– I don't want to have to ask again Jim.

James 'Jim' Burke is sitting outside the hospital on the hot white grill of steps. The cashier from the flower shop has just finished work. She sees Jim sat on the steps. The flowers are at his feet. The bundle has come loose and many of the petals lay darkly curled around his feet. The remaining petals appear harried and baked under the sun. The cashier bends down next to him. It is clear to her that he has been crying. She takes his hand. James Burke looks into her eyes, mouths the word *don't*.

– Please you don't want to, please, he says.

The tone of his voice is astonishing. The girl believes it, steps backward and slips down the stairs. Her back is arched over the base of the steps. She lies groaning, her ankle twitching against his foot. Quickly people come to help her. James Burke stands up and begins walking towards the lighthouse. He is so lost in his thoughts that he does not even notice the figure following behind him or the mechanical cricketing sound of the figure's hand as the stainless steel clanks together with each falling step.

3

START
REPEAT, 1982

He knew that when things ended, it took a long time for them to reach that end. That the way things ended was often the difference between dying and being murdered.

Henry watches the pile of hair that his mother has cut— that his foot *herds* underneath the square legged stool beneath him. He feels a sense of desperation clarifying itself in time with the growing pile of hair, a gut tightening anxiety building in the jailing tug of each half-accomplished movement. The central points of his body: stomach, groin, and heart all hurting with this gathering need.

His mother bends over his head. She is crying. Her tears seem random, unpunctuated.

Henry's eyes shutter and close as his mother sweeps more hair into the maw of the scissors. He opens his eyes at the sound of the snip, searching for the drift of hair, imagining that it might be cradled by the air. It is gone, already fallen. He looks at the pile of hair again. The hair has not turned white as he predicted. Clumps of hair that should have revealed the huddled embers of their alarmed severance have only grown softer and more birdlike. Death wouldn't ruffle them the way his shoe did.

A dollop of tear mistakes a fresh spot of Henry's skull. He feels at it. His mother bends down before him, fussing over the line of his fringe. She cannot seem to get a good line on the hair, her two fingers unable to parallel one another, scooting spasmodically to the side, or pressing into each other with vibrating tension every time she tries to close in upon the fringe. Diane snips a wonky line. She says *shit*. At the same time, she places her hands over Henry's ears.

Henry's mother stands up and walks to the bathroom.

He watches her leave.

Diane returns with a pair of clippers in her hands. She ruffles Henry's hair and pushes the switch of the clippers up with the base of her thumb in the other. The air whines around a torch of blades. The razor anoints the child. Henry's head rolls back with the force of the clippers as a full hemisphere of hair is razed to the ground. Henry's eyes swivel into contact with his mother's. His mother tilting his head towards her the moment his lips begin to part.

– Where's...where's dad?

Diane presses a thumb into his neck and carefully shaves the pedestal of his skull.

– You have to be a good boy today Henry, remember you have to be a good boy. Look left, now straight at me.

Diane kneels before him now, the hair clinging to her knees. There is a wash-cloth in her hand and the hand goes roughly back and forth across the pebble of his face stinging his mouth and eyes with wisps of acrid soap. The rag withdraws and Henry's pink face sputters and tastes itself as Diane doggedly tries to hold onto and reflect his expressions, her own face harnessed only by this increasingly panicked searching. The boy's expressions remain a breathy spot in the centre of her vision that she can't quite rub clear.

– Remember you have to be a good boy.

They stand in front of the horizontal mirror hanging next to the front door. Their reflections regard each other. Henry and his mother standing there like two seaside facades well out of season.

*

– There are a lot of new strategies and cost saving measures I hope to introduce. That is once the situation dies down a little. Yesterday was a little better I think. The meeting we had was important to clear the air...though several people had to leave the room with their hands clasped over their mouths emitting these breathless noises after Barnaby, that's my manager, stated that the meeting was 'to clear the air'.

Lawrence risks a grin at Helene who is sat propped up on the bed, a pillow stood vertical between her back and the headboard. If she had heard what he'd said, or even seen how quickly he'd looked over at her, she'd have found it funny, maybe even laughed. It would have reminded her of something she'd liked about him. Helene has instead been distracted by the orange, red and green trimmed trousers Lawrence has just pulled from the drawers. Lawrence sits on the bed and strokes her ankle with his free hand. Lawrence places the trousers on the bed and lifts her foot delicately by its heel and arch, regarding the finely boned foot before him as if it were a glass slipper.

It has been almost a week since Lawrence arrived home in tears, racing to the bathroom and leaving the car mounted on the pavement with its door swung out wide and its paintwork nettled with thorny scratches and an almost sentient stench desperately trying to host itself in the open air.

Helene hadn't asked about it. Instead she waited patiently for Lawrence to tell her what had happened, which he did, twelve hours later at breakfast, bringing her a tray in bed, his face so sad and penitent, a real boy at last. Lawrence displaying the defenceless aspect of children that Helene is near powerless against. His expression invoking a sense of trust she still wanted to be able to give but which she was so sure she'd lost through the successive failures of age. Although failure, she thinks, is perhaps the wrong word after all. It may be contradiction that she means, contradictions interred in the fill of time that seemed to illustrate what little power one had over the rolling script of days that the mind limped along, tried to keep track of, could not trust or even hold down.

James, Lawrence, how did any of this happen? Helene has asked herself in so many ways how one can be honest without knowledge, without clarity or truth or a strong belief in truth, has asked each time without realising that this need for guarantee, for honesty to be pre–formulated, is itself a relinquishment of love's responsibility.

By telling her the story unfiltered Lawrence had asked for her to love him despite himself, she thinks. Lawrence giving her the chance, so opposed to his own hopes, to castigate him, to subtract this event from her feelings for him. So,

Lawrence could still be a child after all, one who suffered all his torments in the grim privacy of imagined transgressions. They could still learn something about life from one another or she could still teach him something real about regret, about its possibilities, about the value it could ascribe to the world. She might still evolve herself in relation to him, she thinks. If she wanted to.

They are so close in this moment to a kind of reconciliation and this anticipation, coupled with the sudden tenderness that Helene feels towards him, demands from her its own gesture. She leans forward and tries to stroke Lawrence's face. They are too far away from one another though for the gesture to be successful. Lawrence for his part leans in after the failure far too eagerly, jutting his chin out and awkwardly extending himself towards her.

Clumsy instead of deft, the weight of their joint awkwardness results in Helene scratching the inside of Lawrence's mouth, her thumb and its insensate bone able to read every bump of his scabbard gum.

Helene scooches back on the bed and looks up to find Lawrence's ever expectant face still hanging there. It was a face that sought, she had always felt and still felt, to default each interaction, a face that threw its banality, like a body smothering a grenade over every anticipatory feeling. She tries to smile at him. The unsettling look on Helene's face makes Lawrence look away and pay close, frowning, attention to the appearance of his ankles shooting out from his favourite trousers.

These trousers, that Helene cannot even bring herself to look over the surface of for fear of inducing a tartan concocted migraine, are currently being pulled over Lawrence's surprisingly athletic legs. He stands and jumps shortly on the spot as he ties the button around his waist. He stretches his shoulders and sits on the bed near Helene's still bandaged ankle. He lifts her ankle and brushes her foot with the back of his hand before placing the ankle onto its velvet cushion.

—Has there been any news from the police?

—I haven't heard anything more.

—We should check.

—What can they do?

—I don't know, I mean are they even looking? I want to know if he's out there or not.

—Me too.

This, less enunciated than a whisper. Lawrence, trying to catch and define the tailing flight of his wife's voice, dives forward and holds Helene desperately in his arms. His head and shoulders ending somewhere ungathered amid her chest.

—We'll be safe one day.

—Lawrence I can't breathe.

Lawrence withdraws his arms as Helene pushes him lightly away. He does not know where to place them now and they fold and unfold several times in front of him. Lawrence slides his hands down his thighs as he looks around the room and clicks his tongue several times. The silence remains. Lawrence performs an itinerary of "waiting" in the amateur style. He puffs out his cheeks, narrows his eyes, runs a hand through his hair.

Helene waits. Lawrence stands up, walks to the French dresser and puts his cotton tailed golfing hat on. He turns to face Helene, his arms jauntily bowed around his hips, and says:

—Today is the day.

And

—I am going to burn through my handicap.

And

—I love you.

Helene smiles, nods, she knows. She can't speak, he understands.

Things, she figured, changed in either geologic or catastrophic time and in–between that, there was what exactly? Non–change, stasis, or rather the imperceptible defacing of what *was* or had been true. Something like that. Perhaps they hadn't ever loved each other. And who is she thinking of exactly when she thinks that? She doesn't know. She had chased after a man, in a way that seems to her now depressingly literalised. A man she barely knew, despite their shared secrets and history, all for the vicarious emotions he aroused in her. Trying to know other people was like looking down the wrong end of a telescope, she thought. They just mistakenly receded to some fixed point until you ended up accidentally close to them, pressed up against them, so that they're suddenly revealed, delved into fibres seemed inhuman and disproportionate and impossible to relate to any concept of 'them' that you might be able to keep in your head. They became a world of immense historical surfaces no matter how pristine the mind's distance might render them.

But here was a man who had really opened himself to her. With Lawrence there was nothing to hide. They were still young, though she felt old in her shame. She could live with that. Could she? Could she? She wasn't though, living, was she? That's what he would have said.

—Are you sure you're well enough for Golf? You're sure all those little brown holes won't trigger something amiss?

—Ha, I'm ok. I'm ok.

Lawrence stands in the doorway. Something has happened or ceased to happen. He doesn't know which. He observes the sensation, can't categorise it, tries to let it go. He looks at Helene. The way she looks at him is recognizable now. Disappointing in a way he can't compute. Hadn't she tried to smile?

He turns to leave, pauses. Lawrence visualising Helene walking up behind him now, her hands resting on his shoulders, each of them no longer really themselves. At last, he thinks, at last.

*

You couldn't expect him to go. You couldn't expect him to go, not really. Mightn't he though? Would he be there? He'd never got on with her father. How could he? Not from the very first moment he stood at the door— the only boy in the congregation with a motorcycle— a moped really, metallic blue with a small engine that sounded like a hornet's nest on fire. Father answered the door.

– Is Diane in? Can she come out?

She remembers her father's curt one-word reply, herself half hidden on the stairs, roused from her bible study by this rare knock and the strange sound of her name in another's mouth. Her hands ran up and down the bannister. She wondered why the boy didn't leave, why her father didn't shut the door. Then Mark had noticed her on the stairs and he smiled and nodded to her in that way of his. This distracted the old man—he'd lost his composure- wasn't used to being bypassed like this. Her father turning to see her there, his confusion knitting into rage, her nightgown seeming to shrink in the flash of his gaze. Diane was ashamed, pulled the bottom of the gown down around her knees, her face turning a collusive, guilt ridden red as she tried to hide her body from His sight, and then when Father turned back round for Mark—

the muscles swimming through his clenched jaw like so many tadpoles— the boy was already gone on his metallic blue bike, kicking it into life and posing on the fumes of his disappearance.

Even then there had been animosity you see, the first young man able to hold her father's gaze and so hers. You couldn't expect him to come. You just couldn't. Mightn't he though, for her? They'd sinned together shortly after his visit, were wed from the start in that at least. She couldn't even remember how it'd happened, a shopping centre, a cinema, something like that. He wouldn't even recognize the sin let alone fathom it. He said it didn't even reach up to their ankles. He took her by the hand one day and they ran. That's how she thought of it. Each road they took flowered into concrete. Cities, what could they do in a city? Dirty and cramped with a baby in her belly, Diane felt like a piece of pollen attached to the soundless, stamen-like trumpets of tenements and offices. Offices she cleaned under fluorescent lights on mornings where she swore she could see the molecules of things fleeing the ghostly structure of the noumenal world. She watched the static composing the office tables and computers writhing around obscenely on the surface of their existence in mimicry of her sin. Static graining the air. Diane looked at her own hands melding with the empty space and what space was composed of. She'd passed out several times while working. There were tests. The fumes from the toilet cleaner were positively criminal. There'd be some money, enough to get them to the next city at least. The moped had died and they needed a car to keep moving. Keep moving. She couldn't. So they were tracked down, brought to bear. God tracked her down, told her what she must do for her unborn baby or her conscience did or her father did…yes he did, sometime in the past, activating some desire in her when she'd broken free, the light of it pulsing red underneath her skin like she was some fucking robot. No, she hadn't been free. When had she felt freedom? Only in those moments that she had gone away from herself but there was no hope of real freedom that way. There was freedom in service, a striving towards and not away. There was freedom in forgiveness. That's why she prayed to Him before phoning Him. Mightn't he though, come after all today? He was born into it too, as much as she, he must have known why. Who was born into it as much as she? He must come. Please, be there. Not even for her? He wouldn't come, hadn't even been to see Jude since, since who remembers when, when her father came that day in a black coat, large black hat, ever present bible in his rough palm. She saw him from the upstairs window. Her father standing there, tears in his eyes, fire in his throat, a large man to the end even in this disappointment. He'd boxed when he was younger, killed men in the war, found god with the same aggressive sense of clarity. He was looking down at his bible, waiting for something. He lifted it to his ear and then looked up at the window. The tears had all gone out of his eyes. He lowered the bible and knocked with customary authority on the door.

Mark answered. Diane stood on the landing waiting to hear her name. The old man looked past Mark and smiled though this time it wasn't for her. Mark had no need to turn: he knew what was waiting behind him. Her father turned and they both followed obediently behind.

In a car on the way to the registry office the baby pounded away inside her while Mark remained silent as the grave. They were out of earshot only as they exited the car. He leaned in as close to her as he dared.

-You've given us away, he said.

-I've delivered you, she said.

Diane looks down. Henry has taken her hand and sandwiched it between his own.

> – I, I don't know where your father is.
> – I don't know either. It's not good of him.

The car climbs and descends hill after hill while Henry counts churches with and without spires. His mother's hand lays large and weightless between his own. It feels as if her entire being has been shelled. Mined out.

The car comes to a stop in a field roamed with crosses and white pebbles. There are no names on the crosses. A crowd gathers and then absorbs the shape of the car. The doors are opened, hands proffered. They take Henry and his mother. Together the mass walks in shambling grief towards the Elder of the congregation who is stood at the head of a cavernous rectangle. Henry and his mother the covalent bond of the crowd.

The Elder begins by telling them that his hands — level at crotch height, fist swallowed by palm— are the pestle and mortar of the soul. He lifts them to show the crowd. His hands embrace and then strangle one another in mad, snaking movements.

-We work against the invisible until we join with it, he says. The crowd murmurs their assent. He looks around the crowd and at Henry specifically. Henry does not feel protected.

The Elder lifts his eyes to the sky and then lowers them in obeisance, his sinking lids shouldering the great pale stretch of it. He throws back his head and begins to sing. The congregation swells in song. Grief evacuates through Diane's body in great, shuddering, fits. A battered outpouring of sorrow unfairly rendering her body its sole obstruction. Henry too is sobbing now. He is crying for what every breath seems to take and then hoard into insignificance. Henry is crying for the great cover up of life. He cries for all this without knowing.

The hymn comes on louder and more insistent.

As if forced down by the weight of their refrain, the coffin begins to descend. The coffin disappeared by the earth in an image that seems to Henry, who is too small to peer over and into the lip of the grave, infinitely repeatable, perfectly formed, and utterly nightmarish. The fit of the casket and the smooth motion of the ropes and that absolute horizon of disappearance are all contributing to the same internal seizure that is paralysing his reality.

Dirt rains over the surface of the coffin.

The man taking the service says

– Amen

The crowd says
– Amen
Henry thinks

– What have we just agreed to?

There is a golf ball of phlegm strung around his tonsils and some boggy fluid ransacking his sinuses. Henry stares around the people utterly dazed.

Hands, whose owners he never sees, wear his shoulder into a smooth pebble against the damp white cotton of his shirt and then leave forever.

Henry helps his mother to the car. Two members of the congregation, a man and woman, are waiting for them there. Their heads are grey but their skin is smooth and taut. Bibles cover their hearts. They are telling Henry to be good to his mother and a kind and gentle brother to Jude.

They lift their heads and look into Diane's eyes. The man speaks while the woman nods grammatically.

> – In paradise you will see your father again, in paradise your son will be restored. This we know. Stay strong sister.
> – My husband, my husband he has
> – Pray that he recognizes the error of his path, for he that walk
> – Mum? Mum?
> – In righteousness
> – Mum? Mum?
> – And he said I am the way and the truth and the life and no one comes to the father except through me
> – Mum?
> – They are telling us to pray Henry. Should we pray Henry? What do you think Henry, is that a good idea? Something to try perhaps?

The grey-haired woman steps forward

> – Yes sister, you must pray. Yolk yourself to god.

Diane looks into the curiously unwrinkled skin

of this woman, into the pupils of her too light eyes and feels a shudder of revulsion. Mark, it was still sin it was still, it was, it...

> – Mum, mum?
> – We're leaving now Henry.

*

Richard Fort has been suspended for his involvement in the James Burke case. He was due to hand in all files and evidence pertaining to this case yesterday at three o'clock. The evidence, such as it is, is currently untagged and scattered around the passenger seat and floor of his car. Richard Fort has every intention of handing in all the relevant material once he has finished copying James Burke's notebook.

The copy he is making is not an exact replica. The series of drawings that constitute the end of the original have been traced onto the opening pages of this notebook. The transcriptions of James Burke's writing have also been selected and arranged to support Richard Fort's reading of the narrative. In the margins of this new version Richard Fort has tattooed his own commentary, a commentary that he has at times allowed to be sardonic, engaged, self-reflective or angrily provoked by the unfathomable abstractions of the work. The tone of his commentary somewhat dependent on his own state of mind and the alcohol content of his blood. For instance, right now every pore of Richard Fort's skin is a tiny, brimming shot glass and he is in danger of spilling himself everywhere. Consequently, the margins are filling with exclamation marks and question marks, anger and self-hate.

Richard Fort has spent the past two nights in his car doing an impression of sleep. The car is parked near a quiet stretch of beach and is half camouflaged by the clumps of beach grass peppering the dunes. The lighthouse is visible in the upper left hand corner of his windshield. Richard Fort half closes his eyes. The world is warm pink then orange sepia. Outlines of warmth and light hover in impossible flight patterns around their objects like UFO's. The beach is empty but for a few middle-aged men sweeping the sand with metal detectors.

Richard Fort places his hip flask on the dashboard, his hands cupping around it to make sure that it doesn't slide off. The suspension of his car has become unevenly seesawed. The boot and backseat weighted down with books, clothes, pillows, a broken lamp, a small tv, a set of dumbbells ranging from fifteen to forty five kgs and a formerly loved stags head tearfully bequeathed to him by his otherwise emotionally distant father on the day of his wedding. In other words, all he could scoop from the pavement when he arrived home seventy-two hours ago to find his wife auditing him from her life.

He had seen from the driveway his stacked-up possessions, can remember clearly the way the anger reconstituted him as he approached the pile. The way that anger turned to fear as he saw his clothes doming under the doorbell, the stag's head turned dolefully towards them as if ashamed to meet his approaching gaze. He remembers seeing the totted up personal, not so special, effects of a life split in ways seemingly too numerous and menial to count. A life so many times removed that Richard Fort had come to doubt his own relation to it. He had thought, predictably, of putting a match to it all, of walking away. Saw the house flared with smog, great bipedal forms of smoke panhandling the sky, dipping into it with the bowled sun till the silted stars shone through. Then in the morning the smoke walking bow-legged, cowboy style, into the faded blue horizon. This after the smoke had reached down into her, held her last breath. This thought saddening him immensely. He imagined this last breath as being kidney shaped, packed into her icy body, ready for heavenly transport.

That is when he saw the lamp. That lamp, it killed him. He felt horrible, outright penitent. He felt that his thoughts were horrible and so it was no wonder, all this. The lamp was laying some way from the rest of the pile, had rolled onto its side, a small hole showing where it had cracked on the pavement.

He'd wanted to speak to her then, his eyes widening softly and deliberately as he spoke. He would have told her that he'd noticed the lamp, the way it had cracked. How it evidently hadn't been thrown in anger. That he could infer from the nature of the fracture and the way the pieces of shattered porcelain were spread out roughly equidistant to the lamp— one chip of pale green lamp still resting on the lip of the hole— that all this damage hadn't been intentional, that there was no motive to look for. She hadn't meant to break that lamp and he knew this, one hundred percent knew this, was in fact trained to know this if not any other thing. He would say that it was just through a lack of care or by accident (he would say accident) really that the lamp was broke like this now. He would tell her that he didn't usually know what to do with his impressions of the world except in accusation— who in all honesty did? — but that now he knew what to do, that he understood, that he was just slow putting it all together and couldn't she please understand that?

His eyes would be huge, pleading. In them she would not even know how he held her. The dream of his wife's kiss came out in an insolvent groan as he tolled into their home's brickwork. The rough finish exfoliating his skin with a mother's skull polishing touch. He was drunk then too. He had been driving. He'd made garbled phone calls from the bar to members of her family explaining the situation he was in, the pickle of it. Something big was coming, he said, he didn't know what to do. Why didn't she love him? The air from their shaking heads swilled in the phone. Who was this they asked? He hung up. There, in front of the house, he was answered in full. Lurching over the pile he spotted something unmistakeable and final, something hurtful and intended beyond the intended and unavoidable hurt of it. A photograph of them, kiss feigned, on their wedding day. The picture weighted down by the band of her wedding ring telescoping his distracted expression.

Richard Fort stretches in the car, his mouth open and dryly inactive but for the occasional ripping sound of his tongue's perambulations.

The back of the car makes a groaning sound. He gets out to check the boot. The bumper is nearly touching the floor. He opens the boot in order to transfer some weight to the front of the car. Beneath some work shirts is his briefcase. The moment he lifts the shirts from the boot the car improbably rises. Richard Fort frowns. He takes out the briefcase. The car does not rise. He throws the shirt back in. He closes the boot. He walks around to the front of the car. There is a figure in the driver's seat slumped against the wheel. Richard Fort had not heard anything, neither footsteps nor the opening or closing of a door. Richard Fort raps his knuckles against the window. He tries the door. The manual knob has been pushed down. The figure wakes up. He lifts up his hands in surprise. Richard Fort can't quite understand what he is seeing.

The man with the forks in his fingers tries to unlock the door. He cannot get hold of the nub.

The door eventually opens. The man with the forks in his fingers is just staring. He cannot speak. He lifts up the hand, stares at in disbelief. The man with the forks in his fingers begins to cry.

– Who did this to you?

Richard Fort's throat is dry and coarse with alcohol. The words come out ventriloquized. The man with the forks stops crying abruptly and looks blankly in the direction of the sound. He reaches inside his jacket pocket and pulls out a tattered card. He stares at it. Richard Fort takes it from him.

– Lawrence Muir? Lawrence Muir did this.
– Yes Lawrence Muir. He did this, partly.
–

The man with the forks in his fingers looks past Richard Fort and towards the lighthouse. Richard

Fort follows his gaze. The lighthouse is a dark slit in the sun.

Richard Fort leans over and reaches around his glove compartment,

> – Do you know this man?
> – I was, we were, friends. New friends who were old friends it turned out. Taking turns. Not yet, not yet. This book...These books?

The man with the forks in his fingers has just noticed the notebook and Richard Fort's copy of it.

> – I'm in there. Did you find me yet? There's two books. Two books? I, we, met at the hospital, thought he was... he was with the woman, the girl. I thought I already knew them. They felt otherwise, I think. I intruded, regretfully, on their intimacy. After that I felt I was someone he knew.

He stops talking. The man with the forks in his fingers lifts a fork towards the lighthouse.

> – I, I don't remember anything else. Except the man on the card, Lawrence...he's the father...He, is someone who goes all the way through. His type still repeats. I also spoke to him

at the hospital. He told me the wrong
way to go.
– Lawrence Muir was there?

Richard Fort feels drunk again.

*

Helene is standing in the kitchen eating a
sandwich, purely for sustenance. Crumbs fall
over the faux marble sideboard. She sweeps them
away with her hand. She is entirely focused on
reading an older version of Jim's notebook. It had
arrived a little over a month ago through the front
door, after the post had already arrived. She
hadn't picked through its contents then, had half
thought to throw it away but, unable, had hidden
it in her lingerie drawer where she was sure
Lawrence wouldn't think to pry.

As far as she can tell, the notebook she has
is an earlier draft of the one Richard Fort had
confronted her with the week before sans the last
few overtly troubling pages. Helene has been
unable to account for the effect those drawings
have had on her or the way they have worked
themselves into her normally drug-erased
dreams. She'd supposed that the sight of them
had made her think that James was dead and that
this was deeply upsetting to her for reasons both
obvious and unspeakably complex. It is true that
her immediate thought when she saw the

drawings was that Jim was definitely dead or gone but it was not exactly this quality of the drawings that had so affected her.

The drawings were unlike anything Jim had done before. They were original.

Jim's work was derivative and repetitive. She didn't recognise him in this.

Plus she knew all the preoccupations and the code names for the people in his life and the jubilant child had never figured in any of them. Had no relation to them. Usually any new phrase, sentiment, or character could be traced back to an earlier incarnation arriving, as they did, weighted with a sense of their own cryptic history. There was nothing like that there.

On first glance her copy follows the suit of her expectations. Helene with a mouthful of bread and an accompanying, derisory, lip smacking act of mastication, mentally underlines the poorly parsed sentences that she's sure James all but fist pumped the air at:

'What difference can it make to understand that evolution has strung us onto linear time and that, like beads on an abacus, we've been set to account for meaning, not to join with it? The hand says there's a difference but that it's confusing. The hand says he can save her. That he could become her.'

'Love places our flaws under the tech of imagination.'

Helene walks to the sofa with the notebook

fanned out in front of her. She sits down and tries to piece the writing together. Helene spies the word soul and rolls her eyes. She scans the rest of the page yawning. She turns one page and then the next. Helene sighs and skips forward another ten pages or so, the sentence regarding the soul finally ending somewhere around the fourteenth page. She looks for any mention of herself anywhere. She scans another twenty or so pages, sees nothing. Helene is about to close the book when a name amidst the cluttered prepositions strikes her. Evelyn.

She frowns at the page, sticks her thumb in its spine, reads on. A change has occurred. There are clear voices in the prose, the words seem to change and come to life as she reads. Something is happening. The writing is, if not direct or clear, at least gesturing towards a world of concrete event no matter how unrealistically cataclysmic.

Helene flicks back through the notebook and finds the end of the first-person narrative, finds the words 'I'm sorry' repeatedly traced over the spine of the book till they formed a wide and glossy wound in the page.

Helene turns back and reads the Evelyn part again and then all the Evelyn parts she can find. The Evelyn in the text is blonde, evidently troubled, significantly motherless and utterly alone. Evelyn wants to disappear. Helene places the book face down on the sofa. She stares ahead for a moment then walks upstairs. She opens her bedroom door, walks to Evelyn's antique cot and peers into the bundle of blankets. Evelyn is asleep under them, her black hair awkwardly quiffed by the action of her chest and the fitful manipulations of sleep. Evelyn's fingers curl around her face, happy in her voyage of sleep. Helene feels silly, placeless, standing there. What could have possessed her to come?

Helene pulls the door quietly to, walks back down the stairs, her hand hovering just above and occasionally gripping the polished banister. She walks into the kitchen and makes herself a cup of tea. Helene stands by the kettle as she waits for it to boil, then pours the hot water into the cup. The bag swells and bobs. She walks to the sofa with her tea, picks up the notebook, and reads on.

The writing has changed again, is dead in some way.

From what Helene can make out in the unlikely largely unaccredited dialogue that serves as the main tool of narrative exposition, Evelyn is trying to make herself disappear through various forms of abuse, chiefly substance and self. She has— the half-baked notes around it suggest— been cursed into re-enacting a life that has echoed down, in smaller and smaller contractions, through time. The people that care about her are also cursed and there is no one around her who isn't similarly cursed and acutely aware of it.

Helene reads 'What if the love you thought you had to give...'

She puts the notebook down on the sofa. Helene feels sorry for Jim. Sorry for his lack of talent. Sorry for her love and the deficiencies of chance. Sorry for his disproportionate emotions, which had evidently lost their elasticity and could no longer shrink around the heat of the real. She saw his flaccid dreams bunched and exhausted in obscurity, dust-gathering costumes only vaguely shaped by the world. Within her sorrowing rivulets of a muted anger begin to flow, subterranean and so far from source they'll never find home, only form lightless and stone-toothed caverns within her dilapidated interior.

The earth drops away, her interior subsides, and a melancholy porosity focuses its lens. Helene rails.

– It doesn't make sense, James wouldn't, couldn't have meant, his own daughter, how could he?

She picks up the notebook.

'What if the love you thought you had to give was really only your own pain and suffering? And the place where you laid your love wasn't a furnace for a consummation of a shared identity but the very blood of life poisoned by your existence in it? What if all your dreams of disappearance had taken on an essential misunderstanding and triumphed alongside it?'

Helene closes the book, sips her tea. She carries the tea to the kitchen, pours it down the sink, places it on the side and opens the fridge. Time for something harder.

*

Henry has heard the phrases oxygen starved and brain injury uttered by the doctor and then repeated by his mother and both understood and not understood them. His mother hearing the same words in her leaden voice had felt a similar confusion though one more consequentially weighted. The doctor is telling them not to think of this as a loss, that Jude was very lucky that they turned up when they did, that if he had spent any longer unconscious and face down in the dog's water bowl while his grandfather bulged and staggered wildly in the soundless discord of a gigantic heart attack, Jude would surely have died.

Diane is trying to feel lucky. She thinks that if this is not a loss then it is an unthinkable subtraction, the remainder of which will forever stand as an unknown quantity. She will live with the guilt of this thought for a long time. It will rise up in her during innocuous moments, as she stirs a bowl of spaghetti or watches a traffic light move through its limited range of commands, or as Jude's uncomprehending face rises towards her in hope and curtailed expectation, she will be pierced by it and the pain will pass through her like a camel threaded through the eye of a needle.

– It's actually very hard at this point and given Jude's developmental age to gauge the extent of the damage. If we're lucky it'll be relatively minor. What is clear just from looking at the tests we've completed is that your son will still be able to live a full life.

Diane places her hand over Jude's forehead. She is surprised by how little hands can really feel. The flat press of her hand on his forehead, the clear separateness of their surfaces makes her think of his body prone under the sheets and the now unfeeling parts of both their minds. The doctor leaves the room. They stand there. Henry climbs up on the chair by the bed. He leans over Jude's face.

> – It's not exactly like sleeping is it mummy?
> – No Henry, it isn't.

They leave the room, walk blindly down the corridor. His mother stops and buys Henry a can of coke from a vending machine. It is a drink long promised and years in the making. The click of the coins in the machine fall through her mind, exist there, and then disappear. There are things that are only things for the moment, occurring or not occurring in the myriad ways of both. Things like her two sons. Diane and Henry enter the car park.

Henry is drinking the can of coke. It is the

coldest and most exhilarating drink he has ever had. He thinks

– I will remember this forever, as the bubbles strip his throat.

Henry runs ahead of his mother, waits by the car, his foot tapping with intensity.

– I could break through to China, he thinks

He calls for his mother, Henry feeling too there for time's drag.

Henry's mother has stopped to talk to two men. Henry can only see the back of them. There is something familiar in the way one of them opens their body as if to capture his mother. Henry creeps towards them.

Diane is saying to Lawrence Muir

– If I could work more hours, if there was anything more you could use me for. Everything is so expensive and my father, there are debts, and my husband, my husband has, well I don't know where, and Jude he, well you know but...I, I, I,

Lawrence has, through a series of calibrating head nods, managed to normalize his posture after his extravagant display of compassion had gone unconsummated.

– Who is assigned to your son?

Diane looks up at the man next to Lawrence and then at Lawrence with confused hope.

– Have you met Doctor Raymond? He's one of the finest private doctors in

England.
– In all of Europe.

Henry's mother glances furtively again at the Doctor, her hands smelted into a pot before her throat.

> – Beech, a Doctor Beech, sorry, is
> looking after Jude.
> – He's a fine doctor and a good man, if a
> little pessimistic in his prognoses and
> conservative of method. If you write
> your name and number down here I'll
> arrange a time for you to bring your son
> to my clinic, pro bono of course.

The doctor smiles at Lawrence Muir as Diane bends to write her telephone number on his prescription pad. The smile retracts into a thin-lipped concern as she raises her head to thank him. Henry is staring at the Doctor. He can feel his grandfather's voice reciting bible verses though their content escapes him. He drinks the last of the coke, crushing the can in his meagre fist. Ezekiel Chapter 7. He tosses the empty can into the bushes without looking. Revelations... anything. His hand becomes a gun. No one notices. Henry quickly becomes regretful and self-conscious re: the littered can. He remembers that he is a guest in this, in god's world, and that he should behave as such. The gun devolves into a hand left stranded in the air.

Diane turns to see her son squatting in the bush, mud and knees slopping against each other like clumsy open-mouthed teenagers. She calls for him as he grips the can. Walks over and yanks him to his feet, the can rolling out of his fingers and away. Diane turns and says her goodbyes to the two men thanking them both simultaneously.

The two men watch the car stream out of view.

– Did you, did you just come on to her?
– You disapprove, Lawrence?
– I'm just, well I just think, poor woman and... Don't get me wrong you were fine but...
– You were flirting with her also or would have liked to. When she said 'anything you can use me for' your heart leapt no? It was visible under your shirt. Even the child noticed it. He maybe wanted to kill you then. Perhaps you have a bee for the tortured women only. Yes, maybe that is it.
– Now wait a second.

The Doctor has started to walk towards the hospital. Lawrence does not move. The Doctor turns around, cocks his head to one side, and opens his arms to invoke an imaginary crowd. The imaginary crowd is evidently on Lawrence's side. Lawrence feels larger, encompassed, begins to sense a firming presence of morality in his self.

– I am sorry Lawrence, a truly poor joke.
Forgive me. It was a good round of gold
today. I almost felt that I was going to
lose. Your game is coming on leaps and
bounds.

Lawrence feels his new size to be ridiculous,
his emotion to be questionable. He lowers his
shoulders.

– You really think so?
– Today I thought I lose. Seriously. It is
because of that thought only that I win.

Lawrence beams, all but skips, to catch up with
the Doctor who is now turning slightly away
from him. Lawrence begins to talk about the
improved motion of his swing and the new clubs
he has read about in Amateur Golfers Weekly.
Doctor Raymond shakes his head and smiles.

– You don't agree then?
– Sorry my friend, what?
– About the clubs and the aerodynamic
latex handle?
– Oh, no, they are too something? The
real golfer, he is here already

The Doctor points at Lawrence's heart.
Lawrence's heart swells airily.

*

Helene is three quarters through a bottle of wine she definitely shouldn't have opened. She has read the majority of the notebook while pacing around the kitchen. She is still pacing around the kitchen though the book is now up-ended on the living room table. At one point Helene had wondered if Jim was even aware of the whole, like, Freudian symbolism of having a lighthouse at the centre of his story. This coupled with the fear of and longing for disappearance that nearly every sentence went out of its way to describe only added weight to the various convocations of the broadly identifiable phrase 'fear of intimacy' or 'castration complex' that kept angrily circling her head.

She'd turned a page to find a six-page rebuttal of that 'anticipated' reaction interspersed with a little fretting and fairly pitiful attempt at bargaining with the reader. Helene wasn't totally convinced by the writing's obvious desire to avoid such an interpretation. Highly emotional things were unconvincing she felt, feeling terrible herself. Evelyn is awake and in front of the television. On it men dressed in the bright skins of unreal animals give cursory examples of friendship to her evident amusement.

– Hey, honey I'm home

The smile is blandly evident in Lawrence's chuckled voice. He stands in the doorway shaking his head at the witticism. Evelyn turns from the primary coloured screen and stretches her arms out towards him.

– Dada

– Hey little sushi roll!

Lawrence sweeps down and places his finned hands under the chubby barely there indents of Evelyn's armpits. He lifts her up and holds her against the centre of his chest, the pulse of his heart against her ear quieting her for a moment. Her thumb plugs into mouth and her eyes close into scribbled stars.

– Now, where's your mum at?

Evelyn looks up and giggles, her hands reaching for Lawrence's hat. Lawrence tilts his head and the hat drops through her flailing arms and into her body. Evelyn tries to tear it apart, laughs hysterically when she finds she can't.

Helene is leaning against the counter, drawing her bandaged foot into a hovering limp. Lawrence walks into the kitchen doorway bouncing Evelyn lightly in his arms.

– You're standing without the crutches. That's so great.

Helene uses her hands on the sideboard to turn herself around in a wheeling, labour intensive, motion.

– It's better, I think

– You mustn't overdo it though.

Helene looks at Evelyn who is inspecting the white bobble of the golfing cap, picking at it with the fingers that she is still learning to apply to the world, grasping the fact of it with an attention that is utterly serene in its indifference towards ends.

    – Look at her, she's so amazing.
    – Well, she's her mother's daughter.

Helene looks up and holds his gaze. Lawrence smiles. She does too and then Helene's eyes flit momentarily to the notebook tented in the front room. In the millisecond of this back and forth Lawrence looks down and away, half embarrassed, a little ashamed. For all of Helene's continued and newly resolute *looking* whatever was just then between them has gone now and no longer is.

Helene hobbles theatrically to the living room. Lawrence overtakes her and places Evelyn in her pen. Together they sit down. The notebook is before them on the table. Neither pays attention to it though Helene can hear its impounded presence in the echo of her blood, can feel the bass of oxygen behind each called out wish of a thought.

Lawrence is talking about the cleaner to Helene. He says that perhaps Diane could come in more regularly and for longer hours, help out more with Evelyn.

– She needs help and we need help and we can afford it, he says.

Helene for want of anything to say only frowns and nods. Lawrence places his palms flat on his knees. He stands and walks to the telephone. He turns back to Helene as he lifts the phone's receiver to his ear. Helene remains upright on the sofa, staring ahead at the mute cavorting of the television screen. Lawrence dials Diane's number and waits, the phone's ring deepening in its insistence like evidence of a tree's age. He depresses the phone's hook with three of his fingers. He had dared not let it ring another second. How long has he been standing there? He looks again at Helene whose head still seems stiffly positioned in silent reproach. He caresses the dial with the tips of his fingers.

> – You were a long time playing golf, Lawrence

Helene says this as she leans forward, picking up the remote and covertly pocketing the notebook. She sits back.

> – We went to the hospital after. Our Doctor needed to pick up some paperwork

Helene glances back at Lawrence whose smile is an attempt to disarm the hardness in her eyes.

– And that's where you met her?
– Bumped into her
– That's where you bumped into her?
– Yes

Helene leans forward again and drains the dregs of her wineglass and points the remote at the television screen. Canned laughter fills the dead room. Lawrence is stood with his jaw lobbied into his neck and his arms open in an expression of indignant shock. He is holding the telephone's receiver out towards Evelyn's pen. Evelyn pulls herself for the first time into a standing position as if ready to answer the call, her body at rest against the presiding net of her unsure future.

*

Richard Fort is lying on his bed in a cheap hotel room trying to sequence an all encompassing sense of regret. His thoughts are disrupted by the physicality of his heartbeat. The wild gong of it announcing life to him in life's most finite terms i.e. as a barely audible, scarcely existent thump happening outside of his understanding in a universe wholly indifferent to such understanding. Richard Fort's heartbeat making of each formerly treasured memory a shattered,uncontrollable thing.

The duvet frowns under his back. Richard Fort asks

-How, how did this happen?

The man with the forks in his fingers, they'd gone to the police station together. It had been a terrible mistake. They'd arrived, a ghastly tarot pair, at the reception desk all out of breath and ragged, collapsing against each other. Richard Fort with a wad of files in one hand and Lawrence's name on his lips. Richard Fort remembering now the grim patience of the secretary, his clipped tones designed to send them flying like toenails back outside where the car with its jerry-rigged bumper was still visible through the glass. They'd insisted, loudly, vigorously. The man with the forks in his fingers had rapped out his reasons on the front desk.

    – Richard, I don't think it's a good
    – Just do it.

The officer at the desk had buzzed reluctantly for the divisional officer. The divisional officer appeared a few moments later from an adjacent room, eating an apple and glancing up at them from a file. His chewing slowed, slopped, the hard bodied apple in his hand pausing in front of his lips.

This a recurring image in Richard Fort's current index of horror. Richard Fort said that he was here to hand in the files on the James Burke case. The divisional officer looked at him blankly. Richard Fort said that the man with the forks in his fingers needed to give a statement, to be questioned in regards to this.

> – Ok, we can do that. Would you mind waiting outside for us?

Richard Fort waited outside the station. He'd come to a realisation as the air unsubtly coaxed him towards a wall. The woozy energy of his drunkenness had been cooked out, its tired residue basting his eyes with regret, leaving him breathless and with a headache on the steps of the station. It was all so implausible. The point wasn't that he had believed or disbelieved what the man with the forks in his fingers had said, he hadn't believed it all, but that he did have reason to believe that there was something strange about all this...

A junior constable came out with two polystyrene cups filled with tepid coffee. He handed one to Richard Fort and lit up a cigarette. The junior constable was a young man with a face like a potato that had been scoured against a brick wall. The rest of his body provided little variation on the theme. They drank the coffee together in silence.

The young man looked down at Richard Fort and told him to either go home and drink about another thousand cups of coffee or to go sleep it off. This was the message he'd been told to pass on, he said.

On the bed, briefly synced with the memory, Richard Fort mumbles

– You sleep it off. I'm your superior, I'm superior, you can't

The junior constable splashed the dregs of his coffee over the grey worn steps, half washing away one of the palm tree shaped bird shits there. He threw the cup down the steps and crushed his cigarette underfoot.

– Superior? Aren't you suspended?
– Like this, to me

Richard Fort had shrugged.

The young constable's acne-blared forehead made a shuttlecock of the sun's reflection. He gestured to someone behind the glass doors of the station. The divisional officer stepped out of the front door in a long stride, turning his torso to face Richard Fort while simultaneously looking away and towards the sun.

– Your wife is on her way to pick you up
– No, I'm going.
– She's coming for you
– Are you holding me for anything?
– No
– Then I can go
– I can't let you drive that car.

The divisional officer looked at Richard Fort for the first time.

> – You're to report back here tomorrow at 9am and you're to be charged with gross misconduct. You've been drinking.
> – What happened?
> – The man is a lunatic. He didn't even know what year it was. He thought this was the future. What did he say to you?
> – That Helene and her baby were in danger.
> – What?
> – The missing person case, harassment.
> – Ah yes. You were supposed to halt your investigation several days ago. I don't suppose your friend in there mentioned the curse to you?
> – No, I mean, that wasn't the important thing about it. Obviously he's not well. But the connection is, that's something isn't it?
> – You'll have a chance to explain tomorrow at the tribunal. Your wife is on her way
> – I'm not, I'm not going with her. I'm leaving.

He'd walked to his car, looked up as he opened the door, saw the divisional officer gently hold back the constable. It was all over now.

He'd gone to Tesco, filled carrier bags with vodka and crisps and packaged sandwiches before driving to a bed and breakfast. He thought about his wife, what they would say to her when she arrived at the station, what they must have had to tell her to get her to come. He'd drank the thought out, poured another, closed his eyes.

Time passed like this, like that. Richard Fort was getting *there*. He continued to drink until the world and his body were forgotten, until his self became a glowing filament of abstraction, a light stopped against and bounced around the prism of memory and memories of memories that burned in little emblematic fires around his heart's periphery. The fires burning until everything was ash.

On the bed Richard Fort fondles his cock while half asleep and pushes himself up the mattress. It is 8pm now. The glass is empty and the sandwiches crusted, staled by the air. He is sprawled on the bed, fingers tweezing parts of his hiked groin, an image of his wife behind his eyelids. The image of his wife calling him on to some humiliating pleasure. He'd wanted her so much. He still did.

They'd been at school, in the same year group. She was troubled but cool, Richard Fort had been neither. After school she was only troubled. He'd found her again outside of a local punk concert. She was crying and smoking pot. Richard Fort in

uniform, a bobby then, and she with the ripped
school shirt and safety pin piercing.

He'd sat down with her, said

> – You don't belong here
> – I know

And then she'd looked at him properly,
recognizing him at last

> – Neither do you
> – So neither of us belong now

He'd driven her to her parents' house in a nice
leafy middle class area, the utter serenity of which
rendered the turning light of his siren less
anachronistic than strangely beautiful, as if the
stillness of the street could absorb and filter any
sign towards its own neutral glamour.

She thanked him for not arresting her and
laughed. He said anytime, if you want to talk,
anytime and she kissed him on the cheek as she
backed out of the car.

He pursued her after that— called her the next
day— followed a line of devoted enquiry even
when it was clear that she'd be happy to branch
off, deviate. She couldn't understand his devotion
and its continual recurrence seemed to her at
times tragic, farcical, and finally endearing and,
after a while as life or something like its outline
intervened in each of her friend's lives, his was
the only pull that continued to manifest. Even

then she could have taken or left it until she took it, half out of boredom, finding her own feelings towards him starting to take a kindly shape and then, soon after that, there'd been the accident and their futures seem to have been decided.

– It might be a happy thing, she'd thought.

They'd married so fast, she started to say towards the end, had to until it turned out they hadn't, mightn't have. That phantom in her belly even now brought her to tears. She told him over breakfast that it wasn't only at night that their baby called to her. She said he was in this room right now, had been in every room since. She said I'm not mad, why won't you listen to me? All he could say was:

– We're here, we're still here.

– You're not hearing me even. Why are we still here? How are we together anymore? Why were we ever? I feel like I'm cursed.

Richard Fort had loved her for so long that the love once attained suffered the problem of all ends in life, suffered the sheer impossibility of them. Ends were appearances. These things that seemed like definitive answers could at best, when gotten close to, inhabited, only become a framework, a budgeted expenditure of joy, before the next distension peaked and shattered them in turn. With so little to recognize in each other, how could they ever hope to find one another again?

Richard Fort had said that he was sorry,

smashed a tea cup on the table and left the room. Coming back into the room, the wounded pride still pouring out of the words, he would say

> – Because it's important. We're still here because it's important.

Their lives together had continued despite being maritally derailed. Lives propelled by their own coarse weight but slowed by the enervating crash of vegetative weeks and months. Richard Fort at the helm, marshalling their freighted spirits into a pathway of boredom along an axis that could no longer determine its point of convergence.

Days of soup and television followed.

Over soup he would try to expel the silence by complaining of his weight, point out how his chin was beginning to recess. It was as if his life was slumping out of his body, the inner sag manifesting itself. She'd say there were more pressing things to consider but would find herself at a loss to say them. She'd say she wished she'd had a chance to study before they'd married, had started to repeat this often, when she spoke to him at all.

Richard Fort would joke by saying that when he ate he felt that he was directly feeding the pouch of skin under his neck, that he imagined it siphoning the food from his throat, that it gribbited with pleasure and need. It was the silence, his own, that made him say it.

These were not even the end days.

Richard Fort groans in his sleep.

*

The man with the bandaged fingertips can see himself, marked by candlelight, cogitating in another time. He can provide proof of God's existence there, he's sure.

In the here and now though things are a little different. The interview at the station had not lasted long, he couldn't prove anything. He had understood their frustration. He knows what it is like not to make sense of himself. A doctor had been called and the forks removed almost painlessly and then they had driven him here, to this institution. Placed him in this room, told him to wait for processing.

How long has he been here? It already feels like forever. Everything is already forever, he thinks.

The man with the bandaged fingertips is sharing the room with a woman who resembles his mother. They have not spoken though the resembling woman has on occasion regarded him with a look of benign indifference in which a blank spot of kindness had seemed on the verge of dilating into recognition. He cannot remember when she entered the room.

The man with the bandaged fingertips stands

and faces a wall. The woman that resembles his mother is kneeling with her hands on her thighs in the centre of the room.

The room or cell holding the man with the bandaged fingertips and the resembling woman shares the replicate look of hotel rooms in which a sort of violent subtraction has occurred, so that it feels as if the room itself exudes a malicious and domineering sense of self awareness about its own blank reserves. There is an iron bed and a rug and an empty sideboard on which a television might once have sat. The room is obviously missing something. It is as if a piece of furniture or a murder victim had been removed or as if, he thinks, murder was a type of furniture.

The room is near colourless, lit with a weakly cast fluorescent light emitted from a single strip in the centre of the ceiling. There is a small square window in the upper left of the boxy room but it provides no light. In fact the square of grey seems curiously close as if occupying the window physically, as if the sky were somehow wedged into that surface in an act of compression that served to confirm the impossible hardness of the room.

There is another, larger and mottled, window set into the door of the room behind which hurried shadows traffic past, darkening in flashed proximity. The man with the bandaged fingertips turns towards it. A shadow breaks off from the rush behind the door and the light in the window dims and grows dark. There is someone behind the door watching them.

The man with the bandaged fingertips walks towards the wall. As well as being afraid he is conducting an experiment, he has realised that the room they are in is entirely without shadow. Neither the bed nor the sideboard nor their bodies cast any impression. He places one hand slowly against the wall waiting for the wall's surface to pit with shadow. His hand meets the wall.

*

Helene awakes fully upright and surrounded by a world of resemblances, her own image juried against her in the dresser table mirrors. The mirrors stationed around show a woman open gowned and wearing a loose sash of moonlight, her hands cut off by the boundary of the frame. There is a grainy object protruding upwards in the forefront of the mirror barely visible in the lamp lit room. Helene squints toward it. She looks down. The pen falls from her hand. Her other hand crabs around the piece of paper it is shielding. She flattens her hand and pulls the piece of paper towards herself. Helene can feel the slide of it, the weak seal of her palm sweat acting as an adhesive to the paper. She lifts her hand slowly. The paper falls away.

There is a stick figure and a lighthouse

scratched out in biro on the paper. The stick figure is a child. The stick figure has a shiny black circle for a mouth. Helene lets her hand drop to her lap. Through the gap in her robe a thatch of pubic hair smooths around her knuckles.

A group of crudely drawn lines is stabbed underneath the drawing. The lines are traumatised, matchstick piled, bundled against each other. A breeze travels over Helene's body. Her body is filmed with sweat. The sweat is full of information that has passed through her skin. Helene feels outside of herself, sieved. She soaks coldly back into her body.

Helene leans forward toward the mirror, sweeping back her hair with both hands. She runs her fingers smoothly over her eyebrows. They stop suddenly as if having drawn a question. The paper is reflected in the mirror. Amid the stabbed lines she begins to see a raw calligraphy emerging. She leans into the mirror, her hands spooning back her face. Helene blinks then grabs the pen and scribbles out the name. She grabs the paper and clenches it in her fist until her nails dig into her palm. The blood moving under the fat of her palm depicts a sunset. Her nails paint migrant birds of blood onto this sunset. She opens her hand. The paper is ranged with mountains, circled with birds. Helene bunches the open slit of her dressing gown with her free hand and turns around in the chair. The room is as she remembers it, though of course she cannot remember it.

She watches the slow, silent heave of Lawrence's chest rising like a soufflé under the sheets. She listens for his breath and cannot detect it.

The alarm clock reads 3.20 am.

Helene stands up still holding the paper. She walks downstairs and opens the French doors. The night air hardens her skin. In the distance the lighthouse partitions the horizon. Helene climbs over the hastily erected fence. She works her way down the cliff, confident that this time she will not fall. Her feet are bleeding. Sand pixels the cut. Helene's toenails are smithereens, resembling eggy shells clinging to some parboiled and filmy skin underneath. She doesn't notice until the sea air breezes over her. The sting of it makes her falter and Helene stumbles towards the shore. She allows the freezing salt water to ride up over her feet. She walks into the lick of the water towards a loosely moored paddleboat. Her feet are numb all the way through. Deep within their surface an obscured warning light of pain flashes outward.

Helene knows the pain is the last warmth of her and is lost in it.

The water rises to her waist. Helene can no longer tell where the sea starts and her skin ends. Her surfaces seem both extended and dissipated, the borders of her body impossible to locate and she feels that there is nothing in her world now but this sense of surface and its impossible location. She rows to the lighthouse.

*

Richard Fort wakes up. It is 3:20 am. His copy of the notebook lies open on his chest. He sits up. Sitting up turns out to be a mistake; it reminds his brain to hurt. The notebook falls to the floor.

He thinks about having another drink. The sense of shame remains within him, comes on slow and desperate, its tide ruled by his full and moony heart. He looks down at the notebook. The image of the lighthouse addresses him. He looks at it a long time. He picks the notebook up, weighs it in his hand.

Richard Fort stands and walks unsteadily towards the door.

*

A little girl is running around the room weaving in and around the resembling woman who is pointedly ignoring the child. The little girl is holding a bundle that she tends to occasionally by pulling back the lip of the blanket and squealing with delight at its contents.

There is a light pouring through the room's window, spotlighting her, bending as if in water wherever she runs. The little girl runs over to the man with the cheek pancaked against the wall.

The little girl hooks a small finger in his cheek and giggles. She shows him the bundle. Inside the bundle is a baby girl with hair that changes from black to blonde. The little girl laughs. The light following her abruptly vanishes.

The little girl is now tapping the resembling woman on the shoulder. The man with the bandaged fingertips watches. The resembling woman receives the blanket from the little girl with an expression of profound gratitude. The little girl puts her small fingertip in mouth and daintily rocks her foot back and forth in front of her.

The resembling woman jostles the bundle in her arms happily. She leans in and makes a cooing sound into the blanket. The resembling woman pulls the lip of the blanket and stares into the darkness there. She frowns. The resembling woman places the bundle on the floor and unfolds it. The blanket is empty.

The little girl laughs. The resembling woman crows.

In the heat of her scream the figures become shadows burnt onto the wall. The room returns to itself or rather it is as it has always has been. The little girl is gone. The empty sky is wedged in the window. The man looks at his hand. The resembling woman looks towards him. Her face is twisted in grief.

*

Helene is sat in Jim's room smoothing out the creases of his bed with her hand. The rain had begun as she rowed. Her arms levered the oars against the water and then the heavens opened. She could barely make out the lighthouse through the din.

She leans down and lifts the telephone up to her knees and starts to dial. She will ask someone if she is sleepwalking. The phone goes straight to an answering machine. Her own voice and Lawrence's awkwardly harmonising in her ear. Helene places the telephone on the bed. She is remembering the last time that she slept with James Burke. They were right here. They had lain here together, the world cushioned around them like an open palm. They would have, she remembers, roughly fifteen minutes before it resumed its grip.

She had asked him what he thought the bottom of the sea looked like. He said that at the bottom of the sea there lived a creature composed of shadow that covered the ocean floor.

Nothing ever touched the bottom of the sea, he said, things only fell or were pulled into this creature. He said that the creature gestated its own progeny from inception and that every thousand years the new creature ate its way out from the centre joining with and consuming the old.

Helene smiles and rolls away from him. He'd

rolled after her, held her in those skinny arms and made promise after promise to her. Then the night came with its putting on of clothes, the chill of the room infringing their outlines.

The lights in the room fritz on and off, this eternal fritzing of things Helene thinks.

Helene stands and wanders towards the stairs. A sadness is drawing Helene up through the lighthouse as if through a syringe and she feels the tug of it now, a movement into the hollow. She climbs the stairs, stands in the lantern room.

She walks around the lantern and then out towards the balcony. She holds onto the wet rail and looks towards her house. She can see that Evelyn's light is on. Lawrence must be awake.

*

Richard Fort has landed on the Lighthouse's island. He vomits into the surf. His shoe fills with water. His stomach continues to trampoline. Great swatches of rain are sweeping in from the sea, the rain so hard that it washes the air, pins down the muck, returns the dust to the earth and shapes the figurant remainder. Richard Fort straightens up, skull drawn by the wind, his skin flagellated by rain. He drops his torch, light whirls around his feet. He bends wiping his mouth and lifts it towards the lighthouse. The torch's beam flows through the broken strips of police tape and into the open doorway.

Richard Fort climbing the lighthouse stairs as fast as he can manage.

*

It is as if the resembling woman has lost something. Her eyes widen and the mouth draws an invisible circle around itself. The anonymous man screams.

The resembling woman is standing now. Her forehead is beaded with sweat, elbows jerking wildly. The resembling woman begins to fold and break into herself like a chicken entering a coop. Her elbows dislocate, her forearms windmill and crowing the resembling woman drops to the floor as if through a hole and then it is over.

*

Richard Fort passes the living room, out of breath and clutching the handrail, he pulls his body up the metal stairs. The torch slips from his hands, falls clattering through the lighthouse. The notebook is still in his pocket.

Richard Fort staggers through the door of the lantern room, the dust pluming around him. Helene turns around, slips a little, her hands clutching the balcony rail as she bruises her hip against it.

– James?

Richard Fort, drunk and blinded by dust, whirls towards the lantern.

Click.

PART 2

4

THE LUPE
VELEZ
EXPERIENCE,
1991

Evelyn stands under a weeping willow tree a few feet behind Lawrence. The branches and leaves ruffled by the wind reel their stuttering shadows like old time projections across her face. Lawrence, noticing her absence at his side, twists his shoulders to look at her. She is every inch the advert of a child, reality at cinematic play over her skin but restrained from interfering, from delving into, the larger canvas of her expectant youth. Lawrence beckons with his arm and Evelyn steps forward into the bright clean light. She takes his arm, leans against him. Lawrence takes the weight.

Lawrence's face with its delicate features suffering the distension of lived flesh, an autumnal skin sagging with time, expends itself in a reproduction of alert sorrow as he glances down toward her. Evelyn's shoulder length black hair frames a face removed today from time's machinations. Soon her body will emerge to meet the future on grounds she'll believe to be her own, he thinks. All this will start to drop away, has already. The protective casing of puppy fat withdrawing now to release the finely drawn jut of her cheekbones, enunciating the architecture from which her adulthood will hang. Lawrence recognizes, faintly, weakly, that even now there are questions in her uncurling, developing their own heartbeats and minds. Their transparent circuitry ready to mature into the obfuscation of her personality's skin.

After all, she had asked to come here, had asked in a voice unlike her usual formulations of want. A troubled or perhaps just exploratory ask, something considered and trembled in the words she herself hadn't understood. A want without tenable equivalence in the world.

Of course she would want to see her.

Lawrence looks away from Evelyn at last. His

insides try to thumb a ride up his trachea. He is not holding her hand. Somehow it has become agreed between them that this is something that they no longer do. He imagines it as something they will laugh about later on, in the future, when she is older and where he might relate to her a little better.

> – This cemetery, it's umm very
> prestigious. The willows here, a famous
> poet, he once wrote about them

He steps a few feet ahead of Evelyn now, crosses his hands in front of him. It has been so long since he visited, longer still since he brought Evelyn.

> – I forget what he said

Why is he saying this?
They arrive at Helene's grave.

> – Your mother, your mother she is
> asleep here. She is asleep, she shouldn't
> be, there's a place for us all.

Lawrence's face slopes down, a handle bar of skin crimped over hunkered-out teeth and raw-weathered gums. He knows the coffin is empty, that underneath that peat and dirt there's a box with nothing in but a photo of Helene, a dress flat but for the broken pleat of an irregularly tilted zipper— the one he broke with hands that lacked diligence and care enough that night she first came to him for help— and a vial of the seawater, corked and not at all murky, that must have claimed her when she fell.

Lawrence stands a little ahead of Evelyn now. He is detuned by grief, his eyes starred into their sockets, his face trying hard to not be a face, its unstable expression visibly fielding his grief.

Evelyn walks towards him, moves to slip her hand quietly into his. Lawrence is unaware of her movement and overcome with emotions. He throws his arms up into the air, batting away Evelyn's love-foraging hand and catching her with an elbow to the bridge of her delicate nose.

The daughter's blood falls in apples of clot before her mother's grave. Lawrence scatters the idle wildlife with one truncated shout of OH SHIT.

*

Henry is in bed depressed. His whole being contained in a low-level hum of general sadness, punctuated by the occasional surge of a pain that's almost appreciably audacious in scope and execution, and which seems to reach through him towards an end that he himself could never grasp. It is, he thinks, as if there is another body trying to conceive itself within him. One larger and older and possessed of some ancient evil.

Henry wants to die. Not yet, please. His hand flaps for a book to train his mind with for a moment or two. A book that will help him stay alive. The library had strangely never been off limits. Someone messed up there, he thinks.

Henry tries to remember how long he has been like this. He only knows that at a certain point he had become conscious of the pain that he is in. That his moment of consciousness had always been pain.

Even before the onset of puberty he had developed a constant unerring fear of death. Not his own but others.

In his prayers for instance he would reconstruct the crashed cars that he imagined remoulded his mother every time she left without saying goodbye.

Force the metal to unbend, the creped snouts of the cars to smooth into a sun buttered sheen.

The blood to re-equator life.

Chips of glass to singularise into a gleam.

His mother always came home safe.

He remained a melancholy child at heart, one who still paced the rooms he'd learnt to walk in. He continued to experience a profound guilt at masturbating in the showers of a swimming pool aged thirteen though never caught. Guilt at the way the shame fed into the excitement of the act.

Guilt became the only emotion large enough to touch god with.

Henry is losing his faith. It is massive and

alienating and weird. He doesn't know how to exist.

He spent whole afternoons running into his bedroom wall. Throwing his shoulders against the immoveable, was it the future that he hoped would shatter him? When Henry throws himself into the wall he imagines achieving permanent nerve damage, imagines that he is slowly turning himself into an unfeeling thing that just is in the world. Life, he figured, was a costume existence occasionally wore and like all costumes the dull and conscious weight of it came to outweigh the joy of its affect. He picks up his notebook. Everything he has written is terrible. He throws it across the room. He picks another book up. After five minutes the lines start to blur in his eyes. He sits up on the bed, and puts the book down. He doesn't want to sleep anymore.

His Grandfather has begun to appear to him in his dreams of late. In his dreams his Grandfather is sat in a rocking chair, a rocking chair that Henry would later be able to identify, in what he refers to mentally as a well Proustian moment, as one that he had passed countless times in a department store window that had closed down and reopened around the same time that his Grandfather had died.

The Grandfather in the dream in the rocking chair was speaking to a boy in the room who was Henry but with whom Henry did not identify with in any kind of centralised way or seem to inhabit physically in the dream.

The old man's voice in his dreams was calm, not self-consciously calm or measured, rather his voice followed the natural pitch, modulations and evolutions the particular subject had brought to bear on it. Likewise everything quantifiable about the old man's presence was entirely consistent with itself and one could not even say that the lack of drama in his tone was itself dramatic or that the speech was inherently boring because of its commonplaceness or that it was indeed commonplace. At this point Henry, as the displaced consciousness of the dream, became aware that he could no longer remember or understand what his grandfather was saying.

All that he could really say was that something occurred in their relations. In the relations between the Grandfather that spoke and the boy that was both Henry and not. A change that was real and emanated but from which intent and causation had been liberated. The dream would end in the next moment when Henry suddenly became himself and when he became himself, when he became the boy in the room who was Henry, he knew that he was Jude and for a moment he understood what the old man had been saying or trying to say and then, upon leaning in to hear, he would wake in his bed and feel at his face in the dark.

He had told himself this dream so many times

that he could not admit any deviation. *Who am I*, he'd thought often, almost reverentially. There were lies in all of this, in the question most of all. Embellishments, formal innovations, they crept in as he pulled himself into the light of his fictions.

The sheer ego of his misery was breathtaking. Who was he? He was a kid who was in fucking earnest. About what? Life and how to live it? Suffering. He rethinks that. He doesn't know about suffering. He doesn't know about anything, idiot, retard, ugly.

His life was, he was sure, a prolonged sabotage of joy. I, I, I, he, he, he...

Henry hyperventilates into a pillow. It's not working. He tells himself that he has no sense of proportion. That everything is in his mind but then where is his mind if all this is in it? He hears the front door violently rattle, imagines the glass shaking under the blows raining down upon it, sees himself coming loose. Mum and Jude must be out by now. He drags himself to the door. Behind the door's frosted windows is a shape he can't quite credit. He pulls the door open.

> – What you up to? You look like shit,
> were you masturbating or something?

This punk kid from school, Fiasco, walks in. They're only sort of friends. Henry doesn't know what to say. Fiasco is already halfway up the stairs. Henry follows, pointing to his room.

Fiasco strolls in and looks around its space admiringly. Henry watches him stalk around the room. He's got a wedge of CDs in his hand, grabbed from a tippexed rucksack. Fiasco sits on the bed and looks at Henry.

> – Do you like Guns 'n Roses?
> – I don't think I'm allowed to listen to them.
> – Listen to this.

Fiasco puts the CD into the player.

After a few minutes the singer tells Henry that Henry is going to die.

> – I like it.
> – This isn't bullshit.
> – Ok

Henry isn't exactly sure why Fiasco is here. They'd spoken a few times before, had once out-improvised their entire class in the cumbersomely titled 'creative art' lesson they'd ended up taking together by way of intellectual default. That being such a strange and uncharacteristic gesture on his part that had been, even more uncharacteristically, received by classmates and teacher alike with applause.

Creative Art was for the kids who didn't draw well enough to just do art, or couldn't sing, or lacked the mixture of confidence and annoying personality traits (confidence, they had openly wondered) that would have merited taking drama by itself but who also didn't feel like running around outside under the sadistic auspices of the P.E teacher. A teacher who had spent whole lessons making them squat against a wall while he fired the five aside ball at any head he'd spied flinching at his faux drill sergeant routine that, thinking about it, he probably lived 24/7. The fuzzy yellow ball of sun ricocheting off heads, wincing noses, splatting eyes or landing with a crash either side of their jangled to fuck with minds.

– Why does it have to be so yellow? It's killing hope for me.

Creative art had been for the kids who didn't want to, or couldn't, do anything. Henry remembers walking in late one day and seeing Fiasco kicking the keys off of a keyboard while videoing himself. The teacher couldn't control them. The other kids in the class were the equally sifted remnants of the year group. Henry hovered around Fiasco, listened to his improbable stories and found his own gift for invention. He could be funny or something like it around Fiasco. Fiasco who he felt set himself up to be believed in.

> – Give me your lazy, give me your
> untalented, give me your narcoleptic;
> give me the fat, the useless, the weirdly

double-jointed.

This being an audio recording Fiasco and Henry handed in as their end of term project. The piece called 'creative art' and recorded over Henry playing guitar with an effects pedal they'd found at the bottom of the store cupboard.

Still, they hadn't seen each other outside of class or even suggested it, his mother's biblical maxim 'bad associations spoil useful habits' having presided over Henry's lack of social engagement and Fiasco never having apparently even thought about it. He's not even sure how Fiasco knows where he lives much less has any idea at all where Fiasco lives.

> – He could murder me and just leave,
> Henry thinks.

Fiasco sits down on the bed and rummages his hand underneath it. He pulls up a couple of paperbacks and a bible.

> – The good book. What's good in the
> good book?
> – Well, some of the stories are pretty
> messed up. Like in one this guy gets
> tricked into sleeping with his daughter
> and then nothing is really made of it. It's
> just something that happens or
> something.
> – Haha, what?

– Yeah really. There's another one that's actually a pretty awesome story with Jesus.

Fiasco winces and slaps his knee and all but hoots at the idea of this causing Henry to wrinkle his forehead, perspire a little.

– Go on then.
– Listen, just listen. Jesus meets this guy who by today's standard you'd have to call wildly schizophrenic.
– By today's standards.
– Yeah and he's been cutting himself with sharp rocks and speaking madness and generally being very animalistically scary.
– Eating his own faeces and whatnot.
– So Jesus walks up to him.
– Calm as you like.
– Oh yeah, he's as cool as a cucumber.
– haha
– and he says, because he knows instantly that the man is possessed and not just mental… though I'm assuming that being mental wasn't a category back then, so he says demon what is your name?
– Holy shit
– Now you have to imagine this very disembodied, basically inhuman, voice

coming out of this severely disturbed schizoid individual who is completely in the grip of what turns out to be this, I dunno, cabal of demons who, by the mere fact of surfacing enough to organize this disembodied voice, fractionally release the possessed man's soul to the extent that the man finally shows up in himself, in his body, in some, I don't know, quality of fear in his eyes.

– Is the possessed man's mouth moving or not moving as the demon replies?

– That's entirely up to you.

– And does the bible describe the man's soul's agony at being consciously trapped or are you embellishing?

– Embellishing but it is heavily implied
–

– So the demon says to Jesus 'We are called legion for we are many.' Note the single voice. That's creepy as.

– We're going to use that.

– Huh? So Jesus he commands them to release this man from their possession. The demons begin to beg with him to let them stay. They don't back chat or anything

– They don't throw down at all?

– This is the son of God we're talking about.

– They should have known better than to even ask.

– Damn straight except Jesus does throw them something resembling a bone because he sends them flying into a herd of pigs.

– Is it a herd of pigs?

– I guess

– Not a murder of pigs?

– No, not even an unkindness of pigs

– A presumption of pigs?

– haha but anyway, anyway he casts all these demons into these animals

– Who have done nothing wrong?

– Well, they're just animals.

– And Jesus was just Jewish.

– It made sense for the animal to be a pig in the story is what you're getting at I hope?

– At that particular time, yes. Who was sympathetic to the pig back then? It's narratively convenient.

– Point taken. So he casts them back into these pigs who all immediately rush over the edge of the cliffs in one colossal bacony suicide.

– Then what?

– The man thanks Jesus, Jesus heads off to confound some Pharisees, and we're on to the next episode.

– What a guy. We should use this story,

imagine it from the point of view of the demons in the pigs running towards the cliff's edge. That would be fucking awesome.

– I always wondered what happened to the guy afterwards. Was he just fine, how did he cope with what happened to him?

– Yeah I guess the Demons pretty much raped his soul.

– Exactly, you're not just going to live with it. On the other hand you've just met the son of God so maybe that becomes the point of you but either way you're reduced I guess.

– That's something else we could use.

– Use for what?

– Our band. The one we're forming today.

*

Lawrence is dabbing at Evelyn's nose.

– Home time I think

They wander through the pretence of forestry, through the willow trees with their coarse hair entangling in the mope of breeze and towards the unfenced perimeter that bends around the slanted road, fresh tarmac and concrete so new and terminal looking as to seem chromed. Evelyn nods and follows Lawrence towards the car. He tells her that she can sit in the front today if she likes. She slides her body into the passenger seat dangling her legs in the egg-shaped space before her. She slips her hand onto his as Lawrence puts the car into gear. She says *Dad I love you* as he turns the key and the car shirrs into life. Through the windscreen the moon, in its waning gibbous phase, curiously blue and trooping away from the sun, hangs like a monocle in the morning light. Evelyn moves her eyes back and forth between the sun and the moon connecting a line of light between the two. She closes her eyes mapping the distance between her lids, waiting for the world to decompose into her blood. Lawrence turns the key back and stares at the wheel.

    – There is something I need to tell you.

Lawrence's eyes mist up. Evelyn glances at him and then looks through the windscreen towards the sun.

    – Your mother, she was taken from us.

She stares at the sun. She draws a circle around the sun with her eyes, connects the circle to a triangle. Blinking and moving her eyeballs she draws two large homunculus arms and legs that get stuck to the wavy lines of hair that her eyes stroke onto the makeshift girl's head. She draws another, larger, stick figure of a woman.

Evelyn closes her eyes and seals the image. She opens them.

> – There was a man, he took her and he will never be brought to justice for her leaving.

The little girl made of light floats around her vision, drifts away, becomes a skeleton.

> – She loved you more than anything in the world and you have to believe that.

Evelyn looks up at Lawrence. There are tears in her eyes and she wants him to stop.

> – You look more like her every day.

Evelyn pulls down the mirror in the passenger seat. She stares at this slat of herself. In the corner of her eye there are remnants of light. She closes her eyes burying everything. She opens them to see Lawrence reaching for the key in the ignition.

> – And you dad?
> – No little sushi it doesn't work like that. I can't very well look like your mother we weren't related like that. Ha, what are they teaching you at that school?

Lawrence starts the car and wheels it into the road, chuckling to himself.

> – But dad?
> – Yes sweetheart?
> – In school the other day we were learning about eye colours, how you get them and…

Lawrence restricts himself from turning towards Evelyn, restrains himself from teaching her about the notion of rhetorical questions and the silent, meditative, space they implied.

> – Really? How interesting. Now your mother had the most beautiful eyes, like you… not like my own boring brown ones and I think that actually her father did too but her mother did not…or the other way around…there's a whole…thing… deeply scientific and real around it… and so you see often the science you get taught at school, it's not strictly true there are levels to it I think and does that answer your question?

His head nodding supportively, Lawrence thinks of the colour photos he has kept from her. She'd have seen some but when? When he was careless, before he'd thought things through. Before he burnt them along with that weird diary she'd kept.

– Now, did you know that I know a little girl who is going to McDonald's with her dad right now? Shall we play road Pac-man? Let's go.

Lawrence changes gear, the car smoothly taking to the gradient of the hill. Evelyn looks around at Lawrence who is looking at the road and smiling fixedly as he swerves the car into its middle, the little white lines of the road pilling under the car and Lawrence going chomp chomp chomp as the car passes each of them.

– We'll get those ghosts!

Evelyn doesn't say anything, her pupils wide with love in the shocking shaved emerald of her iris. She loves her father, so what? Who cares what anyone says.

5

ANNIVERSARIES, 1993

Evelyn stands in class to accept her award. She steps awkwardly into the spare, near hexagonal, spaces irregularly plated by her year group's crossed legs. She steps on a hand here, stumbles against some thick knees there, all the while artlessly apologising to the rows and rows of fellow students planted like malevolent and surreal cabbages in the hall. Her chestnut hair has the ill-defined cut of her age group, the fringe an armoured visor that her pale hands rearrange nervously as she totters forward.

Evelyn has won an under thirteen short story

competition and her form tutor had insisted she allow the school to co-opt, he had said recognize, the achievement.

Evelyn's story was about the man on the moon and a young orphan girl on earth. The girl was the oldest child in the orphanage and things did not look good for her. She hated the daytime because she was always alone and an orphan. Every time she made a friend they left. She had 'given up the ghost of friendship.'

The man on the moon was also lonely because there was no one to talk to on the moon, not even his own echo, what with it being space and everything. Also, he had weight problems. Over the course of a month he would shift slowly towards obesity before dieting to near anorexic levels and this unbalanced his moods, made him accusative and paranoid.

One day, on her birthday, the orphan girl tied a wish to a balloon left over from the communal birthday party that was held once a year.

The balloon floated into space. The man on the moon fished the balloon out of a lake of stars. The man on the moon read the wish and held the paper to his heart for he had been answered. Written on the paper was

> Hello my name is Lucy, I live at 31 South Street Orphanage. I would like a friend. Will you be my friend?

The man on the moon wrote a reply in the affirmative and sent it back to the orphan girl.

The man on the moon sent his letters by shooting star and the orphan replied by sending balloons that she stole from the orphanage's supply closet.

They wrote to each other many times a day and were soon as close as two people linked only by letter could be, for they exercised themselves in clever revisions of their thought, forming new opinions and sharing their freshly investigated lives. They wrote their selves to each other. There was a bond.

The little orphan girl though never told him the balloons were stolen for she was ashamed and feared both the moral implication of her actions and also what might happen come next communal birthday when the deficit of balloons would no doubt be discovered.

Her letters to the man on the moon during this time took on a regressive quality and the man on the moon was perturbed at the underlying lack of self-esteem evident in their description of the world.

One day— the day before the communal birthday— the orphan girl was caught taking balloons from the store closet and locked in her room. She could not reply to the man on the moon's letters now or ever again it seemed for the orphanage stopped ordering balloons as punishment. The little orphan girl was now more unpopular than ever.

The man on the moon didn't understand what had happened even as the orphan girl tried to mime from earth the sequence and meaning of the events that had befallen her.

The man on the moon peered through his telescope, which was the most powerful telescope to have ever existed but which was nevertheless not strong or advanced enough to aid him in deciphering her poorly developed charades skills.

The man on the moon sent many letters over the course of the year and one night, in a frenzy of loneliness, he sent over a hundred. On that very night a couple driving by saw the shooting stars, and intrigued by the unusual meteorological activity veered off their usual course and drove towards the orphanage.

They found the orphan girl crying in the middle of a circle of fallen stars. They adopted her on the spot and that very night she drove with her new parents to a house far away in the country. The man on the moon could not find her with his telescope and he began to madly send letters like 'ninja shurikens of stars' down to earth.

The little girl for her part had not even thought of asking for a balloon or anything else for she was 'not in the habit of asking' and for a little while, in the disorientating excitement being cared for by the people around her produced, she forgot all about the man on the moon and his letters or any of her abandoned sorrows.

It was a few months later on a warm August day, on her first real birthday, that the little orphan girl, surrounded by presents (one for each lost year) and her new brothers and sisters, remembered her previous traumatic existence. Her sorrow was no longer 'unvisited'. She remembered that the man on the moon's letters had been the sole source of comfort to her and that he was the only one who truly knew who she was then and that he was, moreover, directly responsible for the current happiness of her situation while he himself was most likely frantically lonely and in an even arguably worse situation than he had been before they had begun exchanging letters, due to the accredited pain of loss. The girl scrawled her address on a card, sealed it with 'apologetic tears,' attached it to a balloon and sent it into the sky.

The little girl would receive no reply. In years to come the man on the moon seemed to be the fanciful invention of a deeply lonely but gifted child. The years before her adoption by the Mclucky family had solidified for her into a 'different world,' one that she only liked to inhabit anecdotally, making of it a packaged item in the gentle sell of her personality. She no longer believed the childish story her adoptive parents told her about finding her in a ring of fallen stars. She lived out her life and on balance it was 'slightly better than average, the upward part of a curve.'

The man on the moon watched her for he had, after many years of searching, found her with his telescope. He watched her and hoped for her and held back a fierce sense of disappointment in her to the day she died.

The man on the moon had received that letter but never read it, for in the desperate frenzy of his loneliness he had sent so many stars to earth that he no longer had any light by which to read. He had held that final letter in his hand until it turned to space dust and floated away 'like a galaxy in miniature'.

This had been the first draft. Evelyn had tacked on a happier ending in which the little girl put on a display of fireworks and trained to be an astronaut.

This ending hadn't satisfied her but it had stopped the newly installed school therapist's concerned frown from being so frequently directed towards her. She of the splashy fat body, mohair cardigan and private school education. She in fact a former 'uniquely sensitive pupil' of this school too. Evelyn ashamed of her meanness, of her judgement of the school therapist whose presence in light of her shame is even more oppressive and whose supposed openness and trust seemed unable to imagine, thus cope with, even the possibility of Evelyn's thought being so viciously weighted.

And so Evelyn found her thoughts exiled in taboo for whom could she tell of her repulsion for this figure.

And who could tell her that it was the form of

her hatred and not its content that had resulted in this untenable situation?

The teachers beam at Evelyn from the margins, attempt to guide her toward the makeshift stage. She shakes the headmaster's hand and takes the certificate that she had already received last weekend in a formal presentation. The headmaster looks down at her. The headmaster nods up and down then smiles apologetically to the crowd.

Evelyn is unsure what to do next. The headmaster impatiently gestures towards a long wooden bench at the side of the stage filled with other recent recipients of academic recognition. Evelyn sits next to a boy in the year below her. His name is Geoffrey Hardy and he is captain of the junior debate team. He smiles at her.

The headmaster begins a long speech on the notion of community and giving things back. The things the headmaster wants the private school to give back seem largely unquantifiable and abstract.

Geoffrey Hardy is tilting his winning speech towards Evelyn while smiling and nodding at her. She takes it from him with a sense of automatism that briefly awakens her. She looks down at the speech. It is entitled 'the importance of homework.'

The assembly is open to parents and Evelyn scans the back row for signs of her father. Lawrence of course couldn't make it but she spies her adult smiling and waving towards her in the front row. Diane there, waiting to walk her home, all but bursting with pride at Evelyn's achievement. Evelyn looks down at the speech in her hands and reads.

The school bell rings, classes and year groups are summarily dismissed. The hall empties until only Evelyn, Diane, the headmaster and Geoffrey Hardy remain. They are all waiting to leave except Geoffrey Hardy who is taking a curiously long time to gather his belongings.

The headmaster strides towards Diane and shakes her hand.

> – You're doing a wonderful job
> – Thank you

The headmaster looks away and then around before leaning in

– We are a little concerned about some of the content

Evelyn joins Diane at her side. The headmaster looks down at Evelyn and then up at Diane.

> – Perhaps we should talk another time,
> at parents evening?

Geoffrey Hardy waves at them as they leave. Evelyn's balled hand presses into Diane's palm like a wedding ring. Evelyn tells Diane that she is going to get a £50 book token for winning the competition. She tells Diane that she wants to buy the collected Chronicles of Narnia, The Hobbit and an illustrated version of JM Barrie's Peter Pan with the token.

Diane squeezes her hand and asks her if she wouldn't like to buy a bible with that token too.

> – I don't have to get a bible if I don't
> want to. Dad said I didn't have to. He'd
> be angry.
> – You're right, I don't know why I said
> it.

She squeezes Evelyn's hand.

Evelyn is at home twirling a furry pen around the lined paper of her makeshift diary. She is wrapped in a blanket she's had since birth and from her window she can see a newly erected park taking shape and beyond that the small cove of woods where her mother's grave is.

Evelyn tags her emotions in a few lines of execrable poetry and then begins doodling in the margin and around the page. The doodle is of a ghost, white sheeted, and triangularly trimmed at its floating base, with two droopy holes for eyes delineating the head. Evelyn stares at the sheeted figure. She draws another and then another until the page is filled with them. Something is missing.

She draws a speech bubble for the first ghost. Inside the speech bubble she writes 'ghost?'

She draws speech bubbles for the rest and writes the same question in each of them.

The page fills with ontologically concerned ghosts.

There is a knock at the door. Lawrence comes in and stands in the doorway, keeping his distance. Evelyn knows what his distance means.

> – Hey Sushi roll, how was the assembly?
> – It was ok
> – I'm sorry I couldn't make it
> – That's ok.
> – I'm so proud that you won.
> – Thanks dad. What was your favourite part?
> – Of?
> – The story?
> – All of it, I liked all of it.
> – Which part specifically?
> – The ending, I thought the ending was great. Dandy.
> – Really, the ending? I wasn't sure. What did you like about it?
> – Sweetheart, I really am very tired. I loved it. You're amazingly talented. Your mother would be so proud but right now I have to lie down.

He shuts the door. Evelyn looks at the page and says 'ghost' out loud and to herself.

*

Henry is at the beach with Fiasco. Fiasco Velez's real name isn't Fiasco Velez. His real name is less important than Bruce Wayne. They have been smoking wet spliffs in the drizzle and damp of a September Monday for hours. They have laughed about this, about having nowhere to go, about having to do this.

– When winter comes, we'll be lost.

The tide crowns around their trainers. They are gesturing wildly, shouting joyously into the sea, their profiles cast forward, each of them trying to disrupt the perceivable limits of their world. It is as if they want their faces to take on an aspect of that distant brim, to force its cancelling line around their own misshapen horizons. They are trying to experience the phenomenal. Henry tells Fiasco that the sea is part of the phenomenal.

– If the phenomenal can be divided that is

They have been talking about their concept of 'the phenomenal' for three hours. The two of them previously having waxed lyrical for two hours on the wrestling icons of their youth:
– I have never ever liked Hulk Hogan
For one hour on Indiana Jones and the Temple of Doom:

– My little sister shit herself when that

was on
– I wasn't allowed to see it, or
Ghostbusters, or Karate kid.
– You're making me sad.

Their thoughts are like a breadcrumb trail the birds have been at. They have yet to sleep. The two of them walk through these weird abandoned gardens, climb a dirt hill and amble towards the suspension bridge. The bridge is the final stage in their ritual, the final place where the phenomenal may be contemplated. Fiasco draws the tip of a cigarette from his pack with his mouth and offers the pack to Henry. The cigarette rises up, partitioning Fiasco's fringe as he lifts the lighter to his mouth.

Their hair is jet black and long, uncombed, their pale noses occasionally rippling the matte surfaces like an iceberg in the river Styx. They're dressed in clothes a single devolution away from being rags. The inseam of Fiasco's jeans are sealed with industrial masking tape from the crotch to ankle, Henry's army surplus jacket tattered and stained with mud and blood from his self-harm.

– Did I ever tell you about my Granddad and the action men?

Their conversations were like the games of children, performances that supplanted the hard angles of reality. Except, where a child's habitation of fantasy might have edged around the limits of their own inarticulacy, Fiasco and Henry had developed a frighteningly paced but equally closed lucidity. Their dialogues of escalation illuminated a dedication to logical conclusions that tended towards absurd negation. Or so they told themselves.

Henry finishes his story. They are laughing and shaking their heads. Fiasco now recounts a story about his childhood, about a brown duffle coat that he'd thrown atop the school library and the various indignities that ensued.

They didn't really like their childhoods but they wanted to like themselves, who they were now. Fiasco had loved being a kid but everything by the age of six had already started to seem bullshit. At age eight something had already felt completely gone, recessive. The harsh grammarian of experience interjecting early on as his mother remarried, his brother left home, and he grew wild. Fiasco contracting an Edenic variant of nostalgia during this period. He longed for his younger state as Adam must have. He liked and was fierce about the state of childhood as only an exile can be while Henry couldn't find anything he wanted to remember. Still, credible parallels, narratives, needed to be drawn between who they wanted to be now and who they were then and so they went about retouching their pasts with the wild theory of their imagination.

They walk into the centre of the suspension bridge and sit down.

– Hey, do you know Winston Churchill jumped off this bridge?

– He did not.

– He did, he did it to join a gang.

– Bullshit

– It's true. Or something.

– That something is extraneous or something

– You're an extra anus.

– Or something

The lighthouse is visible through the canopy of trees. Fiasco points towards it.

– That'd make for a cool final scene in a zombie film, like the last hideout or something. The final scene could be shot from the lighthouse's point of view just as thousands of zombie's heads monk out of the water.

– Cool, but I'd want the lighthouse to have something evil about it though, like in the Shining, something supernatural. It looks kind of inherently nasty.

– Did you know a policeman committed suicide there a while back?

– Really? I remember my mum told me something pretty bad happened up there but I didn't know that.

– For real. There was a scandal, everyone thought he was having an affair and that he'd killed someone and he couldn't hack it.

Henry tells Fiasco that he has to go home to look after Jude and make lunch.

– When's band practice again?
– Mum's taking Jude for the weekend and it is the daughter's birthday dinner up there on the Friday... so, maybe Saturday? You found a drummer yet?

*

The depressed sigh of the school bus is audible from the kitchen and Henry rubs his eyes with the back of his hand. He stirs the dried-up tomato clotted mince into a thick cyclopic eyeball in the frying pan and checks the fomented water in the pan of bowtie pasta. He lifts a pasta bowtie from the pan and watches it slip limply back towards the steaming inch of water. He turns the heat up.

He dries his hands and puts the lid on the pan and walks towards the door, stopping to check his bloodshot eyes and spray himself with a bottle of air freshener.

There is a woman accompanying Jude to the house. She has a hold on his forearm and is walking faster than either of them is comfortable with. Jude's head moves in an uneven rotation as he takes in portions of the guttering, a slash of sky, a cascade of gravel disturbed by the bump of his shoe. He laughs at the world. The woman raps her knuckles on the door, taps her feet, and then makes a grab for the purely decorative brass knocker. Her fingertips brush it slightly as the door swings away from her.

Henry looks at the stern-faced woman ahead of him, at her balled left hand and, frowning, returns the gesture of solidarity. There is a pause as the woman lowers her hand, relaxes her fist.

The woman says hello to Henry. She says that she is here to talk about the day, about how Jude has behaved today and whether that is really the way for him to behave. She mentions a bible and ....

> – Oh, he doesn't like the paper, the feel of it drives him crazy
> – Well if that had been all perhaps we could overlook it but there is also the small matter of Jennifer Fishily's hair and Jude having the sparklers and bubble gum in his possession in the first place.

Henry can smell something inedible wafting through from the kitchen and mixing with the chemical drape of the air freshener. He feels nauseous, flustered. He tries to concentrate on what the woman is saying that Jude has done. She is saying something about behavioural strategies and a code of policy while Henry concentrates hard on his breathing to keep whatever blood-cloaked evilness is inside him from manifesting itself on the woman's blouse. It's not until he's able to follow her gaze down towards Jude's alkali eyes that the sense of overwhelming horror subsides.

Jude calibrates himself and grins at Henry, then continues to look around the frame of the door.

The woman looks up at Henry who is still looking at Jude and smiling. Henry is thinking about the way Jude looks at things. It is one of his favourite things to think about, the way Jude regards the blindness of objects with an expectancy that seemed to shrug reality out of its stupor, as if the world thought to only cursorily remember itself in his gaze.

Henry looks at the woman who is smiling fixedly at him now. I'm way too stoned, he thinks.

> – Do you know when?
> – Sorry, what?
> – Do you know when I can make an appointment to see your mother?
> – I, I can pass the message on. She works a lot.

Time eels around his brain, gorged with worry. He is worrying that this woman can tell he is stoned, that the kitchen is about to cavort with

flame, that he needs his mother, that he needs this
lady here, that he needs them both more than he
could admit. He is scared that this woman, her
name tag says Jean, he is scared that *Jean (God,
Jean)* will discover this need, will contact places,
will take Jude away.

— Is that, is that smoke?

The woman shuffles her gaze around him.
Henry has kept the hallway meticulously clean
even as the rest of the house has shifted into
collage. He does not turn around.

— It's not smoke. It's a bug bomb.
— You have bugs?
— It's a science experiment. Home
learning. I'll pass the message on.

Henry pulls Jude inside and closes the door on
the woman. He waits by the door listening for
the sound of the woman's footsteps. Jude is telling
him that he wants to take his coat off. He tells him
this by pulling at the sleeves of his coat. Henry
counts to ten before hearing the woman's
retreating footsteps.

Jude continues to admonish his coat as he
wanders towards the kitchen, fascinated by the
confusingly bad smell and the rattling hi hats' of
pot lids. Henry jogs past him and turns off the
gridded network of hobs. He lifts the lids from
the pan. Smoke geysers into his face.

Henry peers into the blackly webbed pans. The fossilised looking spaghetti could be trying to explicate string theory while the mince in the pan makes him think of an old billionaire's brain I.E totally corrupted.

Henry looks at the food and then at a picture of the food sans the cellular torture.

> – Jude mate, lunch is rubbish today. Shall we get chips? I think there's still some money mum left.

Jude nods vigorously, clapping his hands. Henry leans down and buttons Jude's coat up.

> – Not so hard. You'll bruise me ears.

Henry models a soft clap. Jude claps softly back at him, the clap gradually growing faster and faster, accompanied now by a demonic giggle, until Jude's hands are a blur.

> – No need to be sarcastic. No, mate, don't pull at your coat you're going to need it if we're going to the shops aren't you?

Henry turns around and lifts a still tied trainer to his foot, banding the heel around his sole.

> – I'm well going to get a battered sausage, You're getting Fish bites by the way.

Jude stops and looks up from the dark immersive curve of the pan he'd been interrogating and lets his mouth drop open in disbelief.

> – I'm only kidding Jude, saveloy it is.
> – C-O-D
> – You can have a battered sausage
> – C-O-D
> – We well can't afford fish Jude, it's like four quid. Don't give me that face.

Jude persists with the face.
– Alright, alright.
They walk to the chip shop at the end of their road, past the children kicking a football against the pavement's kerb, and past the fresh and racist graffiti adorning the corner shop's wall.

Henry orders a fish and chips and a portion of chips.

The man behind the counter begins to shovel chips into two paper packets that the chips X-ray on contact. The chip shop man shakes a copious amount of salt over the two portions. The spray then settle of the salt over the chips makes Henry happy in quantifiable ways, in the arc and gravel of their fall, in their dissolution in vinegar and fat. The caramels of potato laying thick and prone, hulking out of their paper shorts.

The man behind the counter places a piece of battered cod on top of one portion of chips and then wraps it in four precise movements into a neat, seeping, bundle.

– Anything else?

Henry checks the money in his pocket and makes a rough guess at what lays in his palm. He looks at the price board, tries out some numbers in his head. He looks at his palm. He looks at the price board. His maths is kind of haphazard, more an estimation of his luck than any actual calculation.

Henry frowns, starts counting out his change laboriously. He accidentally meets the man behind the counter's eyes. The man behind the counter's eyes look boiled in the red crushed hang of his forehead.

– Can I get a pickled egg please?
– I don't know, can you?

Henry glances again at his hand.

– Umm, yeah?

Henry silts the change into the chip shop owner's hand.

Henry and Jude are walking home. Henry bites into the dripping pickled egg. Vinegar pipettes into his mouth. Henry spits the egg out of his mouth and begins to retch. He throws the remaining egg into a nearby bush. Jude is laughing hysterically. Henry turns to him, eyes watering. He shakes his head, his cheeks dimpling either side of a girdled grin, his smile synched around its middle.

– I was only forty pence short of getting the battered sausage you know. Do you think he'd of let me off if I'd asked?

Jude shakes his head. Henry opens the gate as Jude skips ahead of him.

– Yep, me neither, what a mean man eh Jude?

Henry unwraps Jude's dinner for him on the table and helps him sit down. Henry goes to the kitchen for Pepsi and glasses. Jude looks at Henry's mound of chips and then at his mound of chips. Jude picks up the fish see-sawing atop his skittered portion. He tears the batter embossed fish roughly in two, messily transferring half to Henry's plate.

*

This is not his usual Friday evening. What is he doing? Is this normal? Geoffrey Hardy is wandering in the vague direction of Evelyn's house. It is her birthday today, he knows. Not that he's been invited. No one from school was invited. These things get around, especially when you're not invited.

He feels positively twittery inside. He is excited in a way that feels both electric and lobed with portent, a real metaphysical weight groaning between his legs. His hands act out his thoughts which bark CUT like a director every time his daydream tries to bridge the immense plot hole of reality. What is he doing? What will he say? He will simply say CUT. Someone will open the door and, but who, and then CUT. He will peer through the windows, Evelyn will notice him as she blows out the candles on her cake and then begin screaming CUT.

Geoffrey Hardy is almost transparently pale, pigeon-chested, with elongated limbs that he tends to exert an enormous amount of conscious control over. He avoids running and loping at all costs. A forked lightning shaped vein partitions the left half of his face. The vein is an organic shoot sucking remorselessly at his cheek and belching through the empurpled capillaries. The day is cold and a wind sweeps in from the sea turning his head toward the road. He touches his cheek. These headaches he gets some times, they wipe him out. Cut. Geoffrey Hardy is wearing the glasses that his mother would like him to exchange for contact lenses or better glasses at least. He pushes their chunked out frames up his nose, lowers his head, and walks on regardless. He is a man of ideas.

*

Fiasco is being told by his mother that his stepfather says he can no longer live under this roof. He's just woken up. The first thing he notices is that his window is open and that he is cold and that there is a strange oaty-looking stalactite forming on his windowsill.

– Sorry what?

She tells him again. Fiasco still doesn't understand. You need to leave, she says. You vomited all over the car. He's furious. He thinks you did it on purpose. I had to stop him coming in here.

That would have been a first, Fiasco thinks.

> – Your dad is going to take you in.
> – Mum, please. I don't want to.
> – It's done. Where, where are you going? Where are you going?

Fiasco has left the building. His mother stands in his room watching him stamp across the garden, the systems of her body snowed in with doubt. She stands there for a long time, her hands tensed around nothing, the blood of them pushed up in little whited out banks around the pitted palm.

He walks to Henry's house. Henry is confused when he sees him at the door. Fiasco asks him if he still wants to leave.

> – Where?
> – I'm sick of all this shit. Let's go. Let's go now. We've gotta get out of here. Bring Jude as well.

They walk into Henry's room. Jude is sat on the bed. He gives Fiasco the metal salute, horning two fingers out like a bull. Fiasco returns the gesture. Jude laughs and then lets out an extravagantly voluminous fart that sweats through the air.

> – Thanks for that, Jude seriously.

Jude laughs again. Fiasco tells Henry what has happened. Jude presses his hands together like a therapist praying towards their own powers of analysis.

> – What the fuck, Where does your dad live?
> – Miles away.
> – Stay here for a bit if you want to.
> – Yeah?
> –

Henry tells Fiasco that they have to leave in a minute for 'birthday dinner' of all things. He points to his gift lying in a nest of ripped up paper as proof.

> – You're giving her that?
> –
> – That's shit.
> – Just pass me that tippex. Jude put some music on
> – How come you have to get her a gift?
> – I don't know. We didn't even have

birthdays when I was a kid.

– And your mum made you buy one for her boss' daughter? This is cheering me immensely.

– Well she gave me the money.

– And you're giving her that?

– And pocketing the money.

– Seems fair. Will there be jelly?

– It seems highly unlikely given that this is a 'birthday dinner'

– She'll be what, thirteen, fourteen and no jelly.

– I know it's a crime

– Well it's not as if you ever had jelly

– But I knew I always wanted jelly and that's the crucial and overlooked difference here I think.

A car horn rips determinedly through the air in two runty beeps. Henry wanders towards the window. Through the window he can see his mother sat in the passenger seat of a car he does not recognize, he frowns.

– Jude get your coat, we've got to go.

Henry gives Fiasco the house keys and promises to get back as soon as he can. He walks to the nest of paper, closes the scraggly ends of the torn posters around the gift and seals the package with a large canyon of tape.

*

Geoffrey Hardy is sat at the side of the road. He is throwing stones at the pavement's kerb. Geoffrey Hardy knows roughly where Evelyn's house is and he knows what car her father drives but he is lost and confused about his own motivations.

He sees a car approach. Geoffrey Hardy stands up— plunges his hands into his pockets— whistles for want of a better idea. He begins to stroll away. Evelyn is in the back seat of the car next to a teenager who Geoffrey Hardy would probably classify as 'a homeless' under different circumstances. The car passes. Evelyn sees Geoffrey Hardy. She watches him as the car passes as if it were he riding by, he in motion. The car pulls into a drive four or five houses up. Geoffrey Hardy glances back. The people spill out of the car and stare at him. Evelyn waves. He walks towards them.

CUT.

Henry, Lawrence, Henry's mother, Jude, Geoffrey Hardy, and Evelyn are sat around a steaming joint of beef.

They are sat like this

Diane

Jude

Vegetables

Lawrence   Beef   Evelyn

Gravy   Geoffrey Hardy

Henry

Lawrence leans over the curlicues of steam and draws them through his nose, electric carving knife and pronged fork castled either side of his expression. Henry has never seen anything like it outside of a comic book, the steam railroaded into Lawrence's nostrils. Passing from one dead body to the next, Henry thinks. It's kind of gross and metaphorically unhygienic. Lawrence rotates his wrist forty five degrees and then slowly, with the same masking enthusiasm, lowers his head to regard the roast. There is a pause in which his face stretches and pins itself in mock ecstasy. Then the long pronged fork needles the meat.

Henry picks up a fork and clamps it in an upright fist, bangs the table with it and smiles. He is showing off. His mother's raised forehead and pursed lips chide him but in truth she's more charmed than angry. Henry's still feeling the excitement of hanging out with Fiasco. The characteristics he's siphoned from his friend spreading his own thoughts colourfully around the darker pigmentation of Fiasco's tightly bound affect. He turns and looks at Evelyn. Watches her, really.

Evelyn has hardly spoken since they entered the house and her breath is slow and heavy like a glaze added to an already glossed over world that she can't enter any more than the magazine she absently thumbs the surface of. Her palms resting flat upon the pages, the warmth of her hands fogging the laminate paper. These prints of herself moving and disappearing like lone cumuli across their images' sky as she turns the pages. Henry can't help but wonder what's wrong with her.

Across the table, Jude's playing with his already gravy dunked fork. He is laying it across the table's edge and measuring the distance with his fist. Henry can already see the potential arc of its twirl turning and clattering into the tasteless family portrait that's hung, staggeringly poster sized, just behind Lawrence. He can see the wipe of gravy briefly whiskered in the broken glass. Poster Lawrence growing the old Fu Man Chu as gravy beads down the overfilled cracks while Real life Lawrence, watching on in shock, comes to confront this image of himself, his shit eating grin turning shit eaten, the electric carving knife swinging around in his hands like an emasculated chainsaw in parodic horror. Henry and Jude make eye contact. They begin to ripple with barely suppressed laughter. The idea of the joke inflates, makes a demand upon their sense of reality, and presses itself against the curve of action like a bladder.

Jude reasserts his purpose. He adjusts the angle of the fork, feels out a geometry beyond his ken but estimable in life and raises his hand above the teetered tines. Diane calmly removes the fork in a single action from under Jude's falling fist. She has not looked at either one of them and is still listening with seemingly endless intent to

Lawrence recalling something that he— Lawrence— can't quite recall the purpose of recalling... now that he thinks about it. Henry can't figure out how she does it, any of it, come to think of it.

> – Something about the price of bread in the local corner shop was it? Diane says to Lawrence.
> – I'm...ummm

Diane waiting for this confused pause before shooting Henry a single frame of her, in no way subliminal, you-best-be warned face. Lawrence turns towards Henry.

– Actually Henry that reminds me, I wanted to talk to you about your living situation... about Jude and you and your mother's future and the house. I understand that you're going to, hopefully, be finishing your A levels soon and well I've formally offered your mother a full time position here, including board, and of course there's room for Jude so...

Henry straightens up, stops smiling. He tries to look intently at Lawrence without judging him instantly. Jude tilts a confused, lopsided, grin towards Henry but it hangs there unacknowledged, begins to age alone and quickly. Can Henry not see him? Jude begins to get upset. He makes a series of swallowing sounds, it looks as if he is trying to invert his Adam's apple. Henry doesn't look. Jude rubs then clutches his face. His carefully trimmed nails searching for unsafe passage under his cheekbones, body trembled around the chair. He needs someone to lean over and loop their arms around him, to hold him until he stops struggling, until he can feel them, till the irregular bumps of his emotions are worked out against the harder presence of another. Jude stares at his mother.

Henry can feel his mother's attention trained on him. He couldn't move to escape if he wanted to. He's only dimly aware of Jude's discomfort writhen somewhere in the flame of his own.

Diane picks up where Lawrence has stopped

> – I was thinking perhaps that it's time for Jude to come here, to live here permanently and then you can, the house could pay for lots of, if we sold it you could go and

Jude lets out a yell, slams his body against the table. Henry is glassily focusing on the family portrait behind Lawrence. His mother is in it.

> – I don't think now is really the time, he says.
> – When is?
> – Why now mum?
> – Mhmm, Lawrence says bending over the meat and thumbing the switch of the electric carver upwards.

– Why now?

Henry says over the buzz, looking at the portrait.

Geoffrey Hardy watches the saw separate the beef joint, watches the chipped spray of carcass fly around the teeth of the blade. He gets this funny feeling in his groin that's a Venn diagram of pleasant/unpleasant with all the attendant, off season, feelings of each floating around his peripheries. He looks over at Evelyn whose stillness is only interrupted by the rise and fall of the breath inside her. The renewal and sink of it appearing as a purely indifferent phenomenon residing in her near dormant presence. Geoffrey Hardy realises that Lawrence is asking him a question and that the question is an attempt to change the subject and that this represents an opportunity for him to make a positive impression. Geoffrey Hardy looks over at Lawrence and says

> – Well, when I grow up I want to
> manage my own business
> – That's very impressive….
> – Geoffrey, Geoffrey Hardy and I'm very
> sorry to impose on you like this
> – Man, how old are you? Henry says.

His mother revs a 'hmmm' at him. Geoffrey Hardy looks at him blankly and then appeals to the adults in the room with a look of surprise. He watches Henry watch Evelyn as Lawrence begins to layer the stepped meat onto the longboat of the serving plate.

Evelyn too is looking at the portrait, at herself there.

The Evelyn in the poster is a few years younger and there's an enthused expression on her face that the synthetic exposure of the picture, its unnatural configuration of white space and luminous fashion, can't fully co-opt or mask. Evelyn holds her plate out towards Lawrence. Her expression is empty, untouched, as if there had been nothing recognizable in what she looked at, as if she hadn't been looking at anything.

Henry stares at his plate. He looks again at the poster and then over at Evelyn and feels that it is hard to tell which is under glass.

– Diane, would you mind serving the vegetables?

Henry's mother begins serving the carrots, the peas, the sprouts, the cauliflower cheese, the broccoli, the roasted parsnips and the potatoes (whose ratio to person has been calculated then doubled, Henry's mother still with a nagging concern over the extra mouth's impact on the overall weighting of the meal while simultaneously congratulating herself on the mounted abundance of roasted potato).

– Should I do the gravy as well?

Lawrence looks at the gravy. He is surprised to find it on the table. He is surprised at his surprise.

> – You do the gravy, he says, none for me though.

Henry's mother pours it. Lawrence looks away faintly nauseated at the sight. A bad memory snaking through his guts.

Henry asks Lawrence who the 'other man' is in the family portrait. Lawrence composes himself.

> – It's a family friend, our doctor in fact.
> – Oh, right.

The gravy winds around the potatoes on Henry's plate and then slows into a drip as his mother tilts the jug upright.

> – He's been very supportive of this family.

Henry's mother dunks Lawrence's plate with gravy.

> – Diane!

*

Fiasco is at Henry's house reading. He finishes the book and then imagines how he would have written it, how it could have been better. Fiasco plays a film in his head that he has just made up. Things explode meaningfully in it. A desert spreads across the world. People start to think other people are mirages. It's perfect. It turns out the desert is God's screensaver and it's filling up the world cause he's not looking anymore. That's the twist. He gets started on a prequel 'People just want attention'. He gets bored of the idea once he's worked out it is 'all purgatory, all the time.' He gets an idea for a song. He looks around for a paper and a pen and begins to write some lyrics. He hums the tune. He listens to it a few times. He imagines himself on stage. He imagines an unplugged version that's even better, with piano, bass and maybe a cello, that'd poignantly re-contextualise the song's meaning in light of his aesthetically anti-aesthetic and semi-deliberate fuck ups.

He places a tape in the VCR and watches the scene in Dawn of the Dead where Blade's character says 'I see you chocolate man!' to Peter ten times in a row before he gets bored.

He looks through a few things Henry has been reading/writing. He laughs out loud when he sees Virginia Woolf's 'To the Lighthouse.' He puts it down. He picks it up. He reads a few pages. It's ok, not his thing. He looks at Henry's writing. There are some good sentences but it's still, ugh, 'poetic.'

He grabs a pad and a pen. Fiasco starts drawing a lighthouse. He gets into the drawing. He sketches a dead policeman hanging in the tower.

He draws the cliffs. He draws the silhouette of the dead policeman projected over the white walls of a plain mansion. He places the picture in Henry's notebook. He looks around the room. He picks up Henry's guitar. He plays the same chord over and over again. The atonal chung of the strings is the only thing that soothes him. The next hour passes.

*

Pudding arrives. Diane unpacks a stack of glass bowls and then, from out of her pinny, hands Evelyn a small pill. Evelyn's hand hides it.

Henry looks away.

> – There's jelly! Henry says.
> – And trifle, his mother says.

She leans on the table.

> – It's your birthday Evelyn but I think
> Henry might enjoy this dessert more
> than you even. We never got to do much
> of this when he was younger.

Lawrence's hand extends across the table towards Diane's as she talks. Her hand moves away and towards a large ladle. Lawrence's palm caught in the no man's land of the table, between table mat and dessert. Henry visibly ignoring Lawrence's gesture and instead concentrating upon the bellied dance of jelly as it slides around the bowl. Lawrence's hand searches for a bottle of wine and unscrews it. Henry scoops orange jelly into his bowl, the three large suns of it shivering like cooled lava.

-Manners, his mother says.

He tilts the bowl towards Evelyn who remains impassive. He extends his arm towards Geoffrey Hardy whose fingers pinch the rim of the bowl bringing it down cautiously to the mat in front of him. Henry's mother serves Evelyn a scoop of jelly, a scoop of trifle. Jude pushes his bowl away and leaves the table.

–

Geoffrey Hardy and Henry are already three spoons deep into their jelly.

– Um, ahem. Excuse me…

Geoffrey Hardy peers up from behind his glasses, lowers his spoon to the table mat. The vein in his cheek continues to feed into his mouth even after he has swallowed. Lawrence lifts a wine glass and clinks it with his fork three times. The stem of the wine glass breaks. Henry looking up as the glass slaps and bobs upon the trifle's custard before sinking down into the jelly where it hangs half suspended in an orangey dawn.

– Oh dear, Lawrence says.

Henry's mother leans forward and picks up the trifle from the table. She walks into the kitchen holding it at chest height. She walks towards the pedal bin in the corner of the kitchen and presses her foot on the pedal. The lid ratchets open. She upturns the trifle into the bin. It lands sloppily. The spongy mess of it horribly birthed over cracked eggshells. Diane relaxes her face incrementally.

– One, two, three, four.

She walks in and takes the bowl of the glass from between Lawrence's hand and wraps it in three carrier bags and places it behind the bin.

– There, she shouts, no harm done.

She walks out of the kitchen. Lawrence is looking after her. Her face does something to reassure his face. Lawrence claps his hands.

– It's time for presents!
– I believe Henry's got you something Evelyn.
– Oh, isn't that nice, Lawrence says.

Henry begins to dig around in his rucksack. Books and sweet wrappers spill out. He brings up the poorly wrapped, scotch taped bundle. The 'wrapping paper' stuck to the surface of the actual present. He gently tosses the package towards Evelyn and smiles.

> – Thank you, she manages.

Her fingers work the bitty wrapping from the present. It's obvious what it is after the first torn piece of paper.

> – There's a tape of some stuff I think you'll like or think you should like ha-ha-ha on there.

Diane looks at him. Henry looks up at his mother.

> – Don't worry there's no death metal on it.

His mother says:

> – I can see that you've really thought hard about this present.
> – Well, you know, I try.

 Evelyn puts the headphones into her ears, cupping the freighted Walkman in her lap. Lawrence is saying something about classic rock, about a band called Herman's Hermits and the British Invasion. No one is listening. Evelyn presses play and the world changes in front of her. The people at the dinner table become something she can look at. Their expressions momentarily free of her mind's heaviness and filled with ambivalent resonances. The music investing in them a silenced and movable beauty their previously too announced presences had drowned out.

She takes one of the earphones from the tiny cove of her ear.

– It's amazing, thank you.

Lawrence says,

– Let's not forget about the others!

Lawrence looks at Evelyn until she clicks the stop button and puts the Walkman on the edge of the table and removes her hands from the table.

Diane gives Evelyn a powder blue skirt and some make up and some hand cream. These are politely greeted with mild surprise though in truth Evelyn and Diane had gone shopping together earlier in the week, had produced a ranked list of items and purchased them together that day.

Lawrence reaches under the table and produces a large two foot high, apparently weightless, package which he holds expectantly on his lap. Evelyn stares at the package. Inside Evelyn there is a sigh breaking long before the shore of her body, arriving flat and unwrinkled and only a little too quickly into her eyes. She knows what the package is, of course, and what will be required of her when she opens it. She's not sure how much it's going to cost her, at a physical level, to do something she can no longer really see the purpose in. There's just so much she'll have to wade through to give the response that he needs.

– Actually, I, I have a present too.

Everyone turns toward Geoffrey Hardy. Lawrence's grin begins to cramp in his face. He turns his teeth towards Geoffrey Hardy.

Geoffrey Hardy's face becomes a patchwork of embarrassment. The vein a glaring stitch in the redly quilted skin, rustically enjoining the separate flanks of his graded embarrassment, glowing faintly neon amidst the edged pinks, and revealing its royal threading amongst those clayed scraps.

– I, well, I just bought it, I wanted to drop it off that's why I was…If not I was going to give it to you at school and…um I hope you like it.

He passes over a small, professionally wrapped, origami clasped present that reaches through her fog and which she carefully opens to find an incongruously brown, unmistakably masculine, leather notebook replete with a thick stolid looking pen.

– I thought you could write your stories

in it, if you're still writing stories. It was
the most serious looking one in the
shop, that's why I bought it. I umm
didn't want to get an ink cartridge pen
cause they just slow you down I think
where as this type is really functional
and still neat and not stupid and pink

Evelyn weighs the notebook in one hand and the
pen in the other. She lays them both down next to
the Walkman and smiles.

Lawrence leans forward holding his present by
the scruff of its wrapping and begins to waggle it
towards Evelyn. He moves it back and forth on its
side.

From behind the package he says,

– Don't forget me, in this strangled
singsong voice,

like a children's tv presenter strangely choked
with real emotion. Evelyn leans forward and
places her hand on the package's head. She looks
up at Lawrence and opens her mouth enough to
dimple her cheeks. It's enough for Lawrence who
beams down at her and withdraws his hand and
sits, finally, at the head of the table to watch her
unwrap his gift. Without drawing the package
towards her Evelyn splits the wrapping between
her two hands so that the husk of it zippers away.
Luminous colours swirl into the room. A plush
multi-coloured horn protrudes between two

nonplussed plastic eyes that are in turn attached to a sewn up face that droops colicky over the stitched-on swirl of a belly.

Lawrence takes the collective silence for held breaths. The sheer unbridled scope of the unicorn's cuteness and largesse grabbing their lungs by the reins, he determines, as it had done to him that rainy Saturday morning he and Evelyn had spent discussing her medication by the arcades.

The unicorn two feet high, madly pink and purple, rainbow horned, vinyl hoofed, is sat between the large crystal bowl of orange jelly and ice cream. An insanity of fatherly confections covers the table spread.

Evelyn feels the white background of the tacky, professionally modelled, family portrait blindly expand and open towards her like the corners of everyone but Lawrence's expectant, incredulous eyes.

Evelyn exhales. Really it is the tide of herself going out. She leans forward and holds the tip of the Unicorn's horn and then leans back into her seat. The unicorn following her hand tilts into a palm that closes around its neck. Evelyn looks at Lawrence, she swallows. She is trying.

– It's lovely isn't it Evelyn? Henry's mother says.

Evelyn nods. She looks up again at Lawrence and leans forward in the seat. If she just speaks everything will be ok, Henry thinks. Evelyn opens her mouth, her tongue slides backward under her teeth, the 'th' sound on the cusp of existence. In his chair Lawrence grows excessive in anticipation.

The 'a' and the 'nks' hang in the space created for them but fail to sound there. Evelyn moves back suddenly. She frowns. Lawrence looks confused. Evelyn looks confused.

She says:

– Where's Jude?

Diane calls for him. She runs to the stairs and calls then into the front room. The French doors are open. Henry joins her there, freezes. Lawrence and Evelyn arrive followed by Geoffrey Hardy. Everyone walks into the garden. When they see the gate unlatched at the end of the garden they begin to roughly know the as yet un-weighted shape of their fear. The shape falling things trace in the air around themselves.

Henry's mother and Lawrence arrive at the cliff's edge first. They have stopped calling Jude's name now and slow at their arrival. Evelyn follows in tiny bound footsteps that break anxiously into girlish hops every sixth or seventh hurried step. Henry's lagging behind, his knees are crushed cans. He stumbles over. His hand tries to signal the air. The air turns thick. He leans against his breath, his heart pummelling the earth that he's just met beneath him. Henry sits up. He puts his head in his hands.

– There he is, there he is. I've found him.

Lawrence calls to Henry again. Diane runs back into the house. Henry scrunches his eyes hard as she passes, so hard it is as if he is trying to cram them into his brain, to get away from the world, to enter the socketed tunnel and stay there. Shapes keep appearing in the darkness.

– Henry, I need your help

And that is Jude he can hear now, a mad hee-hawing sound of pain following on the air after Lawrence's voice.

Henry gets to his feet, runs towards the cliff's edge, stands next to Evelyn and looks down. Lawrence has dropped down to a tabled ledge and is stroking Jude's whimpering body.

– What happened?
– He must have fallen.
– How?

Lawrence turns Jude's body around

– Are you sure you should be doing that?

Lawrence holds Jude's body.

Jude rolls around the arms he's held in, his mouth blackly foamed and dusty. His torso keeps crabbing up to the sky, lashed by power lines of nerves fallen from the transmitting pylon of his spine, wild nerves that force his neck to arch and eyes to level with the sea. Blood bridges around the creases of his mouth, fastens behind his ears. Lawrence holds his head, strokes Jude's hair forcefully back. Evelyn is staring at Jude's tongue, at the black trumpet of blood horned like a wormhole in the space of there and at the wriggled body through which it passages. She cannot stop looking.

*

Fiasco is scrabbling around his pocket for change. He doesn't know/cannot understand what is taking Henry so long. He looks through Henry's music collection. Mine is better, he thinks, no doubt. There are some 'core' albums but the points of divergence are telling. It bodes well for the band, he thinks. Tensions are important. Not a bad title. Fiasco imagines calling an album 'Crushing Dissent.' He works with its meanings for a while until it's elastic enough to fit any of his purposes. Nihilist or ironically fascist.

– We're a metal band now. So we need to find a jazz drummer with fascist tendencies.

He wants a beer, badly. There's not enough money in his pocket. He combs the house for spare change. Didn't I do this with Henry a few days ago, he thinks. Fiasco carries on looking. He finds an old bottle of gin with an inch or two left in it. He takes the cap off and put his nose to its rim. He sniffs and wipes the bottle across his nose. He isn't sure if acrid is the right word but it's the one he thinks of. He pours it all into a squared tumbler with the pleasing weight to it. He mixes it with water from the tap, feeling the glass heavy. The telephone rings, the sound painfully lighting up the strip crease of his brain. It doesn't stop. He sips. The phone ruins his concentration.

What the fuck?

The telephone continues to ring and ring.

Fiasco doesn't pick it up. The world outside his head's not cleared for landing. He sips the gin. He should have just soaked his hoodie in it and chewed the sleeve, he thinks. He thinks about the painting 'Gin Lane.' The telephone won't stop. He is stood in the hallway, his thoughts rising and falling under the faint levelling echo of the telephone's tides. The answering machine turns itself on. Something's happened, Fiasco thinks.

*

Does he fear loneliness more than resentment? Regardless Lawrence strides the corridors of the hospital with cyclopean focus. He is attuned to the action of his body, feels in each exhale a failing life and in each inhale its battered saviour. He turns his head at the hint of footsteps and frittering lights, is primed to fire questions at errant nurses, to gesticulate manfully at competing inpatients.

Resentment, why resentment?

Well he's left them, but then he is *looking*.

Still, he could not have sat with Henry and Diane any longer, lacks their expertise at waiting.

She knows that. In truth he'd found something ghastly in it though he's at a loss to clarify what. Had found them engraved somehow, burnt into the situation, their true form of waiting captured by the event and then, when they re-appeared to him in some indifferent gesture, there they were: a delving of dust hiding a reality scoured clean by waiting.

Waiting for what? Time to tell. Tell what? That there are no doctors in this hospital. Where the fuck are all the doctors?

He'd already dropped Evelyn off at that boy's house, it'd bought him a half hour but when he returned they were still there, in the exact same attitudes he'd left them in. Henry studying the light fixtures above the awkward plinth of Jude's bed, Diane sat like a captive bird with all her emotions pressed up in mute sediment against the mesh of her skull.

It was more than he could bear.

So he rallied. That's what he did. Rallied. Found inner resources of outrage and tinted them with despair and declarative action.

– I'm going to find a doctor!

That was, how long ago now? If it's long, it'll be bad and if it's short then all the worse.

Around the corner he spies an oasis of soft shadow, the mirage of a doctor's lifted stethoscope twirled between fingers on the wall of an adjoining corridor. Lightly jogging now, preparing his monologue, Lawrence turns the corner but there is no doctor, only an old business card on the floor that he stoops to pick up with all the letters scratched away on so that only the number of his work is legible. He frowns.

Ahead of him, coming in the opposite direction, he sees a doctor round into a room.

*

Geoffrey Hardy's mother fusses over Evelyn like a doll. Evelyn for her part has tried to cede to this estimation of her, has become still and pliable, her upper body an aggregation of tilts and prods.

Evelyn holds the unicorn between her legs, her thumbs indenting its starred nape as the mother once again pushes Evelyn's head forward, gathering her hair and streaming it through her painted nails. Evelyn's eyes turn towards Geoffrey Hardy asking what eyes tend to ask on close examination.

Geoffrey asks his mother if she might get them something for lunch.

His mother leaves the room. Geoffrey Hardy rises and sits next to Evelyn. The unicorn turns an increment towards him, a ruler of light sliding down the two plastic ovals of its signified eyes as the head tentatively regards his lap. Geoffrey Hardy stares down at Evelyn's hands. He leans over and lifts up a finger from the pile in her lap then takes her whole hand and places it in his.

He manages to look over at her. She is looking out at him from the corner of her eye. Geoffrey Hardy looks away towards the television which no one has turned on and in which their curved imitations spread unsteady as petrol on trembled water. Evelyn squeezes his hand. It's not what he thinks but it probably means more to her. On the television he watches her image begin to cry, to shudder forward, the hands wrung around the unicorn's throat, the whole room displacing itself in ripples.

*

– Well, what do we have here?
– My son, doctor my son is he
– He's umm, let me see, yes your son, it says here that he is going to be fine.
– Yes?
– Well we'd still like to keep him overnight for observation. Now I believe you said to my colleague that he fell
– Yes, he, somehow he, he fell down the cliff. Part of a cliff. He, somehow he got out the gate and then he
– What's going on? I see you've finally decided to turn up. I've a few words about to say about this establishment.

This is why I went private

– It's a hospital not an 'establishment'

– He fell. Then he fell. Lawrence, sit down.

– Is he going to be ok?

– As I was saying we need to keep him in overnight for observation and of course you'll have to speak to social services, they'll be quite….keen… I imagine

– This is an outrage

– Lawrence!

– Just exactly what are you accusing us of?

– Mum?

– Sir it is standard protocol in an incident of this nature

– I won't have it

– Sir, it's in your best interests to co-operate

– Mum?

– This is an outrage.

– Sir, you're making a spectacle of yourself.

– What do you mean, what nature?

– Well if it turns out your son intended to harm himself then

– Harmed himself, harmed himself, what are you saying?

– Has your son exhibited any signs of depression at all?

– Depression?

– Yes, has his behaviour changed
recently at all, mood swings, a lack of
pleasure in things he would normally
find pleasurable... to say the least of it.
Depressed, down in the mouth, visited
by a black dog etc

– But depressed?

– I don't quite understand.

– You think, Jude, You think he's
depressed? Doctor he,

– Your son is quite capable of
depression, as capable as he is of
happiness or pleasure or well, lots. And
as I said if it turns out to be the case that
your son tried to harm him self then
Social services will of course have to be

– That's not what I meant. I don't think
that's what I, is that what I? Harmed
himself, harmed himself, what are you
saying? Depressed? Do you think he was
depressed?

– I don't know mum, I don't think so but
then

– Then what?

– I don't know, have we ever, I mean do
we, we're not

– What?

– Have there been any sudden changes
in his routine or...

– They wanted to move him out of his
house.

– He was going to come live with me
– He doesn't live with you already?
– Well, yes but I work a lot of
nights…and some days so my other son
looks after him a lot
– I see

The doctor leaves the room. Lawrence is telling them that he will go hurry up social service so that they can all go home. Helene and Henry nod impassively, Lawrence giving them a little aghast look before leaving the room.

– He's going to be put into care.
– Mum, What?

Henry asks his mother if she would like to pray with him. She shakes her head

– Don't you believe in God anymore
mum?

The question holds Diane in place. Her resistance gives way to exhaustion as she spreads into the place marked by the question.

– I know there isn't any devil but hope.
If god exists he doesn't want us to be
happy. Not like this, not in this world.
– I don't believe in him either.
– Are you trying to hurt me?
– You just said, I thought…

– I'm not happy am I? I didn't, I made a
mistake
– Jude is going to be ok. I know about
you and Lawrence, I, I understand. Isn't
this what you want?
– No one has ever had any interest in
what I want. That's the real truth.

*

Jude's asleep on his back and tucked into a
narrow hospital bed situated among five other inpatients' beds who are likewise either asleep or
worse and whose prone forms are similarly cubed
in little isolative tents. The pale green curtains
dividing each patient from the other are topped
with rings attaching them to an overhead rail that
imperiously maps the room.

A nurse looks at his face through the curtain
and leaves. Jude's face is clouded with bruises like
a British weather map.

A ceiling fan with several of its blades missing
copters like a Sycamore seed above him. There is
a dissonance cradled in the speed and hum of the
turning fan and the serene elegance of its rotation
in his dream filled eye. Jude's hands rise up
toward it then fall to his chest. There are shapes

in the darkness and a way of seeing these shapes that his mind follows.

Jude is in jail. Locked up. This doesn't make sense because Jude is also the Sheriff in this dream. A criminal asks him are you the Sheriff or are you the Detective? Jude doesn't know. The difference is, the dream says, one protects and the other puts humpty back together again. Jude takes a while to decide and then he notices that he's wearing a hat and a rhinestone shirt. Decision made. Henry arrives to break him out but as soon as the cell door opens they are captured by a malignant setting. Outside the cell the world transforms into the conjunction of sand, night sky, and sea.

There is a horse on the beach and, in the near distance, the lighthouse. Neither Jude nor Henry are on the horse or present in what the dream sees. Cowboys aren't meant to be by the sea. Jude is on the beach now. We have to get to the park, Jude shouts. There's no one else around. Something is dripping through his hand. He looks down to see a crushed egg there. Jude is becoming transparent. The lighthouse is growing darker. Jude is disappearing in his own dream. The beach is filling up. He recognises everyone and doesn't. The lighthouse is a spinning top. Everyone else is becoming more real.

*

Henry enters his house, there's a note from Fiasco. He's been given a trial shift as a kitchen porter at The Crows. The Crows is a pub that they've often viewed as constituting their future. It had been their best attempt at romanticising the fatalistic. Fiasco's joked that they'll likely find their fathers there. That they're probably friends. Fiasco in fact claiming in all seriousness that he had seen someone who could be Henry's father drinking there.

The plan had been to apply for a bar job and then stall on the passport, if they even bothered to ask for one given the fact of the place. Meanwhile Fiasco would use his sticky fingers to pilfer money from the till to buy them shit.

> – You wouldn't have to steal and I won't tell you what money is mine and what money I steal, that way I'll spare you the ethical discomfort
> – That's very considerate of you

Henry puts the note down. He makes a decision to get fucked up. He experiences an exhilarating flood of depression. He looks around the house for a bottle, there has to be something. He gets lucky in the back of a cupboard. For something to do while he drinks he grabs his notebook.

Hours pass and everything comes closer to the surface. Everything gets the bends.

Henry's thoughts are a physical presence in his body and they believe in his body the way a mental patient believes in their straitjacket I.E in fits and starts. He's hunched over a glass of supermarket vodka and some old computer paper that's full of fragments of ideas, expressed like equations, in a language he understands only through its evocative powerlessness. Or something.

He puts down his biro and rubs his eyes. He can feel the tears walled behind them and the way his emotions keep getting jerked back towards the image of his mother in the hospital and his own heavy silence and the thought of Jude falling, jumping, falling. He doesn't want to, he didn't. Henry picks up the pen.

He walks around more stunned than numb, in general, he thinks. He hopes.

It's 3 am now but the distinction feels important. He swallows a mouthful of vodka and squints at the blank wall ahead of him. Stunned. It's roughly the same type of qualitative difference that one might be tempted to state lies between that of seeing and watching. At least it would be, a temptation to state that, for those types of people who spend a great deal of time and effort attempting to make these little semantic differentiations to themselves in order to get closer to some internal, highly personal, lexicography that they secretly hope might outlay some kind of key to both themselves and the world. Though the two, themselves and the world, tend to get a little confused in this type of head. In Henry's at least.

In this case stunned, he thinks, doesn't imply the same enervating, dead, anti-sensation that numb might. The contradiction at numbness's heart lying in the fact that the real pain and torture lies not in the encroaching numbness but, rather, in the phantom sensations of feeling within that numbness, as in the famous cases of lost limbs.

Numbness of course, he reasons, is only truly detectable to something feeling, to the feeling thing that is pushed up against it. The real open ended wound of the numb person's pain he figures, is that relation between an unfeeling horizon (the limit at which memory itself is forgotten, disappeared, time-dissolved in empty repetition) and the need for the still living parts to continually offer up themselves up in sacrificial rituals to the very pain that was instrumental to their incipient numbness. However buried and impossible to face this real pain is it had to be called upon, invoked, by the numb person in order to know they were still alive. On the outposts of the body, Henry thinks, everything gets reduced to an edge of feeling.

Henry writes down:

Memory (the awareness of being)

Remembrance (the awareness of having been. A degrade of memory.)

So, Henry thinks, trying to get back to himself. Whereas numbness might stand in relation to the very loss of loss and the plain lumpen fact of all your emotional sensations being replaced by an inert spiritual death by degrees, to be stunned is more like being jammed at a procedural level. There are too many frequencies and they're all equally loud and internally generated to pay any attention to understanding any one. It's better than being numb, he figures, even if it's more pathetic.

Is Jude numb? Am I?

It's all fucked. Jude.

Henry rubs his eyes, waits out a tide of nausea before letting his hand rush out to light a pipe that'll pretty much erase everything he just thought. When and if he happens upon this thought again it'll seem brand new and just as revelatory. He'll half recall the sensation he had the first few times on thinking it and then briefly wonder if this continual forgetting and the anxiety around it might somehow be related to evolutionary mutation. That's a go to.

Looking back down at the page he tries to make sense of what he's been writing. The image of his brother begins to show up around the margins. That's still there.

Henry stares harder at the page.

What was he thinking again? numb = people, where?

Yeah that's right, other people. Take other people, for instance. Take Jude for instance. Trying to know people was like looking down the wrong end of a telescope. They just mistakenly receded until at some point you ended up accidentally close to them, pressed up against them, so that their suddenly revealed, delved into fibres, seemed inhuman and disproportionate and impossible to relate to any concept of 'them' that you might be able to keep in your head. They became a world of immense historical surfaces no matter how pristine the mind's distance might render them.

Same old shit thoughts.

Fiasco bounds through the front door and into the living room.

– Was he there?

Fiasco trips then rolls around on the floor.

– Hey what's up?
– Was he there?
– Hahaha, no.

Henry doesn't ask anything else about the man that might resemble his father.

– You ok?
– Ummm, I don't, there was something

with Jude… are you? Are you alright?

Henry's watching Fiasco's jaw move in and out along the roll of his molars like a possessed chest of drawers as Fiasco explains to him that a man in the pub gave him speed, made him take a large quantity of speed from the end of the man's knife while loudly declaring

– the man that is

That he was fucking animal

– A fucking animal, that's what he said. A fucking animal. Voice like Bob Hoskins.
– You got any left?

*

Jude's brain glitches and ravines. His consciousness shooting up from under a quickly draining pool of sleep, emerging as if thrust into a wholly foreign and terrifyingly present world. He has to get out of here. Jude turns his head in the direction of the sole dispatch of light. He makes out the soft cuboid of light reflecting dimly between the beds. He looks at the ceiling, at the blades there. The room is dark in that blue way that makes the world glow dark. Jude cycles his legs out of the quick of the cover and sits up on his plank like bed. His bruised body sort of sloughs around his fencing bones and his spine bends in the shape of an old fashioned walking cane. Tentatively Jude lets the oval of his big toe spread a cloud of heat across the marbled floor. He robes the curtain around his forearm and surveys the ward. There is a TV playing some gaudy sitcom at a low, indistinct volume in one of the other cubes. In the flickering editions of light from the TV's rapid camera cuts, Jude can make out a man sat up in bed with one starred hand lying static and darkly fisted in his crotch. The light from the TV grows brighter, or lingers in an unbroken shot, so that the man's outline emerges as an after image, more burnt onto the darkness than actually there. The man is wearing his own dressing gown as opposed to the thin blue, pigmented by a thousand collated night-sweats, hospital issue that Jude is currently sporting. The arm that isn't ending blackly around the man's crotch slides in degrees from its position on his thigh. A TV remote clatters against the floor. The man's shoulders and neck follow the weight of the hanging arm. The hand in the crotch pulling a hard left as if steering suddenly away from something fast and oncoming.

Jude holds his breath. No one comes. He walks to the door avoiding the light and then turns back to the curtain with the man. A sustained burst of canned laughter from behind the curtain increases in intensity as Jude's hand reaches towards it. His hand feels at the curtain then releases it, sending a fluttering pulse towards the ceiling. That's not the way. He doesn't need to see this. He stops. He pushes open the door of the ward.

Jude walks down a corridor that is empty and fascinatingly rowed on either side with windows full of a night dumped with stars, stars heaped and combed through the dark like spilt sugar, while the corridor, with its graphics of space and air rendered blocky by artificial light, dims out onto endless repetitions of itself. He finds himself at the entrance. No one notices him. He leaves the hospital.

There are two places he could go right now. He has to choose. He has to choose where he wants this dream to end. He is going to meet his brother at the park. He knows his brother is there waiting for him, can hear Henry calling, knows his brother's worried expression, sees those smooth hands cupped around that thin mouth, sees the fields green and bathed in white light, feels all this developing within himself. He is sure his brother will be there, at the park, where he is now within him.

*

The end of the cigarette pricks Henry's knuckles with an itchy heat. He's standing at the bottom of his garden looking up towards the road that twists out of view, the sound of cars in the distance somewhat like the ocean. The sun is coming up and Henry, frozen electric, wants to feel that age-old contact.

He did about three hits of body hollowing speed an hour ago only to be quickly informed by the sallow gloss of Fiasco's face, all light having exited from his eyes and pooled into the slip of his cheeks, of Fiasco's urgent need to lie down.

– Are you going to be sick?
– I haven't thrown up in weeks.

Fiasco's inside journeying towards sleep through the concentric hells of his flaring neuronal pathways, his trainers thrashing around the never washed duvet that Henry has lain over his shivering body. Henry can hear the soft murmur of fuck, fuck, fuck worming through the house. Fiasco's got a twelve hour shift today that's due to start in about three hours.

– He'll never make it, Henry thinks, or if he does...he'll be a hero?

The light in the garden moves from ambience to bravura. Strange remembrances of his father rise up in him now, probably error strewn or else tonally filled in with his grandfather's presence. Henry remembers his father with a yellow, plank length, spirit level in hand. Father's knuckles baggy and swollen and rowed like the faces of alcoholics frowning at something beyond the reflection of the bar's mirror. Something stunned and unsaid making up the silence between them. He sees grey grains of metal, flaking paint, the inset bubble slipping around the chamber. Spirit level. His father's other tools were appropriable as toys in as far as Henry had imagined being able to utilise them as weapons but it is the spirit level, entrancingly named but boringly configured, that he sees now with that uncanny, split frame, quickness of a memory less recalled than extracted like a rod from some internal reactor. He feels the absence of its extraction, the pull of it into vision, the hole in his self its quietness had plugged, flooding with space.

His father's hands there, no face, definitely his father's hands though (those knuckles gurning out at him) showing him the bubble sliding around. His father's real knuckles grained like the metal. Under the yellow paint there was iron. Under the skin, dirt. It raised questions of constancy, of dirt and metal, of depth and time.

His father measured something with it Henry just couldn't work out. He didn't see anything there. His father started putting everything together, forming something, a cabinet or a stool or something, right there in front of him. He'd tried to encourage Henry into this world making. Henry was not forthcoming.

His father had lain the pieces of the would-be object out, assembled and then disassembled them in front of Henry. Still, Henry couldn't figure it out, couldn't visualise how this thing worked. He picked up two unrelated parts, banged their blunt ends together, twisted elegant protuberances with a surge of impatience, became gradually and creepingly aware that the awkward force of his wanting was hurting the thing that he wanted and that, furthermore, he could not stop violently, obscurely persisting. He tried to give up, couldn't. He turned the mute unconstructed things in his hands against each other and began to cry. His father's hand reached out to slow his own, pushed it gently towards the floor but then held it there distrustfully. Henry looking up to see his father's brow rearrange itself into a familiar set of rifts and canyons.

His father's frown tended to make every other expression he occasionally held seem worse than mask-like. The frown itself was monstrous in its possession of his father's face. The face seemed to grow or rather emerge from underneath the frown, the frown having arrived already fully matured while somewhere in there the cracked seeds of his father's eyes fell dryly open.

His father re-assembled the chair or cabinet or whatever in front of him and then slowly, by or with a sigh, disassembled the… what *were* they making? He can't even recall it.

Henry had tried one more time to build, he remembers, that day or another. He'd gone real slow but still made a mess of it. Had got one uneven joint stuck in another, almost immediately bending a screw in the process so that when his father tried once more to take it apart the wood cracked in sharp censorship across the soft curses his father's lips kept absently forming.

– Has anyone even told him about Jude?

Henry flicks the butt of the cigarette into the neighbour's garden and joylessly lights another. Narrow juts and wide spotlights of sunbeams appear to emerge in roughly circular, mindlessly searching patterns in the dip of the garden. Every light struck object seems to suggest to Henry a secret hidden in the contouring illumination suspended around them. Though these objects in truth emanate nothing but their own inviolability. Henry sees it that way and doesn't. The garden looks amazing or dull. Special or, he doesn't know, 'average' or something. Every appreciation is interrogative. He smiles, sort of, his lips shaping into an equal sign balancing whatever.

He knows every time he approaches a thought he ruins something.

It all just arrived as a joke. He's levelling out.

No one imagined happiness, he thought, couldn't conceive of it except in small triumphalist moments of fleeting resignation. That's not quite right. No one adequately imagined the *conditions* of their happiness, only its supreme effect. That's not right either. This is bullshit. No, it was true. Happiness wasn't an ambition he'd ever known anyone to have. Who talked critically about happiness except in the negative?

The emotion was so vaguely signposted it may as well have just been an idea, an idea that lacked the drive and ambition to evolutionarily take or which was just so frighteningly misunderstood and possibly dangerous to life that it was currently being dissected in some Area 51 of the soul. Or something. Henry's running out of himself. Soon he'll just be a disconnected whirr. He can't let that happen anymore. There's got to be something inside of him. He can't believe what his mum said was true, he has thought of her. He can't understand what possessed Jude to do that either, if that's what he did, though it might possess him too, one day. Henry wants to think this. That he could kill himself. It feels important. No it doesn't. That's the point.

He's never taken much time to imagine Jude's interior life. That's what Henry's just thought. That's not to say he hasn't thought about Jude. He has, all the time. He's cared for him, they joke.

There is a link there. The same with his mother. Who suffers for our lack of imagination?

He doesn't want to think his brother could have...what if he'd imagined his brother more, would Jude have felt realer to himself? Is this ego? To even think that, was it ego?

What part of any of this was true? He hadn't cared enough. Henry could say that. He could say that and it would be true.

Henry walks up to the garden gate and unlatches it. He's going to see Jude, he doesn't care what they— whoever they are— will say, he'll sleep on the floor of the hospital and when his brother wakes up he'll be there. He'll run through the fields and past any guards.

He will be with his brother.

*

There's a hardened whip of chewing gum lodged between Jude's toes as he wanders barefoot through rims of metallic light and bushes reared up in shadowy arachnid hunger. As he walks along the side of roads where drains crease his soles and lodge unspeakable matter under the cliffs of his toenails.

Jude turns down now towards the park situated in the crotch of two intersecting hills that connect one council estate to another and just beyond which lies his home.

The park crowns out before him.

Where is his brother? Jude cannot hear or see him anymore. Everything is becoming too real. The park is a greasy slick of mud laced plastic bags and jettisoned clothes that frighten Jude with their suggestion of desperate, vanished bodies.

Through the wrought iron fence of the playground there's a swing that— chain foreshortened by the iron bar it's swung round— hangs tilted and bat winged some eight feet in the air. Jude pushes his head close to the bars and grapples towards the gate.

The heads of impaled dolls are staked either side of the playground's gate and another two sit unanchored high up on the concrete shoulders either side of it. Henry, Fiasco. There are more dolls' heads spread across the breadth of the fence, alternating along the row of throat-ward aimed spikes with unmatched decapitated infant bodies of every race.

The eyes of one blonde baby blush close as Jude indents its forehead with his thumb, the eyes opening again as the gate swings back behind him. The soft tarmac of the playground dimples under Jude's footsteps, the chewing gum spiralling out of his toes at last and sitting like a melted key on the distressed surface. Jude lays down on the merry go round and closes his eyes, his feet lilting the ground as a steadily spreading incline of light rises over his body, tucking him in. How could Henry have missed him? He does not understand, he begins to sink into the light.

    – Jude? Jude! JUDE!

6

BEGIN
BECOMING
REPEATING,
1997

It's the last ever day of school for Evelyn. She's bunking off. She's not with anybody else. There was no one she'd have even thought to have asked. The last day of school, she thinks. It's bullshit.

She's sitting at her mother's graveside eating her lunch and sipping from a small bottle of vodka discreetly sequestered in her bag. There are a few rabbits running around the willow trees that circle the small courtyard. The trees' dense overhang is pillowy with light, the sky above rectangular and transparently deep enough to believe that something could be teleported into its surface. Down there in the secretive ground was its entry, she's sure. She touches her bob of hair, newly bleached blonde this morning, the tingle of peroxide still buzzing around her scalp, and glances around headstones that declared loves lost and life's short-handed achievement. A cushion of moss laying over every hard truth in the area. Still, it's not a wholly unpleasant place to be and Evelyn comes here a lot to think about her life and to talk with her mother whose absence seemed at the very least approachable here. Not that she actually talks out loud or anything, it's more like they're watching t.v together and she believes her mother can intuit her mood and thoughts via a psychic proximity. It's dumb, she knows.

Evelyn finishes her ham sandwich and brushes the crumbs from her skirt. She brings the vodka out of the satchel and grabs her lighter. She turns the tape over in her Walkman, rummages through the small satchel again and pulls out a baggy looking joint. She arranges the objects around her skirt and then chooses three. She presses play on her battered looking Walkman with one hand and lights the joint with the other. She loves this Walkman, loves its Star Wars junk aesthetic, loves the pencil shaded tippex coiling around the chunk of its body and spelling her name in a cramped hand. She loves how shit it is. How the shittiness retains the subversive function of its action. The Velvet Underground's Sunday Morning bends the air. She looks at her mother's grave, runs her hand over its gravel. She uncaps the vodka. The grass leans towards her in time with the vocals. Evelyn can feel her mother's spirit through the music. Then the music stops and the breeze is just one more ungoverned thing happening to her. Evelyn's eyes start to feel cold. She wipes them with her sleeve. She's losing it.

She checks the tape, takes the batteries out, licks their top with her cracked riverbed tongue then recoils— makes a face— takes a large sip of vodka after a quick look around— pulls another, similar face— before placing the batteries back in the Walkman and pressing the play button down hard with both thumbs. There is a brief chewing noise followed by a sagging, vanquished groan.

Evelyn infers out loud that nearly everyone she has ever talked to is a prick. She apologises to her mother, thinks about her father, about her father and, well, what to call her now? Dad's girlfriend I suppose, shudder. She thinks, mum I miss you.

She sits for another half hour or so on her knees, smoking pot and sipping from the vodka. Evelyn crying in fits and starts, and leaving the moment she becomes too conspicuous to herself.

She starts to walk up the hill towards her home

and then stops. It's the last day of school for fuck's sake. She stares at the Walkman, assumes an attitude of prayer, makes a wager, presses play. A distended noise winds into the outro of Teen Age Riot from Sonic Youth's Daydream Nation.

Evelyn turns around and walks down the hill almost smiling.

*

They knew that work was bullshit and that unless they were famous they'd always be poor.

Fiasco is behind the drum kit in Henry's room tensely playing a short, pissed off sounding drum fill that took him all of six months to nail while Henry crouches over a replica fifty pound Telecaster and scrapes his pick up the low E string.

– Have you got lyrics for that one yet?

Fiasco holds up a bunch of crumpled computer paper he'd stolen from his job at the warehouse. It had become a principle to write only on stolen paper.

– Can I see them?

Fiasco shakes his head. They both laugh. It's a private joke.

Henry and Fiasco are in Henry's bedroom doing exactly what they have been doing for the past four years i.e not really practising but rather talking about the band, theorising postures. Hence the shit amps, Henry's 85% tin ear and Fiasco's ever continuing level one proficiency on guitar, bass, drums. Fiasco even— at a stretch— considering taking up the keyboard. He was always the singer though, even if you would never know it from their 'rehearsals.' His gimmick, and this was the joke, was that he would never ever sing— not once— at least not live or where anyone including the band could see. That Fiasco would stand as a symbol of pure attitude, as total punk. It's a silly idea but one that they're totally behind. It doesn't matter much. It's this, right here, which means everything to them. These few hours where Fiasco isn't angry and frustrated and Henry's depression is only a buttress for their fantasies as opposed to a vice and where for the first time, in what always seems like forever, they don't feel lonely.

> – Can I sleep here tonight?
> – Yeah but Jude's here so I can't get too wasted.
> – That's fine. Hot dogs for dinner?
> – No more living hard.
> – Is that the door?

Henry goes downstairs and opens the front door. Evelyn's behind it fiddling with her Walkman. She tries to hide it as the door opens.

She looks up at Henry from behind a nervously arranged tangle of platinum hair.

> – Hey, she says
> – Hey
> – Hey, she says.

Evelyn doesn't really have a reason to be here, she'd not even thought of inventing or even considered the need for one. She had just thought about being here, made a bet with herself, and now here she was. Evelyn was sure that her own reasons, so obscure to herself, would have crystallised in Henry's reaction to her. That he would at least invite her in. Henry stands mutely in the doorway.

> – How's Jude?
> – He's at your house isn't he? He's coming tonight
> – Oh yeah

Her coming here was a series of things that had happened, that were meant to continue to happen without having to address themselves or their motive. Henry looks back down the hall and rocks on his heels.

> – You coming to dinner this Saturday?
> – I think so.

Can't he see, she thinks. If he could see he'd

have something to tell her. Still, how is Henry meant to know or even care enough from where he is in relation to her life?

There's something Evelyn doesn't know the how or what of to say and something she can say, that had been contained in her mind in some formal afterimage of the more expansive impulse, a hastily constructed concession to reality, a gesture to the practical in the manner of a day dream. Henry starts nodding his head at the silence and fractionally inching away from the doorway.

> – So, see you Saturday probably then? Henry says.
> – Oh yeah, I um just meant to say I can get you ecstasy for Saturday if you want it.
> – Haha, what?
> – I was umm, I was thinking of getting some for myself and I just wondered if you maybe wanted some. Was just, I thought, maybe Saturday night would be cool.
> – Are you alright?
> – Do you want to or not?
> – Um, can I let you know?
> – Yeah just let us know by Saturday morning.

Evelyn turns around and walks up the hill.

Henry closes the door slowly, watching Evelyn start up one hill then turn around and walk halfway up the other before turning back again. Evelyn still rolling around the bowl of the hill as if trying to find her level as the door finally closes. Henry thinks:

– That girl is fucked up.

He goes to his room. Walking up the stairs his body begins to parse the story forming in his mind with a series of nods, frowns, and open palmed confusion. It's a genuine attempt to understand what just happened but by the time he reaches the door it's sheer routine.

– Hey, Fiasco says as the door opens, hey so can I stay here for a few nights?
Then

– What's that face about?
– Ha, The girl my mum lives with who is like sixteen I think, just offered to get us some pills on Saturday. How mental is that?
– It's pretty mental. What did you say?
– I said most likely no.
– What? Let's get some, why not?
– Cause it's mental.
–

Fiasco begins to riff. Henry listens.

– This is an opportunity. You see middle class kids always have the best drugs. You know a middle-class kid and they've probably got connections. I mean how would we meet a dealer who isn't a total scumbag? They wouldn't make themselves known to us, we'd be a liability to them. It's true. Are these the kind of people you'd want to do business with, they'd ask themselves. It doesn't make sense for them to trust us. We're bumpkins really. You have to like dance music and being around people or know someone posh to get good stuff and if they're not posh or like dance music they're probably a girl going out with someone who wants to move to London for fuck's sake.

– I'd move there

– Well, bully for you. All I'm saying is rich people's problems are different and none of our concern. Now buy some drugs off your potential step-sister. Let's just get fucked up. I mean why not?

– Yeah, fuck it I guess.

– Wait, would we have to hangout and take it with her? Cause that would be weird.

*

Saturday already, Diane thinks. And tomorrow…

She doesn't go to Church or preach any more, lives in sin though she still believes in forgiveness. Her beliefs have long since detached from her actions, from the hope of action.

Her life wasn't up to them, to either of them, belief or action. Change occurred, Diane realised, in either geologic or catastrophic time. Moment to moment there was only exhaustion, boredom, a mist of iron pain hived greyly into the heart of things and layering into darkness there. Her prayers still willed and called upon turned against her, no longer left her with the clean and assured feeling they once did. As she believed they once did, when? Her prayers congealed in her thoughts, rarely left her sight, disappeared from her attention only to hide and then reappear in the inanimate material of the house creating these strange, inappropriate, relations with the ephemera of the day. Rain joined on windows would activate a meditation on poverty in Africa, the shadows across the room at a particular time of day might pertain in the waning of their scaled forms to the dreams and fears she held for her children and the cutlery draw, if opened and closed at the wrong moment and containing an upturned spoon stretching her reflection around it, might engender a prayer for an acceptance of her ageing body other than time's. All these signs capable of dialoguing complexly at once in the interrogative cell of her wishing till she closed down or found hope.

Diane is cleaning the house. She had almost broached the subject of hiring a cleaner, thinking of it first as a joke but then later fixating upon it, upon the various indignities of her position so that the surfaces upon which her hand rubbed or buffed shone with pain. The house and her, there were all manner of transferences. It was she felt her closest friend but also a monstrous child with attachment issues, a hernia hanging outside of herself. She is looking out through the French windows towards the lighthouse, the windows polished to reflect the interiors so that Diane sees through herself and onto the roiling sea in which the sofa and her hips dip like wreckage. She runs the vacuum across the surface of the sea. It is seven thirty in the evening on a Saturday night. Jude's upstairs banging away at his drums, Lawrence isn't home yet— isn't likely to be home for hours— Evelyn's gone to the cinema with some friends and Henry is god knows where doing god knows what.

She looks up at the windows towards the lighthouse. A speck of darkness seems to separate itself from the lighthouse. Diane frowns, perhaps it is just a piece of dirt or lint trapped on the window, a fly or a beetle pausing on glass. She steps towards the small, dark, full stop of a thing trying to place itself in her thoughts. The Hoover brings her up short. Diane turns and yanks the cord of the vacuum towards the table with the elegant walnut finish. The vacuum detaches from the wall, Diane looks round at the French windows. The moment the room sifts into a padded quiet the black spot hits the window. Diane drops the vacuum, the glass buzzing angrily as the house's interior, interior to her mind, shakes as if underwater.

*

Lawrence isn't at work. He's at a bar rehearsing private and unconvincing affirmations about his chances of getting through tomorrow without anything like today happening. This time he means it. He means it. Lawrence has made some poor investments. He has made some poor investments at the behest of his friend the doctor in said friend who now appears to have scarpered. Lawrence has bitten off more than he can chew, chewed more than he can swallow, swallowed more than he can digest and shat more than he can stand for one lifetime. There is the house to think about. Oh my god. The house...will be fine. Of course it'll be fine. Fine.

Also he's lonely, very lonely, exceptionally lonely, one might say. He's a widow after all, a widowed man no less. Lawrence runs his finger around the rim of the glass and then rubs the finger into his gum, so lonely. Except, he isn't really, he has Diane doesn't he? Still there was something missing between them and it wasn't children. That's for damn sure. Then what? She had given herself to him without his having to ask, comforted him silently, acquiesced when he started to show signs of his despicable hunger and yet and yet. He had nothing more to ask. That's a problem. That's a problem? That's, a what?

Lawrence had considered Diane for all this time as a gift and had treated her as such. She had given herself to him and what, if anything, had he done for her?

He had committed to her the way he committed to objects, stationing her in his house like a grand piano. He has never opened her. She has never been his. Lawrence wants to take her again in the act of his giving.

What could he do? Lawrence looks into a figurative distance.

Well there was that.

And after all doesn't he want someone to explain himself to, to share his burden with, someone with whom he might enlarge his life by laying it next to theirs? Lawrence tries to peer through the idea. He likes it. The idea meets the alcohol and produces a silencing thunderclap of happiness. Lawrence sways very slightly as if to a slow waltz in his deafness.

Also, there's her house.

Lawrence shakes his head, that's not what he

means. That's not what he wants to mean. Lawrence feels sick. He feels terrible. Why, he could die! What if that was a part of it?

It can't be. I'm not that person really.

Lawrence congratulates himself and downs his brandy. His heartbeat swims in a breath of memory. He is trying to find his way back to the way the idea had felt.

Someone to explain himself to...the thought takes on the quality of a dream and Lawrence feels that he must act now in order to grasp the immaterial, act now or, perhaps, in just a moment.

Lawrence orders his fourth brandy to preserve his excitement and asks for a taxi.

He bends over the glass trying to engender nostalgia for this particular moment, this end of 'that' time. The years , he thought, had passed and were popularly remarked upon as being bad. The populous of his pains, the remarks and glances they had born in the media of sorrow had helped shape him in ways that he had found comforting for what he feared were the basest reasons. The ones he couldn't bring himself to name. He downs his brandy, squeezes his mouth together several times and waits.

The taxi arrives and Lawrence, less committed now, asks the taxi driver to take the scenic route home. The taxi driver winds down his window. The whip of air stings Lawrence's eyes.

– The scenic route, if you don't mind
– You have money?

A tear rolls down Lawrence's cheek.

– I did.
– You have money? Money?
– Yes, sorry, I lost some recently, but of course I can pay

The taxi driver shakes his head at Lawrence. He says

– Gambling?

And then
– Very bad.

The taxi driver winds the window down, makes a turning towards the promenade. Lawrence looks out towards the sea as the car stops at a traffic light, as three figures cross unseen ahead of him, their figures a single frame spliced meaninglessly into the final edit of the day.

One of the figures is a girl's. The girl's hand at her hair obscures her profile as the car passes, Lawrence still staring out the passenger window— the expression on his face held somewhere between moony nausea and tearful determination— half catches sight of this movement and there is something so familiar in the half caught gesture of the girl that Lawrence's own thoughts are disrupted by a sudden but in no way unfamiliar stab of tenderness. The shock of the felt familiar takes a few seconds to decipher itself into a question and when he turns she's no longer in view. The tenderness persists, he knows now. He taps the taxi driver on the shoulder, say's I'm going to do it and then leans back into the seat grinning. The taxi driver shakes his head.

*

Diane still doesn't know how to react when Lawrence comes home, cannot remain seated at the sound of a door. She turns the television off, quickly unearths her cross-stitch from under a pile of magazines and stands looking towards the door. Lawrence lurching with his coat on in the doorframe.

He asks where Evelyn is as he takes the coat off.

> – She's at the cinema
> – Are you sure? Who with?
> – Girls from school I think
> – Oh, I didn't think she had any friends at school.
> – Teenagers always think that
> – Ha, teenagers.

They each glance around the room, Lawrence trying to find her eyes. Diane sits on the edge of the sofa and begins to pluck at her cross-stitch.

Lawrence feigns a gesture towards the television.

> – Were you watching something?
> – No, I was working on this
> – I thought I heard voices
> – Well I had it on in the background.
> – You ought to relax
> – Yes, well.

Lawrence nods knowingly, steps forward, opening and closing his mouth several times, his face recalibrating each time as if harassed by some imaginary and more able interlocutor. Diane puts her cross-stitch down. Lawrence walks towards her, rounding the table in small steps like a dog readying to settle. He stands to the side of her legs and stoops slightly. He lifts her hand by its ring and index finger.

He gets down on one knee.

> – Diane, I
> – Lawrence, Lawrence I don't know
> – I do. Say it. Say it, please.
> – Lawrence...there are, there are complications
> – If you mean Henry and Jude we can work it out.
> – But after last time
> – That was years ago.
> – There are other complications too. I'm a married woman.

> – Not for long... and then one more
> time again, forever

Diane's heart pounds and she can feel the slosh of blood canalled in her ears.

Lawrence, however, is keenly aware that the rough fibres of the carpet are making indents on his knees that he just knows are going to be red and itchy and impossible to ignore and which will inevitably detract from his savouring of the moment, though given the continuance of silence and all things being equal the peak of his confidence is essentially a flat line waiting to happen.

Conversely, Diane's just realised that Lawrence has failed to produce any little black box which might substantiate his gesture in light of the sour fragrance currently sailing out of his puffed cheeks. In the long French doors the sun divides into two.

> – Tell me that you don't love me
> – Lawrence, I

*

> .   – This is great. I'm having a great time.

> – What do you think it means?
> – What do you mean?
> – That we feel great

– It depends what you mean by mean
but at a base level we're actively
changing the chemistry of our brains or
something.

– I think I'm having an existential crisis
re: the role of free will in all this

– You can't have an existential crisis on
ecstasy.

– It must be laced with something.

– Think of it this way. You've chosen to
do this, whatever this is

– Can I just consent like that?

– I think reality is pretty non-
consensual anyway

– What? Oh. Um… Wait a
sec….yeah…never mind.

– …

– …

– This is great.

– Yeah

They're sat at the beach under rags of clouds
suppurate with sun. Strange vegetative forms lean
towards a declining light. Henry, Evelyn and
Fiasco in turn beginning to feel the effects of what
they've so cavalierly ingested. What they've
ingested being several mgs of a more than usual
lysergically laced amphetamine.

Wind scampers around the beach and jumps
through their hair growing furious and emptier
in found form. Pale swarms of attendant sand

encrypt their faces as a heat, inborn, crawls through their scalps into the liberate air mating at last with the beach in little gorged buttons of moisture.

Each of them inhales deeply through their noses. Fiasco says

> – We need music, to no one in
> particular.

Evelyn takes out her Walkman and a purchased that day portable speaker. The Ramones I Wanna be Sedated gets swamped in the sea's feedback.

> – Good choice
> – Thanks

Evelyn hasn't spoken for a while. To be honest it has been hard for her to break into the conversation and their attempts to include her have either taken the form of closed questions— trotted out in little rat-a-tat-tat bursts of polite enquiry that inevitably ended with some enthusiastically gestural, but ultimately silent, acknowledgement of her entropic answers— or at the end of one of their many self referential anecdotes into which they'd generously carved out a fraction of a beat for her to throw her own narrative hat into their ring should she have, you know, felt so inclined.

Still, even before the drug started taking her feelings apart and making of them two large parentheses flooded with indiscriminate good tidings, she'd decided that she liked hanging out with the two of them. It was strange for her to be in the company of two people who wanted to think of themselves firstly as geniuses, then as waste, then as urchins, then as punk (not punk rock), then as shoe shines, then as pick pockets, then as academics then as rock stars, then as writers then as anything other than what time and chance had fixed them as. Saw in this refusal to acknowledge the world outside of themselves an almost ideological denial of reality. It demonstrated, to her mind, an admirable quality of resistance. Still what she's really waiting for, she's just this second realised, what this must have really been all about, she thinks as her thoughts begin to take on spatial qualities, as her body becomes a mind, and the visible parts of her body start to more and more resemble a jagged cliff face beyond which lies— at last revealed— the orgiastic and total distance between her and what she assumes God is given her atheistic conception of that word I.E God being synonymous with some infinite and inevitable and possibly disinterested power/experience— what she really wants, she now knows, is a chance to ask Henry about her mother. She's heard the story of her first word and how he used to carry her through the house a thousand times from Diane.

– Not down the stairs though, he was always very careful with me.

She wants to hear what he has to say about her mother, wants to hear it while she feels like this specifically.

– I'm boiling

Fiasco begins to roll the cuffs of his jeans up. He takes his shoes and socks off and walks towards the shore. Fiasco kneels down at the edge of the shore and pretty much head butts a little nook of water. He stands up shaking his hair, whooping and shouting for Henry and possibly Evelyn to join him. He walks up to his knees in the sea and places his hands on his hips. Fiasco doesn't look back. The only thing that is different is that the emptiness feels amazing, he thinks.

> – You want to go in?
> – It'll be freezing.
> – C'mon

Henry stands leaning towards Evelyn but looking at Fiasco and she feels his hand closing gently around the bowed bones of her forearm, a sightless grip not quite there in its accidental tenderness like that of an oddly weightless elderly man or woman whose age puts the world out of view and under water, who barely remembers meeting the world with clarified force except in the slow inexorable failings of form that ghost their reality. Evelyn can feel an ache radiating and incorporeal under each whooshed sensation as she stands— practically unaided, as if by suggestion alone— an ache like a crackling snow drenched fire sifting the half fulfilled air around it into damp vapours that cause electric rifts in the sky which branch into nothing. Dead ends. The world brought crashing down as a matter of course. Evelyn has to catch her breath, rein in her thoughts, that were not thoughts really but rather movements destined only for themselves.

– Hey don't worry.

They walk into the sea.
Ahead of them up to his waist, a bracing clutch of water flagging his heart, Fiasco's awhirl with his usual verbal energy

– I'm pretty much fucking agog looking at that. He points towards the lighthouse.
– Postcards from the phenomenal: Wish you were here, Henry shouts back.

Henry turns incrementally towards Evelyn, his eyes tracking down her body's profile as her hand moves fractionally towards his. It feels like the sea parting. Evelyn turns her body towards Henry, squeezes the tips of his fingers.

– I, I wanted to ask you about my mother. What you remember of her?
– Not that much.
– Please, anything

Henry looks at her holding his fingers. He breaks the hold and puts his arms around Evelyn and presses her against him till their two heartbeats punch towards one another. She looks up to the sky. Her face empties out. She doesn't know if this is love though it seems as close to it as she can imagine.

> – This is what I remember of your mum. She hugged me once like this. I don't know why, I don't know why I remember it even. I just remember that, that and she would read to us sometimes.

Fiasco ambles back toward them laughing, *what the fuck* he thinks. Henry pulls him in. The three of them grapple and happily stumble around as a large wave bundles them over.

Evelyn feels so inexplicably happy and charged.

> – Fiasco
> – Yeah?
> – I'd be dead without you man.
> –
> – I mean it though, I don't know, you saved my life I think. Or something. Really. Listen, I'd be dead.
> – No, really. Now we really should be thinking about stealing that boat.
> – What boat?
> – That one.

–

– Why aren't we doing it already?

The three of them wade towards the small wooden boat loosely tied to the pier. Fiasco pushes the rickety boat into the water. Henry falls out as he tries to pull him in as Evelyn sits laughing and gripping the seat as the two boys in sync, and with mirrored faces of excitement, climb in either side of her.

The boat turns like teacups around the shore before slowing into a woozy lope. They paddle around and around in trembled circumference, their steered circles eventually winding out towards the lighthouse's island.

*

Diane sits up in bed and places the novel she's been reading on the slight slope of her belly. Lawrence is downstairs in his study sulking. She'd told him that she needed to think about it but that, yes, she did love him, very much. Diane already knows what her answer will be, knew it the moment she'd shut the door and was finally alone. She turns on her side, places her head like a filling into the cavity of the pillow. She will marry Lawrence, of course she will.

Diane considers turning onto her back but doesn't. Instead she lies on her side, drawing her knees up under her chest like a child. The book slides towards her teeth through her parted breasts and enters her mouth like a nipple. They will have to talk seriously about Jude and Henry's future. They will have to give them every chance.

She turns on her back. The book is wedged uncomfortably under her right hip.

Lawrence is speaking loudly to someone on the phone. She reaches behind herself and places the novel on the bedside table. She sits up against the bed's headboard. She listens in, trying to analyse the frequencies and rhythms of Lawrence's murmured, pitch muffled voice in order to somehow infer from its deviations and assertions the position he, Lawrence, is taking up in whatever the conversation may be about. It could be good or ill humoured though the former is more likely. Henry's mother mentally leans in further, making up words that might fit the fluid and cryptic puzzle of the conversation. She thinks:

> – He is panicking about our
> relationship.

This guess hazarded at for all of thirty seconds until the classical music CD, the one that had come free with the Sunday paper— glue tri-blobbed on the front page so that one had to rip the cardboard sleeve from the trailing paper (the headlines still messily lacquering the cardboard)— starts to play "Hall of the Mountain

King" at an eavesdrop censoring volume. The music almost in comical chastisement of her attempting to listen, a judgement of chance she feels. Henry's mother remembering now how Lawrence has, at the last three dinner parties she has catered for, enthused over the "Hall of the Mountain King," declaring it his favourite ever piece of classical music.

A guest asked him if he didn't think it was rather a commercial and overplayed choice.

> – That's what I like about it, how it's
> played. It's very likeable and that's not
> appreciated enough I don't think. I mean
> I do think. I mean….

Henry's mother catching her good-natured but still rolled eyes in the three mirrors of the room's dresser table again. The dresser table that Lawrence had installed in the guest bedroom several years ago once it had become clear that it was in everyone's best interest if she stayed.

Diane laughs a few times in front of her reflections, each division barking a little further into self-consciousness, as her eyes skid over the mirrors. Diane, physically uncomfortable now, finds herself again admiring the quality of the dresser table as she wriggles around the bed.

Helene had taste.

A few years have passed since a thought like that would have directly troubled her though she can't help but worriedly scan it for any trace of materialism. It's there, as it often is, but it feels like something else.

– Helene was a nice woman, I liked her, she was a nice woman, I did like her, I did, I did. And, well, what she, what she...unforgivable really.

She has forgotten about Lawrence's phone call, his voice ridden out in the music below and woven into her blind inner movements.

Diane tries now to hold her gaze in the dresser table mirrors but there are too many gazing. She is outnumbered. She was outnumbered from the start that she cannot remember realizing. Diane flosses her image between each of them.

She selects the mirror on the left, consulting occasionally with a flick of her eyes, the flawed interdependence of the other mirrors. She is satisfied with what she sees until she isn't, till her life filters in and possesses the reflection.

She will discuss Henry with Lawrence tomorrow, he will have to agree to listen and then, afterwards, agree even if without understanding, and after that she will talk to Henry about her plans, about how her plans will be the first step he takes to reaching the potential he's always unquestionably, she will be sure to say this part, possessed but never even been allowed to show. The dispossession of the present will be coming to an end, she thinks, like a thief in the night.

The thought is a comfort, her hands wrap

pleasurably around her body. The bed is finally warm, her legs moving fluid under the duvet as she shuffles her torso gratefully under.

She will sell her home, move here permanently, officially, finally. A list appears. Of course first assessments will have to be sought, things questionably quantifiable will have to be quantified, memories and water damage ticketed into receipt. Henry won't want to come with Jude, she knows this, has of course anticipated it. Besides he is too old to move in with his mother now, was too old several years ago, and he can't expect to be living in that house forever, it is not practical. He will understand this, she thinks.

-It is time for him to do something with his life at last.

Henry has given up an awful lot he should have a chance.

His mother wanting him to be free even as that freedom scares her.

He is not a bad boy.

She has been researching colleges and universities, courses that may interest him. He enjoys reading at least, she knows this.

-He inherited that from me.

What else though? From the bed she leans out a hand and turns the lamp off and rests her head on the airy pillow, the vague outline of which she is still able to make out in the darkness. There's the 'band' he's always talking about but, really, how serious could that be, she wonders, they'd never even played live. Her head centres in the pillow. She closes her eyes and conjures Henry's image, bombarding it with her vision of the future till the sovereignty of each relents and gifts her some ideas. Except what emerge are not ideas at all, they are only wishes vaguely hypothesised and tested amid the biased variables of her hope.

She's broached the subject of his future before of course, pinning the conversation like a lapel to her posture so he could know what was coming,. She'd been surprised and a little taken aback by his reaction. Henry's mood detonating into exasperation at the mere mention of what he might do with his life. It reminded her of her husband in ways she'd care not to recall.

I was much weaker then.

She will talk to Henry, persist past his discomfort. They will negotiate each other's hopes.

(Henry always on the verge of saying in these moments, he has told Fiasco, that he was explicitly told that he would never ever die and that it is slightly rich to now suddenly expect him to have planned for the future given his previously casual relationship to its repeated ends. Henry never having actually thought of saying this at the time, any of the times. Henry instead only telling Fiasco it is like he had thought of saying that at the time, which is true enough he figures. Or at least truer once he had said it to Fiasco and the idea had taken hold. They both understand how this works.)

Diane's mind slowly but powerfully begins to sway into sleep, her thoughts like a body of water on the verge of being spilt, the trebly surface of her reason interrupted by the evacuated base of her mind. He will have to listen, listen to me.

Just

Listen.

*

　– Duhduh duh duh nananuh nananuh
　duhduh duh duh nanana nananuh
　duhduh duh duh nanana

I got out of that one, he thinks. Marriage, he thinks. Ha-ha, he thinks. Lawrence presses pause, then looks up at the ceiling. He turns the volume up slightly and replays the song from the beginning. He presses repeat on his cd player and lifts his empty glass above him like a conductor's baton and then stares at it.

He fetches a bottle of brandy from his antique globe. The drink cabinet gifted to him by Diane last Christmas after she had overheard him complimenting a very similar but by no means identical model from one of the many magazines he regularly subscribes to. The magazines having initially each been selected as a strategic way for him to bone up on the interests of his bosses but then, increasingly, he found himself ensnared by the introductory offers and the pleasant weight and promise of post.

The magazines taking up an inordinate amount of his time and space. Lawrence often retiring to this study under the guise of work only to read through, order/archive, all his growing enthusiasms.

He picks up a copy of Horticulturalist Yearly from the desk and flings it next to a pile of antique watches weekly that in turn displaces a neat stack of The Karma Suture, a magazine devoted solely to deconstructive readings of apocalyptical outsider artists from India. Lawrence looks around the room.

He looks at the phone under his hand, how did it creep there? Lawrence has practised what he would like to say to his friend the Doctor. He has blown off steam, spouted airy bile through all the ventricles available to him except the one under his hand.

Now he need only have the courage to tell it to a machine.

He pours himself a drink.

*

The uncovered light bulb swinging around the lighthouse's living quarters is so simultaneously harsh at its core and ineffective in application that the room's tone seems stagey and in-between enough to physically demarcate the gap between their straining high and the room's dour reality. They trudge around aimlessly, drying their feet to sludge in the dust, the room puffing up around them, absorbent. Their hearts no longer feel volcanic.

In fact the room and its dust only serve to remind them of their bodies in wholly unremarkable ways, in the retch and spit of irritated lungs, in the mortal leash of a hacking cough.

Walking around they slowly begin to ease the clamped fingers from their mouths— suck whistling air through barely exposed front teeth, grit growing around the enamel.

There's a bare table near the centre of the room, a bed frame shunted to the left, and some mouldy books bowing a rotten looking pair of planks near the bed frame where a telephone— its receiver an eyebrow of dust arched ironically over a dialled eye— sits evidently disconnected from source, a coil of muted and frayed copper wire trailing its ending. That's it.

The last thing Henry wants to see is a spider. That's all he's been able to think since they climbed the stairs. The world's still seemingly mixed from paint and his brain keeps moving like a thumb after the scan of his eyes but the illusion is pretty much over now. It's boring and seems overly committed to its life span.

    – Is this going to end soon, he thinks

And

What was that crawling there?

And, while rubbing his eye with the palm of his hand,

    – What is this light behind my eyeball,
    just where is that coming from? Fuck.

Fiasco and Henry sit on the threadbare rug at the centre of the room smoking a joint. Evelyn is wandering around, the decaying grotto ambiance momentarily having triggered some latent potential in her flagging high. She keeps feeling a faint pulse of amazement that her physically tired brain contextualises into an uncanny sense of familiarity. She knows this place, she feels.

    – I feel like I've been here before.
    – It's a dump.
    – This is bullshit.

Evelyn hesitantly pokes the tower of books. She half expects an outbreak of bugs to fritter out, patrol the border of their enclosed and previously undisturbed ecosystem, bug extremities raised like pitchforks. Nothing much happens except her fingerprint clowns in the dust. Evelyn thinks something the sensation of which is that her body is a clownish version of some other her, one that exists in some other place. Weird.

She pushes a tower of books over. The noise jolts Henry whose brain ricochets against his skull, whose thighs tense, whose arms jag and make his skin feel like a parenthesis.

What the?

Evelyn looks over to them.

Sorry.

> – We're going upstairs, you want to come?

Evelyn picks up a book, turns it around in her hands.

–

*

Lawrence wakes to find himself disassembled, folded up, flat packed. He is peering through his lap or rather his entire torso is occupying/ struggling to fill the space that his lap would normally constitute. He had dreamt that his shoes were boats are sailing towards separate horizons.

A staunch believer in first things first, Lawrence tries to sit up straight. He bangs the back of his head on the lip of the desk, ricochets down and then up, pushing himself away from the table. Sitting up and rubbing his head he regards the desk with a mixture of suspicion, reproach and longing. He pulls the wheeled chair towards the desk in an awkward tiptoeing motion that feels, and that he knows would appear to be, grossly pathetic.

Lawrence chances a look down at his lap.

His legs have remained in a wide unyielding V and there is an ominous detuned pain moving laterally across the fold of his lap. He hears a door closing and then the start of a car. Diane must be on her way out, probably to 'run her errands.' He looks at his watch. It says six thirty am. He places his palms on the desk and lifts himself slowly up. It takes him a total of eight steps to turn around and face the door.

Lawrence strides towards the living room like a cowboy. Entering he sees a card sitting on the table with the elegant walnut finish. Lawrence rolls like a seaman towards it.

Inside the card there is a simple YES written in Diane's unmistakeable penmanship followed by 'ps I have gone out for wine and potatoes.' Lawrence takes a few moments to understand before the sudden onset of realisation sets about tearing his brain a new hemisphere.

*

– Do you think it still works?
– I don't know. Should we try it?
– You stand in front of it. Do you think this is where the guy hung himself?

– I'm completely imagining this coming on and it being the phenomenal.

– I can see the light punching a perfect hole through you.

– I'm going to stand in front of the cliffs,

– You'll be a shadow on the face of the phenomenal.

–

– Recently I've been having an old daydream.

– The one where you wake up and no one else exists?

– The first thing I'd do is go round the houses letting all the pets out.

– The most troubling thing about that fantasy is that you have no inclination to look for other people

– I'd have to be suspicious of them.

– Why?

– Firstly my own survival is either an accident or 'peace at last.' Maybe I won't want to be interrupted. But that's not the old daydream I mean.

– So what is it?

– Well it's not so much a daydream as a belief.

– Go on.

– I believe that I've been everyone. That's my new…belief? I can fully and properly believe that and one day I'll figure out the how of it.

– That sounds more like a curse.

– No, I'd really know there were other people and how they/I felt. I'd be god and everything, no matter how terrible, would be fair and practically blameless. It's an idea that would redeem the world

– You wouldn't even exist then. If you were everyone you wouldn't exist cause everyone would have been you

– Nuh-huh, Fiasco says

– Seriously, how could you be said to exist if you'd equally been everybody. It means everybody has been you. I don't think it would work, there'd still be this completely inexcusable force that it'd be impossible to be identical to. You in that moment couldn't be you.

– Well, I wouldn't exist like this but man that's the dream though, right? Shit, you've depressed me now.

Evelyn is downstairs in the 'living quarters'. She is lifting one of the loose floorboards and tentatively reaching her hand underneath. She can feel something lying there. Her fingers push the object around and then pinch it. She draws the thing out through the slat by a wing. Her hand and the object come out wigged in dust. She blows the dust from her hand and hears the sound …paper. In her hand is a book, a notebook with pale faded pages. She's opening it just as Fiasco and Henry come down the stairs. They look tired, older now. They don't even ask what it is she's holding.

– Home time?

Morning spreads in tides of blue high above the beach. A quake of light cracks the vanishing rearguard of soiled cloud, draining night's pigment from each shadow below. The grey of the warming sand effervesces into the sky, a dull gold warming in the tarnish.

They say goodbye to each other on the beach as dogs and their owners make faces at their shivering manifestation of 'misguided youth.' Fiasco points after a jogger who has just ploughed through their intimate circle of ill-health,

> – There but for the grace of god huh?
> – We should form a terrorist cell against her.
> – Ha! I got some things I need to do. Later.

Fiasco begins to walk away. There is a shadow on his heart. He has had a good time but that time seems to have been done with him and he is keenly aware of its leaving.

– You still have my keys right?

With his back to them now, Fiasco raises the keys

upwards and continues to walk. He is thinking that he just wants to walk around for a little, be alone. He is thinking about how some people he liked in books, films and music died in real life. He is thinking that perhaps he should die in real life. Fiasco doesn't believe in depression but he likes to consider suicide a neat alternative to the pestilent have-to of living. Not that he's miserable or anything, don't say that. He's just angry and sometimes, when that burns out and all he can see are the charred and near unrecognisable remains of things he'd either like to take a hold of or be held by, he can get prone to dark thoughts. He knows what he wants to do now. He wants to go home.

Evelyn is asking Henry if she can stay at his for a while.

> – I don't want to get home while my dad is still in.
> – Yeah, of course.

She calls a taxi, says she'll pay. Henry's impressed.

Henry's house is cold and there are milk bottles with carnations of mould reeking out of them is the first thing Evelyn notes on arrival, that and the practised way Henry literally kicks a path through the front room towards an enjoining pre-existent trail of rubbish that leads toward and around the fortified settee. He asks her if she wants to sleep and she nods her head and he shows her the way to his bedroom and says that she can sleep there if she wants.

– Where are you going?
– Um, I've just got to get some stuff

Evelyn takes her jeans off and slips into the single bed. She places one pillow against the wall and scootches up next to it. The wallpaper is bumpy. She presses her finger against one of the bumps in the wallpaper and it is hard and fashioned like a piece of rice that has been trapped underneath the paper though, in fact, it is actually part of the wall paper's design. Evelyn has no earthly idea why anyone would choose to decorate a room like this.

– Hey, Henry says as he comes in holding a sleeping bag and cushion, you ok?

He puts them on the floor and asks her if there is any music she'd like to hear. She says Sunday Morning by the Velvet underground. He puts it on and gets into the sleeping bag.

*

Lawrence stands relatively sedate and half asleep in the glass pillar of the shower. His sleepiness rests against him hugging his shoulders and gently gifting into the biceps. The pain in his legs has diminished or fused with the rest of his worldview.

There's a different attitude in his body, one interiorly vanquished, unconsciously happy and nuzzling into the cushion of his dozy fat. There's the half finished— second of the morning— brandy au lait resting on the toilet's tank which Lawrence looks over at occasionally, giggling at the idea of a good idea coming to short sighted fruition.

Lawrence's cheeks rise around his eyes in a dim smile. He turns the bronze nickel-plated tap anticlockwise, there's a rude coughing in the pipes and then the first pelt of cold water renders the day a dead weight again.

The events of the last twenty-four hours slip over him like oil on water, their surface enjoining blackly over his dawning lucidity. Every thought comes up covered with yesterday.

– I. I. What?

Yesterday and the futures it placed in motion lean heavily against him, their conspiracies of consequence all insinuate and tangled and whispering into his ear things he realises that he already knows and that the freighted voice worming inside him already knows that he knows.

Lawrence takes the weight. He still has hope.

In the innermost quarter of himself there is still hope.

Coming out of the bathroom Lawrence can't help but notice that Evelyn's door is open and then that Evelyn isn't in it and then that the room doesn't seem to exhibit any evidence of having been inhabited in the past eighteen or so hours.

Lawrence looks around the room. The room is immaculate. Could she have come home and already left? How could he know? There are no pictures or posters on the wall. The sole cuddly toy retained from a life full of proffered cuddly toys is sat all lonesome between fattened pillows. The cuddly toy Lawrence has always suspected Evelyn, when drunk in a certain way and considering his daughter, of whole heartedly despising. It kept around, he figures, for the sole purpose of reminding him of her resentment.

The rainbow horned unicorn openly mocking him it seems with its downcast, half mooned pupils, with its immaculate and barely petted fur. Love is a bald spot, he could think.

Lawrence stretches out. Where could she be, who is she with? His arms return to his waist, the pleasant rush of lactic acids and relaxed tendons lighting the hearth of his muscles. His hangover, his dressing gown and the revivifying brandy au café au lait conjuring a rare synthesis of mood. Lawrence feels both early evening and mid morning with all the louche transgression of the former and the investigatory precepts of the latter. He knocks the rainbow unicorn from its perch. The unicorn falls flat on its horn. Lawrence contemplates the chest of drawers. Didn't she, hasn't she always, kept a diary?

He stands up, looks the drawers up and down, and tries the first out of supposedly idle curiosity. It won't come free. Never mind, he thinks. He sits down on the bed and, stretching out a hand, casually tries the drawer again. It does not come free. He places his mug on top of the chest of drawers, cracks his knuckles and goes at the drawers one more time with feeling. Coffee slops slightly out of the mug. Coming clear the drawer reveals a tangle of bras, a lattice of pants and a small pink bullet shaped object from the future that has suddenly started to buzz. He says oh god out loud and tries to close the draw that has now come off its runner and refuses to realign itself. A small puddle of coffee cascades into the gap, gathers in the suggestive crease of some frilled nothingness. Lawrence, still jimmying the drawer in an attempt to find the necessary but lost groove, can't help but see this fresh polka on the dot of clothing. He doesn't want to know any of this.

fuck fuck fuck fuck

The groove is found. He runs the drawer shut. Lawrence Muir rubs his face. He swears four different swear words three times each. At least the buzzing has stopped. He reaches for the drawer and opens it slightly. He looks in. He shakes his head. He closes the drawer. He rubs his face. The drawer buzzes.

Lawrence stands there thinking and staring straight ahead at the empty patch of wall where a mirror used to hang, the patch of wall pallid and tan lined. The mirror laid flat across the bedside table, dressed in feminine powders. A decision has been made.

Lawrence picks up the coffee cup and wipes the top of the chest of drawers with the sleeve of his dressing gown. He turns around and walks out of the door closing it carefully behind him.

Of course, he thinks, just leave. Deny all knowledge.

*

– You don't have to sleep on the floor.
– It is pretty uncomfortable.
– I'll move up.
–

Henry gets into bed next to Evelyn and turns shyly away from her. He'd planned to sit in the front room, smoke a last cigarette and try to come to terms with tonight, his life, his dreams, reality as a whole, whatever. He'd given up halfway through. Same shit different chemical constitution.

Evelyn stares at his back. That lasts a few

minutes. Henry rolls onto his back. She lifts her head and lays it on his chest. That settles it.

They just kissed, two clayed mouths mashed into a formative embrace that doesn't quite take. There wasn't enough moisture to keep them together for more than a few seconds so they stopped, felt at each other's necks with the open palms of their mouths then acknowledged and laughed at the drug's side effects. Evelyn adjusts her head on his chest, rearranging the thin sheet of skin over the tent of his ribs, her hair a forested shadow against it. Evelyn acting all sleepy now, shifting around so that she can find some optimum spot to rest in. Her body is wriggled slightly further down the bed than Henry's and she looks up at him from within her cowl of duvet. Henry is looking up at the ceiling, so Evelyn can really look. She inspects the shifting plains of his profile, the little obelisks of his nostrils. The thought makes her smile, the heat of which Henry somehow detects. She sees the mooned eyeball, glimpsed above a dune of cheek, swivelling down towards her and then up at the ceiling again. She smiles again.

Henry starts to talk about something he likes to talk about with Fiasco since Fiasco is usually the only person he likes talking to.

> – What do you think is at the bottom of the sea?
> – Which sea?

– Umm, the deepest one or something?
– I don't know... 'or sumthin' why do
you guys always do that?
– It started as a joke about how, ha, how
clever we are. You'd give or pretend to
give a really comprehensive description
or analysis of something and then
pretend not to care about it, you know
dismiss it or something. Then we did it
so often that this or something became
so integral to our own, like, futile sense
of contingency that now we're not sure
what it means anymore. It's like we're
aiming for a phenomenal ambivalence...
or something.
– I understand.
– Or something?
– Or something. So the sea...? I'm
guessing you have a guess.
– Our current thinking is that there's
like one giant creature there, covering
the whole sea floor.

Henry continues, yawning, talking to himself
as his voice is pulled into the music and Evelyn's
amused disinterest.

– It's prehistoric and practically
immortal, the source of life and death
but also fucking horrifyingly basic.
– It's weird to think of all that pressure,

all that weight, she says.
– Yeah to think that whatever you drop into it won't even reach the bottom. It'll just disintegrate or something.

Evelyn turns around to face the wall, taking Henry's arm along the line of her hip as she moves.

– Isn't that just the night? She says.

*

– Mum, it's ok.
– Drugs, it is drugs. Drugs and crime and your son. All holding hands like faggots. Why else, in the morning through the window with those eyes?
– Mum? I
– ...
– Mum?
– ...
– Look at his pupils. Just look at them. I told you. I told you this is how he was going to end up.
– Mum, he's hurting me.
– I'm not
– Let go
– Ok
– Thank you.

– You need to get out. Thief.

– Mum?

– …

– Mum?

– He's a fucking junky. Get out now or I'll call the police

– Mum?

– No, go upstairs. I'll come once he's gone. He has to go, he has to. Or I'll ring the police. Listen I'm sorry I grabbed him. Stealing from his own family though, it's hard to take.

– I wasn't, you're not

– I said get the fuck out. Upstairs, I'll make sure he leaves. Tough love they said, that's what they said. Remember, you heard them say it we both did.

– Mum, where are you going? Where you going?

– Leave him, you have to leave, he has to realise tough love, remember love, tough love, leave him, tough love, tough love, c'mon, shush now, tough love, yes, tough love, this way love

– Mum? How about any fucking kind of love? How about any kind of love?

– You fuck should get the fuck out of here before I fucking come back. Cunt.

– Mum?

– Shhh, love, love don't worry he's going, tough love, it works, he's going.

– Mum, mum? Oh Fuck this. What have I even done?

Fiasco is cold as fuck, his clothes are damp and he's still about forty five minutes to an hour's walk away from Henry's house. Not to mention the fact that he's having to walk back across the beach cos that's where his righteous indignation just up and dumped him. Added to all of this he's got no fucking money, not even enough shrapnel for the bus or a fortifying corner-shop pork and pickle pie. He's also pretty sure, given the complete lack of jangle engendered by his staggering limp, that he's lost the keys to Henry's house. Plus, it's right now started to rain and, oh yeah, he's just realising that he needs a shit.

– What have I done to deserve this?

He hadn't done anything.

Ok, so he'd broken into his stepfather's house. Not that he considers that bastard to own anything. His mother also lived there ergo…something. He had only wanted to lay for a while in his old room amid the posters and comics and memories he hoped were left stored there.

He was planked halfway through the kitchen window, gripping the sink, when his stepfather appeared at the end of the hall. Fiasco tried to scrabble away, slipped. Crash. Landed on his hand.

Now his wrist and fingers have swollen up in their casings. The various parts of his hand segmented like a balloon animal and which he could probably fashion a poodle out of with his working hand, he thinks.

– Oh fucking hell John

He should have gone with Henry and Evelyn. Why didn't he? She was the kind of girl who'd pay for a taxi and not resent anyone who couldn't chip in more than a nugget. A top of the hill girl. They got a taxi together didn't they? I bet they did, all the way home, her paying. They're probably eating hot dogs right now and wondering about him.

The beach is all but empty except for a man sat on a bench up ahead. The man sat on the bench up ahead is definitely a tramp, Fiasco thinks. The man on the bench up ahead is wearing a pair and a half of pale blue pyjamas and several raincoats and is periodically pitching forwards into his lap like some waterfowl to feed at the end of what is, Fiasco confidently surmises, some quality trampagne nesting between his legs. Fiasco is considering sitting next to the man on the bench and 'assuming his place' in society.

He adjusts his walk to align with the bench. Drawing closer he tries to casually swerve away upon seeing the man's bleeding hand. It doesn't work. The tramp with the fucked up hand bleeding in his lap looks up at Fiasco. We know you, he says, standing.

The tramp with the fucked up hand points towards the lighthouse.

> – Again and again. And again I'm
> nobody, you see. I'm nobody. You're
> nobody either. Remember? All the
> bodies. So many bodies. In the sea. In
> time. We're already here. There. You're
> nobody, no body, nobody, no body
> remembers.

The tramp with the fucked up hand nods and then sits down on the bench. The tramp with the fucked up hand begins to scream. He doesn't seem able to stop.

Fiasco backs away, sketched out, his good hand balling into a fist just in case.

Fiasco is still walking over an hour later, his pace having slowed, his body having succumbed to the flashlight of pain strobing along his nerves. He's nearly at Henry's now. He's exhausted.... feels caught up in his own skin, weighted by its drag and proliferation, a skeleton rushed against a mouldering dam of flesh. The soup of blood in his mouth seems to have grown its own freshly set skin. Fiasco's tongue moves around the blood's tentative consistency to break it, to stir the skin into a hello, into a swallowing nod at the people he passes. There are parents with kids on their way to the park whose eyes he can't meet.

He walks down the hill to Henry's house. He stops at the door. Now what?

Fiasco can't make it through a window like this, that much is obvious. There are too many people around and the swell of his arm is beginning to freak him out. He tries to let go of his arm to knock but the pain is too much. He leans his forehead against the door. He butts his head three times against the wood. Each knock is gentle but incrementally built, the head sizing up the door. Fiasco draws his neck back in preparation for a fourth and final effort. This is the one. Stepping back something cold and fluttering tumbles past his kneecap and gets caught in the cap of his trouser leg. He stops. Fiasco shakes his foot and the keys spill out.

– Hallowed be MY name, Fiasco thinks

*

Henry is half asleep and navigating a three dimensional labyrinth within his mind that's thinly rowed and purple treed when the sound of a waterfall— followed by the creaking of his bedroom door— collapses the walls and trees therein one after the other until there is only the fuzzy near dark of his eyelids and a thin pass of colluding light expanding in front of him as his eyes and brain languidly succumb to some deeply buried curiosity about the world. He opens his eyes to see Fiasco standing in the doorway winking and grinning at him. Fiasco holds his clawed hand up in an 'O' then saws the space inside that 'O' with his other hand's forefinger. He removes his foot from the door and backs away. Fiasco's face is a mask of backtracking pain as he exits, as if the obscene gesture had cost him more than Henry could know. Henry gets halfway through a thought/amorphous feeling about that before re-orientating himself in the lost aspect of his now subtly turned dream.

Next to him Evelyn is on the moon in hers, resting in its craters, the world a beach ball impossibly balanced on the tip of her nose. In her dream Evelyn is suddenly terrified by the beach ball's deflations, its inward lunged suck. She wakes up gasping, reaches for the bottle of water in her bag and accidentally pulls it over, emptying its contents. She falls back asleep.

Fiasco is walking down the stairs, 'real life' he thinks. He goes to the fridge and searches it for alcohol. Surprisingly, he finds some.

He sits down on the sofa with a 6 pack. He puts the six-pack in his lap. He pulls a beer from the six-pack by gripping one beer between his knees and pulling the remainder of the pack with his good arm. He places the depleted pack next to him on the sofa. The chosen beer stands up in his lap like an erection. Fiasco reaches into his crotch with his good hand and pulls back the ring pull while parting his knees slowly and lifting the can from the rim with the same clawed hand that is pulling back the ring pull. There is that pssht sound and its imagined sustain within Fiasco's mind and then there is nothing but the throat bellowed with beer and the can swinging back against his palm with a soft pat.

Satisfaction, Fiasco thinks.

It's more ironic than bitter or rather it's too resigned and comically tired to be anything but a skewed appearance of bitterness's energy. He laughs out loud.

He'll repeat this thought and laughter a few more times in his memory, the meaning of them both capable of being variously and differentially graphed, before lying down on the sofa, half finished can of beer directly sighted on the oddly nice coffee table, and sleeping there. Fiasco's hurt wrist sticks out from the sofa like a broken oar in the staidly pooled air of the sitting room.

*

Henry is pretending to be asleep as Evelyn pulls the pile of her clothes into brief comets of colour across the peeling façade of the wall. She tiptoes out and down the hallway, clothes wadded under her arms, wondering where the phone is hidden. Who's that snoring on the couch?

Henry, having imagined or misheard some errant creak in the house as the sound of the front door opening and closing, rolls over and reaches under the bed. He feels at a book, it is slightly damp and palm sized. He lifts it up. Henry is already frowning so that when he tries to frown again on seeing the unfamiliar notebook his eyes close and he feels a profound and worrying sense of mental displacement and possible retardation.

The door stirs the room. Evelyn enters and sits on the bed. Henry's already rolled over on his side, the notebook hidden and cool against his chest like a muscle. Quite why he's finding it necessary to pretend to be asleep escapes him. He's well practised at it though, it's like hiding in a cave and imagining there are giants outside, only his face is the cave and the world is only one thing. Evelyn's looking at his face, probably, he thinks. He starts to make vague waking sounds, stirring slightly and then falling back from wakefulness into sleep, travelling away from her. His face and the stopper of his mouth a stone he makes murmur.

Evelyn looks out of the window, dangling her bag between her legs. She reaches into it and whisks her hand around its contents. Vague objects turn and repeat on her fingertips. She pinches one or two of them. Inconclusive.

She's peering into the lip of the bag when the duck honk of the taxi disturbs her. She pulls her things together, takes a look at Henry, closes her eyes, and breathes out in a controlled sigh. She opens her eyes and leaves.

Evelyn's dress and hair are bedraggled, her body's ephemera mixing with the taxi's air. She smells of a sweat upon beach, doggy, her forearms and thighs damp and chaffed, the cuffs of her jacket and elbows studded with sand felted in suspicious circlets. She doesn't get why Henry was pretending to be asleep before she left. She could have said something, though, could have 'woken' him. She digs her hand into her rucksack. Where is that book? He must have been pretending, either way he'd chosen to be asleep, she's sure of it. Why would he do that? She's angry and worst of all her thoughts have started to take on Henry and Fiasco's cadences and that simply don't augur well... or something.

Shit, I must have lost it.

– Hey, this your house?

–

– This very one?

– Yes

– This your house yes? Do you know the time?

– Sorry?

– Your father, you must worry your father. You are sorry? I am sorry. He is sorry. You not so much.

– I worry my father?

– You worry your father. Cost money

too no doubt.

– Are you asking me if I worry my father?

– Your father, he worried. Made his own mistakes, probably. But you, you worry your father. Now. No support. You see yourself clearly yes? This is what I'm saying. It is very clear to me now and I repent as a father myself for the feelings that had overcome me before when this man sat here and I had thought him the very lowest of beasts

– Listen how much?

– But have you ever considered the cost?

– It can't be over a tenner

Evelyn closes the door, thinks: this is something I can tell Henry and Fiasco. Dammit.

Lawrence doesn't turn around as Evelyn clatters through the door, kicking off her shoes and tracking clotted sand into the room. Evelyn lifting each ankle in turn to unpeel damply socked feet. Her bare feet sinking into the soft sponge of the carpet. The brandy bottle is fully visible on the table with the fading walnut finish to the left of him. She sees it. Lawrence's expression is hidden but the mood of the room isn't. Evelyn doesn't know, or have any way of guessing, that Lawrence has been crying. Or that his sobs, intermittently suppressed then issued forth, have brayed Lawrence's gums horsey. Lawrence in fact having had cause to fashion a bridle rein from his biro. To bite down on something real.

> – Dad?
> – Dad?
> – Dad?
> – Ri've had a brit of a shock.
> – What's wrong with your voice? Why won't you turn around?
> – I've been very rwarried. I'm rangry.
> – What?

Lawrence takes a spittle covered biro out of his mouth and places it on the table with the fading walnut finish. He turns to face her briefly.

> – I'm angry, I've been worried.
> – What's wrong with you dad?

Lawrence, looking away for effect,

> – What is wrong with you?

Lawrence becoming aware that the biro has leaked when he sees the oily crack in its middle leaking on the table. He feels with his hands and tongue around the damp corners of his mouth. His mouth black and purple, downward smeared. In his white dressing gown he resembles a Pierrot clown gone to domestic seed. He is too drunk for this to throw him off now.

> – Where's Diane?
> – This is about you and where you have been and what you do. Where have you been?
> – With friends.
> – And what did you do with your friends?
> – Well to start with we all had unprotected sex on the railway line and then after we jammed bloody needles into our clits to make sure. What do you think?
> – I can smell you from here. What have you been doing?
> – I can smell you from here. I can't believe you're drunk at this time. I'm so unbelievably fucking angry at you right now.
> – Who are you?
> – What?
> – You're no child of mine.
> – I'm tired, I'm going to bed. I can't even look at you right now.
> – I'm sorry, I'm so sorry…

Lawrence listens for the slam of her door but hears none. He thinks about that top drawer. He wonders what Evelyn will say and what he will say and what Diane might silently think or publicly do. What tone of air might crumple from her lungs and in front of whom her reaction might tumble. He wonders and wonders. Lawrence reaches out and cradles the brandy in his empurpled hand, fingers running up its body. He thumbs the cap from its neck as if the stopper were a knot of stress to be massaged free. Lawrence wearily rolls the glass around in his palm, 'aerating it', the liquid moving in an embarrassing bath time slosh out of the glass. Lawrence puts the bottle down and dabs the spillage with the side of his finger. He brings his fingers to his lips and shushes at the table. His teeth run purple.

A bird flies into the window. Lawrence thinks 'huh.' He walks to the window. The bird is flapping around on the floor. It turns onto its back and starts applauding him. There's bird blood on the window. The bird's heart stops beating, its wings arrowed up in prayer. Lawrence sips his brandy. The sky becomes overcast. The room dips into grey but Lawrence remains at the window lifting the brandy to his eyes, looking out through a world he's willing sepia. Lawrence remaining outside of it in the brilliant white of his fear.

*

Henry's in bed flicking admiringly through the

pages of the notebook. The notebook's prose was, to Henry's befogged eyes and low lit mind, a mixture of these awesomely overwrought passages of existential desperation coupled with weirdly analytical authorial interjections that tried to posit the biographical how and reasoning why of the rambling pseudo narrative contained therein.

These interjections succumbing as the notebook went on to the 'impossibility of understanding' and the authorial interjections, so calm and assertive of cause at the start, quickly devolved into a series of questions ending in the last few pages with a flick book series of increasingly desperately scrawled why's and quick unexplained exclamation marks that contained in the brevity of their stroke a mad velocity of unreason.

If it hadn't all been written in the same brusque seeming handwriting Henry might have initially thought of the text as notes for a kind of psychological case study. As for the actual story, if there is one, he's lacking the capacity to pay it any kind of real attention. Still, he's sufficiently charmed to make a fairly educated guess at the narrative. There's something about a disappearance and a curse and a mysteriously sad child and a lighthouse surrounded by stags of rock. His guess is that the detective, the one investigating, is going to begin to be drawn into the main body of the text.

It's this framing device of the detective investigating and judging the notebook's 'author' that is instantly intriguing to Henry. It suggests that though the rest of the novel was kind of hermetic in its sincere lack of emotional proportion the inbuilt criticism of this other narrator provided a way out of, or at least a parallel, to the angst, to this 'failed sublime', though there was, he'd later come to believe, a substitute for depth in this alternation, in the endless counter to contact of suggestion. Still later, he'd come to appreciate the gravitational pull the two narratives exerted on one another. In the end it wouldn't mean anything, like a memory that you're sure was a dream and so inconsequential, forgettable. He's feeling that meaninglessness now as his comedown starts in earnest, as the tentative and vulnerable preserves of his body start to force their usually invisible labour into his sense of self. The emotionally worrying shape of their demands amassing exponentially in his mind before suddenly ceasing at their peak though they have in fact only retreated, are waiting, biding their time, in some neutral conclave of battered kidney to revolt again.

Fiasco's sat up on the sofa trying to fashion a sling from the six pack's plastic rings as Henry lopes into the room, notebook wedged underneath toxic armpit, face blanched and tribally scored with pillow marks. Fiasco loops one distended hole around his head and pulls it gently down around his neck. He forces his swollen forearm through the bottom left hole and wincingly lets the weight of his arm slowly bungee the plastic. It's pure theatre.

Fiasco acknowledges Henry with jaw jut, nod, and the start of a winding vowel that dives voraciously into chatter.

> – What would you call your autobiography?
> – Portrait of the artist as a postmodern young man. It'd be a cleft roman. You?
> – 'Fiasco Shrugged' It'd have a picture of me and then a cut out of everyone's face that I've ever known on my back.
> – Bringing you down.
> – They're my burden.

Henry's wondering if reading Dostoyevsky has condemned his personality.

> – I'm wondering if reading Dostoyevsky has condemned my personality.
> –
> – Condemned, get it? You can tell me about your arm now
> – I think it represents a definitive break with my family.
> – I don't think that break's purely representational though. It may be approaching the limb in itself.

– I don't like doctors
– Who likes doctors? Only women in sitcoms.
– That was a pretty sitcom line in itself
– You think so? Thanks.
– I'm still not going. So, ha, what happened with your sister?
–
– Nothing?
– Not much.
– Oh, so it's not much now is it?
– We messed around a bit. It got weird quickly.
– Why?
– The obvious reasons.
– She's not actually your sister.
– Yeah but she's really young and I've known her since she was little. That's weird.
– So it's a moral question, is what you're saying?
– I'm… ugh…is this normal? I feel like shit off a stick.
– I think you're using that phrase wrong, do you even know what it means?
– Use it in a sentence?
– It's going like shit off a stick. It went like shit off a stick. Emphasis on the shit. So, what are we thinking off-license or pub?
–

– Pub then hospital?

– As much as that's a respected and time honoured tradition and while I do, as you well know, very much advocate tradition

– Oh yeah, of course, your love of tradition is well documented, there's been 'some talk' of it in recent times

– Well, even with that in mind, I still think we should go Hospital then Pub. Think of it as a continuum and not a starting point.

– But we've been to sleep.

– Meaning?

– We brought a unit of our experience of time to an end.. the night is over. We're starting all over again. We've got to ready ourselves for the onslaught now.

– We're going to the hospital sober. Also the night is eternal…or something

– Will there be needles?

–

– There's no fucking way I'm going.

– Your hand looks like dead uncooked liver that's started to develop nails or something. I swear your thumb looks like a single pygmy tooth developing in the midst of some suffering meat.

– Fuck off. This hand is going to well pull a Prometheus.

– There's blood in there, see in that hard

little pouch that's just ballooned there
– Prometheus frowns. You mean this bit here?
– Yeah when you touch it like that it looks like it should wobble but it doesn't.
– What fluid is that?
– I dunno, liquid bruise?
– I feel wretched. You still look bongoed.
– I'm thinking your hand would make a pretty cool photo for an album.
– An album by who?
– By us
– Which us?
– Smart dumb punk us.
– I always felt that was closer to the truth than intellectual pseudo punk us.
– Pseudo intellectual punk us is my favourite.
– Why aren't we a metal band?
– A general lack of proficiency, the way we play you'd think we hated sound.
– Sound and time, especially time. I fucking hate time.
– We should take a photo. Can we do that?
– C'mon have I ever had a camera?
–
– Yeah, that's right, that one time…and what happened?

– We took pictures of ourselves smashing your room and then we smashed the camera by throwing it against the wall.

– That was with our old drummer right?

–

– Why did we do that?

– We decided that the visual world was a lie and that a record of a lie had to be crushed

– That was during our disability phase?

– Yep, specifically our 'fuck the eye' phase.

– Talking of images, I saw this apocalyptically weird looking tramp on the way here.

– Yeah?

– He was getting very excited about the lighthouse

– Phallically excited?

– Fearfully excited…phenomenally excited you could say.

– But might you?

– Firstly I'm disturbed by your line of questioning. Secondly he had these fucked up fingers and he was claiming to recognize me… this was not your run of the mill tramp.

– Hands like yours?

– No, it was just the tips that were bleeding and all torn off. He sketched me right out.

– How old was he?

– Trying to guess a tramps age is like imagining what your lung really looks like.

– So not young?

– No, actually i don't remember his face at all. Why?

– No reason.

– So I've been meaning to ask, what's *that*?

– Were the italics in your voice necessary?

– Sadly I didn't even mean to do that.

– It's something I found.

– Pass it here.

*

Diane has received at least three to four more marriage proposals phrased as grammatical commands in a desperate voice from Lawrence over the last few hours. Since she had arrived back to see his gothic countenance swaying in the window. The last marry me had been smooshed syllabically into a pillow that she'd neatly traded for her stomach in a single deft switch. The switch thoughtfully timed with her breath so as not to wake Lawrence. That and to preserve the integrity of the drool threading out from his mouth so as to avoid any spatter coding itself onto her skirt. The drool like a line let out with each slacked promise of love. Diane's white top an index of their boggy mass. She stands up and looks around the room and then leaves the room.

Jude peers into the room. He had heard a sound of some heavily rotten, organic thing, being plunged into a larval hum and had wanted to investigate, to know it. He pushes the door fully open, feels the stale air backdrafting towards him. Lawrence is coughing and drooling and trying now to hide his head away as Jude approaches. Jude sits on the bed and takes hold of Lawrence's hand. Lawrence's other hand moulds around the surface of Jude's. Jude looks at the hands. He puts all his emotion into them. He honestly couldn't say whose is whose. Another hand gently weights his shoulder. He turns and follows the stream of flesh, the rivulets of fingers pooling into the reservoir of her kinked wrist that gently brushes across his face.

Diane knows now, it's ok. It is all going to be ok.

Is that the phone?

*

    – Hello
    – er hi, is that Evelyn?
    – Yeah it's me

– Oh hey it's Henry

– I know

– What? Er sorry. I'm not so good on the phone. I hate hospitals. What you up to?

– Not much, the house is kind of crazy. Where are you, did you say…

– It's loco huh?

– Crazy will do, it is not as fun as loco

– Ha, I'm at the hospital with Fiasco

– Shit, what happened?

– All our families are taking Shakespearean turns at sucking. Hey, did you leave a book at my house?

– I might have

– Is it yours?

– If it's the one I think it is then I found it at the lighthouse.

– Really, You didn't write it did you?

– What?

– …

– Why?

– There are characters in it that could be us

– Shut up. What are you talking about?

– Do you want to meet up today? We're going to the Crows in a bit.

– That place is a dive.

– Nah, it's what you're into, it's what you're about. You've got to see this book, come by in a few hours if you can. Bye

– Why were you pretending to be asleep

earlier?

The light on the phone has already marked its transition to red with a short high pitched beep that simply disappeared, rather than faded, by the time she got the words out to no one. The emergent dial tone as monotonous as her sense of bewilderment. Evelyn looks at the phone, what the... what is he talking about? Did she even hear him right? Is she hearing it now?

She walks back up the stairs and past the room where Jude, bound by the loving arms thrown loosely around him, watches her disappear in a heartbeat.

In her room now, locked and secure, space repurposed with the sound of the Jesus and Mary Chain, Evelyn sits on the bed and reaches for her top drawer. She removes the strategically positioned vibrator from the bed of clothes there. It was meant to act as a kind of nuclear deterrent to any breaches of trust, a sort of mutually assured destruction that would still leave the real secret and big questions intact and untold. It had evidently worked. She notices the stain on her underwear.

Someone had been looking through her things.

Dad. He must have been looking for something. Drugs?

She feels around the bottom of the drawer until her fingers alight on a thin wooden box. Lifting a pile of delicates she extracts the box by the lid which hinges perilously open, revealing in its swing a large plastic baggy containing three other baggies of various sizes that contain in turn about a quarter of weed plus a packet of tobacco and rizlas, three to four more pills, and her locked diary. She takes out the baggie with her diary and her weed and then, after a minute's pause, shoves the pills in her pocket as well. She rolls a joint and smokes it by the window, her eyes inadvertently drifting down the hill and in the direction of her mother's grave.

She tamps out the joint on the window sill, sprays some cheap perfume around her bedroom, takes a long shower. She goes and knocks on Jude's door and then opens it. He's asleep as usual. Typical teenager, Diane would say. Not quite.

– Are you pretending to be asleep?

Jude rolls over grinning, his mouth wet at its peaks. He's pretty much in love with Evelyn. Everyone knows it. He's happiest around her and Henry though the differences in this happiness tend to be glossed over, ironed out, by everyone around him which proves frustrating for Jude in ways he's still struggling to come to terms with.

– Thanks Jude, thanks a lot. You know what's going on with my Dad and your mum?

Jude gets up, his hands fastening around his

wrists. He has something he wants to say. Whatever it is makes him cradle the air. He can't get it out. They stand looking at each other.

 – Seems about right.

Evelyn smiles, kisses Jude on the cheek, and leaves.

She is walking downhill towards The Crows. Her hair is tied up, still wet after the shower she'd taken while stoned. The air in the house once she'd got out seemed to have softened, she thinks. There was a quietness to things not even sound could have displaced.

She walks with her head down against a wind frosting her brain into forked thought, persistent pain. The concrete has the look of elephant skin, a near dead elephant dreaming of water, and the sky behind her is the colour of a flayed peach and she doesn't know what to think about anything at all, really. All that intimacy and then…this.

She told herself it was last night, the chemicals, some bullshit about liking someone. She blinks out a tear or two. That's probably just the wind or something.

The black shed-like building of The Crows rises into view, entrenched by benches topped with snapped umbrellas the colour of washed-out bird shit. She walks past a man, his head lolling and his body inclined to the roadside, teaching the infrequent traffic to trace around the possibility of his fall.

The clientele of The Crows, she knew, primarily consisted of alcoholics, a good thirty five to forty percent of whom had, in the past, displayed overtly violent tendencies which in turn had led to them being barred from every other licensed establishment in an eight mile radius.

She knew all this because Lawrence had for years been trying to get the place shut down. Years ago he had taught her the word 'blight' in describing it.

The problem was that the Crows' regulars, who accounted for ninety nine percent of their business, knew they had nowhere else to go. Unless they moved to another town they'd have to, if barred from The Crows, resort to drinking in parks, small lame ones cordoned off like a playpen or, worse, at home amongst their families if they had any. They were on, as far as they could manage and mostly unconsciously, their best behaviour.

Evelyn stands outside. She lights a cigarette then smokes it without thinking anything at all. She crushes the cigarette out. Everything comes back to her.

She takes a breath.

*

Fiasco, slung hand teased around shoulder, strides towards the pub cajoling Henry who stands, staring out from within the rust of his hangover, torpidly contemplating a grey square of weathered pavement the way he's read other people might a Rothko. Except what he's experiencing is only the organ groan of his emotional possibilities['] organic predicates. A kind of squalid dying as opposed to capital T- Transcendent, capital D- Death... or something.

> – Shit man, is that your dad over there?
> – I don't think so, but umm it could be. Look what it says here...
> – That notebook is cool and all but I need a drink. Hey look, it's the Notorious B R P! Hey Notorious what would you do if you ever met your dad?

The Big Red Pepper aka the head cook, today firmly situated on Carvery duties, stands behind the sneeze guard considering the question. Broken yolks of sweat slide off the curvature of his chin and drop sizzling onto the roast as he leans forward while wiping two large knives against each other mock thoughtfully. Fiasco begins to laugh.

> – Man, are you not amazed by what it says here?
> – I could get into it or something but first I want to know what the Big Red

Pepper would say to his father were he ever see his father again

– I'd walk up to him all grateful looking with genuine tears in my eyes and I'd say 'hey dad, hey daddy, where have you been all my life?' and then I'd knock him the fuck out.

– I knew it, haha, I knew it.

– I don't think I'm going to do that, Henry says

– You want me to?

– That's very kind Notorious B.R.P but no or something. I'm not even sure...

– Hey look man, that's Evelyn. Oh man, she looks out of place here.

– Hey Evelyn, Evelyn!

– Oh fuck, that's the Big Red Pepper's Dad coming in behind her. Shit, he looks proper drunk.

– How do you know that's the Big Red Pepper's dad?

– He's been coming in lately

– But when the BRP said that if he ever saw him again, I thought it meant that

– They fight every time. It's like one all. Where is the Big Red Pepper?

– Shit, he's over there. So what you're saying is

– Yep, this has all the qualities of a potential decider

– What's going on?

– He's over there drinking Sambuca, the
Big Red Pepper has been drinking
sambuca! It's going to kick off.
– Hey guys
– Sorry Evelyn, I think
– HEY DAD, HEY DADDY, WHERE
HAVE YOU BEEN ALL MY

A chorus of OOOHs fills the room as the Big
Red Pepper gets knocked back against the bar.
Evelyn turns and hurries towards Henry and
Fiasco.

– What the...
– Hey man, we should maybe...

The Big Red Pepper turns now, unfurling his
girth across the bar, grabbing something from
behind the counter, the bottle almost hidden in
his palms, the neck of it poorly disguised by the
long sleeves of his chef whites. BRP Senior, who'd
recoiled from the force of the blow he'd managed
to land in on his son, follows in now barrelling
towards 'the *overgrown sperm'* of his son.

The Big Red Pepper though has only been
playing possum and he brings the bottle in his
hand across in a wide curve of warning. A
mixture of alcoholic sweat and osmotic hog fat
have, however, created a greasy resin around the
entirety of the Big Red Pepper's skin. The Big Red
Pepper in truth is almost waterproof with fat and
the slippery lacquer over his slick slurred skin
causes the bottle to turn in lucid right angles out

of the palm of his hand and towards his father's face.

The clunk of the bottle erases the room as it slips from the Big Red Pepper's hand, connecting with the ear and jaw of his father but cracking only as it hits the floor.

Improbably BRP Senior's still standing though he's holding his ear and making wet lumpy sounds. The pub is a mixture of hyenas and the agog. Men stand with their necks jutting out over their pints. A collective decision is being made though what'll end up being decided is, as usual, only the directional flow of aggression split seconds in the making.

– His own old man, disgraceful.

Running forward now, breaking through the ranks, desperate to avoid the brewing cataclysm, the Saturn bellied landlord with short legs and tiny tapering feet, fag in mouth, tries to intervene. He's caught by the hammer clawed bone of BRP Senior's elbow rising up to ward off any potential pacifistic concern, blood slapping out of the landlord's nose and onto the floor as his mouth fumbled cigarette belly flops into the puddle of sambuca that snorts greedily up the trouser seam of Big Red Pepper Senior who crashes now around the bar, winged with flame, as BRP Jr tries to catch and smother his father with his flame retardant whites though the fire is spreading around them, has grown hungry enough to sustain and sift through the waves of beer slapping down upon it. The Big Red Pepper and another regular succeed in dragging the now charred BRP senior to a table at the side.

The Big Red Pepper's father drinks heavily from a pint someone else has kindly let the Big Red Pepper proffer in their stead. The fire however is stubbornly persistent and beginning to demonstrate a fairly rapacious attitude towards the rotting beams of wood, scaling them like ivy.

– No need to worry

The newest alcoholic in the room strides forth like an amateur colossus. He aims the fluted nozzle of the extinguisher at the heart of the fire. It lets out a fart and a dribble of foam.

– Get another one

Another one is thrown to him. The newest alcoholic in the room depresses the handle. The extinguisher whines the air.

  – Ice bucket. Ice bucket!
  – Shirl, It's just over there Jesus.

Fiasco reaches around the bar and pulls out a bottle of Jack Daniels as the barmaid grabs the large tub of scum drenched water instantly slopping three quarters of it around her heels. The flames continue to make progress around the perplexed regulars most of whom have yet to *make a stand* for their own lives and remain seated if increasingly focused. Fiasco's balancing the bottle of jack in his sling, as he tries to explain why they ought to exit quick smart.

> – There'll be a stampede when they remember.
> – What are you talking about?
> – They all got used up at last new years.
> – What did?
> – The fire extinguishers. Everyone was racing each other on the chairs. Almost everyone in that room was there. It's going to dawn on them like a motherfucker in a minute.
> – I don't want to be here.
> – Sorry Evelyn.
> – Yeah, we're definitely going now.
> – Where?
> – Let's decide outside no? Or we hang around here waiting for a subtler if more chaotic atmosphere to loot in?
> – It's a nice evening. I'm just saying we could sit outside somewhere and that we should be mindful of where that place is.
> – LET'S GO. SERIOUSLY.

*

Diane and Lawrence are in the front room. Lawrence is sipping herbal tea. He has one of Evelyn's baby blankets coddling his midriff.

Helene loves him and they're going to get married. Jude comes down the stairs, enters the room. His hands are dirty but no one takes note. He sits down in front of Lawrence. Diane gets out a pack of illustrated cards and kneels on the floor just across from Jude. She begins to lay them out, face down on the carpet. They are going to play pairs. Happy families might have proven too complex. They should have done this more often, at least as much as they suggested, Diane thinks.

Jude picks up one of the thick wooden cards, second row left of middle, and yawns. The picture on the card is of the Incredible Hulk defenestrating a tank in a military compound. He picks up another from the upper right corner. They're not of the same suit, this card depicting Thor having just released or beckoning his hammer from its position in the foreground of the picture. The enlarged, rectangular, winterish grey base of the hammer positioned in the foreground of the picture suggesting that it is has been aimed at or is being retrieved from the card's viewer. Jude still finds this awesome.

– Go again Jude.

Jude looks up and gives his mother a withering look and returns both the cards. He picks up the card second from left in the first row. It matches the first card he took of the Incredible Hulk defenestrating a tank in a military compound that increasingly resembles a car-park. He looks down at the cards for the position of his first choice. The cards jigsaw and multiply. He can't remember. Jude turns over the card in the upper right corner. The flat of his fist smashes down on the floor in frustration. Lawrence places a hand on Jude's trembling shoulder.

– My go now Jude

Lawrence picks the card second from the left in the first row, stretching his hand forward and flipping it neatly between two fingers. He leans back against the chair. Jude turns and looks at him, his face disconsolate and exhausted looking, the energy in them harried and scratched to pieces as they watch Lawrence stroking his chin confidently. Still, there's something about the way Lawrence is stroking invisible hairs beyond his chin, which soothes him.

Lawrence moves forward again, resuming his ogreish stance over Jude's shoulder, and points to the card just right of the middle in the second row making out that he can't quite reach it and gesturing for Jude to turn it over for him. Jude sighs and turns over the card to reveal Iron Man, replete with traditional Hawaiian lei necklace, blasting out of a volcano with a grass skirted baby in his arms. Lawrence widens his eyes, slaps his forehead head comically and squeezes his cheeks between his two hands. Jude looks at Lawrence and lets out a stuttering laugh. Lawrence lets out a long 'nooooooo' that tips Jude into hysterics. 'Noooo', Lawrence repeats as his fingers cage around the escaping sound, closing at their tips over the bridge of his nose, all ten of them pointing downwards now at the correct card left from middle in the second row. He rocks back and forth so that Jude can follow the not quite subliminal message he's aiming to impart.

-Nooo, no, no. It's your go now. Still, you won't get it. You can't find it. You can't

Jude, laughing, quickly turns the two cards back over. He turns the card left of middle in the second row around, letting out a yelp of pleasure at seeing the Incredible Hulk defenestrating a tank in a military compound that resembles a car park. Jude brings both hands together around it and beams triumphantly at Lawrence.

Diane says, go on Jude you can do it.

Jude looks back at the cards in the first row. His body stiffens. A long moan conceives itself in a flash of neurons, the weight of its crossing over into his body bringing Jude's face tensely sloping down, his mouth crimping at the edges, forehead crumbling. He has glimpsed something sad and dark at the limits of his understanding and it has followed him back. Lawrence glances at Diane

-Aha, you'll never find it! I will win, mwah haha

He says, gently shoulder barging Jude so that Jude falls left and forward, his hand alighting on the card second from left in the first row. Jude looks furiously back at Lawrence who looks up and stares at the ceiling and whistles, his eyes dropping down to flick from Jude's confused and angry face to the card trapped under his hand.

Jude catches one of Lawrence's glances. He remembers his hand. He looks at his hand and then at Lawrence. He thinks about what could be underneath them both. He's got it. He picks up the second Hulk and lifts it like a trophy at Lawrence whose head drops between his hands.

Diane observes Lawrence as he looks up smiling gently at her. She can see all the kindness in him, there beneath his face that too often closes around it disclosing nothing. She thinks of the three of them in sunlight, holding hands, maybe even in Tuscany. She sees Lawrence's face, happily clowning, playing the buffoon, the gentleman tourist dressed inappropriately for the weather but happy and in love. She sees it and it is real but it will never happen, not purely like that at least. It's enough for her to have seen though.

People have trouble accepting the kind of kind they are, she thinks.

– Jude, we're getting married and I want you to live with us, if you want to?

*

– Are we turning into Goths? I think I'm going.

– Because of the ghosts?
– Yes, but also because I'm not a Goth and I don't particularly like hanging out in graveyards. I think I might just head off.
– And the whisky?
– Pass me your pint glass.

Fiasco tips about a half pint of whisky into the pint glass and then downs it. He pours out another half pint for Henry and keeps the little that remains in the bottle. He turns on his heels.

– Where are you going?
–

Henry and Evelyn sit on a nudge of grass three to four feet from her mother's grave. They watch as Fiasco passes through a bank of willow trees, tearing down their branches with bad tempered yanks, his left hand occasionally disappearing as he puts the bottle to his mouth.
– Is he ok?
– He's had a rough day. You want some of this?
– Maybe later. You want some of this?
– Yes.
– You roll up.
– I can't very well, you better.
They're sat alternately sunned and shaded by the cloud shattered sky on a bank of grass that rises like a dune and rings the graveyard. The distant, fencing willow trees rise mournfully in

their direction, bustled by a wind that eventually upends her Rizla, spilling its cradled contents over the crease of her jeans and onto the damp earth. She leans forward foraging for tobacco and pot in the long grass. Henry turns Evelyn's Walkman around in his hands, unwinds the headphones and sticks one in his ear and tries the other in Evelyn's who says hey and bats his hand playfully away. Henry insists though and Evelyn relents letting him press the machinic pebble of it into the runic gap of her ear.

> – There's no tape in there, she says licking the gummed edge of the joint and smiling, there's some tapes in there though.

She lights the joint and passes it to him, pulls the bag containing the tapes in front of her. He clicks down on the play button. Evelyn looks up at him and he passes the joint back to her. There's a whir and a grind and then nothing. They notice the silence and then the grains of non-silence composing it. Henry raises his eyebrows and nods towards the graveyard. Rabbits appear in front of them like disparate beats of nature before springing scattershot towards ridged turf, their skeletons elongating under muscle lubed skin as they pour into the ground. All around animals call to each other without voices, with scent and choreography.

Evelyn stops looking for a tape, though she hadn't at all been looking but instead feeling around in the bag that contained them, her gaze trained on the graveyard and trammelled by the potential heat of Henry's. She takes her hand from her bag.

Her eyes stop on her mother's grave. A rabbit sniffs the stone. She blinks, it disappears. She passes the joint over to Henry. He hadn't been looking at all.

Evelyn rubs her eyes, opens her mouth.

> – Whenever I see a rabbit I think how detachable their skin is. How much of their face survives.
> – That's psychotic Evelyn
> – Ha, you think so? I just mean in comparison to a human face
> – A skinned human face?
> – It's just like a wet sack… from what I've gathered.
> – From private research? I'm horrified.
> – No, from horror films.
> – It's weird having a body, I guess, like being stranded in time.
> – Or something?
> – Nah, really.
> – Tell me
> – What?
> – Well… I didn't understand what you said, elaborate

    – Ugh, I'm embarrassed.

    – No, go on.

Henry wants to bring up the notebook, what he thinks he's seen in it, but he doesn't know how, doesn't have the 'Goddamned tact' as one of his too obvious heroes might say. Also he knows something is expected of him now… plus he feels humiliated. He'd said something he meant insincerely instead of something he didn't mean sincerely. He might have said something he meant with insincere bravado and that might just have worked but he hadn't and now who knows what he must look like. That stranded in time line he came out with, what the fuck was that? It sounded so tritely poetic. He meant it though, he could explain. He could. Ugh. Fuck, he thinks.

    – Umm, he says.

He's so clumsy, she thinks.

    Here it goes.

        – Well I guess it seems strange to be so locatable and at the same time have no real sense of proportion. Also mentally, you're here in your head right? But that voice isn't you, it's just like some organizing principle, a bureaucrat. That's my theory. And then also there's that feeling sometimes, the kind of thought that is a space and it's nowhere and it seems like such a distance from this place that doesn't exist to the outside world. So yeah, having a body or being aware of having a body is weird, makes it some kind of threshold for itself. As for time…don't get me started. I remember…someone said it was like a big picture and we're like one encrypted pixel in it or something.

– Are you still religious?

– Are you still on medication?

– A fair bit, yes.

– Sorry, I didn't mean to. It's a bit of a sensitive…

– It's ok, but are you? I'm just curious

– Nah, I mean. I've sort of talked about it with Fiasco and I think I still have a religious 'character' but as far as god goes I go or something.

– What?

– My character is always religious but without a belief. Like I still believe in something transcendent. I just don't know what it is.

– And Fiasco, what's his character?

– He's a fervent believer in his service to and consequent exile from reality, both taking the form of an angelic crime, but at the same time he feels the absence of the god he wants to kill. He's a young but world weary man with a volcanic

soul allied to a defrocked knight of faith.
It's a classic pairing.
– What are we talking about now?
– The characters we'd be if you could
flatten out and siphon the world and our
conflicts into an epic yet coherent
narrative. What's your character?
– I don't think I want one. What are you
going to do next year?

She's a little bored of being on edge plus
Henry's forgetting how to be. He doesn't quite
work without Fiasco, he thinks, gets both carried
away and more contrived. He doesn't think
Fiasco feels the same. He's always Fiasco. This
being the essential oversight of their friendship,
namely Henry's inability or unwillingness to see
beyond Fiasco's character, his performance, and
to see that character as some fixed surface
uninterrupted by event. Fiasco had taught him
the semblance of a shared identity but Henry had
never questioned if the anger that made it
shimmer, that was held in place by Fiasco's
charisma and articulated in humour and
vandalism, might have been sourced somewhere
other than an idea meshed with instinct. Had
never wondered if the magnetic pull hinted at
by this union was the sign of an unattended
implosion out of which his friend radiated, was
broadcast, and if Fiasco might in fact be
somewhere else entirely.

He knew the details of Fiasco's life and their narrative function but not their import or their significance.

What would it take for Henry to realise that other people existed?

Evelyn scratches her arm. Is she bored?

– Just read and get drunk. Hangout with Fiasco and Jude. We figure this summer we'll become writers. It's the cheapest option.
– Do you think you'll always look after him?
– Jude?
–
– It's more like we live together
– mhm
– But yeah, well until the band takes off and then we thought he could come with us on tour, sell t-shirts and that.
– When do you think that will be?
– The end of days?
– How is Jude? He's been spending more time at ours lately.
– He's ok I think. Better. Mum's been keen to spend more time with him, so that's good.
– Can I ask you something about him?
– I guess.
– What happened after he fell? All I know is that he went to hospital, got out,

you found him and then what?

– Do we have to? It was ages ago.

– …

– What?

– I never know anything. Why can't I be part of a conversation? It's fucking annoying.

– They said he was depressed, that he might have been acting out. We all had to meet with a social worker for a few months. Not so much now. They even tried to find my dad.

– Did they?

– That's a mystery. No one ever said. There's this alcoholic in The Crows who Fiasco reckons looks a bit like him i.e me via a lifetime of disappointments but really I don't think he's here. Anyway, we all agreed that it wasn't a good idea to uproot Jude so things were more or less the same except the house is cleaner now.

– It is?

–

– What did the social worker say to you?

– She wanted to talk about careers.

– I thought they were keen for you to study

– Yeah, that too. I was always good at English at school and I'm finishing my a levels after how many years now but I

don't know what I'm going to do. I could
do them and look after Jude at the same
time but now what? The only reason to
go to university would be to get out of
here and I can't.
– Why?
– I don't know anyone who's been to
university. It's weird. Who cares?
– What about Fiasco?
– Fiasco's a genius.
– Would he say the same about you? You
guys just don't want to do anything.
– What can we do? We just want to be
geniuses. We have an understanding
with the future. We don't believe in it, it
doesn't believe in us. There's an accord,
a perpetual. In the absence of the
phenomenal we must be like swill in the
trough of the perpetual. That's…
– It sounds like bullshit
– It's a way to cope but it's also who I
think we are…

Evelyn rolls her eyes, moves closer to him, his
profile obscuring her mother's grave. There's no
one else here, nothing but her loneliness. She
looks up at Henry.
    – Aren't you tired? She asks. Henry turns his
head towards her, tilts his head quizzically. She
leans across and hooks an errant wisp of dyed
black hair over the track of his ear that'd come

loose as he'd shaken his head. Henry's smile crumples. He's a sucker for any kind of tenderness. Evelyn reads this in him, sees it in the metamorphosis of his features, in the sudden reflector of his drowned eye, sees the thought buttoned into the rising emotion.

– Of what?

– Thinking about your self.

– Ouch

She strokes his hair again, flattening her palm against his temples. He moves against the wave of her palm. Eureka. A fat tear escapes the trap of his eye, slicks his cheek almost joyfully.

– Yeah, I am.

Evelyn's fascinated. It's a strange feeling not to be the weakest, to draw strength in relation to another. She doesn't identify this, not right away, there are too many endorphins and too much information to screen for any kind of interpretive insight. Right now, there's only the two of them and these misread feelings of want.

– Sorry it's not very masculine.

– It's not but that's ok.

– Ha, it must be because of yesterday.

– When you're with Fiasco, you're different.

– Better?

– Yeah, that's what I meant.

– He's really the only friend I've got

– I don't think that's true

She tries to kiss him. He's so dumb and stoned he's not sure what she's doing. He eventually kisses her back. She withdraws. Henry feels so fucking grateful that he's sure it must seem repulsive. She leans back in, weights her hand on his chest and... does she know what she is doing? She needs some proof of her life and, so what? So what, she wants to.

*

Lawrence sits on the side of the bed, pulls off his socks and slides into bed. Jude had seemed happy to him, there was that at least. It had made him feel good to hear Diane say it. She had said it so happily, so naturally and of course that kind of emotion is infectious and they had all felt her happiness and been moved by it. The room swayed with joy, he remembers. But Jude's reaction couldn't just be put down to that of course, to the sound of it. Jude understood. Ramifications were grasped, he thinks. Lawrence pulls the sheet under his chin hoping the movement will stave off the thought he can feel building towards articulation: What if he hadn't understood, what if there had been no ramifications grasped, what then?

Lawrence occasionally worrying that he might think that Jude's reaction to 'news' was entirely predicated on the tone of voice his mother employed in the telling. Lawrence deeply afraid that he might believe this on some essential level and in doing so reduce Jude's status within his inner cosmology to that of a pet. It was the worry that had produced the thought, the possibility for the thought, but now it existed to him. He'd renounced the thought the moment it occurred, of course he had, but it had occurred and re-occurred in the immortality of doubt, that is to say possibility, in the shared non-existent space of the infinite and potential. Someone might have something to say about that but why should they? Lawrence wholly distrusted the thought, he loved Jude sincerely, and he couldn't be held accountable for every thought that existed in his head. Could he?

He needs to concentrate, to feel the cool of the sheets, to forget to remember. There was something else maybe, happy thoughts.

Lawrence had been happy downstairs, he remembers. He'd been happy and then he had felt sick, had felt the loathing come on. It had come on all of a sudden, building, hot sick in his chest. He doesn't want to remember why.

He'd looked around at Jude and Diane, he remembers. He hadn't had that thought about Jude then. The room swayed with joy. The light was slow and thick. He was so happy. He'd thought 'family' and then that was it, the turning. He felt ill when he thought it, first on the sofa and now in bed. Hot bile forks his ventricles. Lawrence groans.

He tries to squeeze the thought out through his eyes. Crushed, it only becomes more jagged. Family. There'd been a guilt in that word that he hadn't been strong enough to hold off facing, if strong is the right word. Had he said that to Evelyn? How could he. He had. Where is she now, who is she with? He turns over on the pillow, feels something cool and like a shelled tooth against his cheek. He raises his hand to his face, the hand surfing over what feels like a burst sodden pillow that'd been left out in a drain. A smell to match.

Lawrence opens his eyes to see crow brain peeking through blood-matted feathers, his finger testing the hole, two piercing accusative eyes menacing the life out of his.

*

The sun had already started to set, the graveyard darkening by percentiles in the immediate aftermath, the sad pathetic fallacy of everyday life writ large. Henry had pretty much ejaculated straight away, apologizing as he came then driving his head into the freshly shadowed grass.

She tells him it's ok and it is, kind of. Don't regret, don't worry, it doesn't help. Evelyn willing this for them both. Henry's a carbonating composite of guilt and shame permeated by a weakening field of elation. He doesn't know what to do. He feels so exposed and the fading remnants of his orgasm degrade into abject humiliation. He turns over and stares at a patch of grass between his legs. Don't fucking cry, don't fucking cry. Or cry, go ahead and cry if that's what you are. He looks up at the sky, thinks about the bible, God's wrath. Sodom and Gomorrah.

Evelyn doesn't know what to say. There's no directive here to guide her, for her to read like music. She remembers now why they're here, the strangeness of before bringing into focus the possible lunacy of the moment. She needs reassurance that this wasn't awful, that it was still good, that she could choose.

> – What was all that stuff on the phone?
> – Nothing, it was nothing.
> – It was about that book I found.

– Forget it.
   – Can I have it back? You said I was in it or something?

> – No, it's hard to read but it's definitely
> E and H… and you found it at the
> lighthouse and
> – And what?
> – Well that's where
> – Where what?
> – Where your mum, where she
> – Where she?
> – …
> – No, she died in a traffic accident

– I'm sorry. I, that's not. Don't go.
– Fuck you.

Evelyn stands up, looking furiously past Henry. She didn't want what she had wanted. How many more times? Evelyn walks off.

Henry fumbles around his coat.

– Wait. Take it, you found it.

She turns back and rips the notebook out of Henry's hand. He watches her leave.

*

The sea is a deep noon coloured abstraction. Fiasco's bandaged outline walks across the shore of this darkness leaving tracks he hopes end somewhere mysterious and that someone, anyone at all, might look at and then wonder about the person who made them. Lines of form— his holey shoes and the sea's tattered brim, his hand and the skeleton frames of distant ferries— lean together complicit with the night's crushing of difference. He's tired and clinically lonely, causatively fucked anyway you looked at it.

The pills he lifted from Evelyn's pocket and the bottle of cider he's letting swing from his clawed fingers were two bad ideas relating to a larger overarching instinct for this *type* of bad idea conceived and trained via experiences that were themselves the result of other peoples' bad ideas

and poorly conceived instincts. He wants to sit
down but his legs continue to move habitually
towards some unknown goal. A bench hovers
into view up ahead like a dream staggered with
hope and fears, lit from above, cased in light,
weirdly and evocatively tilted by his hobo shuffle.
He looks up at the street lamp, his blurry eyes
making a ferris wheel of it. It's been waiting for
me, Fiasco thinks. He crosses the sand and climbs
up to the promenade. There's no one around.
He sits down on the bench. The sense of relief is
overwhelming. His body evaporates until a pain
in his hand twinges him forward. Fiasco crouches
over his lap, staring wide eyed at the concrete.
There is a pebble by his foot. He begins to laugh.
He realises he was here, by this very bench, just
this morning. That he's sat exactly where the
tramp was sat and in the same manner, with his
hand balled into the crotch the rest of him is
hunched over. Maybe the pebble was even here
before. He looks toward where he'd come from
this morning and is surprised to feel his face take
on an expectant expression.

What was he expecting? Fiasco laughs at the
thought. To see himself. But he had already seen
himself. He looked because he expected to see
what he had already seen, inside. Time and time
again. He tries to think around that thought.

-No body is nobody.

Fiasco begins to imagine that the tramp with
the fucked up hand he'd seen before was him

from the future, driven mad by crossing timelines, by being everyone, that the tramp with the fucked up hand had briefly recognized his younger self and tried to warn him of, of what? Something. The lighthouse, that boring notebook Henry kept banging on about, Evelyn, himself, Henry, something.

Yeah.

Still there was nothing about the tramp that had seemed familiar this morning, nothing that he could relate to his own experience. Over the years though, with the loss of identity taking its toll, perhaps he had or would grow compassionate and afraid and then, finally, mad. Destined to repeat key events, and in an effort to find his way back to sanity, he'll begin to loop in and out of his current life ending them both.

So that's what's in store, he thinks vaguely amused.

Fiasco extends himself on the bench, stretches out his legs, watches the sea as his vision bobs along the tide of alcohol and drugs. He rides a brief crest of a swampy high, feels the sturdiness of the bench spread underneath him and admires its crudity.

– Cheap seats for the phenomenal, he thinks looking at the sea. He recalls a conversation he had with Henry re: appropriate metaphors for the phenomenal.

Their starting positions had been: Henry for 'the phenomenal inducing potential of outer space, its mortifying distance' versus Fiasco who was arguing for the 'Sea as an analogue for doom, a repository of nightmares and bliss.'

Fiasco felt that the universe was altogether too barren. The phenomenal had to encompass life, the entirety of it, to scrub clean and absolve life of itself.

Seeing as life was never identical with itself, with its expression, life in its unadulterated self-annihilating rapaciousness, its striving, had to constitute a portion of the phenomenal. It thus followed that the phenomenal had to occur within or directly affect or radically alter life even as it left life annihilated in its wake.

For Fiasco, and latterly for Henry then, outer space was awesome but not phenomenal.

The universe, they supposed, was mostly post-phenomenal unless aliens were discovered, they agreed. The sea as the evolutionary source of life coupled with its destructive powers, its shifting surfaces and untold atavistic depths thus better worked as a metaphorical *precedence* for the phenomenal though of course all metaphors for the phenomenal, which was also the death of metaphors, were bound to fail.

– Fail phenomenally.

They hadn't put it all quite like that but they might of. Idiots, he thinks. A half smile rides across his face, a hazy barely intentioned grin that, on closer inspection, is clearly premonitory of the attack he's about to suffer. The grin growing slowly disfigured. Fiasco´s hand throbs from a place he can't identify then spasms materially. His stomach lurches and protests.

Here comes reality.

-Merde

He murmurs this to himself a number of times, his lips lagging behind his thought processes which consequently shut down till there's only a skewed perception of the beach, the sea, the horizon, Henry, himself, humankind in general, the tramp, life et cetera warping around his insides in nauseated, non-pictorial throbs. He vomits wetly. He grips the bottom of the bench and feels something there scrape and puncture his already hurt hand. He's torn the skin off a fingertip on it, the finger coming up red as an ice-pop and stinging. He punches the seat underneath him in wild frustration, near crying until his fist sobs into something, till his fucked up hand aches as something outside of him, as something he might touch with his other fingers and fail to understand. The hand as other.

The pain sobers the nausea for a moment. There's the lighthouse up ahead and a rumble of the train high above and only in his imagination. He needs to see something other than this. He tries to imagine the lighthouse on fire. The lighthouse a tramp's cut open tin-can hat billowing into the sky. He sees the smoke milking the stars then the sound of the train, of a motorbike, of the wind, promises escape. Fiasco looks for it.

The pain of his hand invades and informs the cramp flexing around his stomach. He twists around on the bench, the smear of his sight rendering the lights of the cliff 'mansions' fluid and tracked into the night, the train of them pulling away at light speed as he swivels back towards the sea. He vomits again. Strings of spaghetti dread the bowl of his jaw. He wipes his mouth with his sling then pulls up the bottle of cider he'd bought, washes the vomit out of his mouth and thinks of other places he could be. They're all tv places, the future. He vomits again. He looks down at his sick. It's purple as. Fiasco feels sober now but that's relative. He puts an island of gob into the lagoon blue vomit, watches it fizzle away. His chest jogs through a few shudders of feeling. He pinches his numb hand, tries to lift it tenderly onto his lap. It immediately becomes a claw.

He looks up and watches the thin cord of lights reflected in the water struggle against the crease of waves. He's sick of it. He takes another swig of cider inadvertently piling some into the fold of his lap, marinating his crotch. Fucking hell, enough. There's still some money in his pocket though not enough. Enough for a drink when he got... where?.... He could just skip the train. Anywhere. Enough.

Just leave. There was family in Scotland, on

some remote island maybe. He could join a trawler, live an isolated life and learn how to be quiet, marry an equally quiet woman, then live in near silence in a cabin with his wife.

Fiasco sees his wife helping him with his coat as he enters their cabin, as he comes out of the howling wind and into their simplified space. The snow outside cabled on the window ledge. The snow inside clamped to his boots, breaking into clumps over the carpet as he walked towards the chair nearest the fire. His haul of fish hanging from the hook icily soldered to his hand. She, his wife, would look without reproach at the piles of snow wetting the floor. He would see the chunked ice and look at her face and his muscles would thaw, his blood untwist. He would bend down and pick up the largest chunks of snow with his raw hands and throw them out the still battering door while she swept the melted ice into the hissing fire. They would eat a loaf of bread and a fish soup together at the table and then sit wordlessly by the fire all evening. The two of them warmed by the flames and the fierce unspoken love between them that would, almost imperceptibly, ignite then quickly die down in the damp tinder of their thoughtfully pragmatic gestures.

And Henry, he thinks, where would he be? In another cabin, two and a half days walk away, perhaps with his wife. They'd all see each other once or maybe twice a month at an *inn* equidistant from their cabins.

He wouldn't leave, not yet.

He had to believe in Henry and Henry had to believe in Fiasco. They were best friends. That had to mean something. They could go together.

People that left, for whatever reason, were the worst.

Unlike Henry he'd known other people, had another friend, a friend that left. Left how? He's not sure, drifted from sight somehow and into something unforgiving.

Fiasco had been Henry to that friend. He had borne witness, taken cues.

Henry didn't ask questions, perhaps he didn't know. Fiasco had just appeared that day and declared they were a band though at school they rarely talked outside of that one-shared lesson. Henry had never asked why this was, he just kept telling Fiasco that Fiasco had probably saved his life that day until they both believed it. Why not? It could be true.

He never spoke about his life outside of the story he'd built with Henry. It wasn't about Henry's feelings... he'd probably have found it interesting whereas to Fiasco it was, to some extent, deeply distasteful to think of bringing up. He had become this self with Henry—who he had also been— and he wanted to stay, to change history by refusing time.

Fiasco then, hovering between two avatars of

his self, desperately needed for them both to be ok.

He closes his eyes and then he's lost. The remembered sound of a train wakes him. His knees are underwater and chilled numb. He turns back towards the cliff or he thinks he does, he can't make it out in the darkness. He looks for the light of the houses, of the streetlights failing against the shore. They're so far away he can't tell the true from the false.

He kneels down in the freezing water. He splashes his face.

– This is dogshit. I gotta, I gotta go see Henry.

*

– What is the meaning of this?

Lawrence holds the crow up in the middle of the sitting room. Jude looks at the bird with clear disappointment. He'd wanted it to wake up, to wake up right.

The front door unlatches.

– Evelyn!

Lawrence turns to see her, the crow hanging limply from his fist.

– We've got some wonderful news.

*

From the wooden gate and through the overgrown shrubbery and under the eerie dullness of a cloud matted night, Henry spies a forlorn looking leg snaking out across his garden patio.

– Fiasco?

Henry imagines Fiasco's head resting atop the doorstep and, smiling, sees his bent ear folded into the step recalling 'Rodin's bastard: the failure of the thinker and the thought.' They'd come up with that together. Henry had supplied the reference and Fiasco had run with it. Henry photographing Fiasco done up in military grey face paint and surrounded by beer cans felt tipped in grey that Fiasco had carefully strewn around the 'plinth' of the doorstep in a 'representation of chaos.' Had they actually done that, or just imagined it? He couldn't remember that or the difference.

–

Rain falls incrementally then plain hard. Droplets form protuberances at the base of Fiasco's lobe, ears of rain dissolving into the silence elaborated by their pattering strikes.

– FIASCO, hey Fiasco, Fiasco?

Henry's palm strikes and rocks his friend's shoulder. He notices Fiasco's face, neck, hands, forearms are all mottled like something inside had broken and started to seep through. He tries to pick him up, can't, Fiasco ending up somewhere around his knees and perceptually elongated. Henry puts him down, sort of. Fiasco slumps uncomfortably forward. Henry fumbles for his keys, unlocks the door then drags Fiasco into the hallway by his armpits. Henry's scared. He's scared and paralysed. This is what he remembers of being a child and it still seems like the truth. Henry's trying to remember the American teen drama he watched that involved giving someone CPR in a non-humorous manner. Having said that there may have been a dog involved. Fiasco's legs are still in the garden being lashed with rain.

Henry kneels down above Fiasco and leans in. A droplet of rain slides down Henry's forehead and 'romantically' off one of his eyelashes as Fiasco opens his eyes and reflexively jerks his head away.

–   What are you doing? Were you going to kiss me?

–   I thought you were…

–   Easy prey?

Fiasco rolls over his legs kicking out like a dreaming dog's.

– This is no good at all man.

His fingers are trembling in their sling. He sticks them in his mouth. A taste of splinters and sand gravels his palette.

– Help me up?

Fiasco trembles towards the living room spilling clods of wet sand as he goes.

Henry's sat down, leaning forward, kneading his hands into his thighs. His eyes fret and grow intermittently glassy. He's not thinking about himself, for once, and then he is. Fiasco's eyes are parched, completely bald, the skin starred around them in barren creases.

Henry forcibly brings himself back to the moment, fails. He can't believe himself. He can't stop anything. Yet he worries all the time. About the wrong things though. Henry starts to worry about that. This isn't the time. It's always the place. He still considered every worded thought a prayer or rather every idea he ever had was still formulated in a beseeching tone directed towards an arbitrary but still judgemental infinity. It wasn't spiritual so much as obsessive compulsive. Please let him be ok.

> – What happened?
> – What happened, Fiasco repeats
> mockingly through the pain.

*

Evelyn is in her bedroom. The door is locked. She's just showered. A new start for us all, Lawrence had said. She opens her top drawer, her hand scattering underwear that falls down over her piled clothes like snow caps.

Outside the wind sounds like hunger, like an abstract form of a concrete feeling augmented by a suffering actuality. (Or something). She takes out a pair of underwear, puts her feet through them. She notices the stain across their inside, her thumb explores it. She lifts them to her nose and smells coffee and alcohol. Disgusted she throws it across the room. She lies down on her bed. She doesn't want to think about what that could mean right now or if she's insane or not. She doesn't want to think about anything at all.

Evelyn holds the large unicorn to her belly and feels a slight burning sensation between her legs. That was so stupid. She rolls over to the side of the bed and digs under the mountain of towel, jeans and trainers for the notebook. She pulls it up and starts to read. What could he have meant? She reads for ten to fifteen minutes.

This is all gibberish, she thinks.

– Fucking incomprehensible shit.

Evelyn hurls the notebook towards the wall. What had Henry been thinking? She'd managed to make out some of the scrawl but had found no concrete mention of herself in the pages. The handwriting resembled a crippled fly walking across the page and the dead emotions of the reeking prose that she could understand seemed so antithetical to her reality and so in thrall to their own hysteria that she couldn't see anything in them.

Evelyn stares at the digital clock by her bedside table. It is eleven thirty. She lets the lights blur and split in her eyes. Evelyn observes herself drawing with the lights, as has always been her habit, but her eyes move with an unreal slowness like a boat pushing off. She feels a heaviness surround her that she warms to like a coat. She falls asleep, wakes up. What's the difference anymore anyway?

The clock reads 1.11.

There's a knock at the door.

– Is everything ok?

Evelyn slides under the covers pulling them up to her cheeks. The unicorn rests next to her head and facing her. The unicorn's cheer grimaced face seems, under the present circumstances and many others, mockingly insane. Evelyn flicks its body so that it faces the door.

– I heard a noise

– Come in, she says.

Lawrence opens the door slowly. A triangle of pale light soaks into the carpet. Lawrence's rounded shoulders, hunched and cast loosely forward like the 'lowest of the low', take up a degree of the light like a maths problem. Evelyn rolls her head from the door to the ceiling.

Lawrence is wearing a pair of bunny rabbit slippers and a silk dressing gown that has, over the years, shrunk around the hairy expanse of his gut and pectoral excrescence. That's one reason among many for her staring at the ceiling.

He steps into the room and draws level with the chest of drawers, affording them a suspicious glance before continuing.

– I, I wanted to apologise.

His eyes cross the carpet sweeping up and along the duvet's hem. He's distracted from searching for the hurled object by the sight of the unicorn's plush head resting next to Evelyn. Evelyn with her face flatly revealed, with her body disappeared into the thick cover and her head displayed on the pillow and under his gaze. Her face within which almost all the stages of her growth seemed in this moment not only traceable but recoverable. Evelyn's brimming eyes tip towards him for a moment then return, still brightly distillate, to the ceiling.

He walks hopefully toward the bed and sits on its edge. Shiny navy blue silk shirrs upward across the arid paleness of his goose pimpled thigh and rolls into the gathering crease of his waist.

> – Sushi roll, he says, and strokes the side of her head. I was horrible earlier.
> – I know.

Lawrence goes on to tell her that he is sorry, that he was wrong to talk to her the way he did and to say those things— 'what things exactly' Evelyn wonders, half remembering— and he tries to tell her that he knows all of this, the marriage, the idea of a 'new' family, must seem strange but that he has a sense, a desire really, for happiness, for everyone's happiness, maximum happiness for all and he knows— believes *in*— the secret of it and that all of this, everything that is happening, is part of it, even if he can't explain quite how exactly.

He tries to say this, or something like this, but the only clear and coherent part of his fumbling words comes towards the end when he says 'I love you sushi roll,' and strokes her hair again.

There's silence and then Evelyn turns her head and looks at him and says I know and then:

– Dad, I want you to be happy.

Lawrence tells her she shouldn't have to be concerned about his happiness. He looks downwards and then notices the way his hands are absently curved around each other.

> – I hope you know how proud I am to call you my daughter.
> – I don't know how you can say that.
> – What…
> – Dad, I. I
> – What's that?

Lawrence's neck has grown rigid, each anterior muscle hunched and tightly shimmering, jostling for space amid the once broad stretch of his nape. He wraps his hand around the back of his neck and feels it for the first time as something breakable, a brittle transport of spine fragilely networking into the nobly crude helmet of skull. Lawrence's neck having flared and hypertrophied as he caught sight of the notebook spread out in the angle between the walls.

He hasn't heard Evelyn, hasn't noticed her reaching towards him when he really needed to. Lawrence instead experiencing every classical response to danger at once. Confusion reigns. Lawrence fights the urge to launch himself from the bed and through the door by standing up and pacing slowly before the chest of drawers.

– What's that?

He nods toward the notebook, he can't point, however casual he's trying to be. His voice is different, she thinks. It's not just that he hasn't responded to her but that the attention and emotional range of his voice doesn't even seem to even include her anymore, instead positioning her outside of its command as obstacle, object or opponent.

– What?

Evelyn is hurt and her frustrations speak through her but they fail to convey anything about that hurt and frustration except their existence.

– That, what is that?

– That? It's nothing

– What is that?

– Just fuck off.

– Evelyn!

– It's, it's nothing. It's just something old I wrote that I got frustrated with. Why do you even care?

– Where did you get it?

– It's mine dad

– Please tell me where you got that.

– It's mine, I've had it a long time.

– That is not yours.

– How would you know? You don't know anything about me, you don't even care!

– Since when, since when has it been yours?

– I don't know since, since I got this? Remember that fantastic day dad, happy families?

Evelyn sat up in bed now and holding the unicorn roughly by its head in such a manner as to suggest that the unicorn was her decapitated foe.

> – Geoffrey gave it to me and you gave me this. She throws the unicorn out of the bed.

Lawrence flees the room shouting

– I've always cared.

*

His mum just phoned him with the news. She told him Jude was going to try living there again after the wedding and that Jude might even go to some kind of college, that he had expressed interest in that and that there was still time for Henry to look at University courses for September if he wanted to apply somewhere. He might even get some kind of dispensation considering his age. Henry said he was happy for her and he found that he was. He could tell his mother's words were improvised around a feeling though they came out clear and her voice, lighter than usual and tinkled with laughter, rang with a happiness that seemed to momentarily open and distil the surface of his own occluded feeling. There was a dinner tomorrow at the house, he had to come. He asks if he can bring a friend, his mother says if he has to.

He puts the phone down. The tunnelled banks of his confusion subside and muddle the feeling.

He looks at the Word document he'd been working on and frowns. Fiasco's asleep on the sofa, the sound of the phone having triggered only the slightest of groans in him as he called for a mother, the universal mother of his childhood who was indistinguishable from care and the consolation of pain. Henry won't remind him of it.

He'd managed to take off Fiasco's shoes, build a rampart of cushions for his mashed hand and all but swaddle Fiasco in blankets and duvets in an attempt to soak up and dry the dampness of his clothes.

Henry's sat at the table opposite him, typing up and revising his notes so that they address a specific 'you.' He wouldn't know how to characterise what he's been writing. It doesn't seem to be a story, more like a riddle whose answer existed only in its torturous flight from understanding. He imagined the 'you' of the reader as the unifying repository of his disparate thoughts, that they would be moved and in this movement be able to peer past what he, as its author, couldn't move beyond.

Really he's writing to Evelyn and to Jude but only as a pacified audience, as elements in his over pleaded case, his complex wish. He stares at the phone and then at the Word document and then at Fiasco and then at the open door of Jude's room. He gets up and makes himself some blackcurrant squash and reads over the five vaguely connected paragraphs.

If everything is material then it's not immaterial that a loss makes thought physical. There's something here that's real even if its expression isn't. Lies are the clearest thing imaginable. That sounds like a contradiction but isn't. That could be a lie but I promise it isn't.

In the scaffold of these words there is a tower. It rose from the sea. This voice is from the tower or is the tower. This, like individual lives, isn't equivalent with itself.

The tower is in pain. Pain is cone shaped. Because it has got a voice I can funnel its hollow. Speaking here is a symptom of the poison that could provide a vaccine. It raises ethical dimensions. The world is my body trapped in the tower.

A feeling that's completed in death weaves the loose ends into a demented quilt that covers this roughly pegged interpretation of the world. An outline too large for the soft cover of our lives is stirring within all of this making little ruptures or winged schisms that aren't in themselves violent but do alter everything. These creases are memories detaching and becoming the world. Hiding in time and landscape they set a quest. A quest is a holy mission that is also a narrative. The tower recedes, its one yellowed eye searching behind crumbling brick. Sight caresses the outside with hidden agendas looking for nooks to deepen with. It deals in light to exchange with the black matte pupil of the world. In becoming what is seen I enter into this exchange to plate a body in light hoping to subvert the towers spell.

There's a silent body that runs through our space. Thoughts slur into this body like backwash. Give it a

*semblance of substance that I pocket like a fixed bet.
The tower's face doesn't resemble his but the cracks I
enter resemble me. If the word is a brake then his head
is a spun pedal reversed by the earth. I'm the text of a
quest that'll make his injured head total like an abacus.
I understand now that there is a task involved and a
sacrifice to be made. I'll be a grub in the ear of a figure
that'll dissolve guidance into action*

Henry finishes his squash. What does this
mean? He feels a strong desire to show it to
Evelyn. He reads it again. This time he can see so
many things he dislikes about himself in it. Fuck
this hero bullshit, he thinks ironically.

He stands up and goes to Jude's bedroom. Jude
is really leaving. He lies down on the bed. He
clamps his arm over his eyes. He should really
shower but doesn't. The sweat and the dirt of the
day clad his skin providing an atmospheric layer
of reality to everything he senses disappearing
around and within him.

*

Jude watches the space in the room silt with
darkness. He feels his thoughts dive, swirl and
then bind with the total depth of this blindness.
His thoughts, unconscious of themselves and his
existence within them, range out across the
hospitably vibrant territories of black. He
conceives the whole room as the wing of the bird
ready to take flight. He is first taken under wing

and then becomes wing. He feels a great shift in the weight of the darkness.

The bird leaves and the night's remaindered. Jude's left behind in the afterimage of black.

His thoughts return, partially, to himself. Remote as his body feels he knows that he is loved, that it is something he doesn't necessarily have to think. He opens his eyes.

There is a struggle towards the light.

*

Lawrence dreams of a fire.

Fiasco dreams of formless monsters.

Henry stares at the wall. He can't sleep, the future is coming and it doesn't give a fuck. The present is confusing but at least it ends.

*

Evelyn sits under her bed covers holding her flashlight like a dagger above the notebook's vivisected pages, the spine of the book visibly rising toward her under the real-shaped heart of her fist. She's reading in a kind of sacrificial fury that's antithetical to language so all Evelyn can comprehend of the words failing to latch in her mind and moving, leaking, like a passed razor through her eyes are their sound and shape. The mouthy awkwardness of their construction and anti-grammar though cause little blips of interference in which a phrase, a mood, an intention leak into her annoyance and depress her.

One of the words could look a little like her mother's name. There was a description of the sun showing its age in reference to a woman's face... Typical misogyny, maybe.

A thought occurs to her. She remembers Lawrence's reaction to the notebook. Evelyn slides herself slowly around to the side of the bed and lets her feet curl into the carpet as she tries to think. All of her notebooks are hidden in the drawers. She takes them out. Each notebook is wrapped in the noticeably blandest type of clothing in their category and comprise exactly the kind of 'outfit' Evelyn would likely be seen dead in. Real funeral clothes. She imagined that were she ever to die from misadventure there'd be that one photo of her wearing something similar, years ago, in a family picture printed large in the local, possibly even national, papers and that Diane, moved by this, as she seemed to be by all large-scale concentrations of a sentimental nature, would invariably dress her in these items in accordance with the public's 'death wishes for the posthumous.'

Death often crossed her mind as a fanciful possibility. She was aware or believed that this wasn't an uncommon feeling just one generally unexpressed, and so with a view of preserving some mystery of herself beyond death and even establishing a way to revise *her*, she had taken to hiding what she considered her real person in the suffocations these items represented.

If she had guessed right and if Diane or Lawrence were to tell anyone about the strange costuming of her notebooks, if they'd only notice, then there'd be fertile ground for …something, interest, a story, and here her fantasy broke down into tangential dreams of literary significance.

This was of course only a minor counter urge and fantasy within the necessity of hiding. She did not want what she had written to be seen by anyone. They'd be hurt. Life didn't really allow for the complex emotions her barbed, and not at the time complexly realised, sentences so haphazardly sprayed.

She unfolds the selected clothes carefully and extracts a notebook from a pleated skirt, embroidered leggings, the interior band of what she could only describe as a bonnet. Each notebook is there and accounted for, each is of the same plain leather brand. She places them back carefully whilst retaining the oldest one that Geoffrey Hardy had given her and leaves it on the floor. She reassembles each pile and carefully places them back in their designated spaces pressing the surface of each gently with a slow rock of her knuckles so that the fabric records a slight indent.

She leans over and pulls the notebook Geoffrey Hardy had given her towards her knees. She picks it up and runs her finger down its spine. They'd stayed in touch, had been roundly encouraged to, after that birthday. Geoffrey, never Geoff, would call round and they'd sit awkwardly across from one another in her room, time barely managing to pass the distance between them.

As puberty set in and took root Evelyn, unable to understand his reticence, tried to scandalise him, openly smoking and drinking in front of him. He'd look so pained that she'd end up feeling ridiculous and vaguely insulted. Evelyn would find herself putting out and abandoning her freshly lit cigarette on the windowsill, or, if she were drinking, quickly slipping the little bottle of vodka, or whatever, wherever and under anything that was close to hand before resuming a noticeably tenser silence for another five minutes or so while Geoffrey sat trembling with a care and devotion that she was able to perceive only momentarily before confusion, shame and a strange sense of rejection set in and lashed out, driving him from the room.

When he was present her confusion seemed clarified only by this kind of superior scorn though in truth she used him to convince herself of the 'real' abnormality of the average. After all he was so strangely conventional in everything except his interest. To look at her like that. It was creepy. When around him, especially during the last few months of his visits, she'd find his rapt, anticipatory silence barely concealed an almost perverse ecstasy in waiting. There was a lack of responsibility for reality in this, she felt.

However, her perception of Geoffrey's openness towards her, its passive affection and lack of expectation, would occasionally emerge in her as a comfort during moments of sadness days and sometimes weeks after she had last seen him. The reassurance of his tolerant concern seemed to vouch for her beyond his capability to understand her and beyond her recognition of its source. She had never made the connection so strongly before.

It was this memory of an emotion and a sense of its discovery that curiously arose in Evelyn now as she touched the notebook he had given her. He hadn't called round or telephoned her for about a year. There hadn't been any instance she could have recalled to explain why this was. His visits had always been unannounced and had begun to tail off in fits and starts so that they had often seemed to have 'ceased' until he would turn up again a month or so later. She found herself wondering openly about his whereabouts.

He of course had always visited her. Evelyn had been to his house only that one time and yet she finds that she can still bring to mind clearly the streets leading the way there. This astonishes her. She could remember them in detail without any emotional interference; they existed in her outside of that day and so what she must have been feeling in the car on the way to his house, what every other memory of that birthday was saturated in and with, had been somehow dissolved or neutralised in another significance.

Evelyn recalls now their reflection in the television, his arm pouring on top of hers and then resting atop it. How bold he had been to take her hand. How he watched her crying in the tv and then turned towards her, her own eyes unable to forget the screen until he whispered her name in a pleading tone of voice.

It was the first and last time she had held hands with anybody other than her 'current' family. She'd gone out places, kissed boys, done things. Still, it was so vanilla.

Did he still think of her? Evelyn doesn't know if the thought is a cruel one or not. Calmed, Evelyn allows herself to look again at the notebook. They're just words after all. She stands up then sits on the side of the bed. She picks up the notebook and looks at the first few paragraphs. They're a description of the pictures preceding them. A description of a person dissolving, that would be nice she thinks, and then 'Who is the jubilant child?' Scrawled, repeated, and stabbed into the page underneath this description.

That's it. The End. It felt like. The notebook seemed to start with its ending.

She puts the notebook down and picks up and opens her own. She hadn't written anything for so long. She aches for the child she was and for who she might have been. Geoffrey had always asked her what she was writing.

She looks at the clock. It's late. So what?

Evelyn dresses quickly, shoves the baggy of weed and notebook into her bag and opens her bedroom door carefully. She walks down the stairs and out of the house. She takes the first of several streets illuminated by streetlamps and follows the clear accord of her memory stretching out like a beam in front of her.

Half an hour later she stands beneath what she thinks is his bedroom window, a jiggle of clod reading her palm. She closes her hand and scatters their compactions against her margin for error. They bloomed or broke up against it. The dirt's impact triggering an instantaneity of light, rectangular and yellow, holding things not yet awoken to its demands.

Evelyn waits with her breath sealed up inside of her and already mined for life. A figure moves behind the window, darkening into presence, emerging into a womanly shape. Formless groans emanate from the house. Now every window from top to bottom becomes a gold treasure chest.

Evelyn dives behind the wheelie bin, her shoulders closing around her chest in an unconscious attempt to muffle her heartbeat. She slips to the floor and draws some conclusions about herself. I'm so stupid, I'm so stupid, these words shuddering through her body. She doesn't hear the footsteps drawing toward her over the gravel.

     –   Hey, Evelyn? What are

   –   Geoffrey, I'm sorry, I'm sorry

   –   Don't worry, hey, don't, there's nothing to be

   –   I shouldn't be here.

He looks over the façade of the house, his eyes shifting quickly towards his mother's room.

     – Me neither, he said. Come with me

Evelyn follows him into the house, her hand curled around his fingers. Geoffrey Hardy can't believe his own behaviour, the daring. He calls to his mother, tells her it was nothing. He's impressed with how calm and automatic Evelyn has become on entering the house and he strives to emulate what he mistakes as her casualness. They enter his room. Geoffrey closes the door behind them, almost leaning against it, turning the lock slowly as if mistakenly drawing the world around its secret pronouncement.

We have to be quiet, he says, but you can talk to me about anything you want. She sits on the side of the bed. He goes to her. She asks him to unzip her dress. She takes it off. Evelyn lays back in Geoffrey's arms. They cover her like vines. The back of her head measures the distance between the root of his neck and the emergence of his jaw and back again. Evelyn falls asleep. Later, this fact will feel amazing.

They lay in the shape of a chair like this for hours, her hair muzzling his mouth, his erection pressed hotly against her. He felt embarrassed by it, really had no idea what to do with it, waited until it candled under duress and then felt mortified by its absence. He can't tell if Evelyn is or was awake or not, if she registered it or not or if he wanted her to. She had and it had made her smile unconsciously and she had rested against it comforted by its warmth and non-action, by the guarantee of who they were. And she slept. She wasn't even that high. She won't believe it.

Geoffrey for his part can't close his eyes for the fact of his heartbeat. He is aware of his body. He is unaware that this body is in his mind that is also his body. The body in his mind which is not his body but which he feels is, is all wrong, lumpen and misshapen and full of dark clues and numbed danger. His breathing also seems to have become manual, something a large percentage of his attention is concentrated on, *he must not disturb her*, and at the end of each breath he feels a void edging closer like a continent that he must hasten towards, take into himself, contain for a moment and then expel before it prises him apart. There's also his paranoia, the air bustling under the door of his room, the creakings of his house that might be his mother's footfall, and everything else that must at all times be watched over and considered. If his mother came into his room or knocked on his door how would he conceal the sweat in his voice?

There is joy too. He admits it without acknowledgement, smuggles it in. The joy passing untranslated through their inert points of contact, surrounding his thoughts like a halo, then archiving itself as thought. He'll have to wait till she's gone to rediscover it and by then its nature will be less artefactual than a relic and even more prone to the revision of his intellect.

Daylight tassels the curtain.

What's a thought other than something we imagine having? Evelyn opens her eyes. Geoffrey presses her against his body so gently it goes by unperceived and then, somehow, magically makes his arms weightless. She shuffles loose of him. She has to go. She asks about the window. Stunned, Geoffrey Hardy doesn't know, he's never thought about it. She looks at his door. He helps her with her dress. The zipper breaks, folds down over his hand. It doesn't matter, she says.

He quickly writes down his telephone number. He tells her that he wants to see her again. He opens his door. His mother has already left. How did that happen? When did it happen? They've barely said a word to each other. Evelyn walks down the hallway and into a field of light. She stops and looks back at him. He beams back into her faceless outline.

He walks into his room, closes the door, and

lies down on the bed. He can't believe it. So this is happiness, he thinks. What can that mean? Soon all this will work itself out, turn to lame desire and then rise far too high until he's a little dog doing tricks underneath it, driven half mad but still believing and then it'll start to lower again, look deceptively possible, and when the night's in reach he'll jump up and rip it apart until what's in his mouth is squeezed out and unrecognisable in the dirt. Geoffrey sleeps.

She had come to him.

On the walk home Evelyn tries to remember the night. She had walked to his house. She had stood skittling dirt that spored like a dandelion against the window, there was light, a woman, Geoffrey, his room, and she had slept there. She had slept. She hadn't told him about the notebooks. That doesn't matter.

*

– It's a new day, sort of.

Henry opens the living room's curtains. Bitty light flutters artfully through the prehensile covering of wisteria and fronds Fiasco's face. The wisteria crowding the glass had once suggested to Henry a conspiracy of wilderness, one that preserved in the hidden interior the lie of his disappearance. It was in this front room that he secretly played, eschewing the outside world of the close where the other children gathered and yelled and turned almost silver as twilight descended and emerged in one blue note across the sodium streetlights. The fever pitch of the children's activity rising towards this stellifying moment while Henry watched or just listened. In either case he'd be drawn to the portal of the window then, his pace around the living room's rug and the weird amoral fantasies of sacrifice lifted and tweaked from television and the bible and which he acted out in turns (now the victim, now the evil then barely the hero) became interrupted or inflected in this moment.

He'd had a sense of occupying some marginal space, being something inter-dimensional, as he watched the children rolling into the bowl of the hill slightly above him, tearing after a loose ball, their features something only to be glimpsed at through the leaves shuffling like a toy viewfinder between measured abstractions and emergent bodies, caught expressions, sturdy limbs.

His Grandfather had planted the wisteria with his usual quiet insistence, something more or less than forceful, to dually obscure the outside world's view and blind the inner so that in secrecy and abstinence they might wait for God alone to penetrate their idyll. After his Grandfather died the wisteria was left to its own devices and grew exponentially until the corner armchair sat enrobed in permanent shadow. After his death the foliage had seemed to hover, sentient, knocking at the window like someone whose faith was bent on murder. It had never once occurred to Henry to go outside and assume some mantle of control. Henry had had nightmares and daydreams and probably Freudian insights about the vines creeping in under the awning and toward him while he slept.

He turns and regards his friend who seems to have merged into and escaped these surroundings like a figure in some, he doesn't know, painting. Which one? That one of a poet…young and dead and laughably beautiful. Henry steps towards him, to observe the cracks of his detail. Fiasco's mouth is set in an uneven grimace and his brow, eyes and lips are all stiffly etched and ringed with sweat, briefly pollened with the light bustling around them.

> – Fiasco?
> – Fiasco can you hear me?

It was Fiasco who'd shown him how to occupy other, more transitional, spaces. The fringe of the town, a car park, the centre of a bridge, the mesh of a fence. This was where their dreams were. He had shown him how easy it was to disappear into the connection of things.

> – Fiasco?

An eyelid snaps back revealing a vein harried ball that swivels and fixes on the dark object of Henry's face. The pupil contracting around

Henry, who senses its lack of agency, knows that without the mind's input that this continuance of the body's function doesn't render Fiasco a reality. The other eye remains closed though underneath the finely encrusted point of its mashed seam Henry can just about discern an eyeball roving around underneath. Fiasco turns on the sofa, his exposed eye rolling dryly back into his skull.

Henry continues to summon Fiasco with a low incantatory repetition of 'Christopher Marlowe, Christopher Marlowe.' Every pain and every attenuated pain in Fiasco's body comes to remember itself as the activate world feeds back wailing into the stems. He lets out a Neanderthal grunting of fucks that dip and rise, groan and bend, evolving and regressing in an aural showcase of the ascent of man according to which pain his attention switches between or begins to approach.

Henry steps back.

> – I'll get you some water.
> – Fah ha ha huck.

He brings a tumbler of water from the kitchen with an added side of reverence for the state of his friend. He waits with his hand outstretched for Fiasco to coordinate, reroute, translate some reserve of control over his reactive body, for the leap over the destroyed throughways of lost time into his eternally present self to be thrillingly re-enacted in a kind of animated stutter. It still doesn't occur to Henry that he ought to be concerned; that his friend needs *his* help. He believes in his friend *selfishly*.

Fiasco's face presses itself into the cushion, smearing its features, the real weight of the stressed fabric against his eyes, its physical and limited resistance, both immensely pleasurable and incommensurable to the consistency of pain funnelling inward after it. His jaw extends into the cushion forming a little pocket of darkened space that his breath heats unbearably and which warms his cracked tongue into a muddy sludge.

Fiasco's tongue:

   – Snap crackle pop
   – Water, you've got to have some water.

An arm identifies itself and in a few heaving motions works itself free from the board of Fiasco's chest. Henry presses the glass into his palm then stands there cautiously protective of the space around it. Fiasco's arm remains partially outstretched, holding the glass heart-high and gently shimmering the water. Fiasco leans forward over the glass and cautiously sips the water. He looks at Henry and tries out a wry gesture of fucked self-acknowledgement that's interrupted by his stammering limbs. He sinks into himself and sighs.

– My clothes are damp

– You were kind of freaking out, I tried
to

– Ugh

– So… how was your night?

– I think I went insane with sadness and
almost got suckered into the
phenomenal or, given the way I feel, I
descended into hell to rescue some
beautiful, mistaken, siren like ideal and
subsequently lost my soul.

– Sadness?

–

– Where did you go?

– Like I said. Like the last thing I
remember. I feel like death.

– How was Oblivion?

– I don't think I was meant to come
back. What happened with your sister?

– …

– Holy moly.

– Man, I've got some news.

– If it's that you're a dirty rascal then
that is no news

– It's not.

– King of the castle?

– Mum's getting married. There's going
to be a lunch today..

– So what's happening?

– …you're invited.

– Oh

– What about after? What are you going to do?

– I thought we'd hangout with Evelyn and then maybe come back here

– After they're married brainiac.

– I dunno

– You're lying.

– They want me to apply for university

– University? Get you. Where?

– I don't know.

– Oh…and Jude?

– They think he'll understand now.

– When are you leaving?

– I don't know man, like I said, it wouldn't be until September anyway

– So you're going to leave?

– What am I meant to do?

– Not leave.

– Why don't you go too? Come with. This place is dead anyway.

– It's not possible, that's bullshit. Now you're with the money.

The room has become something they're in. The world that usually drops away when they speak reasserts itself.

– We can't keep

– What?

– Nothing

Fiasco looks away, finally disgusted. This is unbearable.

> – What about the band?
> – The band is for good you know that.
> – I thought we were going to invoke Marlowe today?
> – You're in no state.
> – What about the band?
> – Maybe I'll find a drummer at uni, if I even get in.
> – Fuck you, fuck the band. Can you find a drummer who'll serve Christopher Marlowe? I don't think so. Fuck you.
> – Are you going to come to the lunch?
> – Am I really invited?
> –
> –
> – There's no food in the house.
> – Fuck you, I don't need to eat anyway. I'm going out.
> – Hey
> – I'm fine, I've got stuff to do.

Fiasco hands Henry the glass.

Henry's confusion is so generative it shortcuts the world or his place in the world. He's either completely alone or not really there. What used to fill that space was prayer and then Fiasco. He leaves the room and enters the kitchen.

Fiasco's confusion and anger is so localised it

destroys him or the world. Either he's not there
or nothing is. Nothing has ever filled that space.

It's all a question of ratio.

Henry fills the glass with water that rushes up
the sides of the glass and over his hand, what's
happening? When he re-enters the living room
Fiasco's already standing up.

> – I've to go see what my hours are for
> next week.
> – If you've 'to go see'
> – Hmm
> – Have you still got the keys?
> – I think so.

Henry opens the door and Fiasco turns his
body sideways toward the door and slips through
it. He keeps walking.

> – Later man, or something.

Fiasco walks up and round the garden without
turning back or raising his hand. Henry goes back
to the sitting room. He sits down on the rug. He
watches the wisteria knock at the window. He
can't think of anything.

*

> – Dad?
> – Yes sushi roll?

– Are you busy?

– Yes sushi roll.

– Oh

– Not too busy to talk to you! Do you remember?

– Can we talk about mum?

– We can keep mum.

– What?

– I mean, I mean, yes of course. We can always talk about her.

– Really?

– Of course.

– Tell me how she died.

– You know how she died.

– Tell me.

– I don't want to think about it.

–

– In an accident, a car accident. A hit and run. They never got the person responsible. It was a… a police officer, a maniac. He was never brought to justice.

– She didn't just leave us?

– She would never have left you.

– And…Dad, are you ok?

– I don't understand why you would ask.

– Do you promise?

– What?

– Do you promise?

– On my soul.

– Are you ok?

– I'm

– About last night
– You're right, I've…I've made mistakes. There are times when I see myself, the way I've acted, if not the things I've done, and I
– Dad?
– I think, is this me? I know that I'm not supposed
– Dad!
– What?
– Can I invite someone to lunch?
– You want to invite a… friend?
– If that's ok.
– Of course.
– Is Henry coming?
– He should be. We told him last night. Part of the family now. It'll be good for him. I think it's what he's always wanted.
–
– You're not excited about your new brother?
– I gotta go ask my friend to come.
– Will I like… them?
– It's a boy and yeah I think so. Dad, you ok?
– Fine, fine.

Evelyn leaves the room and telephones Geoffrey Hardy. She feels excited and simultaneously kind of stupid, goofy even. Her finger hooks the cord and pulls it straight. She weaves it around her finger where it tenses into a sensation which tinctures the effect of Geoffrey's voice brightening the other end of the line.

> – Do you want to come over? There's a lunch.

A cloud of electrical interference hoods the receiver.

> – Crackle es crackle en?
> – You can come.
> – Cr En?
> – If you can hear me come at 1.

She places the phone on the hook. She walks up to her room and enters her room and then walks to her chest of drawers. She opens the chest of drawers and goes through her clothes quickly. She locates the notebook. She opens a page of the notebook. She doesn't recognise the words. All she sees are the crescents of her nails pressed into the page's sides. She bruises the paper. Around the tight bracket of her depressed thumb's field of pressure she looks at the faintly stretched letters arcing outward in the letters of her name. She drops the notebook. She picks it up. She finds the page. She reads a sentence. The words won't hold in her head. She doesn't recognise anything. There's a sensation of blindness in the spaces between the marks. The letters won't adhere to one another. The doorbell rings and its piercing insistence seems so much a voice disembodied and shrieking. Through the floor and doorways and air she hears Lawrence's voice confluent with the words he's pronouncing and the relief of this understanding deafens the curious tone Lawrence is employing.

– You're here early!

*

The Crows is a cordoned off and char-stained skeleton of a building that Fiasco imagines picked cleaned by the wind and standing for years and years. Long enough at least for the surrounding area to regress to a wilderness, a desert, a scalded piece of shit. Then the day would come when the wood beams would splinter, crack, disturb the order of recumbent dust, lay exhausted and unobserved by life bar the occasional, curious twitch in some scuttling insect's antennae informing it of a slight and essentially uninteresting change to its perceivable world. There'd be nothing to remember and no one to remember it then.

He longs for that, silly as it sounds.

There's a truth dirtily oxidising that thought, revealing the arterial thoroughways of its meaning vis-a-vis: Fiasco versus life.

Not that Fiasco would regard his non-ironic willing of a total, self-including, annihilation of humanity as a maudlin realisation. He'd never let it out or tell anyone and it doesn't make him feel bad, it just is...bad. He knows it. He'd never complain. It's never that near the surface to begin with. That's so weak. Weak like Henry. Phoney. Fiasco flattens his hand against the thin layer of skin separating it from his skull. He presses the two conjoined but separate sets of bone against one another until skin can't distinguish between skin. The bones don't even try to link and it'd take a millennia before anything fused. That confirmed it then, not even the same thing was ever able to truly know or even inhabit itself.

In his lap, his injured hand throbs, pulsates, radiates a field of nausea. Fiasco searches for a distraction amid the few spectators who stand scattered and threadbare across the tarnished stretch of pavement and gutter. Their heads are wide and cavernous and hard. For a brief moment Fiasco cannot perceive them as having 'faces' or any sort of front or addressable side. He merely sees sets of features inverted or loosely moulded around holes that flared and deflated senselessly, sucking greedily at air. There was something gaping and useless in their local and general distribution like a pile of barnacles chipped clear from the hull of a wreck that was held together only by the disease they were. He sits down on the curb. This is real hatred. He doesn't want to be a thing that hates. The Big Red Pepper walks over and hands him a beer.

– How's your dad?

– He can do one.

– What now?

– Fucked if I know. This is proper Roobash.

– Anyone get hurt?

–

–

– Also Posh Barry saw you scarper with that whisky

The Big Red Pepper walks off, joining the crowd. The ruddiness of his skin merging with the light behind them, his waist enshrouded in a cloudy wreath of apron, a few bottles rain-tinkling out of his pocket. The Big Red Pepper, Fiasco thinks: A walking sunset.

Fiasco drinks the beer, it tastes bad but it's only a question of persistence he's sure. He designs a tick list.

No job. No family. No friends.

He doesn't know where to go, what to do, or anything at all, except want what isn't and hate what is and he's here and it sucks and soon he'll be somewhere else with about as much say in the matter reacting however he'll react with a probability that disgusts 'him' and which 'he' can't affect and that'll be related to now if only tangentially in a way he can't understand and which he increasingly doesn't care about understanding and it's that, the experience of not caring coupled with the now, that is just too fucking exhausting to continue feeling.

Even then he wouldn't be these dwindling things that propel him. He wasn't the forces that sculpted his life, that shaped him into mush by their ineradicable movements within a context neither force nor life could derive a privileged status from. Or something. He was just a thing, the trace of another, as all things were.

Fiasco tries hard to think about what life could be like. What it would be to genuinely feel something different and how could he? Maybe if I had more money? It's a conclusion. So is history, he thinks.

He thinks: There's much more to me than I've been able to be and then 'this is both impossible and accurate.'

He remembers a conversation he had with Henry. In the conversation they were with the Big Red Pepper and standing below Big Ben. They were chanting who are ya, who are ya as Big Ben began to chime. The sound of the bells drowned out their voices. They were blissfully silenced by a noise that eradicated their own and to which they did not contribute. The amount of sound, its mass, was the same with or without them but they were all together unified within it. It seemed beautiful to him now. They could still do that. There was time to make it real.

Fiasco turns around. He looks up the hill. His feet start shuffling him towards its peak.

*

Henry and Diane stand awkwardly in the hallway as Lawrence bows at a thirty-degree angle with his arm bent subserviently out towards Henry like a waiter at a fancy restaurant or hotel concierge. He wants Henry to take off his coat and fold it over his proffered arm, to take part in a joke that points towards its meaning: Henry belongs here now.

It's a light-hearted joke on Lawrence's part but the longer no one notices, or pretends not to notice, the more sincere he feels in both the desire to acquire the coat and to impose upon Henry the generosity of his spirit.

Henry's seen Lawrence, wondered at his posture, but has been unable to interpret the gesture. He glances across at his mother. Diane too seems at a loss to explain Lawrence's behaviour. She steps forward and touches the rack of Lawrence's arm. She says 'I better get to the kitchen' and then remains standing, her fingers rafted over his forearm waiting for some sign.

His hooked arm momentarily depressed by her touch rises in slow elation. Lawrence straightens up, places his other hand atop hers and smiles. Diane lets go of his arm and walks contentedly to the kitchen. Lawrence's eyes follow her. He turns back towards Henry as if to say something and then repeats his bow with an added flourish.

Henry's hands are dug into his coat's pockets. He's not practised in parting with his coat, relinquishing it, if that's even what Lawrence wants. It's a habit that, like ninety nine percent of his, he's acquired from Fiasco.

– Ummm Hey Man!

Jude skips down the stairs and bear hugs Henry. Lawrence straightens up then repeats his bow for a third time while winking at Jude. At the top of the stairs Evelyn wanders into view. Each face turns towards her.

Henry attempts to catch her eyes then tries to observe them as best he can. They seemed at odds with the rest of her expression. Her eyes were so complexly afraid, so entrapped within their own time, it was as if they radiated through her expression like some alien fragments in the otherwise regulated system of her face. She waves hello and troops silently back to her room.

Henry tries not to watch the space she's left behind.

Lawrence repeats his bow one last time. His arm begins to cramp. He turns his palm to the ceiling and wafts a few traced circles towards Henry, coaxing a certain je ne sais quoi from the air as he speaks:

– Teenagers, he says by way of

explanation.

Jude releases Henry then shimmies a few jabs at his brother's solar plexus. Henry's response is automatic, his hands only blocking the poorly thrown fists that were meant to land like nostalgic jests. Jude frowns. Henry's not there. He interrupts Henry's eyes, enquiring after their meaning till he finds himself there. Henry smiles,

– Hey man.

Henry shucks off his coat. Lawrence tottering towards it as Henry, an accidental matador in the house of his inaugural, though in no way bullish stepfather, turns and half throws the coat into the corner between the hatstand and the wall. Lawrence, having plunged a few steps forward, puts his hands against the wall and stares out from under the jacket as the two boys, oblivious to his charge and subsequent adornment, enter the living room. The two of them no doubt poised to aggressively graze the upmarket snacks Lawrence has provided without so much of a thank you, he thinks. My boys, he thinks. It's just an association, he doesn't mean it or really feel it though his eyes are primed to saucer at its articulation. His sense of self-reproach seems to cut both ways. Make an effort Lawrence, he thinks.

Lawrence shakes his head free of emotion, tries to picture that emotion leaving the tight corner of his mind and diffusing peacefully into the air. He leans down and hangs the coat on the rack. He walks to the living room where Henry and Jude are not eating but instead standing at the French windows looking out over the sea with an air of 'quiet rumination'.

> – You like the view?
> – It's nice man, I like that you can see the lighthouse.
> – Really? To me it's something of an eyesore, dreary. One day they'll knock it down
> – It's not listed?
> – I suppose but I think there are things you could do. Turn it into a flat or some such.
> – Didn't someone die there?
> – That's enough. That should've been enough. To wipe it off the face of the earth.

There's not much more either of them has to say. The three of them look out over the sea for a moment or two longer. Henry feels he should say something about the wedding.

Henry says 'congratulations.'

Lawrence beams at him then gestures for them to sit. Henry and Lawrence sit while Jude continues to look out of the window. They instinctively sit at the furthest possible distance from one another without being directly opposed. Lawrence leans forward conversationally, his mouth opening and closing, but says nothing. He breathes out as innocuously as he can and sinks back into the armchair.

Henry looks away absentmindedly scratching at the table with the elegant walnut finish. He could ask when the wedding is going to be but what's the point? Also, what then? It's an emergency question anyway, one best saved until he absolutely needed it. His mother has not come out of the kitchen though he can almost perceive her movements, the ease with which she locates each pan and ingredient, the near soundless accord between herself and this house. It eats away at him though he won't acknowledge it. Jude tugs at Henry's sleeves and, once he has Henry's attention, picks up and crams some sliced meat and crackers into his mouth. His jaw revolves like a cement mixer. He grins at Henry and then at Lawrence, cream cracker dust and fringes of meat falling from his grin, pebbling his trousers. Lawrence frowns and shifts his posture towards Henry who is smiling at Jude now, the genuine pleasure he's taking in Jude's performance translating to Lawrence as some kind of conspiratorial ploy to undermine him.

– Would you like a snack?
– I'm ok…
– Ok

– but thanks.
– Of course, of course.
– LAWRENCE
– Yes dear?
– LAWRENCE
– YES, D…
– LAWR
– I better go
– ENCE
– YES dear
– Have you seen the …
– They're right there
– Oh
– Everything ok?
– Yes, your mother couldn't find the peeler
– The peeler?
– Yes, the peeler.
– Oh

Henry and Lawrence each wonder what proportion of the meal is already in pre-production, for exactly how long things will seem interminable for. Lawrence divines this connection between them, conceding to its indifferent to mildly hostile source though not without sadness. Still, it's a relief. They'll be able to avoid each other like this for years if needs be. If that's what Henry wants or if that's what he thinks Henry wants.

Jude has washed down or otherwise dissolved

the clingy remainders of cracker and ham— medievally turreted in the sulcus of his canine teeth— with some lukewarm and usually forbidden Fanta, spilt glucose globules of which have fizzed then flattened out around the base of his cup, one or two flopping over the side of the table before pressing their colour into the crème carpet like an aged flower.

Lawrence eyes the damp spots and the table and Henry's hunched and ready to bolt demeanour. He's sat as if he still had his coat on, Lawrence thinks.

> – You can go to the garden, if you'd like.
> Jude seems keen for some fresh air.
> – Actually Jude, I wouldn't mind seeing
> your room. I don't think I've seen it
> since its been all set up.

*

Evelyn is still combing through the notebook when Henry knocks on the door.

> – Evelyn, Evelyn?

She can feel his voice entering her body, taking up shape there, the sound of his voice simulating itself through her*self* in hideous and/or sinister mockery of *itself*, of her, of himself in her. Her skin feels insufferable, itchy and hot, not like something you would want to wear. She pinches her wrist until the skin looks both dead and dazzled like a 1950's flashbulb illuminating some corpse's telling detail.

> – Hello, hey. Do you want to hang out
> with me and Jude?

On the other side of the door Henry just wants to hold her hand, put an end to the weird grief of simple unknowing. This at least could be resolvable, he thinks, though he'll soon come to realise the naiveté of that stance.

She feels bad. Guilty. She knows, or thinks she knows, that it's not fair to feel this way. Why not?

He seemed so gross now. Look at what he has her imagining. This notebook. Those words. Her mother. Could he have imagined what she would feel? Totally Deranged. Go away, she thinks.

Henry backs away from the door. Jude's standing in the doorway of his room glaring at Henry. Henry walks towards him. Jude closes the door.

*

Diane's in the kitchen. She can hear Henry re-entering the room. Lawrence's voice stumbling into conversation, a rumble of words disarticulated from any meaningful structure resolving into a questioning lilt. Henry mumbles something in reply and then the pitch of his voice grows animated.

She opens a pan. A whoosh of steam cleans her face. She wipes her face with her arm. The arm reveals the tears in her eyes and the sweat patterns of her face. She is crying and happy and then just crying. For no reason, she feels. Diane pulls herself together as Lawrence enters the room.

> – I thought I heard something?
> – Is your sonar on?
> – Hmm?
> – I just burnt myself a little that's all. How's it going?
> – Fine, fine. We are talking or rather trying to talk about…things, some things. In general. I feel like I should mention courses but I don't know how he'll react.
> – Leave it for now.
> – Too late.
> – You mentioned it?
> – Yeah, only a little bit
> – What happened?
> – He thought I said curses. Then he asked if I knew anything about the area, if there were any old stories about the sea and the lighthouse I'd could tell.
> – That's good
> – Yes, except I don't. Can't. So we

stopped talking.

– Did you ask him why he was interested in that?

– I thought that might be rude. Also I wasn't sure whether to ask him again.

– Leave it for now.

– How long until dinner?

– Not long.

– I would just like to have something to tell him.

– Stop, it's fine. Talk to him as you would do to anybody.

– Right...and that will help?

– Go, out of the kitchen now, shoo, shoo.

– About fifteen or so minutes more?

–

*

They are sat like this:

                 Diane

                         Evelyn

             Vegetables

    Lawrence   Beef   Jude

              Gravy

              Henry

Lawrence is asking Evelyn where her friend is. Henry raises his head, looks towards the two spare places. Jude's changed into his blue pyjamas. That means he's pissed off, Henry thinks.

– Fiasco can't make it either, he says.
– Please use his real name, Diane says.

The bell rings. Evelyn pushes the table away, whispers I'll get it. At the table they listen to the murmur of voices, counting their registers, something noticeably off in their dynamic. The dining room door opens.

– It's your resident ghost at the banquet.
– And me…Geoffrey
– Why Dennis I haven't seen you for years!
– How are you Diane?
– I'm very well, are you eating enough? You're nothing but skin and bone.
– Well you know whatever I can find …still your food is the only food I would consider to be food or something. The rest is just swill.
– Stop, stop. Join us, we're celebrating.
– Hey man
– Hey man

Fiasco brought out a real charity in Diane. Or rather charity was the only clumsy way she could formulate the impulse and pride in the impulse that his dishevelled appearance always aroused in her. She felt for him in an uncomplicated motherly way that she would never have been able to feel for her own children. That unfettered, deeply sourced, tenderness that was so eroded by the day to day material fact of dependency that it existed only as a kind of distant order was, in her apprehension of Fiasco's vulnerability and his tenuous relation to her, suddenly activated and realised and gratifyingly sincere. He produced an ache in her that in a limited way she could address through kindness alone. She'd expected to dislike him, of course, but never had. She could see what he meant to Henry, Henry who she'd expected to take after her father but who she couldn't help but regard as lacking character... as if proximity to a strong conviction had hollowed out his own, as if he hadn't learnt anything but the gravity of what could hold him in place. She wasn't thinking of how he'd looked after Jude, it wasn't about that. He didn't seem to want anything possible. Dennis at least had a work ethic.

– Come and sit down. Hello Geoffrey love, so nice to see you again.

Lawrence eyes Fiasco warily, has heard him alluded to by both Diane and Henry in strangely fabling tones though the actual content of each anecdote was at best inscrutable and at worst described a kind of lifestyle that he couldn't help but construe as threatening. Fiasco sits down between Henry and Jude. Geoffrey Hardy takes a place next to Evelyn.

Lawrence's eyes thaw at the sight of them sat together.

– Hello Geoffrey

– Hello sir, how are you?
– Very well thank you, and you?
– Very well thank you and you?

Each of them jocularly bows to the other.

Henry's trying to catch Evelyn's attention. She picks at her food. Geoffrey asks her a question he can't make out. She turns to him and, as she turns, Henry notices a picture of Jude hanging on the wall.

Diane is talking to Lawrence.

Geoffrey is chatting benignly with Evelyn. Jude is looking at Geoffrey.

Henry scans the rest of the photographs on the wall.

Fiasco leans across.

> – I was thinking we might plan a trip to London or something. Go shout at Big Ben like we talked about?
> – Umm, sure when?
> – After this?
> – Ok, wait. I'm not sure I can.
> – What's up with you man, her?
> – …
> – Whatever you're thinking is crazy and weird. Let's do something, I gotta get out of here. I need to talk…or something… I feel mental.
> – hmm

Fiasco turns back towards Jude. He raises his

shoulders and gestures with his fork towards
Henry who is in danger of drawing attention to
himself via the subject of his gaze. Jude puts his
elbows up on the table and frowns. Fiasco
considers Jude.

> – So…do you know what's happening?
> What's up with him, with you, with me?
> Have you been me yet? What should I
> do?

Jude sticks a finger into Fiasco's eye and laughs.

> – You're so right. Kingdom of the blind.

Jude sticks a finger into Fiasco's other eye.

> – I see or…or rather
> – JUDE!! You mustn't do that
> – It's quite alright Diane
> – That's very informal
> – What is?
> – Saying 'Diane'
> – Lawrence!
> – You think?
> – A little
> – Huh, I thought informal was like
> calling someone…Darlin….I can't think
> of anything more appropriate…Calling
> someone Sheila… if you're Australian
> and they're not called Sheila…that's
> informal…being Australian is

informal…. That's an a priori category…
if Croc Dundee taught me anything it's
that. I thought I was just using the
correct noun.

The bare plates sit on the table awaiting
command. Geoffrey Hardy stands up and lifts his
and Evelyn's plates. He looks from left to right
just sort of standing there smiling at everyone
around the table. Fiasco takes the last piece of
bread and dips it in the array of juice fogging his
plate.

– Where is the ummm…

Diane stands up telling Geoffrey Hardy how
kind, and not to worry. He passes her the plates
and sits down. She reaches over and begins to
stack the rest of the plates atop each other with
the minimum of fuss.
She watches Fiasco's alert movements from the
corner of her eye as and then looks directly at
Henry's despondent slouch and the piles of
picked at food on his plate. She senses Fiasco
looking at her.

– How is your mother Dennis?
– We don't see much of each other but
it's ok.
– That's sad
– It's always been like that

Fiasco stands up and starts helping Diane clear away the plates. His movements are natural and accepted in precisely the way Geoffrey's were not and he tucks each plate underneath the last with a practised precision. He seemed always to be able to take care of things that were not himself, Diane thinks..

– Actually that's not true. I remember when I was a kid I had these nifty pyjamas a bit like Jude's. I loved them. I remember eating eggs and soldiers. I remember my mum bringing me them and the bread all spongy and I'd press the ends of the bread into the yolk and it'd spill out of the sides and all over my fingers and get everywhere. Some days I'd find these little yellow pastel stains on my pyjamas. They were so fascinating. It was lovely. Then one day she just stopped bringing them. I think I was probably five years old. That's the punchline, that and i'll never forget.
– Oh, Dennis
– It was a joke, kind of. Anyway, I have to go. Can Henry come out to play?
– Ha, Dennis, of course
– I err think I might stay
– It's ok if you want to go now Henry
– Yes, yes by all means go, live your life.
– No, I think. I think I might stay for a

bit. Help clean up or something. There's
no dessert?
– There's some cake
– Man? I, I could…lets go, there's some
band stuff we need to
– I'll catch up with you in a bit.
– But we were gonna…cake? Are you
serious?
– So, when is the wedding planned?
– Where's Jude?

The air in the room stiffens. They call out for
him. Jude wanders back from the bathroom
drying his hands on his pyjama shirt. Air passes
through their lips.

Fiasco takes the plates to the kitchen. He stands
there for a moment straining to listen to the
voices in the dining room. He stops trying. The
door swings close. He feels totally sealed off, in
another dimension. He could just go out the back
door, climb over the fence, skitter down the cliff
and squat like a hermit in the lighthouse until his
existence was a rumour. Why not? Fiasco walks
back into the dining room.

– Next month Henry, we're going to
have it in the garden.
– What?
– The wedding
– That soon?
– Why wait for happiness?

– I guess

Fiasco says goodbye. He thanks Diane and Lawrence for having him and then leaves without looking at Henry.

He walks towards his bench, towards the lighthouse. It may as well be home.

Cake is served in the front room. Coffee's received and drained by everyone but Jude and Geoffrey. Evelyn and Geoffrey are next to each other on the sofa. Geoffrey sits forward. He realises that if he were to lean back his shoulders would sit like a patch on Evelyn's. He also notices with excitement the proximity of their knees. He maintains an open and 'ready' expression, giving in turn a portion of his attention to each person in the room. Smiling anew each time eye contact is established. Geoffrey's hand pats the snailish recoil of the sofa arm.

Henry's slumped in the large armchair by the table with the elegant walnut finish, his back to the French doors. It is the nearest he can get to Evelyn. The cake he has waited for is largely untouched. He doesn't know exactly what he wants but the wanting itself is unbearable. His motivations don't feel his own.

Diane, who has just barely sat down, stands and announces that it is time to clear up.

Jude races upstairs.

Diane laughs then signals at Lawrence to follow her into the kitchen. Lawrence is stood

by the window benignly watching Evelyn and
Geoffrey. Openly looking, smiling.

> – Ahem…
> – Of course, of course

Diane looks at Henry, who is trying to coax
Geoffrey into a conversation about music, and
raises her eyebrows till they roof her forehead. He
ignores her.

> – Henry?
> – Yes?
> – Can you help us with the dishes?
> – Yep

Geoffrey and Evelyn sit and talk for a little
while on the sofa. He leans back, their shoulders
touch. Her arm wriggles out from underneath but
then she turns inwards *towards* him. They form a
little cove. Joy rushes in. They arrange to meet in
the town centre at eight.

Henry dries the dishes, pacing back and forth
in the kitchen, staring at the door to the living
room, attempting to infer something from
nothing. Diane watches him out of the corner of
her eye from the sink, wonders what's bothering
him, if he has quarrelled with Fiasco and if so,
about what?

Lawrence pours a drink for Diane and himself.
He holds her glass behind her. She turns and
holds it in her soapy hands.

Lawrence laughs. She reaches into the sink and then smears a bubbly beard on his chin. He turns laughing and reaches under the table in the corner and pulls something out. He opens a small stubby French beer (Biere Speciale 2.2%) and places it onto the counter next to Henry.

   – That's for you.

Glass is clinked.
Henry downs the Biere Speciale. It is delicious and pointless and then yeasty and pointless.

   – You want another one?

Henry nods.

   – Of course
   – Lawrence, Diane says
   – Yes?
   – What are you doing?
   – Keeping you company

The three of them laugh. Henry can't believe it.
Evelyn and Geoff say goodbye at the door, stare goofily into each other's open, expectant, faces. She lets the door go, watches it close out the space between them. Geoff catches it, bounces it on his fingertips then pushes it open again. Their faces change in all kinds of hopeful and empathetic ways. The door rebounds, passes in front of them. Her hand starts towards it and he sees, or she

imagines he sees, this reflex for what it is. The door closes. Evelyn runs up to her room. Geoffrey all but skips home. That was cool like a film or a poem, he thinks. Henry hears the latch and the thump of feet on the stairs. He counts to twenty.

He places a dish on the rack.

> – I'm off then
> – We need to talk soon
> – Of course

He hugs his mum, shakes Lawrence's hand. Lawrence involuntarily, as if his arm were a pull string, says 'good on you, son.' Diane frowns. Henry barely notices.

> – I'm gonna check on Jude before I leave, ok?

*

> – Hey Evelyn.
> – Hey
> – I was wondering…
> – What?
> – What's…
> – Fiasco seemed odd. Are you sure he's ok?
> – He's fine.

– He seems kind of depressed.

– Fiasco doesn't get depressed.

– What does he get?

– What?

– What does he get?

– I don't know.

– You probably should.

– Can we meet up later? I know I said some things that…

– I'm going to the cinema. With Geoffrey.

– Maybe after?

–

– Do you have that notebook?

– Why?

– Did you read it?

– No

– Oh, but there's. I saw something in it. I want to check i really saw it.

– I threw it away.

– Why?

– I'm really angry with you.

– I don't understand.

– You're an idiot. Did you think it was funny?

– What?

– Actually fuck you. Get away from me.

– What?

– What you said, the notebook. Did you think it was funny?

– I didn't…I can explain

– …
– I don't mean to be creepy.
– Tough shit.

Henry goes home. He unlocks the door. He already knows Fiasco's not in because there's no music pushing itself or him through walls but he calls out again anyway. He calls again.

*

Fiasco waits at the edge of the phenomenal.

He waits some more.

It's coming.

He walks onto the balcony and looks out toward the sea.

There's the horizon moving towards him:

> *Up above*

To the side

> *Down below*

You're too...

There's the phenomenal.

Bye Fiasco.

Would he have wanted it this way, his body barely a homeopathic dose to the sea?

It's been two weeks since Henry saw Fiasco. He'd contacted Fiasco's mum and stepdad. They'd contacted the police. He'd had to talk through the sobs and hyperventilation of Fiasco's mum and her reaction hadn't been what he expected.

Where's my friend? He's gone. Is he alive? We don't know.

The police had come.

> – Aren't you even going to ask about his bank accounts? Have you looked at them?
> – Actually we have.
> – Has he used them at all?
> – Well, it seems that he didn't actually have any money in them.
> – We also know that someone matching his description was seen at the beach around twelve thirty am.
> – What were they doing?
> – Walking across the shore, or rather in the shore. It says here that they looked 'soaked' and 'disorientated'
> – One scenario is that he decided to go for a swim or else just wandered…

– That's speculation, we're of course not even one hundred percent sure that the person seen... but we have notified the coast guard to be aware...

– Have you been to the lighthouse? He might have left something there. He could have written...

– There's nothing there.

He'd cried in front of them then, cried until red welts slowed up under his eyes like lava and cooked the world's substance out of his vision so that every*thing* remaining seemed hollow and poorly configured, threadbare, a grainy pile of atoms ashed into a crater of time. He stopped when he thought what Fiasco would say if he could see him like this. He reached for his tobacco and nearly slid off the sofa he'd been reclining on. He'd had to keep his foot up on the sofa's arm. He'd got drunk, played music so loud it was physical and kicked a wall, kicked it for Fiasco, and nearly broke his foot. For Fiasco. He smoked in front of the police officers because they were police officers and because maybe that's what Fiasco would have done.

– Still, it's possible he's ok

– It's possible of course.

– What can you tell us about his character?

– He was a genius.

– Did he ever use drugs? Was he prone
to abusing alcohol?
– Did he get depressed, angry?
– Angry maybe
– They say depression and anger are
linked

He never made it through any of his cigarettes.
He'd always start blubbering again, lips flicking a
mixture of saliva and mucous that flowed down
from his nose onto the cherry of the cigarette
that his shaking hand dragged around, creating
these caramelised pentagonal lines of snot which
measured from nose to hand until he collapsed
the thread by dropping the half smoked rollie into
an empty beer can. As soon as he calmed down
he'd try to roll another one.

– These people, the detective said
outside.
– You don't think that's sad, his only
friend?
– He's going to burn that house down if
he's not careful
– Nah, it'd never happen. He'd just put it
out with his boo-hooing.

Henry heard them through the door.

– HEY, FUCK YOU

He shouted through the doorframe. He

imagined the second policeman restraining the first. He fell against the door and started crying again. That must have put them off.

The house was a mess. Fiasco's absence revealed it. Henry couldn't look after Jude like this. He was alone.

At night when he forced himself unconscious he dreamt he was running around asking everyone 'where is my friend? Where is my friend?' but in the dream he was Fiasco and his questions became pointed and he never saw who it was that he asked.

He thought of Evelyn all this time, in between and within this time, he thought of her as something other than what she was, saw in her both his guilt and the possibility of transcending that guilt though neither one was very clear to him. Everything was hazier than ever without being in any way more mysterious. Still the thought of her made the connections between his body and mind throb differently. What was that word? Sublimate, yeah.

He wrote her letters when drunk that he didn't send. Thank god. He started to phone her when he knew his mum and Lawrence were out. She'd sit and listen to his trembling voice for a while before finding a reason to leave.

He kept phoning her.

She came round. They didn't say much. He tried to hide it every time he started to cry. He asked her again about the notebook. She got angry and left but the next day she came again and this time she brought it.

> – Why do you even want it?
> – It's your resident ghost at the banquet.

That made her angry, or she was already angry.

> – I'm seeing Geoff now. We're going out. I don't want you to think that there's anything between us, is that clear? You need to stop calling and writing to me.
> – Writing?
> – Fiasco is probably fine.
> – I didn't send you anything I wrote
> – You must have when you were drunk and your obsession with this, she held the notebook above her like a biblical tract he thought, is creepy and weird and hurtful.
> – What did the letter say?
> – It was just a copy of things in here.

He prayed. He beseeched God. His thoughts all prostrate and biblical 'for I know that I am a hypocrite who has offended you,' his face all scrunched up.

He repented for everything. He kept going. He beseeched God for Fiasco, for Evelyn but mainly for himself in relation to them. He didn't want to but he did. He came to no understanding. That was ok. He kept praying, his neck bent towards his stomach, tears ringing the pit of his belly button. God was something like his navel, he thought. That umbilical dip, dead nexus, wrinkled seal, a closed portal that hid his own acrid biliousness and the olfactory pre-productions on which his higher functions sat all regal like…. The gut, in other words, in all its wormy glory and the divine outside that it quivered in darkness against…or…

Wait…have another drink…

It was a joke too. Wasn't it? Staring at your navel. Its ultimate pointlessness well established. It didn't used to be. How many angels on this pin? Fucking none. The same as an infinity. Don't even try. Getting carried away. The beer. Between the fourth or sixth there was a kind of grace period where his sadness maintained itself in a singular state long enough for thought, however damaged, to emerge.

He asked his mother about his father, about the divorce. She said it had been easy. They hadn't even had to talk. She'd had the papers for years. The marriage was going ahead in just a few weeks. Why wait any longer for some happiness?

Henry said: 'I know he sees Jude sometimes'

　　　　– It's different and it's not often.
　　　　– Why doesn't he like me?

Jude comes over for visits with his mum. Henry could see the worry in Jude's expression but he couldn't tell how that worry interacted with Jude's eyes which had grown unreadable to him. When his mum left to unlock the car doors Jude hung around. It was then that he'd rush up and hold Henry in his arms with a power and desperation that Henry couldn't fathom, that swamped him.

The first time it had happened Henry had felt furious and then moved by...what was it, a gesture or an action? And these feelings of shame and gratitude, weakness and strength, along with all the others, continually traded places with one another until he was almost completely ground out, empty. At night he reflected on these feelings while shame slowly trickled through his abandoned state and filled him.

He found it hard to sleep during these weeks. He'd lay awake thinking of how eyes interacted with skin, how fucking alien their composition was. He tried to remember Fiasco's eyes but it was his voice that came back admonishing him. 'My eyes? What the hell is wrong with you?'

Cue everything again.

He read the notebook nearly every day. It was a mystery. Whoever wrote it wanted to convey a feeling so exactly that all they could do was torturously describe what was recognisably indescribable, fluid, alterable from moment to moment, yet distinct from any moment in particular but still ultimately contingent and appealing to the very chance its existence was dependent upon and therefore what rendered it indescribable. Holy fucking moly but it tried. It wanted something. He imagines the letters piling on over a feeling....

BUNDLE!

He imagined the writing as a huge lattice, a net...the sentences and paragraphs as wiring or string and in this system, this trap that hung loose in the world he thought, the indescribable buzzed about, testing the limitations inscribed around it until finally, exhausted or suffocated, it died weighting a few sentences here and there with the temporary outline of its meaning. The meaning was always the same and stood for something eternal that wasn't. Something that stood.

He'd come to consider the second voice, the one in the margins as establishing the notebook's chronology. The first voice had disappeared. There was a schism. The voice in the margins doesn't know who he is anymore and can't understand what he was. Nothing he had believed made sense. The voice in the body of the text has come to know what it is and can't believe it.

The voice in the margins wanted to disappear the body of the first through understanding. The voice in the text wanted to disappear to save the future. Both of them thought that endings were disappearances.

The drawings at the start are a synthesis of these two perspectives, Henry thinks, the third space between enquiry and affirmation. What's left is incomprehensible and real, a dream of a body and nothing else.

It wasn't quite the phenomenal but it still tried to split the atom of his thought.

It wasn't the book though or its contents.

If there just *had* been something real in it.

He wouldn't have let Fiasco down?

Fiasco.

Weeks pass. He has an interview for a university in London. They ask him about his hobbies. He tells them he wants to write. They ask him why and he says it's the cheapest thing you can do and he doesn't know anyone else who wants to do it. They say you know this isn't a writing course? I don't want a writing course...I just want to read.

Somehow he gets in. His mum tells him that Lawrence can get him a job in London over the summer if he wants to go up and get used to the city beforehand. Part-time but enough to cover part of his rent

> – What about the rest?
> – You can get a loan and we'll help you out every now and then when we can.

He says 'I'm not sure'
His mum says:

> – This is exciting. Think about it.
> –

She asks him to clean the house so they can show it to buyers. I'll help, she says.

– I can do it.

Cleaning his room he finds his old notebook and the picture Fiasco drew of the lighthouse. The blood of Henry's body pools in his skull. It is as if the conditions for thought had first broken through the cause and then the effect of thought, sweeping away the raft of self, cracking the institutional grain and trying to pour out through his eyes to get at the world and depart this leashed together body.

He tries to calm down. He can't. A nausea that he'll later, in recovery as a symptom of non-recovery, have to contextualise as profound causes him to faint. He wakes up and vomits. He can't get the stain out in time. His mother comes over and gives him that look. The smell of bleach accompanies the days of his sorrow.

Henry walks to the beach nearly every day. He sits on a bench there. He looks at the lighthouse. He thinks, maybe?

*

Evelyn wakes up and vomits. She eats beetroot and peanut butter for lunch. Diane looks at her askance.

– What?

– Are you on a strange diet?
– No, I just fancied this. I must have eaten it when I was a kid.
– I don't think so.

Diane frowns. Evelyn goes out with Geoffrey. They go to the cinema. He holds her hand. They kiss then touch in incremental stages towards something exponential. They stop abruptly each time. Someone does. Could this be real? Did it mean anything in particular...it wasn't necessarily better but she felt good and at ease which was....better?

She sees Geoffrey, 'Geoff', 'Geoffranistan' nearly everyday in May. He reads the books she suggests.

– I don't like anybody in them.
– Not even Caulfield?
– Especially not him. He's so arrogant.
– You read it all though?
– Yeah

She encourages him to try a joint. He does.

– It's ok, fun even haha

He lets her touch the vein in his cheek. At first it was the same temperature as his lips but the longer she touched it the more heat it radiated until she felt it glowing beneath the soft tip of her finger.

She found this delightful.

The next day she rolled up three, suggested they wake and bake then stroll around town for no reason.

> – I don't feel like that now. Let's do
> something else
> – Really? I think it'll be fun
> – It wouldn't
> – Wow
> – What?
> –
> – I don't mean it to sound judgemental
> – What else can we do?
> – Something different

She tries to stop smoking pot.

> – I don't think you need to stop, he says,
> but I don't understand why you'd want
> to do it all the time.

She starts to smoke only before she sleeps, to help her sleep.

She talks more and more to Geoffrey. At the same time she begins to feel that Geoffrey is withholding something from her, that there is an essential inequality in the way she empties into him.

And what has Geoffrey to give back? He doesn't know, he's simply amazed by her and present to the point of self-abnegation.

By the end of the month Evelyn feels frazzled as if she were forcing herself to be in thrall to something recessive, a fixed horizon. She was trapped in something she couldn't feel the limits of.

> – Do you guys know each other biblically? Do you want to come over and get fucked up? Let's believe in something.

She imagined Henry's voice sometimes on the phone late at night. She felt caught between something she wasn't sure of and a temptation that was disappointing. The next morning she vomits again.

*

Lawrence wakes up and thinks an ampersand. He thinks '& Marriage, *part deux.*'
The doorbell rings.
Catering are here!
He runs to the landing.

> – Evelyn, Evelyn! Catering are here!

Evelyn wakes up and vomits. After flushing she sits on the toilet and holds a small white swab under the flow of urine.

> – C-C-C-CATERING!!
>
> –

She wraps the white swab in three inches of toilet paper and presses it into the bin. She covers it with the rest of the roll.

*

Henry wakes to the sound of the telephone. He picks it up. No one speaks.

> – Fiasco?
> – …
> – Dad?
> – …
> – Evelyn?

The silence is replaced by a tone less inclusive than their silence.

*

Evelyn places the phone in its receiver as Lawrence marches through the door twirling a ladle, a procession of tuxedoed young men and women in tow. There's a monk's haircut of sweat fringing her forehead.

*

Diane picks Henry up.

You're meant to be helping me get ready and you're not even dressed. He puts his tie on, wedges his feet into a stiff pair of shoes, does up the laces.

– There.
– Help me with this.

The netting of her veil shimmers across and beyond her face. She glows. There was in this concealment something that told of her naturally, of the secret truth of herself in this moment, of a faith in a love that reached not beyond but into the unseen.

Henry sees her, if Lawrence can't, she must not mind. She believes in something else.

Diane stands him up in front of the mirror straightening his back with her palm. They look at each other there. His mother smiles through the mesh. Henry trying to meet the world outside of himself for her but *he's* so hard to find let alone summon. He looks into the mirror. They've been here before of course. Except now he's bored into his own reflection while his mum looks angelically liberated from herself. Gone away.

– I'm so happy for you mum.

*

There's a spatter of people, a photographer, a

whole bunch of Lawrence's work colleagues and the lady that does Diane's hair milling around the garden's entrance as their taxi noses up the driveway.

She had never had many friends or any, actually. Strange to be realising that on your second wedding day, Diane thinks.

*

Geoffrey is an usher and as per his *Lawrentian* inference has assumed the responsibility of averaging out the bride-to-be's seating section. He glances towards Lawrence at the altar who nods, with what feels like paternal reassurance, at him in confirmation of his efforts.

– I'm with the groom

Geoffrey Hardy already turning and gesturing towards the row of seats to his left, a polite grimace etched onto his face.

– But I'm with the groom.
– Yes but...we're not really umm that's not how we're seating people
– What about all those people? All of them know Lawrence and those people sat pretty much alone I don't know at all.
– Yes but...
– I'm here for him in all this, we go back a long way

The hairs on Lawrence's neck stand to needling attention at the slopped sound of that voice. He turns and steps down from the altar.

– Ian, Ian, how are you?

– Good, good. Wow, look at this huh? THE LIFE or so they say.

– They?

– The ball chain.

– Ah…aha..ha

– Is there going to be a free bar?

– And your wife will she…I don't remember inviting?

– She left me.

– I'm sorry to hear that

– Do you want to know what happened? Laugh, I nearly cried

– is this really the ti.., or the pl…

– It's a joke really. A joke what happened. I'm infertile

– Oh I see, how…um, um

– It was probably that jestering bitch's faul…

– Ian, you do know why we're here today don't you?

– Of course. Wouldn't even consider adoption. Heartless.. So, this shindig… are you up for making it legendary?

– Excuse me?

– I've a hip flask right here

– So the bar is just over there but it

won't be open till after the ceremony. So you best, you'd better just sit wherever, wherever you want.

The first strains of Lawrence's second favourite piece of classical music pricks his ears, awakening in him a sensation that's 3/5 awe and 2/5 crushing fear and wholly exhilarating. He leaves Ian and floats towards the altar. Don't look back, he thinks. Wait for her here.

*

The Wedding march or Mendelssohn's career albatross, Henry thinks. Not that he'll even pretend to understand, actively won't understand, classical music.

Destroy culture right?

A gentle exterior force undermines that thought expanding through him like a ripple, a physical sensation gentle and inclusive but which carries within its outward movement and inward space the erasing aspect of its cause. His mother's arms are woven through his, pressed into him. I'm supporting her, he thinks. They walk in stilted unison under the banner of tradition.

Lawrence turns to look. He can't help it. He's not rescuing her from death or anything like that after all. They're just going to live together. His foot begins to tamp down the grass then begins to rock back onto its heel before evolving in arrhythmic reaction to the musical *conditions* of the moment, this moment, the event.

Lawrence desperately trying to keep time with the march, to adjudge whether their pace is off, if it is too hurried or too lax, if they will make it in time or be stranded in minor humiliation... On today of all days. He begins to will at them with the musculature of his face and the repressed tensions of his limbs like a traffic conductor that is mentally and physically unfit to direct traffic.

Evelyn holds the rings. Henry can see them piled in her palm like a venn diagram. Her hand opens and closes over them. The way she looks at him and then won't. What is that?

The Vows begin. Henry works through a mental checklist:

> Sickness.
> And its
> opposite.

> For materially better and
> Immaterially worse

> Forsaking, forsooth.

> Reasonable consent.

– I now declare you man and wife.

That's that, then.
They gather for the family pictures.

They mouth cheese at the exhortations of the hapless, overexcited, photographer.

Henry just pretends to.

What?

Mouth cheese.

What?

Snap.

> – Jude! Jude, just pretend to mouth cheese ok?
> – Haheheha
> – You're either mouthing cheese or pretending to mouth cheese or mouthing a pretend cheese

Snap.

Everyone laughs at the mouthing cheese joke even though it makes no sense.

Snap.

> – That'll be a nice picture, the photographer says
> – Blootif-sniffle-snof-ull, croaks Ian through the jellies of his tears.

Thank you, Diane thinks *towards* Henry. Henry soaks it in, his place in the laughter. Lawrence invites Geoffrey for a picture. He stands next to Evelyn. Henry's mood doesn't so much darken as it does implode. He's so embarrassed of himself and ashamed of how he conceived of the situation, what was he thinking? And he still thinks it, he knows that it's all still there…all the pain and confusion wanting to resolve itself in another body, in the dream of a body and his own ego lurking therein.

Snap.

> – Perhaps we might take that one again.
> I'm not sure everyone was ready

Henry excuses himself, goes to the bathroom. He'll leave soon, quietly. Go sit on the bridge and drink with a memory of Fiasco, drink until Fiasco's there beside him… and when he doesn't show? He goes to the upstairs bathroom. He wants to be alone.

Henry sits on the toilet cover. His jaw begins to vibrate, an immense pressure builds behind the buried hemispheres of his eyes, his face becomes unbearably hot. Fuck this, fuck this, fuck this. He kicks over the toilet bin. The bin rebounds off the wall then spills its contents. His head's in his hands as a wad of clean tissue flops out of the bin and unfolds on its lid. There's a slight rattle across the floor. The fingers across his eyes separate a little.

> – What's that?

*

Diane *glides*, connects space, enjoins. She talks

to everyone effortlessly, her hands extending to touch the guests, an easy intimacy established between bodies. Lawrence watches her move through the spaces of the heads surrounding him. Heads whose words of congratulations and double entendres have given way to a more celebratory than usual discussion of their interests. Feeling allowed to watch Diane, to only cursorily listen to the heads' inanity, Lawrence does. His eyes follow her as the conversation connects remotely around him, generating in its last movement some completed feeling. He laughs along somewhere and way behind their laughter. Everything is coincidental to this one thing, this one thing that he gets to see.

Wait. What?

> – You can't beat it as a statement
> – Excuse me, could you move just a little, I can't
> – The RX?
> – The RX yes. It speaks, it confers, it designates. Your competitors will know who you are and that isn't a weakness…with the RX
> – The spin you can get off it *is* poor though
> – A little more to the left, if you could
> – They're working on that, they're working on it.

Diane has just this moment spotted Ian woozily leering at her. Lawrence in turn has spotted Diane spotting Ian woozily leering at her. Lawrence's fully craning gaze pans back and forth between them.

– The thing with the ZX series is that...

Lawrence excuses himself from the enclave of men and enters into the open space of the party. No-man's land. If someone joins him, then what? Something might happen. The circle, briefly ruffled, though seals up.

Where is she? There. She's talking to him. Oh god. No. He'll ruin her mood.

Lawrence watches Diane gesture to catering, sees her disappear behind Jude and Henry and then reappear holding a cup of steaming black coffee. She sits down next to Ian as he drinks the coffee, sips her wine in front of him, her face interpreting, establishing, utterly directed towards him. She touches his shoulder.

To Lawrence's amazement he perceives in Ian's back a whole range of emotional transitions. The musculature quietens, sobers up, droops, resurrects. Lawrence is walking towards them both now. He doesn't have any thoughts whatsoever.

Ian stands up and walks towards Lawrence. They stop. Ian apologizes. For all his behaviour. He says I'm sorry.

He says:

– You're a lucky man.

Lawrence lifts the champagne to his lips, the sun sinking in the glass.

– Yes

Diane comes closer and nestles against his heartbeat. The three of them laugh and look out across the sea.

– I should go

A communal cheer rises as the sun performs its sleight of hand with the sea.
The music changes, increases in volume, opening up across the garden

– Stay

The music attaches itself to the guests, entangling them.
Hands clasp forearms. Arms extend drawing partnering bodies along that inertly protest then relent to the beat. The party unconsciously migrates towards the Marquee. Lawrence feels the pull of his species, his own shining self-consciousness trying to lose itself amid the crowd. He won't dance though, he can't.
Diane's hand clasps his forearm, their arms extend.

Go.

*

– Jude I need you to do something for
me. Do you see Geoffrey over there by
Evelyn? Walking with her towards that
big...tent... Can you distract him for
me? Jude, Jude! I'm sorry. I've made
mistakes. I've always wanted to be a
good person but I get tricked, I trick
myself. And I let you down. I can't
explain. I wanted to know if... If I had
anything at the core of me that wasn't
fucking ugly. Something like a soul or an
instinct that wasn't just cowardly. That's
all I wanted to know and that was ugly
and cowardly. The wanting self, my
fictions. They spread and now
everything is real. I've let you down. I
didn't think about your happiness, didn't
spend time imagining it enough. I don't
expect to be forgiven, that's not what my
apology is about though obviously I have
hope, hope that you can or will in time..
cause I know you must hold it against
me...you're a better person than I am...
But Jude can you do this for me? It's
important. There's something I need to
find out and make up for. Please. I don't

think I'm tricking myself this time. I really hope I'm not.

*

The peak of the wedding marquee is visible from the shore and near luminous against the night. The canvassed structure resembling some ghostly insect divested of its armour in which the shadows of people pulse darkly like organs. Or something, he thinks.

Henry watches a pair of spotlights edge out from the hulk of canvas and wiggle at the moon's soft girth.

He looks down.

The tide traces their feet in compound-eyed foam. The foam spawns tiny staticky mouths. There's the notebook between them. That's all now. It used to be more, he's sure of it.

His existence in the world and its relation to her thought is the appearance of light from a star so burned out that its death reflects back and silvers up the emptiness.

– You should run away with me.
– Everyone knows where you're going.
– But you would?
– It's not yours.
– How do you know?

Henry and Evelyn barely register the wind, the

chill of its presence a mere embellishment compared to the size of the ocean and the magnitude of silence between them. They'd walked down here together from the party. He told her what he'd found and somehow they'd both agreed not to speak again until they were sat.

– How do you know?
– It's not yours and if you quote that fucking book at me one more time...
Anyway, I'm not going to keep it.
– I'm sorry I've been weird
– Even if you can't help it, it's still unforgivable.
– EVELYN!
– Look, there's Geoffrey.
– Does he know?

She shakes her head.

– What are you going to tell him?
– What can I tell him? I don't know. I'll say you used to be my friend and that you lost someone close to you and that you needed to talk.
– Does he know anything about us?
– He knows you got weird about me. And that I looked up to you once.
– When you looked up I saw myself and it made me go weird. I lost sight of...
– You didn't see anything except yourself.

Geoffrey Hardy is still watching from the promenade. Henry stands up. He points at the lighthouse.

> – That thing should be on fire. It should look like a tramp's open tin-can hat. The smoke should be milking the sky.
> – Is that another thing you wrote?

It had taken all his bravery to say and it had been exactly what he had thought of saying but it was fake and it made no difference. Nothing transformed. Could anything be said now? Impossible to tell, though Henry knows he's failed even if the how, when and why of it will continue to elude him.

> – I have to go now.

*

Evelyn and Geoffrey make their way towards the still audible party, the cheers and laughter they heard warped in the distance condensing into something more distinct and less charming the closer they get. Pop music decorates the air like tinsel.

Geoffrey hasn't said a word, hadn't felt the need to once she took his arm and leaned against him while walking away. He can tell she's glad of that. The silence. Besides and also she hadn't turned around to look back at *him* and if she was sad about something, something to do with *him*, did it matter if he didn't understand, did it matter as long as he cared honestly and she was near him? He doesn't know. Neither of them knew.

They enter the garden. The music is louder, brighter, and the sound of people now enframes them. Everything is different on the inside.

There's Lawrence, she thinks. Her father dancing and happy with Diane alone outside the marquee. They're going to Italy for a few weeks. She's so happy for them. She'll do it then. Or not. No, she will, she has to.

Evelyn turns around. She looks at the lighthouse.

The moon just above it.

Fireworks erupt.

The moon is golden in the light.

Honey Moon.

She feels something.

> – What are you thinking?
> – I just got scared for a second. Come closer.

*

The morning slowly appeared in the sky and in the sky's interaction with all the hesitant things of the world. Henry stops and watches a bush withdraw from the light of the sun's touch, ephemera of blue, green and brown tones hovering instead of its true being that was utterly unthinkable but which he invariably stood in relation to. His being also unknowable like any other thing. Everything he saw seemed false and alive in the same way, growing out of confused expectations about the inevitable like the idea of a ghost from a corpse. Was he tired of all this?

He felt an immense blindness at each point of his intersection with the world and he wanted to press himself into that fading and disappear.

He turns around. The lighthouse is still visible in the distance.

– It's all my fault but it can't be.

(........)

– Hey
– Hey
– It's been a while
– It's been pretty much forever for me
– I'm sorry.
– Nah, I heard you calling.
– And you never answered?
– What would I have said?
– So I'm the little bitch?
– You were always the little bitch. Not really. You're my boy. Imagine me beating my chest meaningfully as I say that.

– It's weird trying to talk like this

– Yeah, we never used phones even.

– How are you?

– The same given the continuity of silence but then I was never that glib before so let me rephrase that. All I'll say is the difference is you're definitely older and I'm still me albeit from a distance and augmented by the guilt of generations via this weird thing you're doing.

– So you're wiser.

– That's just another thing you think you know that I can't possibly

– See?

– What?

– I don't know or something. Your superiority seems hostile, you're an argument for something. This, maybe.

– Please put the words in my mouth. Fucking hostile?

– Also that's your job and no, not fucking hostile, just defensive.

– Me or you?

– Now it's hard to say.

– You, I'm nowhere.

– So you're everywhere?

– That's pretty hopeful thinking or something. Is it spacious or specious reasoning?

– I don't know Poindexter

– This is the notebook?

– This is it.

– In that little thing.

– My whole life.

– I call bullshit on that. Now what do you want to know?

– Just what you think.

–

– HA!

– Do you think honesty is the aim? Cause this is pretty dishonest, the parts that I can make out.

– No but I think, the way everything is…honesty isn't truth, life isn't truth so how am I meant to understand..

– Those are real people

– You were meant to be the hero.

– What happened? I hardly figure.

– My ego as per.

– You're getting closer to the truth now. Don't you want to ask me about her?

– What do you know, is she happy?

– That shit is banal, b-a-n-a-l that shit is banal b-a-n-a-l, Bee Aa ENN Aa YELL THAT SHIT IS

– What are you doing?

– I'm appropriating a forgettable yet successful pop song that you've got inappropriately stuck in your head for my own comedic ends. Actually for more than that. To avoid telling you

everything but the truth is forgiving.
That's either consoling or terrifying
depending on your outlook.
– I'm not sure it works, also it's already a
pretty dated reference.
– What?
– The song.
– You are deaf to all reason. Anyway you
can't deny it was a hit and could be
again.
– What were we talking about?
– Her, this, then.
– I want it to matter. To know it
matters. Can you tell me that?
– It either means something you can't
understand or it doesn't. Mean that is.
You're not in charge basically. It's not
what you want.
– How do I know it's really you I'm
talking to?
– What do you mean?
– You could be any one of them, of the
'disappeared'.
– Your laugh doesn't sound quite right.
Also I'm not…. though I'm not me
either. Remember. You're at a time in
your life where you can't transform your
limitations
– I don't blame anybody.
– And you still haven't sorted anything
out? Look at you…

– I know I'm not really thinking of anybody but myself when I think of anybody else. That's fucking lonely.

– Boo hoo.

– Thanks a lot.

– Did I ever tell you about my idea for a ghost called Boo Who? It was about a dead orphan who is trying to find out what he was like when he was alive. In the end he'd rather forget. It's basically an updated version of that *Are You My Mother* kid's book and *The Little Prince* but in no way intended for children.

– Ha, yeah I think so. You told me about that, yeah.

– So, do you know what happened to me? Am I dead, is this death? This empty reconnoitring?

– I'm sorry.

– We were brothers.

– I never knew him.

– So what are you going to do? You've got an insane ego and as a person you're the deserved subject of criticism.

– Did you know I studied?

– How was that?

– It didn't do shit

– In the end you have to pick your failure, that's all I'll say by way of criticism or support. You could be better but you might be worse.

– I'm trying to work out if I agree with you and what difference it makes as I've already decided to do something irrevocable, that is to say real, the way the unreal becomes real i.e without my seeing it and with a logic I can't fathom.
– Where are you? Hey, where are you?
– I'm there.
– Don't.
– I'm there.
– Don't.
– I can't imagine a way out of this.
– Try.

CLICK

Special thanks to Joe Roche and Colin Macklin.

ABOUT THE AUTHOR

Thomas Kendall is a writer from a small seaside town. His work has appeared in a couple of places like *Userlands: New Fiction From the Blogging Underground* (Akashic Books) and online at Entropy and Lies/Isle. A section of this novel was first published on Lies/Isle. Thank you.

ABOUT THE PUBLISHER

Whisk(e)y Tit is committed to restoring degradation and degeneracy to the literary arts. We work with authors who are unwilling to sacrifice intellectual rigor, unrelenting playfulness, and visual beauty in our literary pursuits, often leading to texts that would otherwise be abandoned in today's largely homogenized literary landscape. In a world governed by idiocy, our commitment to these principles is an act of civil service and civil disobedience alike.

CPSIA information can be obtained
at www.ICGtesting.com
Printed in the USA
BVHW092113030722
641252BV00004B/11

9 781952 600180